THE PRINCE FROM A CRUEL SUMMER

A FORBIDDEN ROMANTASY

CURSE OF THE FAE
BOOK THREE

ANYA J COSGROVE

The Prince from a Cruel Summer

Copyright © 2025 by Anya J Cosgrove.

All rights reserved. No part of this publication may be reproduced, distributed or transmitted in any form or by any means, including photocopying, recording, or other electronic or mechanical methods, without the prior written permission of the publisher, except in the case of brief quotations embodied in critical reviews and certain other non-commercial uses permitted by copyright law.

Cover designer: Bewitching book covers by Rebecca Frank

The Prince from a Cruel Summer/Anya J Cosgrove

ISBN: 978-1-997524-00-7

❀ Created with Vellum

Unwanted Gifts

"You've forgotten your own name. Your destiny. Aidan Surtr Summers, I heal you from this sickness, though you shall never thank me for it."

CHAPTER 1
EXILE
BETH

Los Angeles, New World, Present Day

An electrifying roar of excitement fills my ears as I step onto the stage for the encore. Thousands of cellphone lights blink in and out of view, dazzling me. The powerful vibrations of the speakers under my feet are nothing compared to the screams and shouts of an adoring crowd, applause and whistles and vows of eternal love echoing through the stadium.

"Thank you, Los Angeles! You've given us everything you had tonight!" I wave to my fans. "But you know me... I can't leave without a kiss goodnight."

A mix of howls and tearful screams engulf the stage as I take position for the last number—my most popular single, "Summer Kiss."

The mic is heavy in my hand, this song reminding me of the letter and invitation balled up in the trashcan of my dressing room. I left it there minutes before the concert started, and I still can't believe it's real.

The music swells, blowing out all thoughts of despair and

betrayal. The clarity I get whenever I sing in front of tens of thousands is the best drug any Fae could hope for. We're wired to crave attention and devotion from mortals, and yet I don't have to feed on their dreams or collect their souls as they pass to another life to earn it.

I can share their sorrows and joys through music without the burden of ruling over their hearts.

That makes me luckier than most Fae royals.

I reinvented myself a few times since my exile started, from the pearls and frills of the roaring twenties, to the modern sound stages and glitter of pop stardom, and I've finally found something to live for. The fans have become my whole life, all the pain I've carried into this world turned into something useful and beautiful by their love.

I love them, and they love me. And that's enough.

Or at least it should be.

The dancers take place behind me in the dark as we prepare for our cue. The intro pierces the veil of smoke and shimmering lights, and I sing, my magic healing their hearts and mine—if only for a night. There's no doubt this is what I was made for.

Your wind lured me
Under the willow tree
Into your summer dream
You stood barefoot in the stream
As you strung out your lies
To catch imprudent butterflies

My delicate powdery wings
Picked right off the seams
A devil's deal was made
And sealed my fate

They were cruel
The games you played

With my heart
My body
My soul
You took all you wanted
And shrugged when it ended
A liar, a player, a shameless flirt
Let me ask you, Wonder Boy
(Tell me the truth)
Was it all for nothing?
(Ooh, You're nothing to me now)

You knocked on my window
Under the midnight shadow
And smiled like the devil
(Watch out for the devil at your door)
A smarter girl would have turned you away
(Watch out, Watch out)

But I melted in your arms
Spellbound by your charms
I guess you didn't know
How to handle snow

Fire and ice don't mix for a reason
I guess I've learned my lesson
And after I turned my back on you
I never looked back, sugar plum.
(No, I never do.)

Complete darkness takes over, the spell I used to force all the electronic devices to shut down for a few seconds a secret recipe of mine. I slip out of my white dress in one fluid motion and run the length of the stage in the black leotard and harness I had underneath.

Dramatic exits have become part of my brand and made all the more impressive by my perfect night vision, a trait most dark Fae share that confounds mortals.

Every single person on my crew wants to know how I manage to zoom through the dancers and clip the wire onto my harness so quickly and perfectly every time, despite it being pitch black, and it has become a mystery I cater to every chance I get.

The wire hauls me all the way up, up, up.

When the lights flicker back on, I'm no longer at the end of the catwalk, but on the very top of the soundstage next to a giant cardboard cloud with a hidden door carved into it. Mere seconds have passed, and the crowd goes wild.

A giant spotlight showcases my location, and confetti rains from the sky as I blow them one last kiss and exit through the door.

On the other side, I clip my wire to the long safety pole and climb down the ladder. Becky, my loyal assistant, is waiting for me at the bottom.

"Great performance, Beth," she says. "Flawless exit, as always."

I hand over my in-ear monitors, mic, and battery packs, and wipe my dark bangs away from my forehead. Sweat and glitter stick to my hair and neck.

"Another one in the books. Praise the gang for their performance, please. I'm going to change."

"I wish you'd tell me what upset you, earlier."

I offer her a warm smile and squeeze her shoulder in reassurance. "It's nothing, Becky. I just need a bit of alone time." I zip down my knee-high boots and slip through the hallways in my bare feet to my dressing room.

I'm not known for being a diva, but tonight, I need space. I'm going to set fire to my trashcan and order a strong drink. And possibly fuck the sexy bartender that comes with it.

Once the door of my dressing room is securely closed behind me, I wipe the red lipstick off and sneak a glance at the wrinkled envelope on top of the trash. The torn heart-shaped seal fills me with dread, but I pick up the invitation and read it a second time.

> *Dear Miss Snow,*
>
> *I've been a fan of yours for decades, and when I watched your dazzling performance during the live broadcast of Elio Lightbringer's wedding, I knew I had to do everything in my power to meet you. I'm getting married three days from now at the Royal Academy in Augustus, and it's my dream for you to sing "Never to Be" at my wedding.*
>
> *I will send for you tomorrow night at your hotel, and we can discuss terms.*
>
> *Consider yourself my guest of honor.*
>
> *Your biggest fan,*
>
> *Heather Heart*

A downright adorable note if it wasn't for the wedding invitation tucked underneath it. The name of the groom reflects off the silver and gold calligraphy, sharper than a knife's edge.

It's not every day you get invited to your ex's royal wedding. It's even rarer for the poor bride to have no clue of what she's just done.

Immortality has its drawbacks. Most Fae I've grown up with are frozen in time, and I am no exception. We are full of regrets, yearning for something that used to be or could have been. It's so easy to forget to heal when you've got all the time in the world to wallow in past mistakes.

It's been almost a hundred years since I set foot in Augustus, the sparkling coastal town where I got my first taste of blinding happiness and heart-wrenching loss. Yet, the crisp crinkle and faint citrus scent of the invitation bring me right back to the night of the admission trials, fireflies shimmering in the night, the boys of summer ready to shred me to pieces.

A strangled grunt grates my throat as I ball the letter and invitation.

I should leave the ghosts of my past alone, but Winter Fae are used to digging up graves. Even after all these years, I wonder, what would my life look like if I'd gone right instead of left in that damn labyrinth?

CHAPTER 2
NEVER TELL ME THE ODDS
SONGBIRD

Summerlands, Faerie, 100 years ago

A king's pride can go a long way toward ruining your life. A father's ambition is even worse. Either death or glory awaits me in the Royal Academy's labyrinth. I don't think I could face my father's disappointment if I merely washed out of the trials.

Death is honorable. Failure is not.

Whatever happens tonight will determine my entire future. They've gathered the applicants on the field behind the huge maze they built for the trials. All the aspiring students are peppered around the manicured lawn. Applicants are here by invitation only, and I'm the sole common Fae present.

Most of my competitors are receiving one last prep session from their coaching teams, whereas I stand alone. It singles me out and makes me an easy target, the stares of my competitors riddling my pale skin with goosebumps.

Half of them are boys from the Spring and Summer courts, but a nasty-looking Red Fae—an applicant from the bloody Red Forest—

bares her teeth when she catches me looking, prompting me to angle my gaze toward the sky.

Huge round torches tower above our heads, flooding the space with light. The vast majority of the Fae competing in the challenge need them to see.

Fireflies flicker in and out of view on the outskirts of the clearing, the gigantic half arched windows and tall, prickly turrets of the Abbey twinkling behind the maze. I try not to stare at the shape of the Royal Academy's main building, my mouth parched and my lips dry.

I'm hungry for this. I want to show each and every one of these rich, pompous high-borns that I, Elizabeth Snow, am as clever and powerful as they are.

The boys are expected to wear nothing but black shorts, while we girls have been given flimsy summer dresses to cover our black, form-fitting, waterproof leotards—I think they call them swimsuits. The Spring Fae decorated their dresses with bright flowers, but that's a mistake.

Who cares about looks? These trials will certainly include a few sentient beasts, and I'd rather not give anything with fangs or claws a better chance to spot me.

I play nervously with the straps of my leotard, ready to melt into the grass and hide within the crust of the earth. I don't know how to swim—not properly. If the challenge calls for me to plunge into anything more than a shallow pool, I'm screwed.

"Let me through." A boastful voice erupts from the crowd.

My stomach cramps as Ezekiel Nocturna, the Shadow Prince, elbows his way through the sea of supportive coaches. I've been glaring at pictures of him for the last two days. My father was all too happy to present the prize he'd won for me, my royal fiancé.

Fae royals usually never marry so far down the totem pole, but this one was desperate enough to choose me, being in dire need of raw magic to boost his claim to the Shadow throne.

I'm an anomaly in my family. The first Snow with enough power to draw the king's attention and escape the mediocre fate I was born to, or so my father has been telling me since I froze the entire kitchen as a Faen because I didn't want to eat ragout.

A hurried betrothal to Ezekiel allowed me the perk of vying for a spot in this elite school, but I'm an outsider. If I make it through the admission trials, I'll receive a first-grade education. I'll be initiated into age-old secrets about our realm's magic and form connections with people that would not otherwise have deigned to glance upon me, given my lineage, and that includes my brand-new fiancé.

The living shadows flickering along the prince's smooth, tanned skin create an aura of black fire around his tall frame. Men from the Shadowlands are known for their rugged sex appeal, and Ezekiel is no exception.

He's got his father's strong jaw and his mother's silver eyes. I'd be tempted to grin timidly at him if it weren't for his sly, superior smile—the hallmark of a true Fae prince. His no-frills uniform bridges the class divide between us, but he looks like a man who's never worn anything but the finest silk.

He crosses his arms over his chest and eyes me up and down. "There you are, moth. You're not so bad to look at, at least."

Moth is used when referring to a common Winter Fae without any noble blood, as we come from the land of death. It's not considered derogatory, but it chafes my vanity all the same. Ever since I hit puberty, I've had a sixth sense to gauge a man's intentions. Call it a gut feeling or feminine intuition, but I can always tell when a man only pays me a compliment—even a backhanded one—to manipulate me, and Ezekiel checks all the red boxes on that front. Hells, he's not subtle or witty about it.

He purses his lips. "But I don't believe you've got what it takes to pass the admission trials. You're going to fail—or die." He shrugs as though his words are merely simple truths. "And I won't cry over it when it happens."

"I guess you'll know soon enough," I deadpan, my nerves stripping me of my usual carefulness when speaking to high-born jackasses.

"Don't get too attached to this face," he says, pointing at it with his index finger. "I don't care what my father said. If you don't get into the academy, I'll *never* marry you."

"No one is expected to marry a corpse, right?" I crack.

"Corpses take care of themselves. I can't marry a loser. Good luck, moth, but I don't expect to see you on the other side." He leaves with about as much discretion as when he arrived, thundering back to his advisors.

"Wow. He's an ass," a man says, inching closer to me. "I heard he's not the most talented or disciplined pupil. He should worry about his own fate, not yours."

"You're right about that." I spin around to face the newcomer. "Oh—"

The boy is awfully tall, but his posture lacks confidence, and his long arms hang awkwardly at his sides, as if he just sprouted a few inches and hasn't yet figured out what to do with his new height. His platinum blonde hair is in disarray, slicing through the dark night, but it's the wide wings on either side of him that steal my breath. He obviously wasn't on the lawn when I sized up my competitors earlier, and I glare at his outstretched hand.

"Elio Lightbringer, nice to meet you..." he trails off, waiting for me to introduce myself.

I've studied his name, along with the names of every Fae royal. Elio, second-born son of Ethan Lightbringer, the King of Light.

"I'm Beth—I mean Elizabeth Snow."

A luminous smile stretches his mouth. "Your name is on everyone's lips tonight."

My brows furrow. He's right, of course. "Given your expression, my last-minute invitation must have ruffled quite a few royal feathers."

"All of them, I'd say."

I shouldn't trust any noble Fae, especially friendly, gorgeous princes, but my keen instincts remain subdued and quiet.

I crane my neck around, searching for Elio's coaches. "Why are you alone?" As a prince, he's probably been training for this since he came out of his mother's womb.

"I ordered my coaches to stay away." He rolls his shoulders back. "It's nice to meet you, Beth. If it helps, I'm nervous as hell, too. They all expect you to fail, but if I don't make it through... Let's just say my father will take it as a personal affront."

The high-born applicants who wash out are usually relegated to less prestigious positions and never taken seriously as contenders for one of the seven crowns, but it's hardly a harsh fate. If I fail, I'll be trained to become a reaper and lose my only chance at life. That would force my cousins to leave school early, as they would have to work year-round in the mines to keep even a basic, hole-riddled roof over their heads.

We can barely afford the food on our table as it is.

I shake my head at Elio's lack of awareness for his obvious privilege and swat his comment away with a dismissive wave. "You're a prince; you'll be fine. This could completely make or break the rest of my *life*."

"Let's agree that we're both in a tight spot, then. Each trial has a guardian—a seasoned student granted the honor of crafting their court's challenge. My brother is one of them, and he'd love nothing more than to prove his superiority by being the one to eliminate me," Elio explains.

His wings shiver at his back, and in spite of myself, I keep staring at them. Sleek long feathers are interspersed with smaller down feathers that appear incredibly soft to the touch.

"Why don't you just fly over the labyrinth?" I joke.

Elio raises a pointed brow at my suggestion. "That'd be cheating."

I blink at him, stunned. *Is he saying he can actually fly? Or did he answer in jest?*

"You two should stop whining." A melodic, high-pitched voice muses from the side. "I've got worse odds to overcome."

A tiny girl plants herself next to Elio and me, and for a moment, I wonder if she's a pixie or a nymph. Loose brown waves fall below her waist, and she has a steep, slanted nose and big amber eyes with thick, long lashes that don't look human at all. Her red lips, high cheekbones, and chin dimple give structure to her round face.

The applicants are at least sixteen years old, but this girl could still pass for a Faen. We're all barefoot, and my big feet look like sleigh runners compared to hers. She didn't put on the summer dress. All her black leotard is missing is a dance tutu, and she'd be ready to step onto an opera stage as the worlds' most ethereal ballerina.

"Hi, I'm Willow Summers," she chimes.

Willow Summers. Daughter of Thera Summers, the Summer Queen. While all the Fae courts are technically equal, the Summerlands are larger than any of the other kingdoms, more populated, and possess the biggest army. The capital of the entire Fae continent, Eterna, lies at the heart of the Summerlands and doubles as their capital.

Given an inextricable argument between two courts, the side taken by the Summer Court pretty much tips the scale, making Willow the most influential princess.

"I'm Elizabeth Snow. Beth to my friends," I say quickly.

"I know. You're all everyone's been talking about." Willow braces her hands on her hips and stares down the labyrinth.

"What were you saying? About your odds?" Elio asks.

"Only a quarter of all applicants make it through the trials. Of those who don't make it, five percent die trying. That's 0.9 of us tonight."

"You're a... ball of sunshine," Elio croaks.

"I'm not finished. Of the dead aspiring students, only forty percent are female, but of those females, ninety-five percent were princesses less than five foot two."

Elio's mouth quirks. "That's an awfully specific analysis."

"Math doesn't lie. Probabilities are worse than fate. Short princesses are in grave danger tonight, whereas there's been zero casualties in the winged prince category."

"And what are my odds?" I ask, half amused, half terrified.

She tilts her head to the side and examines me. "You're tall and not a princess. You should be fine."

One of the faculty's presiding judges walks onto the stage, and conversations die down across the lawn. The black woman is wearing a ceremonial white toga, her dark brown hair styled in an afro and held away from her face by a thick, golden band.

"If I could have everyone's attention, we have a long night ahead of us," she announces. "I'm Master Evelyn Eros, and if you're lucky, one of your future teachers. Coaches must now leave the lawn. Applicants, please line up in front of our esteemed Headmaster, Idris Lovatt. Since his daughter is among you tonight, he appointed me to rule over this year's trials in his stead. Thank you for the honor, Headmaster." She offers a respectful nod to the man standing right in front of the stage as the coaches head off the grassy field.

The older man's gray hair and thick beard contrast with his dark brown skin. He's got an elegant face and the piercing, enticing gaze of a Summer Fae.

He brings a hand to his heart and shows off his perfect white teeth. "Thank you, Evelyn."

The woman goes on with her speech. "Master Idris will have you draw a numbered tile at random. And don't even think about switching tiles with another student. Everyone must keep the tile they drafted. I, along with the two other judges, will ensure that there's no cheating of any kind. Remember, cheating during the trials is not only an automatic disqualification, but also a serious crime against her Majesty Thera Summers, our beloved hostess."

The lawn seems almost empty now compared to how it was a minute ago, only the twenty-four applicants remaining, and we form a semi-straight row in front of Master Idris, a few applicants peeking out of both sides of the line to watch the others draw their starting numbers.

Willow, Elio, and I are the farthest away from the stage, and we end up at the back of the line.

Elio motions for us to stand in front of him. "Ladies first."

I refrain from narrowing my eyes at his gallantry, suppressing the mistrust in my gut, and stare at the tall hedges beyond the stage as we wait for our turn to come. The holes forming two distinct entrances into the labyrinth's exterior wall give absolutely no clue as to what lies beyond them, the hedges at least twenty feet high.

According to my father and the information he managed to glean from his network of friends, the first two trials should be Winter and Storms, followed by Spring, Autumn, and Light, before the trials end with Shadow and Summer. *If I could only draw an early entrance slot and blaze through the Winter trial… it'd give me ample time to work my way through the other sections of the maze.*

"Going too early has got its drawbacks," Willow declares with the same verve she displayed earlier. "But the last few time slots are the worst."

"Because of the time crunch, you mean?" I ask.

The applicants who go last have to race through the trials if they hope to make it through in time.

"Yes, and by the end of the night, the guardians are in a hurry to get to the afterparty. They're known to be more vicious on the unlucky few who close the march since the poor bastards will be rescued and resuscitated by the judges in a somewhat timely manner after the closing horn. But the first few to enter get all the fresh, active traps."

I could drown before the last bell rings…

"I'm hoping to draw a number between five and fifteen," Willow says, sinking her small hand deep in the purple velvet bag to retrieve her tile. "Ten." She blinks a few times like she can't quite believe her luck. "Only one student who's drawn this tile in recent times has died."

My fingers tremble as I pick one of the last two tiles.

23. I press the rectangular piece of marble hard into my palm, and my stomach churns. *I'm in the very last group to enter.*

Elio reaches into the bag, too, and drags out the final tile. "I'm in the first group."

Willow elbows my side. "What did you get?"

I grimace and show it to her.

"Time will be your true adversary. Less than ten percent of the applicants in the last group finish in time. A ton are severely injured, but none of them has ever died. Silver fucking linings, right?"

I grumble a strangled acknowledgment, wondering what 'severely injured' means for rich, powerful Fae who can easily get the best healers. Are we talking stab wounds or severed limbs here? I can't afford to spend the next month in a sanctuary.

Master Evelyn collects the bag and turns it inside out to make sure it's empty. "Alright. Now that you have your starting numbers, you know the rules. To be admitted to the Royal Academy, you have to come out of the other side before the closing horn blows. No physical objects, weapons, or armors of any kind are allowed inside. Only your magic and the clothes we gave you can cross the barrier. You have one hour after the chime of the last bell to cross the finish line. There'll be no exceptions, however close you are to the end of the labyrinth. The early time slots get more time, that's true, but they have more deadly traps to deal with, so you shouldn't lament your late time slot.

"The labyrinth will ensure that you do not cross paths with each other, but if you were to encounter a guardian, know that they are not allowed to help you—or even speak to you. There will be no interference until the closing horn goes off, after which we'll rescue those who failed."

I paw at the front of my summer dress, my heart in my throat.

"The maze is made so that you don't have to go through all the trials, but three at a minimum, depending on where you enter and exit the challenge," Elio whispers. "You should strive to stay away from Spring and Summer altogether. Those two will be the hardest considering your darkling pedigree, and the viciousness of their magics."

I squint at the prince. "Why are you helping me?"

"I think everyone should be allowed to apply here. It's stupid that only high-born Fae get invited since power is not necessarily hereditary."

Willow nods emphatically at that. "I agree. The way they only allow a teeny tiny percentage of common Fae to study here keeps the vicious wheel of our wicked caste system turning."

"You're preaching to a believer," I say on a sigh. "The admission process is meant to weed out undesirables like me, who have enough magic to succeed, but not the right surname, favoring nepotism—no offense."

Elio fails to conceal a grin behind his hand. "How did you get invited to the trials? My father left out that part."

Willow points at the Shadow Prince's back. "He's the reason."

Elio raises a brow. "Zeke?"

"Yes. If everything goes according to my father's plans, I'll be the next Shadow Queen," I say, my voice shaking over the last part.

"Number one, left or right?" the judge calls out to the girl who drew the number one tile, urging her to choose her starting position.

She picks right, which means Elio has to go left, and the prince waves us goodbye. "Got to go. See you both on the other side." He walks to the starting totem at the left entrance of the maze.

"Winter is on Elio's path," Willow breathes so faintly I almost miss it. "Ice will change him forever," she trails off, her voice carrying a strange musicality.

"So Winter's on the left? Are you sure?" I ask.

She blinks again. "I'm sorry?"

"You just said Winter was on Elio's path."

"Oh." A deep blush brands her round, youthful cheeks. "I get these flashes sometimes, of the future or whatnot. But seventy-two percent of all predictions and forecasts end up to be incorrect."

The first bell rings. Elio and the girl enter the maze while the two members of the second group take their place by the totems.

Willow sits in a lotus position on the grass, and her gaze darts over to my fiancé. "Why doesn't Zeke sit with you if you're engaged?"

I sit crossed-legged next to her and nibble on my thumb. "I don't think he cares much about me."

Zeke drew a middle of the pack starting group, but the Shadow Prince doesn't attempt to belittle me further. He's too busy flirting with a gorgeous Spring Fae with long dark hair and radiant brown skin to bother with me.

Willow nods at that, as if I'm making perfect sense, not at all bothered by the admission. "Eighty-nine percent of all royal Fae marriages are for power—either meant to boost the bride and groom's political momentum or their raw magic, depending on the Fae. Half of those marriages were arranged between the Fae's parents." She bites her bottom lip. "You must have tons of ice magic to spare. No one in my world would dare to entwine their fate with Zeke's, given how weak he's rumored to be."

The crowd starts to filter out after a few bells, each group of two given a five-minute edge over the two following behind them. After Willow is called away, I shift to hug my knees to my chest, trying to get comfortable. I've still got a long wait to go.

The bells ring again and again until the cuticles of my thumbs are bloody. Only four of us are left. We glance at each other, sharing the same ill-fated timing. Oppressive silence blankets the lawn, and sweat beads on my brow.

The two applicants in the group before mine enter the maze, and Master Evelyn finally waves me forward. "Number twenty-three. Left or right?"

I watch the exterior wall again, searching for a clue, but they wouldn't make it so easy as to label the entrances, would they?

"Left." My stomach flips. I've got one shot at a completely different future, and I can't let my father down.

I take my position, and the guy who drew the twenty-four tile takes the empty spot next to the totem on the right.

The three of us are the last people here, now. Most of the crowd probably transferred to the other end, anxiously waiting to see who makes it through—and who will be cast aside.

The last bell of the night rings with a shrill edge in the clearing, and I run into the maze.

Here goes.

It's all or nothing.

The entrance closes behind me, bare branches in the cedar hedge stretching from the heart of the plant and crawling toward one another like skeletons staggering toward the afterlife. The deep *cracks* and *snaps* of the dried twigs shiver through me.

There's nowhere left to go but forward.

Warm tingles of warning creep along my spine as I spot a large thundercloud crackling with electricity up ahead. This isn't Winter but Storms. Fuck me.

Off I go, deep into the labyrinth.

CHAPTER 3
MADNESS AT FIRST SIGHT
WONDER BOY

The luscious jungle I created for the admission trials smells of passion fruits, rain, and impending doom. Clusters of mist dampen the air and conceal an endless string of carefully-laid traps. A catered selection of magnificent, deadly plants are lying in wait to attract and eliminate the most powerful applicants, while the fever dreams take care of the rest.

The odd poisonous snake and a swarm of pyre butterflies even ventured in on their own.

I walk along the banks of the boiling stream that runs along this section of the labyrinth to the moonlit meadow and contemplate my masterpiece. My bare feet leave footprints in the rainbow-colored sand, but if I was to try and cross the stream, they'd be burned straight to the bone. A constant cloud of smoke rises from the waterfall rushing down to the bottomless pond, and the will-o'-the-wisps twinkle in the distance, enhancing the scenery's mystique.

The rules of the trials are simple: only those who cross the labyrinth's exit before the closing horn will join our elite group. I still hold the record for the fastest time, though I have to share the title with a mightier-than-thou, annoyingly talented Shadow Fae.

It's no surprise they decided to pit Damian and I against each other as guardians.

The judges assigned us to the last two portions of the labyrinth, making us responsible for the only two exits that lead to victory. The one who lets fewer applicants through his trial will be crowned the winner, and there's no way I grew an entire rainforest to end up in second place.

Anything goes tonight, except for cold-blooded murder. While the occasional *accident* has happened in the past, murdering the sons and daughters of the most influential High Fae is frowned upon.

Even though we're near the end of the night, only two applicants have made it to my exit. There's barely fifteen minutes left, so I'm pretty confident of my victory.

A woman steps through the garden gate on top of the hill that marks the start of my territory and the entrance to the meadow, and I take cover behind a hedge of bleeding hearts.

I've never seen her before. A long braid cascades over her shoulder to her waist, but half of it has unraveled. A loose black curl snakes along the valley between her breasts, luring my eyes down to her cleavage. Freckles of blood from the previous trial pepper her pale neck.

My prideful smirk falls, wiped away by a sudden tension between my ribs.

She's white as a snowdrop and graceful as a spider, so she's a darkling, but I can't hold that against her—she's divine. I rustle the leaves of the willow tree towering above her to wish her luck.

She squints at the moving branches and maps the scenery with a serious pout, the beauty of the meadow clearly not appeasing her mistrust. The most direct path to the exit is through the marshes, but she's still got to cross the boiling stream or the bottomless pond. Dark Fae seldom know how to swim, a basic life skill they should really work on.

Spiders and snowflakes have not fared well in my section of the labyrinth. None have managed to cross, a few of them stuck so deep in the mud that they'll need reanimation.

Only a couple of darklings are expected to pass these trials, and that's a shame, because it means the odds of her making it out are almost null. I'll probably never see her again after tonight.

Sucks for me.

Lips pressed together, she observes the surface of the pond's black, reflective water for a long minute. My chest deflates as she decides to climb the trellis to go around it. She carefully places a foot on the first rung, the wood creaking under her weight, her fingers testing the weathered vines for a strong grip. I mutter a curse under my breath.

The only safe way to cross was to cliff-dive to the center and swim ashore.

The mature canopy of ensnarer vines snakes to life, spooking her, and she cries out as she pushes off the ledge, landing chest-first at the back of the pond. Watching a beautiful dark Fae drown isn't exactly on my bucket list, and I dig the balls of my feet into the earth.

She beats the water with her fists, arms flailing, and a succession of soft, rhythmic crackles grates through the air as she manages to freeze two large chunks of ice. Using them as buoys to keep afloat, she catches her breath. It takes immense power to sustain ice in this environment, and I let out a low whistle. The ground beneath my feet cools, demanding more energy to melt the ice, but I reign in my fire, curious to see what she'll do next.

Clutching her icy floats, she waddles clumsily toward the beach, but my abs clench as I realize the vines aren't finished with her. Ensnarers don't mind getting wet. They slither along the steep rock cliff to reach the water, the friction of their leaves against the stone mimicking a low, hissing sound.

Ice only makes them angrier and more vicious, but the girl extends her arms to them instead of trying to escape. My throat tightens as they coil around her arms and waist. They'll no doubt choke her before the closing horn blows.

Beads of mist cling to the bell-shaped flowers of the vines as my girl starts to sing. She doesn't sing just any song, but the most sensual and heartbreaking rendition of the ballad of St. John's Eve I've ever heard. The familiar lyrics form a haunting melody, and I can't help but mouth the words along with her.

At sunset on St-John's Eve
At the top of bare mountain
The Summer King lies in wait
Clock ticking down to dawn

Anything can happen
On top of the bald hill
For one night only
Even when it's folly

But demons follow in the king's wake
To prey on Eros' many mistakes
Up they climb, footprints full of snakes
Beware of lies, illusions, and heartbreak

Flower for a spade
Blood for treasure
Gold for a hand
A simple "yes" that was forbidden
A promise that should be freely given
A witch's heart's not so easily mended
As the devil's pride she has offended

At daybreak on St-John's Eve
Gone is the lovers' reprieve
And the chime of a far-off bell
Disperses the spirits of darkness

Blessed Flame. The vines deposit the girl on the shallow beach before weaving back into the trellis, and I press a hand to my beating heart. My cheeks throb like I've been slapped straight in the face, fingers and toes tingling with warmth.

Summer Fae know better than to roll their eyes at love at first sight, but by the Flame, I never thought it would happen to me.

The girl stumbles out of the pond, drenched to the bone. Her wet summer dress hugs her delicious form, and something inside me snaps. Before I can think twice about it, I slither closer to her, the thin but vigorous hedge of bleeding hearts still separating us.

"Tell me your name, Songbird," I whisper through the leaves.

The girl's hand jerks away from the foliage, and she peers through the vegetation. "Who's asking?"

I skip ahead of her with a small laugh and round the corner of the hedge, allowing her to take in my silhouette. If she's alarmed by my stature, it doesn't show on her perfect face. Mist and magic hang thick in the air, but the Shadow mask covering my eyes and the upper part of my face helps me keep most of my secrets.

"Tell me your name," I repeat patiently.

Water drips from her thick braid, her lovely feet covered in sand and mud. She tilts her chin up and raises her brows, not backing down. "Come into the light."

I tiptoe closer to her, and she draws a sharp intake of breath. After a definite pause, she tucks her bottom lip between her teeth and angles her gaze to the side, a fierce blush tainting her cheeks.

I take advantage of her hesitation and walk all the way into her bubble, taking the edge off my forwardness with a smile. "Don't make me ask again."

Jaw slightly askew, she sways from the ball of her big toes to her heels. "I'm Beth."

My tongue darts out to my bottom lip. "Beth. I love the sound of that."

"What about you? Are you a sidhe...or a nymph?" She cracks,

looking me up and down again, her initial embarrassment apparently forgotten.

A nymph? She can't be serious. I'd be amused—if I wasn't insulted. "Neither. I'm a guardian."

Her nose wrinkles, the vibrant shade of red on her face about as charming as her chastising tone. "If you're a guardian, you're not supposed to speak to me until the trial is over."

She springs ahead, but I fall into step with her.

"Go away, now. Let me focus."

"Time is against you. But I could take you directly to the end of the labyrinth," I offer quickly.

The corners of her mouth tense, and her previously nonchalant dismissal sharpens into anger. The dry click of her tongue leaves no room for interpretation. "Why would you do that?"

Her distrust is warranted, and I can't fault her for it. I offer her a wolfish grin, knowing better than to let that seed of anger take root. "Every gift comes with a price."

She holds both hands on her hips and considers me with great care, her annoyance morphing into a calculated glare. "And what would yours be, pray tell?" Her ocean-blue eyes shine in the dark, stealing my thoughts.

"A kiss," I blurt out, sounding more confident than I feel.

I'm such an idiot for bending the rules in the first place, but I can't help myself. There's not enough time left for her to cross the marshes on her own, and if she fails the trial... I can't take that chance.

I'll steal a kiss from her before the night is done if it kills me.

"A kiss..." Her melodic laugh echoes in the fragrant summer night. "Are you sure you're not a sidhe?"

Sidhes are hybrid beasts that inhabit our forests. They can take human form, and if you kiss them, you change into a beast, too. Forever.

"Quite sure."

"That's not a yes or a no. Sidhes are Fae who were cursed by the gods, so they share our blood and can't lie. If you want me to believe you, I need a resounding yes or no."

With a soft chuckle, I give in to her demand. "No, I'm not a sidhe."

"And did you ever change into a beast and didn't know how it happened?" she asks, checking that I'm not in denial about my sidhe nature, an interesting loophole that would have allowed me to answer with a lie.

Oh, I'm in love already.

"No. I swear to you I've never been a beast."

"Are you a guardian, or a devil then?"

I grin at her keen logic. We're in my father's labyrinth, and she's not about to trust the first demon that crosses her path. "Both. One kiss, and I will lead you out of here. You have my word."

She nods in understanding and starts to walk again. "A venomous kiss from a fever dream is a clever way to take out the imprudent. The glistening abs add a nice touch, Wonder Boy."

I chase after her and grab her arm, forcing her to a standstill. "No venom, no tricks. Just a kiss. I swear it."

For a moment, she just stares at my grip on her elbow. The space where our skins touch tingles with magic, our bites of power surprisingly similar. I give her arm a gentle squeeze and slide my fingers down to her hand, taken aback by the freshness of her smooth, creamy skin.

The steady current of magic should reassure her that I'm not a construct of the labyrinth, at the very least.

Impatience and need mingle in my blood, her proximity making it almost impossible to wait. "Take the deal, Songbird. It's a good one."

She arches a sceptical brow. "Who are you, really?"

"Does it matter?"

I hook my finger around hers and pull her closer, my other hand darting out to cup the side of her face. Her wet skin soothes the blaze of my desire, and I hum in approval. I've never touched a Winter Fae before, and the sensation leaves me dizzy, my breaths coming in shallow, rapid bursts as if I'd just run twenty miles to reach her. Her alluring scent, though watered down, still carries hints of pine sap and frozen vanilla, making my mouth water.

"Going once."

This is sorcery, I'm sure. Look at her eyes... I shake my head to regain my composure and lean forward. I've got a good foot on her, which leaves a few inches for her to cross.

Her troubled gaze flicks to my lips.

"Going twice..."

By Hephaistos, I will die if she says no.

Finally, she squeezes her eyes shut and stands on her tip-toes, crushing her mouth to mine.

I hum at the sweetness of victory.

It's not my first kiss by any means, but it sure feels like it. It's all new again, her wintry skin balancing out my fire, and I run my tongue across her bottom lip, begging for entry.

Eyes wide, she pulls away and covers her mouth with her hand. "Now, you have to make good on your promise."

I squeeze the side of her face softly and lean in for a better taste. "I wouldn't dream of disappointing you."

She presses her index finger to my mouth, gentle and yet firm. "You said one kiss would do it."

My forehead creases in confusion. I've never felt such an atmosphere, the plants almost stretching from their stems to sneak glances at us. She *must* feel it too.

"I'm a greedy devil," I rasp, desperate for her to give in. "Let me be greedy with you, Songbird."

She gives a small incline of the head. I would have missed it if I wasn't so consumed by her every move, and smile from ear to ear as I bend down to kiss her again.

Ecstasy runs thick in my blood when she opens her mouth, her tongue searching for mine, their meeting sweeter for the wait. She links both arms around my neck and sinks her nails into my hairline. *Fuck yes!*

We kiss like we've forgotten how to breathe.

Hard and fast and slow and steady.

A kiss of passion. A kiss of fate.

Our magics greet each other. She's the ice to my fire. I'm an unruly flame to the calm, smooth expanse of frost inside her veins. Her taste is fresh and sweet, but also piney, salty, and aromatic. It reminds me of abyssal violas, a rare delicacy harvested from northern skerries that the palace cooks use to decorate wedding cakes.

Both of her palms end up flat to my chest as I grip her waist, and she curses under her breath. Is she pushing me away or feeling me up—I can't tell.

I look down to check.

Our breaths are ragged, our mouths hanging open as she tentatively traces the ridges of my stomach. I nudge her nose with mine, a very real, very enticing scenario taking a life of its own.

Half of my heated brain calculates how much time we have left before the closing horn, while the other half evaluates all the surfaces available to us, the pressure in my groin almost unbearable.

Before I can find a romantic way to verbalize the extent of my greediness, Beth pulls away again, and a burst of ice hovers in my chest at the loss.

"*Tick tock*, Wonder Boy. You have a promise to keep."

Her lips are bruised by the intensity of our kiss. The obvious sorrow twisting her features cramps my stomach, more sobering than a kick between the legs, and the urge to spread her down on the grass slips away like sand through an hourglass.

I link our fingers and pull her along. "Come on. Follow me."

Half-running to give her a chance to keep up, I guide her through the will-o'-the-wisps. The pitfalls of the marshes have swallowed most of the other applicants whole, but I know every inch by heart.

Beth holds on for dear life, and I instantly become addicted to the confident and yet timid way she holds my hand.

The wooden pier separating us from the last corner before the finish line scrapes the soles of my feet as I come to an abrupt stop, my arms instinctively wrapping around her shoulder. "I can't go any further," I say.

Out of breath, she grazes my mask with trembling fingers. "Are you real?"

The way her voice cracks at the end breaks my heart... Like she's saying goodbye.

I twist her hand and press my lips to the sweet underside of her wrist. "Of course, I'm real. I'll see you soon, Songbird."

She stands on her tip-toes and pulls me down for a final kiss, and we devour each other until the pier itself quakes beneath my feet in warning. Time's almost up.

I begrudgingly push her off me with both hands. "You have to go. Now!"

She dashes toward the exit and glances over her shoulder before rounding the corner, the loose strands of her dark braid knotted together. She disappears from view to cross the finish line, and my chest swells with untamed joy, my heart too wide for my ribcage.

Smiling like a lunatic, I comb my wet hair away from my face, the strands heavy with mist and sweat. No one can know about tonight, but now that she made it into the academy, she'll be mine. Darkling or not, I will marry that girl.

CHAPTER 4
MOTHS AND CROWS
SONGBIRD

The closing horn resonates across the lawn. The hedges behind me sew themselves shut, and my heart pounds in my throat. I crossed the finish line seconds ago and struggle to catch my breath, arms braced on my knees.

I've done it. I crossed the labyrinth and made it into the academy.

But at what price, my inner self snickers. My lips are tingling. My hand, my face, my belly... A part of me wants to backtrack into the marshes to look for my handsome devil, but I dig the balls of my feet in the grass.

He wasn't real. Absolutely not. A man as beautiful as that would never give you the time of day.

I blink away the volatile emotions of the last hour and observe my surroundings.

The set up on this side of the maze is identical to the starting point but for the intoxicated crowd in the bleachers. The alumni of the academy, along with the immediate families of the applicants, were invited to attend, but my father remained in Wintermere. His boss doesn't like his personal assistant to wander off, so there's no shouts or howls of encouragement to greet my success.

If anything, I'm probably to blame for the raucous, unhappy clamor rising from one side of the bleachers.

I shake off the urge to cry, waiting for one of the judges to call me out for breaking the rules.

The three of them whisper between themselves, stealing nervous glances at me, but Master Evelyn finally clears her throat. "Cutting it close, Miss Snow. But well done." She stands up and motions for the students laying on the lawn to approach.

I quickly take stock of the small group. Five other applicants made it through before me, and they peel themselves from the large pillows sprawled under the torchlight.

Elio jogs toward me. "Beth! You made it!"

Willow's lips spread in a satisfied smile. "That'll teach them."

A boy keeps close to her rear, his eyes the exact same color, and I figure he's a Summer Fae, too.

Zeke and the girl he was flirting with earlier are the last to stand up. My fiancé looks down his nose at me. "You're full of surprises, moth." He punctuates the statement with a wink, and his gaze trails down my sweaty body, my skin tightening under his scrutiny.

"Congratulations to the six initiates who managed to get through the challenge in time. You've proven yourselves worthy of your place here. I need your signatures in the official ledger." Master Evelyn sets out ink and a quill for us to sign our full names in her voluminous leather-bound ledger. It's a big deal. True names allow powerful Fae, especially royals, to enchant others with ease, but Master Evelyn carefully flips the page between each initiate to prevent us from seeing anyone else's name.

I go last, and the date written at the top of the page catches my eye.

With the scorching humidity, it's easy to forget that it's still technically winter across the continent. Faerie has seven seasons, but it's almost always warm here in the Summerlands. The school year starts right after Alaveen, the season of endings and new beginnings.

The quill is steady in my hand as I sign my full name, Elizabeth Melia Snow.

Once we've all signed, Master Evelyn closes the ledger and holds it to her chest. "I hope you're all ready to work hard and give us your best."

The lump in my throat throbs.

"Now, if the judges would join me in the maze, we still have to congratulate the guardians and rescue the poor students who didn't cut it."

The other judges walk to Master Evelyn's side, while Master Idris clasps his hands together to get our attention. "Initiates, come with me. I will take you on a quick tour of the academy and show you to your dorms so you can freshen up for the feast." From the way he's grinning, I figure his precious daughter is the Spring Fae Zeke was flirting with.

I try to hide the jitters as I fall into step with the others. Only an hour ago, they were on such a high pedestal that I could barely picture myself among them. A searing glow hovers in my chest, making me feel fuzzy and light—yet I still feel incomplete. Pieces of me are scattered along the labyrinth, as if every challenge and trap took its pound of flesh.

Truth be told, I left my heart at Wonder Boy's feet.

As we approach, the grandeur of the Royal Academy ties up my tongue.

The main building is called the Abbey because of its stern, ominous look and its bloody religious past. The main tower rises several stories higher than the four long wings that extend from its corners. Vines creep along the weathered stone walls, covering about a third of the building's surface.

Dramatic arches create a breezeway that ensures coverage from the heavy rainfall this kingdom must receive to account for its leafy greenery.

The initiates gather in front of the main entrance, where a thick red carpet marks the three flights of stairs leading to the grand atrium. I recognize a few faces from the history books among the portraits of the alumni monarchs, the gold plaques beneath them too small to read from a distance as Master Idris escorts us to the center of the room.

The three-story-high windows at the back of the atrium offer a panoramic view of the undulating dark sea beyond. Salty air blows in from an open dome above the windows and kisses my cheeks like a promise.

The academy is located on the west coast of the Fae continent. I've never even stepped foot on a beach or let the sea lick my ankles as they do in my favorite novels. My father always discouraged fiction readings, but I could only read so many history books. Whether it's the Legends of the Breach, the Tales of the Dark Sea, or the occasional new world novel like Moby-Dick and The Blue Lagoon, I've been dreaming of the sea since I was a little girl.

Funny, coming from someone who doesn't even know how to swim.

I force my attention back to my immediate surroundings. A two-floor mezzanine towers above us, and a group of about thirty students huddles on the third floor. Some of them brace their arms over the ornate banister to catch a glimpse of those who made it through the labyrinth, while others are engaged in animated conversations. A few keep their backs turned to the atrium, as if they couldn't care less about the new arrivals.

All of them are wearing cloaks with pointy triangular hoods and jeweled masks. I swallow hard. The academy students possess Shadow masks, high-end tools that allow them to walk between worlds freely through the sceawere, the in-between space that connects every realm by use of reflective glass. They can travel between Faerie, the old world, and the new. They are free to become whoever they want to be.

"The Crow's watching you," Willow whispers. "Do you know him?"

"Who?"

Common Shadow Fae are called crows, and my ears perk up. Maybe I'm not the only commoner here after all. I glance in the direction Willow pointed, scanning the crowd until my gaze lands on a tall figure looming on the empty side of the mezzanine. My breath catches in my throat. He stands shrouded in shadows—a dark spot of raw magic against the modern, vibrant backdrop of the atrium.

His iridescent onyx mask is peppered with broken pieces of polished glass. Despite his eyes being concealed, I know he's staring at me. The weight of his gaze travels across my face, and a flash of unease takes root in my stomach.

Willow leans closer to my ear. "His name is Damian Sombra. He's not really a commoner being the son of High Fae, but he's known for his stern, dark looks, and his complete disregard for social norms, so they use the sobriquet anyway," Willow explains before the corners of her mouth twitch. "He's a graduate student, and he gives my brother Aidan the creeps."

The Sombra province appeared in my geographic studies of the Shadowlands, but this Damian did not make it into Royal Lines, the genealogical reference I memorized before I came. If he intimidates Willow's brother, I should be weary of the way he's staring at me.

"You're Aidan's sister?" Zeke asks in a hushed voice.

My, my, was the jaded Shadow Prince eavesdropping? I didn't notice him creeping into our little group, but there he is, huddling close to Elio.

Willow blinks at Zeke like she's unsure if he's being facetious or just plain dumb. "You know Aidan?"

"A little," Zeke answers quietly.

The brown-haired boy on Willow's heels snickers, "I bet everyone's heard of your brother, Will. Even the moth."

"Of course I've heard of him," I snap. "Aidan Summers is the only known exception to the rules of succession."

The gods usually mark a king or queen's heir upon their death, but not in this case. Aidan Summers' reputation has reached the underbelly of the Wintermere castle, which is quite a feat. Moths don't often gossip about the Summer royals since most of us aren't likely to meet one in our lifetime.

The rude boy finally introduces himself. "I'm Sean Summers, Will's cousin."

"Elizabeth Snow," I grumble.

"Aidan was born in fire and blood, his skin ablaze and the Mark of the Gods seared into his flesh, marking him as Thera's heir *at birth*. Some say Hephaistos sired him himself—no offense to your father, Will," Sean says.

Willow rolls her eyes at that. "Wild rumors, of course. Aidan is no demi-god, I assure you."

Sean's eyes shimmer, and I get the impression he's more than a little infatuated with his famous cousin. He pats Willow's shoulders down with a chuckle. "Will is just blind when it comes to her brother. Sibling rivalry and all that. Aidan holds the record time for the admission trials. He crossed the labyrinth in twenty-seven minutes flat and skipped a whole year, graduating in three, which is unheard of."

"Not unheard of. The Crow did, too." Willow grins. "It really pissed Aidan off."

Damian is still staring at me, and I'd glare at him right back for his rudeness if I wasn't hoping to make friends with another outsider. "Are the graduate students around a lot?"

"It depends. There's five of them at the moment, one for each kingdom besides the Red Forest and Wintermere. They might give us lessons in their respective school of magic when they're not studying off-world."

"Talking about going off-world, when do we get a mask?" I ask, my palms sweaty just thinking about it.

"Before Morheim, if we pass the exams."

Morheim is the season of nightmares, when the sun doesn't rise in the Fae sky for seven to ten days. It's squeezed between Autumn and Winter, so it'll be almost a full year before we get what most common Fae consider the ultimate instrument of freedom. I can't wait.

Master Evelyn joins us just as Master Idris finishes his speech about the various portraits. He was so engrossed in his lecture that he didn't seem to notice the whispers being exchanged, most of the initiates more interested in Willow's inside information than in the feats of long-dead kings. All except the gorgeous Spring Fae, who glowers at us for not paying attention, confirming my suspicion that she's his daughter.

"Everyone alright?" Master Idris asks.

Master Evelyn rubs off a crust of mud from her knuckles. "We had three reanimations, and one badly burnt Spring applicant will probably never recover her rosy cheeks, but all of them are alive."

"Wonderful, wonderful. Well, it's getting late, so I will take the men to their dorms, now, while Evelyn escorts the ladies. Men sleep in the south wing and the ladies in the north wing. We do not tolerate sleepovers between the two, and I do not care if you're not getting along, everyone has to room with their year's comrades," he says with a steely edge to his voice. "Your Keepers will show you through the dining hall and bibliotheca tomorrow and go over the school rules in depth."

Evelyn guides us under the breezeway and into the north wing, which is five stories high, about half as tall as the main building.

"You're a very small group, so you've been assigned to the third floor. There are two rooms with two beds each, but since there are only three of you, one lucky gal will get a private room. Once you decide who that will be, just write your names on the slates hanging on the doors, and your personal effects and school gear will be delivered immediately," she explains.

"Do we have classes in the morning?" I ask.

"No, only orientation tomorrow so you can recuperate from the trials. Classes will start the day after. We follow a clear-cut

Summerian calendar. Three days of classes, two days of personal studies followed by two days of rest. It's a tight schedule, but we manage."

I bite the insides of my cheeks to hold back a flippant comment. Winter Fae work for six days and rest for one, so this Summerian calendar sounds like a vacation, but Evelyn is from the Secret Springs, and the Erosi calendar calls for four days of parties and decadence every week.

"The seasonal holidays always fall within your rest periods, so you can celebrate accordingly." She braces her hands on her hips and adds, "Alright, I'll leave you to get cleaned up. The students' after-party is on the beach right outside. Follow the signs for the Saffron Cove. Congratulations again, and welcome. I'll see you in class soon."

Evelyn moves to leave, and I thread a little deeper inside the grandiose apartment. The living area spans the entire width of the building, with windows opening to the ocean on the left and the gardens on the right.

As soon as Evelyn is gone, the dark-haired Spring Fae skips ahead of me and spins around to face us, her hands clasped behind her back. "I want the private room."

"And who are you to decide that?" Willow quips, her tone sharp.

"Who are you, little thing?" The Spring Fae clearly missed our earlier conversation, too busy playing teacher's pet.

"Willow Summers," Willow declares with a bit of cheek.

"I'm Iris Lovatt."

Iris is the daughter of the headmaster and the beloved niece of the Spring Queen. Since Freya Heart couldn't have children with her much older husband, Oberon Eros, she elevated Iris to the rank of Spring Princess. I read all about it in one of the old royal pamphlets my father smuggled out of the castle for his collection over the years. The gifts bestowed during high-born Faen birthing ceremonies are usually reserved for royal eyes only, but Iris's title is hardly a secret.

Despite her impressive pedigree, Willow is the sole princess of

Summer. That puts them at a hierarchical tie for now, but if I had to choose, anywhere outside these walls, Willow would certainly outrank Iris.

"We should leave it to fate," Willow says as she grows three brown twigs in her hands, one longer than the others. "Let's just pick one and be done with it."

It's generous of her not to press her advantage.

"I'll hold them. So you can't cheat," Iris says, clearly unimpressed by Willow's magnanimous offer.

"That's fair."

Iris gathers the twigs in her hand and makes sure they're even, concealing their true length in her fist.

Willow and I both pick one, and I bite my bottom lip. Mine is longer by an inch.

The two women blink, and Willow laughs. "Oh my, looks like karma has spoken and Beth gets the private room."

"Hmpf," Iris grumbles. "She didn't even want it."

"Cheer up, Iris." Willow nudges her new roommate. "We get the striking ocean view."

"I don't mind switching—"

"Nonsense," Willow cuts me off. "You won fair and square."

I write down my name over the writing slate in chalk and twist open the knob.

All the adrenaline leaves my body as I walk inside the bedroom. It's five times as big as the one I shared with my cousins back home, and the beds could probably fit three people each. Two desks are set in opposite corners, furnished with a chair and built-in drawers. The frills of the textured pillows are maddeningly soft as I comb my fingers through them, the heavy sensation at the pit of my stomach giving a bit of a pulse.

I don't belong here.

Uniforms are sprawled over the foot of the closest bed, the other one stripped to the mattress. One skirt is plain black, another white, and the plaid skirt is black and white with teal accents and little snowflakes in the corners of the pattern. The button-down blouses are made of a slick, airy silk that feels almost liquid in my grip.

Corset camisoles add a bit of frill and variety, likely meant for special occasions. There are also swimsuits, sports clothes, and an assortment of shoes—more new clothes than I've ever owned. My usual attire mostly consists of hand-me-downs from my aunt.

Any of these garments sold at the market would probably feed a family of six for a month. Wishing I could curl into a ball and sleep for days, I abandon the large, oversized bed in favor of the cushioned bench of the alcoved windowsill. I sit down and hug my knees, staring out at the gardens.

Our apartment is on the third floor, and tall rectangular windows stretch along the corner of the building. Beyond them, wild, overgrown but beautiful gardens block my view of the east wing. A forest of tall, leafy deciduous trees tower in the background to the north, and a creek snakes through the bushes and flower beds. Star-shaped flowers as big as my head sag from the branches of the vines creeping above the windows, and the expansive canopy of trees casts mysterious shadows along the walls. The thick vegetation in the Summerlands is eerie, to say the least.

A loud knock jolts me back to reality as Willow cracks open the door, all dressed up and ready to party. A long fishtail braid hangs over her shoulder, and a dress with sequin stripes that imitates the new mortal fashions finishes right above her knees. She arches a brow at my appearance. "The bathroom's free now. Are you alright?"

"Yes. I just need a bit more time."

The door opens all the way, Iris's manicured nails propped against the wooden pane as she pushes in. "Then you can manage alone and join us when you're done. I expect even moths know how to use a bath, yes?" She hooks her elbow around Willow's and tugs her away.

Willow arches a brow. "Is that alright?"

"Go ahead. I'll catch you later."

As I watch the two women leave, I can't help but wonder what it's like for them. They were probably nervous, but the Royal Academy was their birthright. Willow must have visited this school many times, her parents being the official patrons. Same with Iris because of her father's position. It's a wonder they'd never met, actually.

I rummage through my tiny travel bag. I didn't own any appropriate clothes for the hot weather, and I couldn't afford anything fancy, but I did bring one classic black dress. I hadn't realized that my only *good* garment would probably be considered a rag next to the artful and expensive fabrics sewn by the royal tailors. The Winter Court typically values sensibility over artifice, remaining quite sober in their fashions in comparison to their peers.

After a quick bath, I slip on the solid black academy skirt and forgo the long-sleeved blouse in favor of the corset camisole with ribboned straps. The boning hugs my body, the teal and gold patterns making the ensemble shine.

The bustier is a little risqué, but Summer Fae are used to showing skin. Here, I don't have to act like a meek moth.

My mind drifts to the confident, glistening man I met in the labyrinth. When I first walked out of the maze, I felt a desperate, eerie, almost all-consuming need for him to be real, but now I'm not so sure. Guardians are either fourth years' or graduate students, so I'm bound to meet him tonight if he wasn't a fever dream after all. He said he'd see me soon, but what did that imply?

I shouldn't get too comfortable in this gilded, humongous bedroom.

Wonder Boy didn't look like a man who knew how to take no for an answer, brazen as he was to steal not one, but three kisses from me. What if he expects something else in return for helping me? What if he changes his mind and tells the judges what he's done?

I will be expelled within the hour if anyone finds out.

CHAPTER 5
SHARP EDGES
WONDER BOY

"Aidan. Damian. Come." Evelyn braces her hands on her hips. "Congratulations. Per usual, you two have a knack for ties."

I offer her a wry grin. If I hadn't taken Beth through the labyrinth, I would have finally beaten Damian fair and square. While I'm sure it'll be worth it, it still stings. I could take solace in the knowledge that I know I've won, but the whole point was to have everyone else know I'm the best, too.

Evelyn looks down at her ledger. "Only three initiates each, and zero casualties. Great job. It's an art to incapacitate them without killing them."

A dark gloom sticks to Damian's brow. "It might be funny if it wasn't so damn sad."

I bite the insides of my cheeks, determined not to say anything that could give me away.

"Cheer up, Damian. You still won," Evelyn teases.

"A tie is not a win."

"It's almost a win."

Damian licks his lips. "And I'm *almost* smiling."

After the other two judges congratulate us on a job well done, I stop by my room to change and take a quick shower before joining the undergraduate students on the mezzanine.

I sit alone along the banister, my back pressed against the intricate metal work and prop a book in my lap. If any of my fellow guardians walk past me, they'll assume I'm waiting for the initiates to clear out of the atrium so I can head to the afterparty. I angle my face slightly to the side to catch a glimpse of my Songbird through the space between the railings.

She takes my breath away. Even from afar, all muddied up, she's the most beautiful woman in the room—and by far.

I can't afford for anyone to notice my fascination with her, or they might begin to suspect what I've done. I especially can't let Damian catch me staring at her, not before we're formally introduced.

My nemesis doesn't share my restraint and glares unabashedly at the initiates, to the point where they gossip between themselves. The familiar timbre of Willow's voice is easy to discern from the others, and a smile ghosts over my lips.

I always knew my little sister would crush the trials. Our father will finally stop holding that over her head.

After a minute, Damian marches over to me. I pretend to be engrossed in my reading and don't acknowledge his presence until he clears his throat.

"Hey, Damian. Great job out there," I say in a condescending manner.

"How did she do it? Cross the marshes so fast?" he grunts, tucking his mask inside his hooded cloak.

"Who?"

"The moth."

"How would you know how long it took?" I ask with a grin, knowing damn well that it triggers his temper when I answer his questions with questions.

"I asked Diana, and she said the moth left her section of the labyrinth with barely fifteen minutes to spare."

A cold sensation slithers deep in my gut, but I shrug. "She got lucky."

He squints at me, his golden, liquid gaze locking with mine. I swear the man can see inside my soul, and I hate it.

"I can't believe you let Zeke Nocturna slip through your fingers." I purse my lips in a dramatic pout. "Too bad. So sad."

Damian flashes me his best hawkish, disingenuous smile. "Zeke managed to trudge through my trial because he's shadow through and through. It still doesn't make him strong, smart, or skilled enough to claim his father's crown. You letting a snowflake breeze through summer is really the only shocking twist of the night."

My eyes narrow at the overbearing disbelief tainting his voice. If one of us should be suspected of cheating, it should be him. Light Fae usually don't fare well in shadows, and two of them managed to pass his trial.

"What about Elio? Your nightmares couldn't take him? An inexperienced Prince of Light?" I quip.

"You'd be surprised. There's more to him than you know."

"And what about the Spring rose? Or were you too chicken to eliminate the headmaster's daughter?"

He shrugs. "She's darker than expected."

But my questions clearly hit a nerve, and he becomes real quiet. Knowing him, he's replaying every moment of his trial and analyzing what he could have done better. The guy is a brooding perfectionist if I've ever met one.

Mission accomplished. Now, he's picking apart his mistakes instead of wondering about mine. I snap my book shut and jolt to my feet, the initiates now gone to freshen up inside their dorms.

I lurk along the main pathway between the girls' apartments and the beach for the next half an hour and hide behind a column when Willow and the headmaster's daughter walk past. Beth is not with them nor following behind them, and my palms get a little sweaty.

I couldn't have missed her, could I? I hope she's alright, and that Damian didn't ambush her with questions about what happened in the labyrinth.

A few minutes pass as I try to determine if I should head to the north wing, but I'm not sure which floor the initiates were assigned. I'm about to enter the gardens to check when Beth finally appears at the top of the stone stairs leading down to the sea.

My heart almost jumps out of my chest. "Songbird. Hi."

She freezes on the step, her blue eyes wide as I bridge the gap between us. "Wonder Boy..." She tucks a long strand of black hair behind her ear. The waves are slick and glossy, no longer matted together with sweat and blood. I barely resist the urge to comb my fingers through them.

I can't stop grinning, and my chest swells with a rushed breath. It's silly, but I'm a pack of raw nerves. I have no idea who this girl is, who her parents are, or whether she's into me. I just know she's got to be mine, and that's a complicated emotion.

The rational part of my brain urges caution.

"Congratulations," I whisper, admiring her pale skin. No one in the Summerlands could get away with a complexion like that, and I slip my fingers under the ribbon strap of her corset to caress her shoulder and trace the flesh of her arm with my thumb.

Her gaze darts to my hand, her lips parting in surprise—or perhaps warning—but she doesn't speak. Instead, she stares at the place our skin touches.

I offer her my arm. "Let me escort you to the afterparty."

She doesn't move to take it, and my brows pull together.

"What's your name?" she asks quietly.

This is not the happy reunion I'd hoped for. She looks...terrified.

"Hey, is everything alright?" I whisper, unable to understand how the girl who bravely sang my ensnarer vines to sleep and stood tall against a guardian of the labyrinth could be shaking with fear now.

Zeke Nocturna barrels down the stairs and comes to stand beside her, interrupting our conversation. I let my arms fall at my side and offer the prince a nasty scowl as he wraps an arm around her shoulders and pecks her cheek.

"Lizzie, there you are." He lets his arm hang casually between her breasts, and my Songbird grimaces, ever-so-slightly inching away from him.

I have to sink my nails inside my palms not to push him off her, but he quickly adds, "Keep your hands to yourself, Summers. It's my fiancée you were touching."

My frown deepens, and I shake my head. "You're—" My gaze burns into my temptress, a rebellious flame licking the back of my neck as I try to reign in my emotions. "You said your name was Beth."

I'm confused as to how she managed to lie to me. All initiates are full-blooded Fae. It's a consecrated rule.

"My name *is* Beth. Elizabeth," she croaks.

I trace the arch of my brow, feeling as though some grim pixie dragged me to her lair and is using my intestines to replace her harp strings.

Elizabeth as in Liz fucking Snow. Blessed Flame. She's the moth my father fought so hard to keep out of the academy.

CHAPTER 6
SHRED ME TO PIECES
SONGBIRD

Wonder Boy smiles at Zeke the way a snow serpent smiles at a wolf when it steps too close to its nest. "I was only introducing myself. To your...*fiancée*."

As it turns out, he's real. And not at all happy with the reveal that I'm engaged. The mere mention of my surname plastered a disgusted grimace on his face, so he's not into me being a moth, either.

Zeke's arm tightens around my shoulders, and the overbearing smoky scent of his shadows clogs my nose. I shake off the urge to cough, barely functioning. When I saw Wonder Boy heading toward me earlier, I thought I was hallucinating. He's even more perfect without the veil of mist blurring the air of the labyrinth—his amber eyes alight with keen, searing intelligence. The very shape of his body taunts me, his fancy clothes doing a poor job of concealing the muscles I fondled earlier. Add to that the all-too-real masculine inflections of his husky voice...

I'm simply dizzy with how *real* he actually is.

Zeke just called him Summers, so he must be another cousin of Willow's and Sean's, but Thera Summers has twelve brothers and sisters, which makes her family tree confusing as hell.

I quickly run through the list of possible names, scanning him for clues, but there are simply too many Summer High Lords to keep track of. The Summerlands genealogy is more like a confusing game of tic-tac-toe than a clear family tree.

A few strands of Wonder Boy's brown hair gleam in the night like bottled embers. His traditional dress shirt is made of fine, crisp white linen and tailored to fit the contours of his body. Embroidered details near the collar showcase a row of creeping ivy—no doubt the Summers' family crest.

The mask of melted glass he was wearing back in the maze is no longer obscuring his face, and I follow the sophisticated arch of his brow, the discrete slant of his nose, and the alluring groove of his chin dimple. And those full lips... Lips that were hungrily devouring mine only an hour ago.

His amber eyes are guarded, the sharp line of his jaw tense enough to appear chiseled from stone. He looks thwarted—betrayed, even.

The fire in Wonder Boy's gaze could burn down entire cities, flames licking the shape of his clenched knuckles, and I inch away from both men.

Zeke glares suspiciously at the guardian. "How do you know Lizzie?"

I wince at the pet name. Only my father calls me that.

"I don't. I had never seen her before tonight. I didn't even have time to introduce myself before you marched in like a leprechaun eager to protect his pot of gold," Wonder Boy says, the answer carefully crafted to appease my fiancé.

I curse my complexion, the blush on my cheeks threatening to reveal everything we did in the labyrinth. My mind drifts back to our kiss, to the way he hummed his approval against my lips, his tongue seeking mine without restraint. My gaze drops to his long fingers, the ones that held my waist with just the right pressure—enough to make me feel precious and desired, but not intimidated. His cleanly-shaved skin felt so smooth to the touch...

A sharp inhale rocks my chest as I recall how he clung to my hand while we ran, and the way he smiled at me after letting go, as if I were something worth burning the world down for.

"Lizzie, this is Aidan Summers."

Err—what?

I blink. "You're—"

"Aidan Summers." He arches an impish brow, drinking in my reaction. "Do you two lovebirds need help finding the beach? It's right outside by this thing we call the sea." His natural warmth is gone, replaced by something sharper and falsely sweet.

"We'll manage," I croak, my insides boiling as the realization hits—I made out with Aidan fucking Summers, the Crown Prince of the Summerlands. And why did I just say *we* when Zeke was so brazenly marking his territory? I might be engaged to him, but we're not a *we*.

Aidan Summers... How could I have been so stupid? Smooching with a stranger like that?

He told me he was a guardian.

What was I thinking? That I'd somehow stumbled upon the only other common Fae at the academy? He had to be just another egotistical, pompous prince, but this... this is worst-case scenario.

The revelation keeps exploding in my mind, dragging me down a rabbit hole until a tall blond saunters up the sandy stone steps in front of us, shouting, "Aidan! Stop playing with the spiders. I need your key—" The newcomer skids to a stop as his blue gaze crosses with mine. "Whh— Hi! And who might you be? You're not a spider."

"Elizabeth Snow."

A pair of powdery white wings are folded behind the man's bare back, and between the wings, the defined abs, and the platinum-blond hair, there's no question in my mind that he's Elio's brother.

He snatches my wrist and brings my knuckles to his lips. "Ezra Lightbringer, at your service, Lady Snow."

Zeke's nails dig into the flesh of my shoulder. "Fuck off, Ezra. The *lady* is spoken for."

They all know each other, of course. There must be special

soirées for spoiled, cocky princes to plot on how to look so damn good and effortlessly break women's hearts.

A derisive snigger pops out of Ezra's mouth. "You set yourself up for failure, Lady Snow."

"Why? She passed the trials, didn't she? And she's attractive enough," Zeke clips.

Ezra swats the comment away like my fiancé is nothing more than a bothersome house fly and focuses all his attention on me. "You're gorgeous, of course. That's not up for debate, but I stand by what I said. You're going to fail at what you came here to achieve."

I raise my chin. "Is that so?"

"Look at you." He bites his bottom lip and grazes my face from my cheekbone to my chin, as if it's an apple he might pluck from the tree, take one bite of, and discard without a second thought. "With a face like yours, you're meant to wear a crown... But Zeke's unremarkable ass will never touch a throne."

The ethereal glow of his skin is mesmerizing up close, and I find myself hypnotized by the luminous patterns swirling beneath his dermis.

"I'm the only heir to the Shadowlands," the Shadow Prince counters.

Ezra's gaze darts over to my fiancé. "By blood, but the Crow is going to steal your father's throne. Everyone knows it. It won't be long now; he's growing restless here. And if, by some miracle, Damian decides to wait for your father to croak, Morpheus and Hypnos will name him as their true heir."

Zeke lets go of me, crossing his arms over his chest. "You're wrong, Lightbringer."

"Ooh, did I hurt your feelings?" Ezra snickers before he lowers his voice and inches closer. "You, Lady Snow, might as well have bound your fate to my brother, Elio. He's never going to sit on a throne, either, but he's clever and a true gentleman... I could arrange it, if you asked nicely." Ezra looks positively evil as he dips his eyes down to my breasts, his tongue darting out to touch his bottom lip.

"Unless you'd rather be a mistress to a true king than queen of nothing..."

Somehow, in just four sentences, Ezra has managed to insult Zeke, undermine his brother, and treat me like a whore. Zeke grabs a fistful of my skirt to tug me away from Ezra, while Aidan's fists clench and unclench at his sides, as if he can't decide which of them to punch first.

I feel like nothing but a piece of meat being prodded by vultures. Clearly, I should have focused less on the trials and more on how to deal with gorgeous, vicious princes.

"Thank you for this little...chat, Ezra. It's been enlightening." I skirt away from Zeke and slip between the other two princes. My heart hammers as I march forward, ignoring the weight of their gazes, and throw them a dismissive wave without looking back. "See you later, boys."

CHAPTER 7
VILLAINS
WONDER BOY

"I like her," Ezra declares, his eyes following Beth until she disappears between the bushes with her fiancé on her heels. "The Iris chick is smoking, but this one... there's just something about her."

"Iris is Idris' daughter. He'll make your life hell if you try anything."

"And the moth is engaged, so there's not a lot of fresh meat for us to sink our teeth into this year." A wide grin overpowers his face. "Thank the Flame that the Summer Princess is hot."

I click my tongue and bare my teeth in warning. "Where Willow is concerned, consider yourself a eunuch." If he so much as looks at Willow funny, best friend or not, I'll cook his balls and serve them for dinner.

"Just kidding, of course. Will's my buddy, as you well know, and I'm not her type."

"No new girl for you to seduce means you'll get to study more," I joke, trying to appear high-spirited despite my egregious mistake. Ezra knows me pretty well. I can't let him know how interested I truly am in Beth and how I risked my reputation for her to be admitted here. "Evelyn is always berating you to spend more time in the library."

Ezra cringes as if I've just crammed a fistful of myrtle seaweed into his mouth. "Study? Library? I think not. It's our last year, Aidan. We have to make the most of it. Besides, I wouldn't count the first-years out so quickly. The moth won't stay with that tool Zeke for long, not now that she's made it into the academy."

"If Zeke's father isn't an idiot, he would have made a proper deal with her to prevent her from changing her mind." As I say the words, a heavy knot coils in my stomach. *Fuck.* I hadn't thought of that until now.

Ezra licks his lips, unaware of my turmoil. "We don't have to change her mind, boo. Just convince her one night is worth the transgression."

He's beginning to sound too interested in my girl.

"What did you need?" I ask sharply.

"Your key to the cabin."

We built a log cabin in the heart of the gardens back when I was a first year. It's meant for special occasions when we want privacy and don't want to be disturbed. I wove an enchantment over the whole meadow, and only someone in possession of the key can find it. Since we're both expected to inherit a throne, our secrets are a coveted currency. At the cabin, we can talk, laugh, and love freely, away from our father's spies and nosy peers.

I stare at him, unimpressed by his predictable need to put his Faehood first. "The party hasn't even started, and you promised to introduce the new villains."

"Don't get your fiery panties in a twist. I just like to plan ahead, that's all."

I pretend to hand over the key, only to pull it out of his reach at the last second. I'm not a fan of him using our oasis of peace for a random hookup, but who am I to judge? "You can get the key later, when you've done your duty. Diana told me you refused to rehearse with them last night."

"My best performances are always spontaneous, as you well know. Come on, Aidan. I'm horny as hell and optimistic about tonight, though my plans might be shifting as we speak." He glances down the stone steps to where Beth and Zeke disappeared. "Do you think the new girl might be persuaded—"

I answer too quickly, a flicker of jealousy igniting in my chest. "No. I don't think she liked your attitude."

"I like a challenge, but you're right. I should stick to old favorites tonight. The twins let me know they're ready for round two."

The twins, two third-years with wild sexual appetites, have history with Ezra, and I chuckle, happy to hear he's not going to go after Beth. "Have fun." I rub the piece of leather acting as a keychain between my fingers before handing it over.

Some silly part of me wants to hold on to that key, just in case, but taking Ezra out of the equation is worth it. Besides, I'm willing to be patient. After what I just learned, my genius plan to seduce Beth and make her fall in love with me might take a few days more than I'd originally planned.

Ezra and I stroll over to the beach, exchanging playful jabs and lighthearted banter as we go.

The alumni have reserved the north beach, preferring to keep bad decisions away from the prying eyes of the students. As a result, the crew huddles on Saffron Cove, a small, secluded orange beach at the foot of the Lovers' Leap cliffs.

I grab a cloak from the pile on the table next to the buffet, pulling the hood over my head and pressing my mask back in place. The attire allows me to reflect in private as we wait for all the first-years to settle down in front of the bonfire.

The seasoned students are wearing their cloaks and masks, adding to the atmospheric vibe of the initiation kick-off.

When the last of the six initiates has arrived, Ezra plants himself in front of the bonfire, facing the half-circle of students. His gaze is angled downward, leaving only the bottom of his prismatic opal mask visible.

The conversations die in an instant.

"I'm Ezra Lightbringer, last year's Master of Mischief," he announces gravely. "Tomorrow, you will meet your Keepers. They will try to convince you to play nice, follow the rules, and act like good little sheep." He slices his arms in denial and shrugs off his hood and cloak.

The fucker spreads his wide, powerful white wings on either side of him, and the crowd gasps in surprise and excitement.

Ezra might not be a Spring Fae, but he's got his own lust magic, rooted in his godlike aesthetics and sharp wit. My mouth dries up as I catch Beth with her lips parted, ogling him. The way she bites her bottom lip makes my throat bob.

Fuck me.

"We were born to rule, not to be meek. We are the heirs of the gods, the chosen ones, the most powerful beings in the worlds." Ezra raises one finger in the air for us to wait as he grabs a pitcher of Nether cider from the table and gulps down the entire thing. After he's done, he rubs the back of his hand across his mouth and exhales on a satisfied "ha."

The corners of my mouth quirk up at his theatrics.

"Tonight, I present to you your new villains."

Diana removes her hood, her dark auburn hair red as blood in the night. "I am Diana, your Big Bad Bitch."

"And I am Johan, your Master of Mischief," Johan announces, the Storm Fae's skin crackling with electricity.

Ezra nods at his fourth-year friends like a proud mama duck presenting her black, evil ducklings. "Your villains will impart challenges upon you, one at a time, and when summer comes, we will tally the results. The loser will be sorry, and the winner will receive a special prize." He pauses for effect. "A behind-the-scenes tour of our capital, a chance to get a glimpse of the Eternal Chalice, and try on the throne of your choosing—all escorted by our resident Crown Prince: the heir forged in flames, the resplendent phoenix, the legend himself, Aidan Summers."

Ezra motions for me to join him. "Consider yourselves lucky. This is the last year such a prize will be offered."

I walk to the center of the circle and slip off my hood to a flurry of encouraging whistles. "I promise the winner a night of scrumptious chaos and revelry that'll rival the best coronation feast this continent has ever seen."

"Hear, hear!" Ezra cups his hands in front of his face. "Come on, you know what the ladies want... It's a tradition now. Show us your mark."

Claps, cheers, and enthusiastic shouts blare through the circle.

Shaking my head as if I'm only humoring them and not at all flattered, I disrobe and toss my cloak into the fire before unfastening the buttons of my formal, embroidered shirt.

The howls pick up as I throw it into the flames, too, revealing the bright orange phoenix mark scorched in the depression below the v-line on my abdomen, right above my left leg. I hold down the hem of my trousers to showcase the entire thing, my hand covering my crotch.

Most of the girls chant and whistle in cheer, but Willow hides her face in her knees with a loud and dramatic, "Eww."

Next to my sister, my Songbird appears rather distraught by my public display, shielding her eyes with her hand, and my stomach plunges.

Ezra encircles my shoulders with one arm. "Hephaistos branded it into his flesh when he was just a wee babe, and we're all fucking jealous. We're bound to lust after his mark until the day we get our own," he trails off dreamily before raising his cup. "Now, let's show these first-years how to have fun!"

CHAPTER 8
LOVER
SONGBIRD

Huge blankets have been laid on the beach near the buffet, and I'm sitting in a first-year huddle with Willow, Elio, Iris, and Sean. Zeke is playing ball with a group of seasoned students, but by my quick calculations, the entire student body comprises no more than thirty-something people.

The Royal Academy might be a big place, but it doesn't have a large roster.

The flickering torches keep us warm despite the strong sea breeze. The tight knot in my stomach throbs before it slowly unravels, as if the unfamiliar, salty wind is inhabited by healing spirits that have drifted out of their graves on the ocean floor to greet us.

Elio draws patterns in the striking golden-orange sand beneath his fingers. "This sand is so smooth and heavy." He rubs a pinch between his fingers. "And warm, like the sun is still shining."

Willow nods. "Saffron Cove is usually the place students use to get some privacy, given the warmth of the sand and the fact that it... doesn't get stuck everywhere."

"Sounds like you're speaking from experience, Will," Sean teases her. "Go on, spill."

"Err—I wish. Aidan told me."

Sean nods like her answer appeased his thirst for gossip. "Aidan would know."

All my hairs stand up to attention at the mere mention of the name, and I startle at Sean's unexpected nudge, my heart suddenly pounding in my chest.

"Your fiancé is one fine man, moth. Shadow dudes just have a certain *je ne sais quoi*..." he scans Zeke from head to toe, biting his lips. "Too bad he's into girls, because I wouldn't mind taking a peek under his trunks."

I blink to dissipate the heat in my chest.

"Look at her. She's clearly hoping for that peek, too," Iris chuckles, and I curse my complexion once more.

"If shadows get you hard, maybe the Crow swings your way, Sean," Willow suggests with a devilish grin.

"Nah. According to the rumors, the only wave that rocks the Crow's stiff boat—which I heard is an impressive vessel indeed—is Devi."

Iris's eyes dance at the news. "Devi and the Crow? Really?"

"I'm just repeating what I've heard."

"Oh, I'd pay good money to see that," Iris jokes.

Blood still sears my cheeks, burning my face. I'm not a prude by any means, but Winter Fae seldom talk so openly about sex. Only when we've had too much cider and are surrounded by our closest friends do we dare to discuss our fantasies so freely. We'd rather whisper about it.

Our wedding celebrations are scandalous as we watch newlyweds from afar with opera glasses, tasting cheeses and wines. I've attended twelve since I turned fourteen, each leaving quite an impression. My own sexual experiences were all whispers and hushed breaths, biting my lips to avoid being caught with Henri in his bedroom.

But I was warned by my father that Spring and Summer Fae have no such qualms about discussing their primal urges, so it's not a big surprise.

Iris motions to a boy playing against Zeke. "Declan is into boys. He can't shut up about it."

"Declan's my cousin," Sean whines, grimacing.

"I know, but when the pond's too small, you can't be too choosy," Iris quips, and everyone laughs.

A group of four third-years attacks the buffet, packing up almost half the food into containers and slipping them into a large bag. "Hey, rookies! Some of us are hiking up Lovers' Leap for some cliff diving. You want to come with?"

Sean jumps to his feet. "You bet!"

Willow wraps her arms around herself, her skin riddled with goosebumps. "I warn you, the water is freezing this time of year."

I give a confident shake of the head. "I'm out. Though I'm sure the water's warm enough for me."

Summer Fae are wusses when it comes to cold.

"You want to join them, Iris?" Elio keeps his voice as casual as possible, but a hint of red flushes his cheeks, too.

Uh-uh. Elio's got a crush on Iris. And sucks for him, it shows.

She crosses her arms over her chest. "I wouldn't be caught dead cliff diving with you, Lightbringer."

"Why not?" he deadpans, narrowing his gaze.

"Well, you're obviously a virgin, and I don't like to teach. So unless you do some serious homework, don't ask me again."

The mixed crowd of third- and second-years behind us howls and cheers at her flippant response, and Willow and I exchange a cringey glance. *Ouch.*

"She's a real... treat," I mutter under my breath, and Elio's fingers dig into the sand, though he manages a soft, embarrassed smile.

Zeke runs over to us. "Anyone up for some beach ball? We've just lost some players."

I have to admit, glistening with sweat and wearing only black trunks, he's objectively attractive.

"I'm game," Iris purrs, peeling herself from the blanket.

Willow stands and dusts the sand off her legs. "Me, too."

"And you, moth?" Zeke's gaze travels up my bare thighs to the hem of my skirt. "I wouldn't mind seeing you in your bathing suit, running around with that cute ass on display, desperate to catch my balls."

I glare at him through my eyelashes, eyes half-mast. "Alas... I'm not going anywhere near your balls tonight, Zeke."

Elio coughs, and Willow snickers, "Oh, she got you there."

The trio runs off to the ball court, leaving Elio and me behind.

"Wow. That guy will give my brother a run for his money in the womanizing department," he says.

"Oh, I forgot to mention. I met your brother earlier. Are you two able to wear shirts, or—" I pause mid-sentence. Since I've already committed to a stupid, oddly personal question, I decide to own it. "Do the wings get in the way of your clothes at all?"

I examine the wings folded at Elio's back again, the long feathers at the ends tucked underneath his ass.

Elio cracks up at my fumble, and I take pride in my successful attempt to change his mind from the public humiliation he just suffered. "Yes, we can wear shirts. Our wings can actually return to the ether the way magic armors and weapons can, but my father insisted for me to wear them proudly tonight." The light in his eyes dims. "He doesn't want anyone to forget I'm a Prince of Light."

"Only royals have wings, then?"

Wings are part of the secrets and traditions that don't make it into wide-spread literature. One of the many mysteries that'll be unveiled now that I'm here.

"Yes, it's a gift from our god Helios. He's a firm believer in hereditary monarchies, and so he marks his possible heirs with wings similar to his own."

"Are you born with them?"

"We're born *to* them, but we have to practice summoning them. Learning to fly is way harder than learning to swim, I assure you.

And when my father decides it's time to prove your worth, you either fly or crash at the bottom of the Solar Cliffs."

My jaw hangs open as I gawk at the smooth, white curves of his feathers, itching to reach for them. "By Thanatos! You can actually fly?"

"Did you think they were just ornamental?" Elio teases.

"Well... maybe." I shake off the urge to berate him further about his wings or more embarrassing still, ask him for a ride. "Is your father very difficult?"

His gaze darts to the ground. "That's one word for it."

"Mine is very... politically oriented."

"Is that code for ambitious and ruthless?"

"Like with Zeke. My father plotted for years for this betrothal. My magic is strong, so if I hadn't been admitted here, I would've had to apply to Tundra University to become a reaper. But Papa wouldn't hear of that. He might serve the Winter King, but he wants me as far from the Ice City as possible. He wants grandsons and—" I try to find a positive spin to my rather depressing train of thought.

I probably shouldn't talk about reapers, or the Winter King. Fae from the other kingdoms don't like to think about death. They don't like to be reminded that, even though we call ourselves immortals and age incredibly slowly, we all die, too, at some point.

Elio doesn't seem put out by the turn our conversation has taken. "He wants his name to live on after his death. He's not the only one."

"Yes, but royals are supposed to be that way. My father is adamant that his legacy has to amount to something. He's never content with anything."

Elio raises a brow. "And you?"

"I'm grateful to be here. It's a life-altering opportunity."

I'm fine with Elio thinking that my hopes and dreams are driven by my father. The seed of ambition he planted in me has only recently begun to flourish, and I'm unsure how much of it comes from me or if I'm merely being influenced by what he's been telling me my whole life.

"'Work hard, and when you're done, work harder,' is my father's mantra. It's a tiring way of life, but I'm here, so it obviously amounted to something."

"My father's mantra is: 'Reflect your light upon me, or die trying.'"

"Wow. He sounds like a prince."

His brows knit together. "You have no idea."

We watch the waves crash onto the beach, the restless ocean as unfamiliar as the warm breeze blowing at my back. Wintermere does have a connection to the sea, but the coast is prone to freezing arctic winds and ice that span for miles and miles before reaching open water.

No wonder we don't swim.

I catch Elio's gaze. "The life of a reaper must be pretty lonely in the end. Everyone curses them for their work. They don't get to have partners or kids. Aside from their obvious duties, they're not meant to be seen by the living. So I'm really glad I get to come here instead."

He nods thoughtfully. "Becoming a reaper does sound pretty lonely."

"Hey, Elio! Come here! There are some girls you have to meet!" Ezra suddenly accosts us, his swim trunks still dripping with seawater. "They want to go cliff diving with us." He offers his brother a hand to stand up, but Elio leaves him hanging, so Ezra turns to me. "We do look alike, right?"

"Err—kind of?"

Ezra's hair is slightly longer, the coastal wind and leftover salt water giving it quite a bit of texture and volume. Elio's still growing, with less muscle as his body figures itself out. The slightly skewed proportions aren't quite as flattering as Ezra's perfectly balanced physique, but with those abs, the glow-in-the-dark hair, and those ice-blue eyes...

It's a good thing I already have a fiancé. And a secret.

Two girls who look exactly the same wave mischievously at Elio behind his brother's back. Elio shakes his head, his feet digging into the smooth sand for traction. "I'm not interested in whatever twincest thing you have going on, Ezra."

"Oh, come on, kid! They said they wouldn't go if it was just me."

"You know what? I think you should go," I declare.

Elio glares at me like I've grown a horntail and stabbed him in the back with it. "What?" he chokes.

"Yeah. I think it's a fine idea." I discreetly point at Iris in the space between us, and his eyes follow my movement.

My catty roommate is watching the exchange intently.

Ezra crouches behind me on the blanket and wraps an arm around my shoulders. "I was right about you, moth. You're cool."

The wickedly handsome Fae's lure is much easier to deal with in his drunkard iteration, and I grin as I pat his arm in a soothing fashion. "Why, thank you."

He climbs back to his feet, the movement effortless and graceful, and arches a brow at his brother. "Lady Snow has spoken. Shall we?"

"I don't want to have a foursome with Ezra. Under no circumstances. Ever," Elio clips under his breath, still glaring at me.

"Then don't. Iris is watching. Just go cliff-diving with them, and she'll spend the rest of the night biting her tongue."

"I—" Elio stretches his neck to look at the twins. "You think?"

"Elio, come on. She totally humiliated you, and now, she'll be the one left in the lurch."

A sigh whistles out of his clenched jaw. "Oh, alright."

Ezra points to me with drunken emphasis. "You're my hero, Lady Snow. I owe you. Big time."

I wave them off, watching the foursome head up the grassy path at the back of the cove, a smile tugging at my lips. Now left to my own devices, I visit the buffet and munch on some verdant chips and salsa.

Hum. Yum.

Summer certainly has a spicier, more varied cuisine. I bet all the royals get to enjoy their choice of fruits and vegetables year-round, while in Tundra, the common Fae mostly subsist on root vegetables and potatoes alongside their meats. Sure, I've tasted a couple of blood oranges from the Red Forest each year, and I've licked my share of salt rose caramel pudding from the royal cook's spoons when I visited my father at the castle. Lucy was always delighted to see my eyes sparkle at the taste of her batter.

But these? These are all-you-can-eat high-end, fancy delicacies.

It's so good. I could get used to this.

"Don't eat too much, moth, or you won't be able to take flight anymore," Iris teases as she jogs over to get a glass of cider.

Judging by her tiny waist, the girl must watch her figure closely.

I make a big show of licking my fingers and throw her an asinine smile. But she's partly right. I should be more careful about eating in front of the other students, and not because of some fat butterfly nonsense. I shouldn't give them a reason to be reminded that I'm not one of them. That I'm not used to these luxuries. Same thing as with the princes. I can't show I'm not used to dealing with drop-dead-gorgeous, powerful men. I have to take it all in stride so that they never question if I belong here.

The fourth-year Red Fae that made a speech earlier joins me by the wide array of food. She's thin with auburn hair that falls in soft waves, a sharp pointy nose reminiscent of the witches she descends from, and brown eyes that glimmer with mischief.

"Hey, moth."

"Diana, right?"

"It's Big Bad Bitch to you. I was the guardian of the Autumn trial. I saw you leave with all that blood sprayed on your chest and boy, you really blew through Summer." Her unfriendly grin widens. "I thought of the perfect challenge for you. I want you to find out Aidan's full initials. He'll be the judge of your success or failure, of course. I wouldn't dream of having you blab away something so personal."

"Are you joking? He's never going to tell me." I risk a glance in his direction.

My skin warms as Aidan glances in our direction, as if he's heard his name.

"Hey, Johan." Diana motions her friend over, and the man creates a welcomed barrier between me and Aidan. "How many points would you give the moth if she managed to find out Aidan's initials?"

The boy raises both brows high at the scandalous proposition. "I'd say it's worth three times as much as the hardest challenge we came up with."

"I agree. See? This way, you get to fail and keep face. No one will expect you to succeed."

She pats my arm in a condescending manner as she leaves, and I bite my tongue not to reply. *Deep breaths and rise above.* I don't care about some stupid initiation contest, anyway. For all I know, Aidan himself put her up to this.

Our first official meeting doused some much-needed icy water over the possibility of repeating that kiss. Aidan might be real, but his interest in me certainly isn't. And after his... revealing performance earlier, I know he's just playing with me. This must be the kind of game princes play to keep themselves entertained.

It should be a relief, but I can't dismiss the heaviness hovering beneath my breast bone or the itch at the back of my throat.

I feel terribly stupid.

Aidan broke the rules and roped me into his little scheme, and I fell for it hook, line, and sinker. A man so imbued with his own self-importance will expect nothing less than unfailing obedience from a moth in return for his help, and I'll be lucky if all he wants to use is my body.

The pressure of his gaze is a quite literal line of fire crawling across my neck. Not enough to make my skin blister, but the heat quickly becomes suffocating. The sand beneath my feet warms as I refuse to acknowledge him.

If there's one thing I know about my standing here at the academy, it's that I should study hard, keep from talking about the trials, and not make waves.

Being caught in a dalliance with the most infamous bachelor in Faerie would ruin me—destroying my credibility with Zeke's father and my chances of graduating faster than if I openly admitted to cheating at the trials.

A cup of Nether cider in hand, Aidan approaches the buffet under the guise of serving himself a refill. "You're engaged," he says on a sigh.

"Yes," I answer without looking, wrapping an arm around my frame.

"You should have told me."

My eyes bulge, and I glance over my shoulder to see if he's serious. "I thought you were merely a fever dream."

A rogue, arrogant smile warms his face, his gaze focused on the liquid foaming over his cup. "Am I that handsome?"

"Ugh." I move to leave, but Aidan grabs my lower arm, his fire snaking along my skin. It's warm and enticing. I can't look away.

"We have to chat. Privately."

I pull away from his grasp so I can concentrate, the gentle sting of the flames too damn distracting for me to keep my head. "We can't be caught speaking in private."

The last thing I should be doing tonight is leaning any further into that weird hypnotic thrall Aidan's got going for him.

His lips curl down. "Normally, I would agree, but we have to get our stories straight. The Crow is already asking questions about your performance, so we can't afford to wait. Head to your room now."

My mouth dries up. "My room?"

"I'll meet you there in ten minutes." He gulps down the rest of his cup and discards it on the nearest table, walking away without another word.

My head swims. He certainly didn't wait long to come and collect what he thinks he's owed. Well, if he tries to blackmail me into sleeping with him, he's got an ice dagger coming for his throat. But in spite of the boulder in my chest, my skin tingles.

Aidan's piercing amber stare, his long brown lashes, the glistening ridges of his bare chest, and the damn V-line above his godly marks replay behind my closed eyelids like my very own wicked brain cinema.

A small voice inside me coos. *Maybe it wouldn't be so bad to play* — No!

If I'm to be expelled tonight, it might as well be for assaulting a prince than for cheating in the trials.

CHAPTER 9
STALK ME
SONGBIRD

Heartbeats resonate at my temples as I study the small living room and kitchenette. Two studded green velvet chairs and a small sofa are arranged around a table. Out here in the common area, there's enough privacy for my little chat with Aidan.

Before I left the party, I told Iris and Willow I was dead tired and asked if they wanted to come back to the room with me. I'd hoped to erase their suspicions, maybe even keep Aidan away, but they'd refused.

You'll be fine. But no matter what, don't let him into your room. And you should definitely change.

I slam my bedroom door shut and strip off the revealing corset and short skirt, then unpack a loose, understated, form-erasing pajama set from my trunk. The flannel ensemble has a row of buttons down my chest, and high-rise pants. I bet the girls here sleep in silk negligees and lacy underwear, but moths use their sleeping clothes to ward off the cold, not lure in their lovers. Perfect for sending a clear message.

I slip on the pants first and unbutton the top, but my hands suddenly clench the fabric. The fiery imprint of Aidan's gaze travels along my naked back, and my spine stiffens. With a shaky breath, I pull on my shirt and button it down, making sure to secure them all in place, even the one near the collar I usually never fasten.

When I'm decent, I spin around at the sound of a gentle knock on the glass. Aidan has climbed the vines to my third-floor window, his loose grin as wicked as the way he taps, motioning for me to remove the flimsy golden hook that serves as a latch.

I crack open the window. "You make a habit of stalking women while they change?"

"Only you, Songbird." He licks his lips, his eyes trailing down my body. The vines grow, giving him better access as he boosts himself onto the rocky ledge, spreading his arms to grip both sides of the open window. "And I told you I was coming, so… with you stripping in full view of my gardens, I could only assume you wanted me to see you."

My gardens, not *the* gardens. Like he owns the school and everyone in it. Bastard.

"And I assumed you'd use the door like a normal person."

He chuckles, then leaps over the windowsill bench, barefoot and graceful as a cat. "I'm not normal."

Behind him, the branches of the willow tree snake toward the glass, providing some cover as one gnarly sprig inches the window closed.

"What are you wearing? Armor?" he asks.

"It's pajamas."

His lips purse in a grimace like he can't wait to set the whole thing on fire. "If you say so."

He seems far too comfortable sneaking through women's windows, and I cross my arms to create a barrier between us. He's still half-naked, wearing the same dark, laced-up trousers he had on earlier by the bonfire.

The tip of his infamous mark peeks above the waistband, but I refuse to steal a full glance, keeping my eyes firmly on his face. It would be much easier to avoid ogling him if I could just close my eyes entirely.

Aidan walks around the bed, skimming through the tall pile of notebooks and novels I unpacked on the nightstand, before his gaze shifts to the stripped, empty bed across the room. "You got a private room. Interesting."

When he moves to pick up one of my journals, I rush over to him and slam my hand down firmly on the leather cover to stop him. "Stop snooping around my things. You said we had to talk so...talk."

He holds his hands up in surrender and backtracks, shifting slightly to encroach on the narrow path between the bed and the wall. The cramped space prevents me from walking past him and returning to a more neutral spot. A soft, enticing heat rolls off his body, luring me in.

I didn't want him to read any of my lyrics, but this is worse. The only escape is to climb onto the bed, which wouldn't be very subtle.

A smile ghosts over his lips, removing any doubt I had about his awareness of what he just did, cornering me like this. "The Crow knows something is amiss."

The phrase takes me back to reality, and my eyes narrow. "How could he know?"

"You crossed the marshes quicker than Willow. It's suspicious."

I turn my back to him and rummage through my notebooks, picking two at random to cram into the drawer. "Didn't it help him, though? If we hadn't cheated, he would have lost the contest, right?"

"Yes, but he's a real stickler for the rules."

I bite my bottom lip. I'm new here. As much as it pains me to rely on Aidan for anything, I don't have a choice, so I stow my misplaced lust and budding anger away. "Alright. You know the ins and outs of this place. What should we do?"

"Just don't say anything about it. To anyone. And if Damian asks, don't give him a straight answer. Try to answer all questions with questions. He hates that. I'll take care of the rest."

It's a reasonable request, and I nod. "Alright."

We both have too much to lose to leave it to chance. Even though we've reached a quick agreement, Aidan is in no hurry to leave. The bright light behind him forms a halo around his body, blurring into the glow of the flames creeping just beneath his skin.

"You should go now. And in the future, we probably shouldn't be seen together—"

He slides forward, and I flatten my back to the wall, hands held behind me as an ice dagger slowly frosts in my grip.

"Do you love him? Your fiancé," he asks, inches from my face.

"Why would you ask that?"

"Seems relevant enough. Most royal marriages aren't based on love, but you're a moth, so it's not political either."

Coming from him, the word physically hurts, and my abs clench. "I agreed to marry him. What do you think?" I try to infer a yes, but Aidan doesn't look convinced.

"I barely know you."

"Yet you ask very blunt and personal questions."

The corners of his mouth quirk. "Which you haven't answered yet."

"You just advised me never to give a straight answer."

He leans closer, shifting his weight to his right foot, and my pulse swirls. "You fascinate me, Songbird."

My escape path is wide open now, giving me ample opportunity to walk away, but I can't move. I finally understand what the phrase "a moth to a flame" truly means. The gentle light of Aidan's fire feels like a hand peeling away my doubts, my clothes, my sanity. *It's lust. Lust that will get you expelled—or even arrested.*

"Why did you help me? What do you want?" I croak.

"I want to kiss you again."

"But you shouldn't." I grip the hilt of my dagger, but it melts away and drips on my heels, useless.

His eyes soften. "Do you want me to, yes or no?"

"I never thought this would happen—"

"This is not a no."

A nervous hiccup rakes my throat. "You're an insufferable prick."

His bright smile muddles my brain. "Still not a no." His lips brush mine, and my throat bobs.

Our breaths grow even shallower as we remain locked in place for an absurdly long minute, studying each other, him waiting for an unequivocal *yes* to kiss me, and me unable to buy my freedom with a lie.

"This is madness. I'm engaged to Zeke and you're… You should go."

The name makes Aidan cringe, and he draws back an inch. "Do you love him? I have to know," he rasps. "If that's why you're holding back, I *need* to know."

"Are you always this brazen? Or is it just because you know I'm doomed the second you tell someone about what we did? Is this how the oh-so-great Crown Prince of the Summerlands gets girls into his bed—through blackmail?"

"What— Blackmail?" he scoffs, his jaw slightly opened in outrage. "I could get any girl I want without blackmail. And I would never tell *anyone* about tonight."

"Then tell me. Why are you here with me and not frolicking with… bosomed twins like your friend?"

"You answer my question, and I'll answer yours."

I tip my chin up. "You go first."

"Alright," he concedes.

The invigorating spark of victory is short-lived as Aidan braces both forearms against the wall on either side of my face and slides one knee between mine, no longer playing chicken. The feel of his strong thigh pinning me in place is absolutely scandalous, and my lids flutter.

"You are the most beautiful woman I've ever seen. One look at you, and I was fucking hard for you. When you sang, I wanted to tear my heart out and lay it down at your feet. One kiss, and I knew you had to be mine." He presses his lips to my ear. "I want you, and since

I'm the *oh-so-great* Crown Prince, as you say, I'm used to getting what I want."

My will falters, along with any last shred of common sense. I press my hand to his chest to hold him off, not quite able to push hard enough to mean it. A whimper of indecision bubbles from my lungs as I scrape my nails along his pecs. "You're spoiled and unreasonable."

Don't you dare give in, moth.
He's fucking perfect.
He's going to burn you.
Let him. It's only one night. No one has to know.
"A deal is a deal. You owe me an answer," Aidan purrs.

"No, I don't love him," I finally growl. "I don't even like him."

His chest heaves in relief as he kisses my temple. "Now, was that so hard?" He cups the side of my face and angles my gaze to his. "It's been a long night for you, so I'll let you mull this over, but you'll be mine, Songbird. Of that, I'm absolutely sure."

Beautiful, sexy bastard.

He jumps over the bed, and a vine creeps to open the window, clearing his path.

Aidan Summers saunters out of my room through the window with a mischievous, "Nighty night," and my entire body shudders in response, as if his voice is now the rope and pulley to some deep well of lust inside me.

I wrap my arms around my body, suddenly so cold my teeth chatter, and hurry to the window.

Aidan lands with villainous grace three stories below and throws me a wink over his shoulder. A part of me cries out in regret to see him leave, and my hands shake as I secure the window hook into place.

By Thanatos. I sink to the floor and hug my knees, biting my bottom lip so hard I draw blood. The steely taste of it barely dulls the warmth in my belly.

That boy is either the only exception to the Fae can't lie rule, or barking mad. Me, the most beautiful woman he's ever seen? It's ludicrous.

But a dumb, infuriating grin breaks through my shock and awe as I muffle a nervous giggle with the heel of my hand. He might only be into me because he can't have me, but I can't pretend he's not the sexiest man alive. His confident yet boyish attitude mollified my resistance, and I force myself to look away from the bed to avoid picturing what could have happened if I had dared to indulge the spark of madness he's ignited in me instead of snuffing it out.

My cheeks burn as I flee to the common room to pour myself a glass of water from the pitcher in the pantry. I lean against the counter, willing my heartbeat to slow down.

A loud knock at the door of the apartment whips it back into a frenzy as water spills everywhere on the front of my flannel shirt. I curse under my breath and grab a towel to pat myself dry, absent-mindedly heading for the door.

Hand curled around the knob, I pause.

Did Aidan change his mind about letting me escape his thrall? But then, why would he knock on the front door and not just use the window again? *Unless he wanted to tease me some more.*

I crack the door open, and it's not Aidan on the other side, but Zeke.

Your fiancé, my inner voice quips.

"Hey, moth." A dark shirt sticks to his skin, the short beach trousers he had before dripping with seawater. He shifts from one foot to the other, clearly nervous. And obviously drunk. "I've been thinking... Forget what I said before the trials. I felt a crushing pressure to perform and couldn't see straight. I'm glad we're engaged. We should get to know each other more," his eyes scan my flannel pajamas, "to make sure we're compatible." He raises a hand to my lip. "You're bleeding."

I cower away from his touch. I can't afford for Zeke to smell Aidan on me, and I'm not sure how keen Shadow Fae senses are, yet, so I brace my elbow on the door frame, barring him from entry. "I think we should take it easy tonight."

"Now, don't be like that. It's a big day for us, we should celebrate," he says in a low, cajoling drawl. "We deserve it."

I'm trying to think of a good comeback, but what happened with Aidan has muddied my thoughts. "I'm tired."

What can I say that will drive him away, but not so much that he tells his father to call the whole thing off?

"Let me give you a nice massage, then, babe." He slips a hand under the hem of my flannel shirt, stroking my bare side, his fingers digging into my flesh.

While Aidan's touch seared my skin with a disarming blaze, Zeke's uninvited hold makes bile rise in my throat, and my skin ices over where he laid his hand.

He draws back, startled. "Ow. That's cold."

"You should know something about me, Zeke," I blurt out to buy some time.

Think fast, moth.

"Yes?"

"My father wants me to remain a virgin until marriage," I announce gravely.

It's not strictly a lie, of course. My father's old enough to belong to that generation. What's implied serves my purpose, and it's the first statement that popped into my mind.

Zeke shakes his head with a chuckle. "He doesn't have to know. I certainly won't be the one to tell him."

"It wouldn't feel right to sleep with you against his wishes."

This could work.

"Are you serious?"

"I am." We just met. Why would he expect anything different? Fiancé does not equal owner. A line of anger creeps up my spine and spreads to my chest. "Dead serious, in fact."

This was either the stupidest thing I've ever done or a stroke of genius. This way, I get to go to school in peace, study, graduate, and not have to worry about him being too pushy. Marital duties start on the wedding night, not before.

"But we're supposed to marry *after* graduation," Zeke whines. "You can't possibly expect me to wait that long."

I hold his gaze, not blinking.

The pout on his face vanishes in a flash, replaced by a bright, self-serving smile. "You know what, moth? This can absolutely work. You'll do your abstinence thing, and I'll do my thing. We're betrothed, but marriage and commitment start after the vows, right? Don't you agree?"

Wow. We think more alike than I'd thought. If it gets him off my back about being all handsy and possessive, I'm all for it. "I was thinking the same thing."

"Perfect. See? We're getting along already." He pats my shoulder and pecks my cheek before turning on his heel. I watch him leave with an ounce of bitterness and a pitcher of relief.

Stroke of genius, indeed. As long as he doesn't stroll in here expecting me to spread my legs just because his father is paying my tuition, he can do whatever he wants.

What about Aidan? A pesky little voice chants in my head.

Get real, moth. Aidan can't happen. Not ever. Especially now that you have a fake virginity to protect.

CHAPTER 10
FINDERS KEEPERS
SONGBIRD

The next morning, I tiptoe into the common area, my eyes sticky with sleep.

"Hungover, moth?" The most striking woman I've ever seen greets me from the kitchenette. She whistles a soft tune as she fills a boiler. "I thought commoners from Tundra knew how to handle their cider."

"N-No. I just had trouble sleeping." I gawk at the beautiful stranger.

The locs of her sculpted side ponytail are twisted and wrapped around themselves, and their incandescent glow is richer than the blood running through my veins and deeper than flames.

Dark freckles soften her otherwise angular features, with two golden hoops hanging from her delicate ears. Her otherworldly gaze meets mine, and the silver flecks in her irises shimmer with hues of midnight amethysts and polished moonstones.

The golden hilt of a small dirk is hoisted in the dip of her matching bralette, the tip of the blade pointing at her bare navel. Daggers are strapped over her tight black leather pants, and her elegant hands and bare feet show off a regal shade of gold nail polish.

The sum of it all gives her a god-like quality, and my spine straightens, the urge to blurt out effusive compliments almost too strong to suppress. I catch myself wondering what her dark skin would feel like, and a strange lull settles in my belly.

"I'm Elizabeth Snow."

Her brows raise. "I know."

I'm not usually attracted to women, so I suspect this one is the most powerful Spring Fae I've ever encountered. Her bite of power makes me feel all queasy inside, and I smile dreamily at her with my lips parted.

Iris joins us in the common area, breaking the strange vibe.

"Morning, Little Flower," the woman greets her.

"Devi!"

Violet "Devi" Eros. Granddaughter of Oberon Eros himself. Oberon has been ruling over the Secret Springs for over a thousand years. Even the old Winter King is *only* seven hundred years old, and soon to crumble to ashes if my father is right.

Given his age, Freya Heart is actually his third wife—and not Devi's grandmother. With Freya being Iris's aunt and married to Devi's grandfather, Devi and Iris must know each other pretty well.

The two women embrace each other warmly, and Devi presses a quick kiss to Iris's lips. "Congrats on making it in."

Willow inches into the room, her hands flying to her hair as she pats it down in a self-conscious manner. "Blessed Flame. You're Devi Eros."

"And you're Willow Summers, the boss' precious daughter."

Devi breaks the tie between Iris and Willow with that one sentence, reminding us in no uncertain terms who owns this school.

The boiler whistles, and she takes it off the cooktop to fill the teapot. "I'm your Keeper. From now on, I want you to think of yourselves as my sweet baby ducklings, and me as your demented prison mama."

Iris snickers at that, but Devi shakes her head. "I'm not kidding. It's my last year here, and I will not have a trio of horny, impressionable teenagers derail it. Your parents didn't send you here to get pregnant, so drink your contraceptive tea every morning." She dumps a spoonful of tea leaves from a bright orange box into an infuser. "Even the virgin," Devi adds with a pointed look.

By Thanatos. It's only been hours, and Zeke already blabbed? I'll kill him.

Blush sears my cheeks as Devi retrieves four cups from the cupboard.

"You're still underage, so it's my responsibility to keep you honest. No, you can't sneak in a few sips of Nether cider, and yes, you're actually meant to study. Leave the mindless partying to the third years. Those bastards have earned it."

Fae drink wine and beer from infancy—alcohol isn't meant to affect our bodies to the same extent as the mortals—but Nether cider and other stronger elixirs are prohibited until we turn eighteen, the age of majority in Faerie.

"But you're infamous for breaking the rules," Iris argues.

"Breaking some rules will get you expelled, while breaking others will earn you a bad-ass reputation. It's not my job to help you distinguish between the two, so tread carefully. Knowing which rules to break and when and where to do so is an art. Unless you can back up your bouts of rebellion with some serious wits and power, I don't recommend walking down this path," Devi muses.

"Bullshit!" Iris grumbles.

"Little Flower, how many women have been graduate students in the last decade?"

Iris crosses her arms over her chest. "I don't remember."

"You're the only one," Willow says under her breath.

"Good girl. Now, why is that?" Devi asks sharply.

Fire burns within Willow's gaze. "Because equality between men and women is a myth. We judge the mortals for imprisoning their women in hideous corsets. We think ourselves superior because they prevent females from voting and building their own wealth, but deep down, we're not much better. Marriage and motherhood is still thrust upon us at an earlier age, and females are ten times more likely to be challenged and kept off their rightful thrones than men when they are marked by the gods to rule."

Devi arches a brow, clearly impressed. "Exactly. Why do you think they made me Keeper of this dorm when I'm the most famous rule breaker this school has ever allowed to graduate? Doesn't make much sense, does it?" She smacks her lips together, giving us a moment to chew on the question. "Because I'm the only woman who made it into a graduate program, that's why. Until you turn eighteen, your parents basically own you. They can legally beat you or marry you off to someone you hate. So, no drinking until you're of age, as mentioned. No cheating on examinations, no traveling through the sceawere unless your itinerary is sanctioned by a faculty member. You are to exert discretion about what you'll learn here. Enchantments, spells, other court's traditions or private affairs, and so on. So don't think of dazzling your cousins over break with juicy, sordid details."

Devi pauses, watching us closely. "Curfew is at ten, and I expect everyone in their beds by midnight. A few special celebrations are exceptions to that, like the admission trials yesterday, and it'll be made clear that curfew will not be enforced on those nights. If I come here in the middle of the night and find you gone, I will rat you out faster than you can invoke the name of my grandsire.

"No act of violence will be tolerated. You can't enchant your enemies for fun or use your magic against them unless it's in self-defense. We're not here to shred each other to pieces." Her fist curls over the edge of the counter, and a tense breath rushes past her clenched teeth. "And I warn you against spreading your legs for anything with a hot mouth and perfect abs. Times have changed, but not enough for us females to assume our indiscretions are viewed in the same light as men's. They can afford to plow their way to the Eternal Chalice, whereas we have to exercise restraint. If you sample every royal cock there is, it'll quickly become a very...incestuous situation." She bites her bottom lip, balancing herself from her heels to her toes. An odd tension lingers in the air as she holds my gaze. "And if you're same-sex oriented, you're in luck, because no one cares. Just don't go screaming from the rooftops that you're shagging your roommates, and you'll be fine."

A fierce blush creeps on my cheeks at the reminder of how I ogled her earlier.

"Keep your secrets close and your sins closer. Gold and jewels have no value here, but secrets do... A badly kept secret could keep you—or your competitor—from becoming queen. Gossiping away your ammunition is insipid, so don't." Devi's eyes dart to Iris, and I might be reading too much into it, but something in her gaze suggests an admonishment, as Iris's teeth grind in a very unladylike fashion in response.

"What did I forget? Oh, yes. You've already met your villains. It's customary for the fourth years to initiate the rookies. They'll give you ridiculous, dangerous, or downright mental challenges to plot and execute in the next few months and tally your points to pit you against one another. Don't accidentally kill yourself for glory, alright? And whatever you do, never give away your true name."

"But I heard you smashed the initiation record," Iris says, crossing her arms over her chest.

"Well, yes. I'm Devi Eros." Devi flips the twisted locks of her flaming red ponytail behind her head with a cheeky smile, as if her name explains it all.

Given the admiration written in Willow's wide, adoring gaze and the flush on her cheeks, it probably does.

"Now, the bibliotheca and dining hall are in the main building, on the second and third floors. Classrooms are on the floors above. I trust you know how to count, so I won't be showing you around. Don't give me a reason to remember your name, and you'll graduate." She narrows her eyes at each of us in turn. "But if you truly want to become queen, in your own right, and not only through marriage, make sure no one around these parts ever forgets it."

A Faeling flies in from the window, his magic allowing him to pass through the solid glass. "Mistress. You're late for... you know."

The little creature flutters around for a moment, dressed in old-fashioned purple clothes. The outfit is tailored to fit his tiny frame, complete with a crisp collar and a waistcoat. His delicate wings shimmer as he hovers just above my eye level, creating a gentle hum in the air. The old Winter King has a Faeling. I was unlucky enough to be in his way one day and received a chiding I'll never forget.

But this one isn't irate at all and throws us a timid wave. "Hello."

They say Faelings are born to serve. They die if their master dies, and they wither when kept apart for too long. Their personalities develop to account for the flaws in their master's character, so they can counterbalance it. The fact that he seems to be a nervous ball of anxiety and a sweetheart should serve as a warning that Devi is neither of those things.

"Thanks, Percy."

Devi strolls out without further instructions or a word of good-bye, and the door closes behind her without a sound.

"She's...intense," Willow breathes, clutching her necklace.

"She's right. It's not called the Royal Academy for nothing. Everyone here wants to rule, and those who don't end up with a crown will always wonder what could have been," Iris says before walking back into the room she shares with Willow and slamming the door shut.

"Oh my Eros! Did you see her?" Willow braces herself on the small kitchen island, as if she can barely keep herself upright.

"I know. She thought I was into her because I stared so much. I'm so embarrassed."

"Don't be. Everyone does it. My brother once said that meeting Devi for the first time was like being kicked in the groin while a nymph goes down on you. He was right. I still have goosebumps. Look."

"He said that, eh?"

The soft glow that had been hovering inside my ribcage vanishes as Devi's magic stops affecting me. The departure of that strange, lusty thrall leaves me cold, disoriented, and annoyed. That last bit of information stings in particular. I don't want any more reasons to think about Aidan's cock, especially not in relation to Devi—or nymphs sucking him off. So much for me being the most beautiful woman he'd ever seen.

Letters are sprawled over the coffee table, and I walk to the living room area to pick up the three out of the bunch that have my name on them. They look drab compared to the ones addressed to my roommates. One of the letters meant for Willow, written on gold-dusted paper, boasts the seal of the Summer Queen—a crown circled in flames.

"I'm supposed to make out with Devi for the challenge. Publicly." Willow shakes out her hands. "But that's so—I'd simply die."

I examine my letters. One bears my father's seal and is written on typical Winter Court staff blue paper. Another bears a moth seal and is folded in an overly fancy manner, just the way my cousin Marjorie would do it. But the third remains a mystery.

"They tasked me with finding out Aidan's full initials," I say, tearing open the blank seal.

Willow gasps. "Even if I knew them, I would never share my brother's initials. Do you know why Diana would choose that?"

I weigh my words carefully. "She wants me to fail. She said so."

Willow furrows her brow, her expression turning serious. "Reds are vicious, but don't worry too much about it. It's just a stupid initiation thing, anyway."

"Exactly." My gaze darts to Willow's bedroom. "What did Iris get?"

"She wouldn't say."

I unfold the letter, my eyes quickly scanning the page, and my cheeks warm.

> Dearest Songbird,
> I hope you had a restful night, though I have to admit I couldn't sleep a wink. Your voice, your smile, the taste of your kiss... they've kept me awake, until I just had to pick up a quill.
> Since we won't be able to see much of each other, I figured I should write to persuade you that I'm not some flimsy, good-weathered stalker—scratch that, admirer. I meant every single word I said, and I won't let something as mundane as a bogus engagement come between us.
> Miss you already,
>
> Wonder Boy

The handwriting is not at all what I would expect the calligraphy of a Fae prince to be, and my heart tumbles past my feet when I realize Willow is standing on her tip-toes to take a peek. "Who's got you blushing like this?" she asks.

I press the note to my chest. "No one."

"Wonder boy... Beth Snow, don't tell me you've got a beau pining over you at home?"

I nod sheepishly. My cheeks burn at the falsehood, but Willow doesn't seem to recognize her brother's hand, and a wave of relief washes over me.

Her eyes widen. "Oh, I love a tragic romance. Was he very crestfallen when you broke it off?"

"He hasn't truly gotten his head around it yet."

"A fighter. I like that."

"I tried to discourage him," I say quickly.

"But did you mean it?"

"No," I admit with a twinge of shame. "Not really."

"Then you can't fault him for not giving up. By the Flame, have you ever thought about how twisted our society truly is? On one hand, women are supposed to play hard to get and make a guy work for it, but we're also expected to marry someone our parents chose for us—the richest man who'll take us and is most likely to achieve greatness. The whole thing is disgusting."

"I agree."

We exchange a quick smile. *If only she knew...* She's about to add something, but a knock at the door startles us. Willow skips over to open it, and my lips part in surprise as I see my father standing in the doorway. I never expected him to drop by.

His gray hair is slicked back, and he's traded his usual uniform for his fanciest suit. But the knot of his tie shows a bit of wear and tear, and the sleeves are slightly too short.

"Papa!" I scurry over to the door. "This is Willow Sum—"

"Princess, it's an honor to meet you," he says, bowing at the waist in an overly formal manner for the setting. Such formalities are probably expected of him during official ceremonies, but here, it feels downright ridiculous. "I'm Paular Snow, but everyone calls me Paul."

I mask a cringe with my hand. "Come on, Papa. I'll show you my room."

But Willow is a true princess and knows how to handle such gestures. She smiles and offers him her knuckles to kiss. "I'm glad to meet you. Beth is talented and smart, and that reflects well on you, Sir Paul." She gives us a gracious nod. "No need to cower in your room, Beth. I'll leave you two to talk."

"You're too kind," he replies, his face brightening.

Willow closes her bedroom door quietly behind her, and Papa relaxes a bit. "She calls you Beth already?" He looks down at me with a soft smile, his mouth slightly agape as he takes in my pristine Royal Academy uniform. "Oh, Lizzie. I'm so proud of you. I knew you weren't born with your mother's face and that god-gifted ice magic for nothing..."

I trace the golden lines in the cushions of the sofa as Papa walks to the windows, gazing out at the ocean. The unshed tears of joy in his eyes rattle me. He's not much of a crier.

"Your mother would be so glad to see how far you've come..." he trails off.

My breath catches in my throat. Papa almost never talks of my mother, a real shame considering she died when I was a toddler. I have no memories of her and barely enough stories of their time together to fill a piece of parchment.

He clears his throat, erasing the emotion from his voice, and turns to face me again. "You seem surprised to see me. Didn't you get my note?"

I show off his sealed letter. "I haven't opened it yet."

His eyes sparkle with pride and something else—something I'm all too familiar with. Expectations. "Making it into the Royal Academy is no small feat. You're on the path to greatness, my girl."

I try to smile but end up just nodding. "Thank you, Papa."

He walks over and sits beside me, his gaze intent and serious. "But it's just the beginning, Lizzie. You've got so much potential, so much talent. You passed trials most of us wouldn't dream of taking on. You succeeded where tons of high-born royals have failed. I know you can achieve anything you set your mind to, but you have to give it your all. No slacking, no distractions."

"I know, Papa. I won't let you down." My voice wavers slightly, weighed down by an anchor of secrets, but I manage to hold his gaze.

"Good. I've sacrificed a lot to get you here, and I want you to have everything I never did. You have the chance to be a queen someday, and no matter what happens with Ezekiel's father, your new status will ensure a better future for Marjorie and Kiro as well. They send you each a kiss."

The mention of my rowdy cousins brings tears to my eyes. I miss them so much already.

Papa places a hand on my shoulder, his touch both comforting and heavy. "I know it won't be easy, Lizzie. But remember, I'll always be here to support you. I just want you to succeed. To be happy."

"I will," I whisper, my voice barely audible. "Tell Marge she can finally have my bed. And that overcoat she liked."

Papa thinks I'm this perfect, golden child, but I cheated. It kills me to lie to him—to everyone—and endure this charade. But he's right. It's not just my life that'll be forever changed by this opportunity, but that of our entire family.

He studies my face. "Are you sure everything's alright? You're quiet when you should be ecstatic. Did something happen between you and Ezekiel?"

I swallow hard, the urge to confess ebbing out as soon as it surfaces. I can't tell him. Or anyone. Not ever. "It's...a big change."

"Is that all?"

I nod quickly to disperse his suspicions. "It's been a lot to take in, but I'll manage, I promise."

"Alright." He pats my hand. "Just remember, I'm always here for you, no matter what." He stands up and glances around the room one last time before heading toward the door. "I'll let you get back to it. Just work hard, Lizzie. You're destined for great things."

As soon as he's gone, I let out a long, shaky breath.

"That didn't last long," Willow muses, and from the mischievous look on her face, I know she was eavesdropping.

"My father is nothing if not efficient. I'm surprised he came at all."

She bites her bottom lip. "You've made him proud."

"For now."

His love too often takes the shape of a hoop he needs me to jump through, but I keep that part to myself.

Willow squints at me, and after a long pause, she finally clasps my hand. "It's decided. I'm taking you under my wing, Beth Snow."

"Why?"

Her smile widens. "I think you've got something special. Plus, my father can be such a small-minded pain in the ass. I'm sorry to say he petitioned for you to be excluded from the school the second you exited the maze."

A flare of anger frosts my chest. If the Summer King despises the thought of me attending his fancy, elite school, I wonder how he'd react knowing his own precious son broke the rules to get me in—and seems determined to seduce me. Hells, Aidan probably wants me because he's consciously—or unconsciously—driven to defy his father's authority.

Willow squeezes my upper arm. "If I can help you shine, and it drives him up the wall, that's a bonus."

I can't help but chuckle, Willow's admission confirming my hunch that the Summer heirs like to rebel. "Sounds like you've got a plan."

"More like a mission," Willow says with a wink. "You have *a lot* to catch up on."

Her enthusiasm is infectious, and despite the whirlwind of emotions the day has brought, a spark of excitement ignites in my ribcage. Maybe Willow can become a true friend, and having a clever, good-natured princess as an ally is not as dangerous as falling for her devil of a brother.

Dearest Stalker,
I got your charming—scratch that, overconfident—note.
But in spite of your ego, I will concentrate on my studies.
Best,
Beth

SONGBIRD,
HOW WAS YOUR FIRST DAY? IN THE SPIRIT OF HONORING YOUR WISHES, I FEEL OBLIGATED TO WARN YOU ABOUT EVELYN'S LOVE FOR POP QUIZZES. AND IDRIS' OBSESSION FOR FOOTNOTES.
YOU'RE WELCOME.
WONDER BOY

My first day went well enough, but I'm onto you, Stalker. I've researched the spell you use to alter your handwriting and decided to try it on for size. Do you like my new hand? And last but not least, are you really trying to buy my affections with random pointers on the teachers?

-S

IF IT'S THE WAY TO YOUR HEART, WHY NOT? MOST IMPORTANTLY: IS IT WORKING?

-WB

Keep it up, and we'll see.

-S

CHAPTER 11
SWIMMING LESSONS
SONGBIRD

As the moon reaches its peak, Willow shifts restlessly in her chair, tapping an absentminded rhythm on the pages of her book. "I can't believe we've spent the entire day in here." She tosses a longing glance out the window. "Don't you think we could use a change of scenery?"

I look up from my notes, grateful for the quiet sanctuary of the bibliotheca. "I like it here," I say, leaning back in my chair and running a hand through my long black waves. "I can't believe the first week is already over."

I've been caught in a whirlwind of ruthless lessons and unsettling surprises, playing catch-up.

Willow chuckles softly. "Tell me about it. But you did better than you think. You've got more magic than most of them combined. You just need to get used to the politics and ridiculous traditions."

I sigh, frustration creeping in. "That's the problem. The others know who's who and what's what in a way that just can't be learned from a book."

I've studied the names, the family trees, the geography of the seven realms and memorized the different political systems of the old world and the new, but my peers know much more. They know who slept with who growing up, who holds grudges, and who to talk to when you want something handled discreetly. What to serve for dinner to insult a guest and get a rise out of them. What gift to bring when you visit a royal you need a favor from.

"It's the unwritten stuff that trips me up."

Willow raises an eyebrow. "You can't expect to simply *inhale* the knowledge that comes with a royal childhood in the span of one week."

"We're still months away, but I'm already nervous about the examinations. And I heard we might get a pop quiz soon."

"Evelyn does love a good pop quiz." Willow waves a dismissive hand, either too aloof to worry or, if I'm reading her right, determined to pry me out of my box of anxiety. "You're more studious than the rest of us combined. You'll be fine."

Her confidence gives me a small boost. "Thanks, Will. I don't know what I'd do without you."

"Probably end up a pariah," she replies with humor. "But alas, you're stuck with me." The legs of her chair scratch loudly against the wood as she climbs to her feet. "Now, let's take a break and raid the kitchens for a midnight snack. We deserve it after the week we've had."

Our fast friendship makes the daunting road ahead feel a little less intimidating, and I follow her to the kitchens, where the Summer sprites are more than happy to indulge their princess' sweet tooth.

The kitchens are empty, the silence broken only by the soft sounds of our chewing. An array of fresh fruit and pastries lies spread across the long wooden table, their vibrant colors contrasting against the rustic wood. Willow and I sit side by side, but I can't shake the feeling that we're not alone.

"Do you feel that?" I glance around the room, a peculiar sensation hovering in my stomach.

Willow's brows furrow. "Feel what?"

"Like... we're being watched." The hairs on the back of my neck stand up, an elusive and yet powerful bite of power rippling across the room.

Just as I'm about to say more, Ezra appears behind us, his presence sudden and unexpected. "What's this? A couple of mice stealing breakfast?"

I jump, nearly spilling my tea cup. "By Thanatos, why would you sneak up on us like that?"

Willow smiles at Ezra as though the two of them share a secret she's not yet inclined to divulge. "Ezra loves to catch a girl off guard."

The Prince of Light leans against the table, wearing a fitted dark shirt that highlights his athletic build, his platinum blonde hair shining in the dark. He tosses an apple in the air and catches it again. "Are you two lovely ladies doing anything tomorrow?"

I chew on a piece of fruit, trying to mask my unease.

Willow leans forward, linking her fingers over the table in a Machiavellian manner. "No. What's going on?"

"A bunch of us are going to hang out in the labyrinth before they tear it down completely." His blue eyes dance. "You two should definitely come. And bring along your gorgeous roommate, too, if you want."

"I'm in!" Willow says.

I force a smile, though my heart isn't in it. "Sounds fun."

Ezra raises an eyebrow, noticing my hesitation. "But?"

"No buts. I'll think about it."

He nods, still grinning in a predatory manner that has all the alarm bells ringing in my mind. "Good." With that, he tosses the apple again before walking out.

Willow watches him go, a smirk playing on her lips. "Ezra might be intimidating outright, but he's a big softie."

"That's *very* hard to believe."

Will wiggles her brows up and down. "He likes you. I can tell."

The rumors going around the academy about Ezra Lightbringer make Aidan sound like a timid gentleman. "Well, I have Zeke, so..."

"It's me, girl. I know you and Zeke have some kind of arrangement. And I'm not suggesting you and Ezra should sneak behind his back, but do give him a chance at becoming friends. He's going to surprise you."

I doubt that. I doubt that very much.

WILLOW FINDS ME THE NEXT MORNING IN MY BEDROOM, FEIGNING SLEEP. I tossed and turned all night, plotting excuses to get out of accompanying her to the labyrinth.

She ambushes me in my bed, barefoot. "Wake up, Beth. It's time to go."

I nestle under the covers, pulling the thick feather duvet over my head. "I'd rather not."

"If the moth wants to stay in the dark, let her be," Iris chimes from the common room.

Willow wraps herself around me, and despite her small size, it feels as though she has nine legs and a tail, her body taking up so much space, crushing me to the mattress.

She lets out an exasperated sigh. "Come on, Beth. You told me yourself that what you need to learn can't be found in a book. I'm inviting you to witness firsthand the inactive traps of my brother's labyrinth. An opportunity to see up close what being a guardian entails. A chance to talk to legends who have gone through it all and passed the exams with flying colors."

"I'm not—"

"I'll stay right here"—she stabs an elbow to my stomach on the guise of making herself comfortable—"until you agree to come with us."

I sink into the mattress. "Oh, alright, I'll go. Give me a minute to change."

Iris is clearly disappointed, which is a plus. But Aidan will be there, and he hasn't replied to my last message—which was *three days* ago.

I haven't seen him all week. After a few days of my stomach jumping every time a tall man entered a room or walked behind me in the corridors, I figured he'd decided to play with someone else, but a little voice in my head keeps torturing me.

It's too easy. What if he's just biding his time?

Nothing has ever come easy to me in this world, aside from my magic.

I'm not sure I can handle any more of Aidan's intense, lashes-to-lashes conversations, or worse, see the proof that he's moved on to grander horizons. Thanatos help me, maybe I've just been making too big a deal out of this in my head. He's one of the many princes here, and with the week I've had, I'm growing accustomed to their lures and overall shenanigans.

Maybe Aidan will look more like Zeke in broad daylight—a privileged asshole only interested in putting me down or spreading me open. Besides, I told him to keep his efforts up, and he downright stopped answering. That was as clear a message as I could ask for.

I put on a pair of black shorts over my swimsuit, but Willow purses her lips as she eyes me up and down. "Oh, that just won't do."

I look down at my chest. "Why?"

Iris rolls her eyes. "Because you look like the poor little orphan du jour."

She's clearly antsy to get going, but I'm starting to understand the confident, bitchy Spring Fae facade is only just that. If she was half as bold as she pretends to be, she wouldn't mind heading there on her own.

"Step aside, Will. I'm done waiting," she blazes toward me. "Stand straight, moth, and look forward."

I've seen Iris fix her hair and make-up, and even do Willow's but this is a first for me, and I gawk as she combs her hands through my frizzled black hair, taking care not to disturb the sunglasses sitting on my head. The curls go from beaten down to perfectly shaped in one swipe. "I can't do miracles, here, but maybe..." she bites her bottom lip, squinting at me like I'm no longer that annoying roommate she endures because of Willow, but a blank canvas.

She drags her hand down the high, u-shape neckline of my bathing suit. The fabric melts from the very austere cut to a plunging cleavage that finishes right between my breasts with a metal ring.

"Your breasts are perfect. It's beyond unfair," she laments.

I look down at my breasts, the round shape of them exposed, and resist the urge to cross my arms. "It's because of all this food I'm eating, remember?" I crack.

"Eyes closed. Don't move." She passes her hand over my closed lids, and when I open them again, her lips are curled up in a smile.

"They're your best asset; that and your eyes. Men love blue eyes. And wear this over your shoulders," she grabs a red, semi-transparent shawl from the hook next to the door. One of hers. "Keep them guessing what's underneath until you're ready to reveal those beauties."

I blush at the compliment. Iris is usually the first in line to criticize my appearance. "Err—thanks."

Willow squeezes her lower arm. "You're a true artist, Iris."

"Ugh. Let's go, now." But I detect a hint of blush on her cheeks, too.

The more I get to know Iris, the more I'm convinced her mother raised her to always appeal to men—something that, despite all the stories I've heard about the Secret Springs, sounds like a harsh, disenchanted childhood. Since Devi's speech, I've done my homework and confirmed that most women at the academy can only hope to become queens through marriage—and that's infuriating.

No wonder my father was so proud to secure the exact same kind of arrangement for me that princesses dream of.

We walk under the breezeway toward the eastern field, where the labyrinth is located. A huge hole has been torn through the side hedge, creating a shortcut to the ornate, creaky iron gate that marked the start of the Summer trial. My ears buzz as the scenery hits me for a second time.

A stream rises from the earth and spills into the pond where I nearly drowned, casting a rainbow over the turquoise waters. The willow tree above our heads provides a welcomed respite from the sun, and Elio set up a tartan blanket in the shade. The Prince of Light isn't wearing his wings today, just short trousers and a loose cotton shirt, and I greet him with a quick, "Hello."

The dangerous mudslides and will-o'-the-wisps that were lurking in the distance the other night have already been cleared out. I cast a begrudging glance at the trellis, overtaken by ensnarer vines, and recognize their distinctive feather-shaped leaves—something I failed to notice last time. I've since read up on the plant that nearly cost me my life. Harmless by day, but under the moonlight, they'll choke anyone who dares to trespass on their territory.

If I hadn't miraculously remembered that singing was their one guilty pleasure, I'd be dead.

The creek running down the hill bubbles into a succession of four small white pools before it reaches the pond, each large enough to fit two—maybe three—people. They've been crafted to resemble the Lunar Cascades, one of the most striking natural wonders of the Summerlands. During the trials, the whole area was overrun with poisonous, luminescent piranhas, but the water looks safe now.

Devi is luxuriating in one of the pools, her eyes half-closed, her gorgeous face soaking in the sun. At our arrival, she blinks and shields her eyes with her hand, her feline gaze lingering on me and my red shawl for a long moment before darting over to Iris.

"Come, Little Flower. I saved you a spot," she calls to her friend.

Iris beams and heads halfway down the hill to sit with her. My eyes wander of their own accord to the narrow beach and the hedge of bleeding hearts where I met Aidan, and my heart somersaults.

He's still there, half-naked, standing with his back to me in front of the hedge like a ghost.

For a moment, I believe it's only a figment of my imagination, but he's actually there, rummaging through the hedge for a... ball? Sure enough, the prince who has been haunting my every thought squeezes a white ball out of the bushes and punches it back to Ezra with the underside of his wrist.

I quickly crawl next to Elio on the blanket to avoid Aidan's notice. "Hey," I breathe.

Ezra, Aidan, and the fourth-years are playing ball in the water, and I can't help but stare.

"Looks like they're having fun," I say, trying to sound casual.

Sunlight glimmers off the warm, inviting skin of Aidan's broad back. Sun-kissed is not a shade I'm used to seeing on a man, and the luster of summer stirs something deep in my belly. In the labyrinth, he looked like a creature straight out of a fantasy, but here, he's all too real.

I can't help wishing I could kiss the tantalizing space between his shoulder blades and write my name down his spine with my tongue...

Elio nudges my shoulder. "Are you even listening?"

I jolt around to stare at him, wide-eyed, and his brows raise in question.

"Are you alright? You're looking a little green."

"Oh— I-I almost drowned in that pond."

He peers over the stony edge. "You can't swim, huh."

I shake my head.

Willow sits on the blanket with us, restless. She keeps stealing peeks at Devi and Iris, clearly irate not to have been invited to their little soak. She plays with her long brown hair, twirling it around her fingers before a groan bubbles up her throat. "Look at her. She's... flawless. Fuck, I'm jealous. I want to be a Spring Fae, too."

"Willow, come!" Iris shouts.

The Summer Princess feigns to hesitate. "Is it cold?"

I mask a grin with my hand. Summer Fae are complete wusses. Devi and Iris roll their eyes in sync, and Willow saunters over to join them.

Down by the beach, Ezra stumbles out of the water to retrieve a stray ball and waves in my direction. Just as Aidan is about to turn around, Diana jumps on his back and wrestles him under the water.

The Red Fae emerges first, and my throat itches. She's wearing two black, flimsy pieces of fabric that shouldn't even count as a swimsuit.

Aidan must have decided to focus his attention on someone not playing hard to get.

It's fine.

They look good together.

I lay down on the blanket, using my arm as a pillow, and force myself to concentrate on Elio, unwilling to waste one more second thinking about Aidan. Him and his damn beautiful back have clearly moved on to bloodier pastures.

Elio is still watching me, marking the page of his book with one finger. The cover showcases black and white piano notes.

"Do you play?" I ask.

"Only all the time," he grins. "Why?"

"I...sing."

He sits up and tucks the book in his lap. "Then I want to hear."

My mouth dries up. "Right now?"

His expectant smile widens.

"Later, alright? If you accompany me on the piano."

"You have a deal."

A brief pause lingers in the air before Elio averts his gaze and starts pulling at the green grass beside the blanket. "So... I heard something about you. I don't want you to say anything, but I thought you should know Zeke is telling everyone you're saving yourself for marriage."

I choose my next words carefully. "Yes, I already know."

A slight tremor rocks his voice. "One way or another, I believe it's not a badge of honor—or anyone's business. In fact, I wish I could have waited, but my father wouldn't tolerate his sons being naive about such things..."

I bite the inside of my cheeks for a minute. I trust Elio. Maybe this is the opportunity to test that trust. If I'm wrong, at least I'll know.

"I'm not, though." The corner of my mouth quirks. "A virgin."

His ice-blue eyes narrow, and a hint of a smile appears on his lips. "You're not? But how did you phrase it with Zeke?"

"I told him my father wanted me to remain a virgin until marriage. He implied the rest." I chuckle softly.

Elio lets out a low whistle. "Oh... You're good."

I bow my head and spread my arms in a mock curtsy. "Thank you."

"I hope you know your secret is safe with me." With a genuine smile, he sinks back into his previous position, legs crossed at the ankles, and returns to his reading.

The tree bristles at a sudden burst of wind, and the soft leaves brush my cheek. I swat the low-hanging branches away, but another crawls down my shoulder to nudge my side.

"By the spindle—"

I risk a glance at the pond beneath my oversized sunglasses. Aidan throws me a discreet look from the shallows before resuming his ball game. The loose grin playing on his lips confirms he's the one moving the tree, and my breath hitches as a big leaf curls around itself to caress my neck.

I disentangle myself from the plant, my heart racing.

While I was wrestling with the tree, Ezra climbed up the hill and now stands right above us, shaking his head to splash us. "Good day for a swim, wouldn't you agree, Lady Snow?" He offers me his hand.

Elio flips the page of his book with a tired sigh. "She doesn't want to swim, Ezra. Leave her alone."

"Tut-tut, kid. Let the lady speak for herself." He raises his hand by an inch, and his features fall as I hesitate.

"I don't know how to swim," I admit.

Ezra's intent gaze softens, and he lets out a short, somewhat relieved breath. "Oh, that won't do." He spins around. "Aidan! Come here!"

Aidan approaches, water drizzling down his body. "What?"

"Lady Snow here doesn't know how to swim."

"Oh, we can't have that. Not when you're the best instructor there is."

Ezra brings a hand to his chest like he's touched by Aidan's words. "I knew you'd get it."

Without further warning, the boys pull me to stand.

They each wrap an arm around my midriff, tugging me toward the edge of the rocks, and I forget how to breathe. I try to wriggle out of their hold, and Ezra releases me, but Aidan tightens his grip and cages me against his rock-hard chest.

I zap his arm with a burst of ice. "Let me go! Gods!"

He releases me, and I shove him hard. "You jerk! Let me at least get this off." I slip off my shorts first and step out of them before removing the shawl.

The boys' smiles fade, their eyes drinking in the shape of my body. A thrill shoots up my spine at their reaction while I bunch the red fabric at Elio's feet, leaving me in my one-piece black swimsuit.

Ezra snaps out of it first and slaps Aidan's shoulder. "Aidan. Let the lady undress, first. Jeez!" he chastises his friend with a big goofy smile.

I narrow my eyes and build a gigantic snowball in my hand. "Let's see how you like your balls on ice, boys."

"I like my balls as they are, thank you." Ezra runs and jumps in a cannonball back into the pond, landing right in the center. Iris shrieks in surprise, sprayed by the splash of his rather dauntless performance.

Aidan's amber eyes dance dangerously.

"I'm not jumping in with you," I clip.

"Yes, you are."

"No, I'm not."

He motions with both hands for me to take my best shot. "Give me all the ice you've got."

I build the mother of all snowballs in my hands, ready to break it over his head.

Quick as a cat, he snatches one of my arms and pulls me into his embrace once more. My body goes slack as his fire melts my ice, the snowball crumbling at our feet.

Aidan nestles his face in the crook of my neck. "I just got back from an unplanned trip to the new world and got your note this morning. I've missed you, Songbird. Hope you're ready for a swim."

My treacherous body arches into him as if to say, *with you, always*. I crane my neck around and examine the constellation of freckles licking the shape of his Adam's apple, the raw charisma rolling off him turning my insides to mush.

"I almost drowned in this pond, as you well know," I snap, trying to keep a straight head.

He grins like I didn't just bite his head off for nothing. "You better hold on tight to me, then."

CHAPTER 12
IVY
SONGBIRD

Aidan turns his back to the pond and falls backward over the ledge, pulling me along with him. A yelp escapes me, and we break the surface a moment later with a loud *splash*. Holding my breath, I instinctively twist in his arms to grab hold of his neck. Even though the dangerous traps and deadly blooms have either been deactivated or lulled back to sleep, I almost died here.

We emerge, and I sink my nails deep in his scalp to let him know how mad I am, but he doesn't appear bothered in the least. If anything, he's more than a little smug. Long, nimble fingers map the slope of my waist as Aidan holds me afloat.

"First lesson: move your arms and legs so you don't drown," he jokes.

"You're relishing this, but I'm terrified."

His lips brush my earlobe. "I would never let you drown, Songbird."

Aidan holds the both of us out of the water like it's easy, clearly a fantastic swimmer, and drags me under the canopy of gnarled roots at the back of the pond. Hidden from the world above, a small alcove offers a reprieve from the sun—and the keen eyes of our peers.

The roots of the willow tree twist and curl above our heads, forming a natural archway framed by trailing tendrils of neon-green lichen that thrives in the shadows. The air is cool and damp, filled with the earthy scents of wet moss and rich soil.

The water is clear enough for me to see the tubular network extend well below my feet before it vanishes into an inky abyss. Droplets plop down from the underbelly of the tree above and create a myriad of gentle, circular ripples across the water. It's like we're in an entirely different world.

Now that we're out of view, Aidan's joyful, carefree expression morphs into something heavy, tortured, and a little dark. "I couldn't stop thinking about you. You have to be mine, Songbird." He squeezes my sides, his ragged breaths rushing out.

Heartbeats pound in my chest, the immediate fear of drowning in Aidan's arms suddenly taking on a whole new meaning.

A flush creeps up my neck. "I-I can't be yours, Aidan."

He presses his forehead to mine, his breath warm against my skin. "Why not?"

I hold on to the closest lifeline I can find. "Because I'm not an object," I manage to whisper, though my certainty wavers. "I'm a person, and I can't be owned."

"Your logic is flawed," he murmurs, his voice low and intimate, "because you own me."

A shudder runs through me, and I press my hands to his shoulders. "You don't even know me."

"I'm following my instincts," he says, and for a moment, I'm caught in the intensity of his stare, my heart pounding in a fanfare that both excites and terrifies me.

"It's not your instincts you're following. It's your" —my gaze darts down between us— "Faehood." I blush, a hot burst of shame searing my entrails. Why couldn't I just say *cock*?

A low, masculine chuckle rumbles up Aidan's throat, the devilish prince clearly amused by the euphemism. "Talk more about my Faehood."

"You're a cocky bastard."

"I'm a prince."

"Is that how you justify your behavior?"

"I'm Aidan Summers. The heir forged in flames. The resplendent phoenix. I was never allowed to be anything else but bold, impulsive, and simply...ardent. People expect that of me. I need to burn brighter than everyone else. So I put on a smirk and forge ahead. It doesn't mean I don't have hopes and dreams of my own. Fears, even."

I crack a smile. "And what does a resplendent bastard fear, exactly?"

"I'm terrified of your indifference. Did you think about me at all?"

He looks so apprehensive, like a negative answer might actually hurt him. *Real.*

A wet strand of hair has fallen over his brow, and I brush it behind his ear. "I did wonder if you'd moved on already."

"Never."

Warmth radiates from his body, a stark contrast to the cool water of the pond. It melts the promises I made myself to stay away from him, one icicle of doubt at a time. Every detail of his face becomes magnified, from the slight arch of his brow to the way his lips part ever so slightly, his breaths growing shorter and uneven as my gaze darts down to the drop of water hanging from his chin. I wish I could dip my head down and lick it off.

The urge to close the distance between us, to bridge that final gap, dizzies me. Just the thought of crossing that line sends a jolt of adrenaline through my body.

"Beth..." he murmurs.

I shiver at the sound of my name on his lips.

The space between us shrinks to barely a quarter inch of wavering restraint and crackling desire. Until neither of us can suffer the wait anymore. I lean in first—or maybe he pulls me to him, the movement unrehearsed, yet natural.

Kissing Aidan is an even worse ailment than I remembered. As soon as our lips touch, I'm drowning again. Not in water, but in flames. In him.

There's nothing else like it.

At once, all the tension that had banded in my chest and knotted in my muscles dissipates, replaced by a blinding certainty. This is right. *Good.* This is where I'm meant to be.

We sink into the kiss, taking the time to discover each other, to the point where I can't even tell where one kiss ends and another begins. I run a hand through his wet hair and wrap my legs around his waist.

The combination of the cold water, Aidan's fire, and the steely ridge of his erection sends a flush to my cheeks and neck. My nipples are clearly visible under the stretchy fabric of my swimsuit, the pebbled peaks hard as stone.

The emptiness in my belly throbs, an ache there urging me to claim this man and let him use every inch of me in exchange for his soul. It's a new and disarming feeling, like I could *claw*, *bite*, and *scratch* at him until he belonged to me forever.

It's too much. Too violent, too carnal, and I recoil from it, spooked.

We both struggle to catch our breath, trapped in a storm that's both relentless and fragile.

Aidan runs a hand from the side of my face to the hollow of my neck. "Woah. Take it easy there, Songbird. I'm a bit flustered, here."

"Flustered..." I caress the back of his neck with spider fingers. "Or *ardent?*" I say in jest.

"Fuck. I'm not above taking you with our swimsuits on. Not completely against a crowd, either, if that's what you're into, but that's hardly how I imagined our first time to be."

"You—" A sharp inhale quakes my chest. The idea that this prince took time out of his day to fantasize about me and reflect on how and when we would have sex *for the first time* floors me.

I press my index finger to his chin dimple, scratching a line down his masculine jaw before climbing to the arch of his brows, taking ownership of his godly face. He's not wearing his phoenix mask now, his amber eyes open and vulnerable. *Definitely real.*

He twists his hand in my wet hair, his arms wrapped around me like the ensnaring vines he grew for the trials—dangerous yet beautiful, steady yet bound to choke the life out of you. I should break free, but he's not letting me go, and here I am, covered in him, already doomed. He crushes his mouth to mine, exploring every groove with his tongue as though he can somehow make up for this disastrous encounter with a deeper, better kiss.

And it works.

So well in fact that I wrap both my arms around his neck for him not to stop. I want him to take me somewhere private and teach me more than how to swim. The heat that ravages my lower belly is ten times as strong as it was with Henri, and after only a brush.

How would it feel if he actually lowered his trunks and tugged away the narrow scrap of fabric keeping me from feeling all of him? How deep would he stretch me as I lowered myself down on his cock? I'd burn to ashes right here.

I can almost see the whole scenario play out behind my closed lids, and he grabs the flesh of my ass as though he's thinking the exact same thing. Somehow, the thought that we absolutely, maddeningly, *desperately* can't do it spurs me on.

"We have to stop," I pant between kisses.

"Yes."

I sink my nails into his scalp to keep him from retreating. "This can't happen, and I don't just mean *now*. You and me, it would be a disaster," I say, half-serious, half-mad. "So it's not just a *no*, it's a *never*."

He smiles against my lips. "Absolutely never."

"Hum-Hum." A loud throat-clearing from behind wrenches the flames out of me, replacing them with a torrent of ice.

Ezra raises a pointed brow. "You two are playing with fire..." He trails off. "Zeke and the Crow just joined us."

Fuck! The madness that was keeping me in Aidan's arms stretches and snaps, the whiplash spreading a fine crust of snow down my spine. I push myself off his chest with both hands and grab one of the bigger roots from the network above our heads to keep from sinking.

I exhale, and the air in front of my face frosts in ribbons of mist.

Aidan presses his knuckles to his lips for a moment before his princely mask clicks back into place. "Who invited them?"

"Devi invited Damian. I think Zeke just saw him heading this way and tagged along."

My gaze darts between the two Fae princes. "We were just—" I huff at my own stupid attempt to lie. Ezra saw us. He saw us, and now he can barter my secret away anytime he damn well pleases. My shoulders sag.

Am I really the kind of woman to squander away my chances to be queen, to have a meaningful life, for a summer fling? As enticing as said fling may seem, it would never last.

Ezra extends a hand in my direction. "Need a knight to get you out of this tight spot, Lady Snow?"

I open my mouth to refuse, but the seriousness of his gaze makes me pause. I can't swim out of here alone, and if Zeke is to see me in the arms of another man, it shouldn't be the one I actually kissed. I nod and head toward him.

"Thanks."

Ezra glances at Aidan. "Stay here for a minute and... calm yourself." He wraps an arm around me, his hold more timid than Aidan's, yet solid. "And you, hold your breath and bat your feet."

Ezra presses my back to his chest, and I abandon myself to his grasp as we plunge under the roots to emerge in the middle of the pond.

Zeke squints down at us. "What were you two doing down there?"

"I'm teaching Beth how to swim. You want a turn, shadow man?

No one wanted you here, but as long as you found us, we might as well make good use of our time."

Zeke curls his fists. "You want a piece of me, Lightbringer?"

"I have zero interest in you, actually."

"Don't taunt me."

"What are you going to do? Wait for me to get out of the pond to punch me?" Ezra cracks. "You can't swim."

My feet bump solid ground, and Ezra loosens his hold. He grazes the nape of my neck with his thumb in lieu of goodbye, still bouncing off insults with my fiancé.

While the two men posture, Aidan discreetly peels himself out of the pond and into the lowest of the shallow pools. He rubs down his face with both hands, the dangerous spark burning in his amber gaze taking a life of its own.

"Enough, you two. Either fight like men or shut up already," Devi clips.

Willow waves me over emphatically, now standing alone in the highest pool, and I move to join her, but Zeke stops me. "Babe. A word."

He takes me aside.

Everyone is still watching, and I think he means it that way. His hand curls like a wolf's jaw around my elbow. "You can't do that, you know?" he whispers.

"Do what?"

He stands a little taller, still speaking too low for anyone else to hear. "Act like a tart with your boobs hanging out, grinding against Lightbringer in public."

A hot, almost suffocating mix of rage, shame, and self-consciousness engulfs me. All three emotions compete for the title role in this hideous play we're enacting, when only righteous anger would suffice. "I was not—"

"Are you hearing me?" he asks as he bends down to peck my cheek.

But I sink my nails in my palms, a hiccup dribbling up my throat.

I know who holds the power in our non-relationship, and it's not me. "Yes."

"Good."

My jealous, possessive fiancé kissed a second-year very publicly this week, a fact almost every student with a mouth has run by me since then, to see how I'd react, and his hypocrisy makes me want to claw at his smug face. An undertow of humiliation ices what's left of my good mood, and I quickly climb to the tartan blanket.

Elio snaps his book shut. "Are you okay?"

"I'm fine," I roar, snapping inadvertently at the only man here who's never put his ego above my well-being. "But I'm done with dumb swimming lessons and stupid, stupid boys. And for clarity, that does not include you."

Elio climbs to his feet. "I'll walk back to the Abbey with you."

Tears wet my cheeks as he dusts off his blanket and wraps it around my shoulders, ushering me away from the others. I must have been under a spell earlier. From now on, I won't let Aidan, Zeke, or any other jackass prince within two feet of me.

The next time I'm tempted to give into my most basic urges, I won't be so quick to forget what the price for being carefree is. It's too expensive for a moth.

One night of passion isn't worth the freedom I can buy with a Royal Academy diploma in one hand and a Shadow mask in the other. Morpheus can strike me down where I stand, but I'm not marrying a misogynistic pig just to become queen. The countdown to graduation begins.

CHAPTER 13
CRUSH
WONDER BOY

"Your trial was vicious, Aidan," Damian says with a grin. He admires our surroundings, his keen eyes able to see past the beauty of the gardens to the traps underneath. "It's a pity they're clearing it out so soon. I see the marshes are already gone..." he trails off.

I keep a neutral expression. "My father wanted the labyrinth to be dealt with early this year. He's planning to host a big party for my mother's birthday."

The Crow scrutinizes me for a minute longer, and I know he doesn't buy the story I've tried to shove down everyone's throats. It's strictly true, of course, but I was the one who gave my father the idea to destroy the labyrinth so we could grow an enchanted forest in time for the queen's birthday. No one will be able to figure out why I was truly in such a hurry to see the place destroyed, the proof of my meddling in Beth's trial erased.

Damian finally gives up and heads toward Devi, who's now lying down on the small beach, and Ezra takes the opportunity to join me in my shallow pool.

"I think you forgot to mention something, *boo*," he whispers. "Come on, repeat after me: I have a huge crush on Beth."

"I have a huge crush on Beth," I sigh.

"Wait. She's the one you've been sending all those conspicuously unremarkable notes to." His carefree smile is wiped out by a reproachful scowl. "There's no doubt she likes you, too. But that was pretty reckless of you both today. Anyone could have—"

"I'm lucky it was you."

"I don't know..." Ezra picks at his cuticles. "I'm kind of jealous. I could slip up if not for the right incentive. Maybe if you mentioned to her that I could be your third, I'd be more willing to forgive you."

"Ezra."

His ice-blue eyes drill holes into me. "It is *just* a crush, right?"

I trail my gaze back to Devi, Zeke, and Diana chatting on the beach and grit a dubious answer through clenched teeth. "I don't know."

Ezra slaps my bare chest with the back of his hand. "Aidan. She's a moth. Your father would never let you court her. Or even date her. Hell, if he knew we were having this conversation, he'd find a way to send her packing. She's only here because she happens to be engaged to Zeke and our fathers are dying to keep Damian off his throne. If that little prince gets too jealous and stupid, it will put her place here in jeopardy."

"I know. It's just... I've never felt anything like it."

"Then get it out of your system *discreetly*. Take her to the cabin. But don't sneak around in public, because I won't take the heat for you again."

"Thanks, mate."

We drift to safer, easier subjects, but I'm still marinating in the emotions that Beth's argument with Zeke dredged up. The brief joy felt under the roots has been destroyed by guilt. I pushed her, and while it allowed me to finally determine that the attraction goes both ways, it was too much, too fast.

Devi joins Damian in the pond, and Zeke flirts with Diana

without a shred of shame after the scene he caused. *What a jerk.* My fists clench at my sides. I could kill the guy just for the way he encroached on Beth's personal space, earlier. She clearly doesn't want anything to do with him. Arranged marriages are the worst.

Ezra shifts in the small pool and erases Zeke from my vision. "Easy, Othello." He climbs to his feet, spraying water all over me. "Come on, let's go back to the loft."

We leave the others behind and make our way back to our apartments. Ezra and I share a loft on the top floor of the south tower, a perk granted by my position. It's still only one floor above the Crow and the fourth years, but it's better than squeezing into an apartment with them.

When we get to the loft, the door is ajar, and Ezra slows down as we near the entrance. "See you later, boo."

There's only one person with enough gall to breach our sanctuary.

The sunlight streams in through the wide, arched windows of the loft, painting the floor with golden light. The view is the best on property—on one side, the endless expanse of the ocean, with a clear view of the Saffron Cove, and on the other, the coastal village of Augustus with its tiny, colorful homes and bustling streets.

"Aidan. We had an appointment, son," my father enunciates slowly, sending shivers up my spine.

The otherwise jovial air of my little world is thick with unspoken grievances. My father stands by the window, his broad back to me as he gazes out at the horizon. His presence fills the room, commanding attention and subservience even in silence. He might only be king consort, but he's still king.

And he hates to be kept waiting.

"I apologize, Sir. I completely forgot," I say, using my best repentant voice.

He makes this sound with his lips and tongue that's equal part disappointment and resignation, like he expected nothing better of me. "It's your last year in school. You have to start thinking about your future beyond the academy."

He doesn't mean my future as king, because he still can't confront that he and mum will die someday, and I raise a worried brow. "Are you saying you want me to choose a wife?"

A genuine grin pierces his mighty exterior. "Blessed Flame, no! Your mother and I think it's best for you to wait and enjoy your unattached bachelor status for as long as you want. You already wear the Mark of the Gods, my boy. You have nothing to prove. And until you're ready to start thinking about kids, you don't have to commit to anyone."

Relief washes over me. "What did you mean, then?"

He crosses the room, the sleek hardwood floorboards creaking under his shiny boots, and stops beside a tall bookcase. "I thought you might want to start shadowing me and learning the ropes of politics. We could start with negotiating your sister's marriage contract."

I stiffen back tenfold at the news and try to mask my reaction with an awkward stretch. "Willow is to be married? Now? She *just* got into the academy—"

I stop myself and press my lips together, knowing better than to ramble in my father's presence. He's not asking me my opinion, he's *telling* me what he plans to do, and I know that expression of his well enough to know he's determined to see this through.

He nods, his brows furrowed. "Yes, and that improved her horizons. She doesn't have the same advantages you do. She wants to be queen, so we'll have to arrange it for her."

"Does she really?"

My little sister being thrust into marriage doesn't sit well with me, but arguing against my father's wishes will accomplish nothing other than to put him in a foul mood.

"Son, every Summers wants to rule. It's the fire in our blood. We have trouble following orders."

I've been trying to hide my discomfort, but he reads me too well.

His gaze sharpens, his tone bordering on anger. "I was not asking *if* she should marry. Merely for you to help me choose her husband."

A metallic taste fills my mouth, my tongue parched and dry. "Who do you have in mind?"

"Ezekiel Nocturna."

"What? Are you joking?" I can't hide my anger or incredulity, my guarded face losing all semblance of reverence. "Are you so desperate to keep Beth out of school?"

His amber eyes burn, the flames within them barely contained. "Beth?"

Fuck-fuck-fuck.

"Everybody is talking about the new girl's engagement to Zeke, and how it earned her an invitation to the trials," I backpedal. "She's all everyone has been talking about."

"Yes, it was quite clever on the Shadow King's part. He asked for Willow first, of course, but I didn't want to agree to anything before his son was admitted into the academy. You know what the rumors were about him. Given his performance, I might have dismissed him too quickly. With your sister's magic, he might just win his throne after all. Unless Damian marries, too, of course."

"Damian thinks himself above such things as marriage." The scope of my father's plan slowly comes into focus. "So Willow gets a throne, and you get rid of the moth as a bonus."

"Moths do not belong in our *Royal* Academy. This sort of precedent is dangerous. I thought I had taken care of it, but she was more resourceful than I'd expected."

"What do you mean?"

"When I caught wind of how powerful she was, I enchanted a tile to make sure she'd be in the last group. Less than ten percent of applicants entering last make it through in time, so the moth had almost no chance of success."

I bite down on my tongue not to make a scene.

"Oh, spare me that look, son." He waves his hand dismissively. "Are you too immature to handle the truth?"

I struggle to keep my flames under control, the heat of my emotions flaring just beneath the surface.

"You are not allowed to tell anyone about this. Or Willow's wedding. Not until things are settled. Swear it, or by Hephaistos, I will throw you in a holding cell until you do."

I give him an insolent bow. "I swear I won't tell, Your Majesty," I reply, though my mind is already racing for a way out.

A hint of magic swirls through the air to seal my promise, reassuring him that I'm not about to go rogue and rat him out to the faculty, but I can't keep this from Beth. She has to know that our cheating in the labyrinth only nullified my father's meddling.

As for the wedding, Willow might skin me alive for keeping the secret, but I'm not sure what good telling her would do, aside from robbing her of her last precious weeks of carefreeness.

The king sits down on one of the three sofas, crossing his leg and laying his ankle over the opposite knee. "Damian Sombra and his prick of a father are about to get a lesson in the importance of politics. That's why we come out on top, Aidan. We don't minimize the role of alliances. The Gods bestow power upon us, but it's up to us to cater to that power so that it doesn't wither and dry like a fruit on the vine."

I sit in the armchair beside him and meet his gaze. "Can I speak plainly, Sir?"

"Go on."

"Zeke is a fool. It's a miracle he passed the trials in the first place, and Willow... You know I love her, but even their magic combined wouldn't be strong enough to best Damian."

His lips thin as he scratches his thick sideburn. "I don't want Damian Sombra to be king. He's too strong, and not malleable enough to be of any use to us."

I lean forward, trying to exude as much confidence and poise as I can muster. "Then leave Zeke to the moth. She's the strongest darkling I've ever met and managed to ice the pond I created for the trials."

My father raises an eyebrow, clearly rattled by the news. "She froze the water in your section of the labyrinth?"

"Yes." I pause, munching on my next words carefully. Am I arguing for Beth to marry Zeke? The thought unsettles me, but I don't want her to leave school, and my little sister deserves better than Zeke Nocturna. "Given the strength of the moth's powers, she's not a trail-blazer, but the exception to confirm the rule. And once she's tucked away in the Shadowlands, no one will give her a second thought."

Sweat pearls on my brow from the effort of phrasing that. I do think Beth is exceptional, which allowed me not to lie, but the overall message was on the cusp of dishonesty.

A thoughtful smile appears on the King's lips. "I trust you, son, so I will take your advice into consideration. Now, if Zeke is not the man for her, we still have to get your sister settled. I do have another idea."

"Why so fast, though?" I ask, trying to keep the conversation going.

I'm beginning to win him over.

He leans back in his seat, sinking deep into the cushions, his leg jittering over his knee. "Aidan... You're a man now, so I will stop protecting you from hard truths. Your sister has certain....quirks that will only become more and more problematic now that she's at the academy. You understand what I mean, right?"

"Yes," I answer through clenched teeth, feeling like my mouth is full of burning, boiling sand.

"And those quirks will get out, eventually. We need to get her married before then."

"You mean to entrap a future king of Faerie?"

"Everyone walks down the aisle with secrets, son. It's just how life works."

The conversation lingers in the air, heavy and unresolved, as I turn my gaze back to the ocean. The waves crash relentlessly over the beach, each new undertow stealing a bit of its red sand and dragging it toward the sea. My father's words buzz in my ears, and I can't help but feel like I'm being pulled under, too. Except instead of being slowly eroded by the sea, my soul and beliefs are going to be chipped, chiseled, or burnished away by the thousands of rules and expectations that define my life.

For a crown of fiery amber I'm not sure I even want.

I thought I did, but now... I want Beth more.

She's in my head.

The way she held my hand in the labyrinth. How tightly she wrapped her thighs around me. The sweet taste of her lips.

I want it *all*.

I hang back at the loft for a couple of hours, trying and failing to think of anything else. Night has fallen by the time I snap out of my Beth-induced fantasies, joining Ezra and most of the fourth years at the Saffron Cove. The festivities are already in full swing, empty bottles of cider already piled next to the fire.

A silvery glow bathes the dark crimson hues of the secluded beach. The ocean gently laps at the shore in a rhythmic, soothing pattern. The night air is warm, carrying the salty scent of the sea and the strong aromas of burning wood and smoke from the crackling fire.

Ezra is playing poker with a bunch of the other guys over a flat rock, while Willow lounges on her stomach, chatting animatedly with Iris, Sean, and a couple of second-years. Beth is not among them, and my nails dig into my palms as I pass by a couple lying on a blanket. Zeke has his tongue so far down Diana's throat, I fear she might choke.

I do my best to ignore them and sit beside Ezra on the sand, joining in as he deals the next round.

"Nice of you to finally join us. Did the old man keep you all this time?" he says the last part softly, so the others don't hear.

I shake my head and offer a small shrug. My relationship with my father might be tense, but Ezra's is far worse. It seems petty to complain to him about it.

When Diana finally leaves Zeke behind, the Shadow Prince joins our circle. He's all flushed, and Ezra raises a pointed brow at him.

"Where's your fiancée, Nocturna? Or do you still have one?" Ezra muses, a smirk creeping onto his face. "It's hard to believe you gave me such grief for touching your girl this morning. What's the matter? Did your lady dump you for your jealous fit, as she rightly should have done?"

"Beth is mine. But that doesn't stop me from having some fun," Zeke replies, a glimmer of defiance in his eyes.

"And she's on board with your appalling behavior?"

Zeke crosses his arms with a faux air of indifference. "Please... the last thing I need is a lecture on loyalty from someone who can't even keep track of which girl he's sleeping with."

Ezra chuckles, a sharp edge to his laughter. "Better to be a rake than a prince whose crown is only as secure as his fiancée's affection."

Zeke straightens his cards and sits on the log on the opposite side of the fire, his legs sprawled. "Beth is lucky I didn't tell my father how... frigid she is." He cracks a devious smile and elbows the fourth-year sitting next to him. "I shouldn't have expected anything different from a moth, right?"

"That's not something a real man should say. Ever," I clip over the rumble of the bonfire.

"Hear, hear!" Ezra chimes in. "You might have the name and pedigree, but she's got the looks, the brains, *and* the power, Zippy. I'd be careful if I were you. I'd think you have just as much to lose if she rescinded her promise—if not more."

"Settle down. It's just us guys," Zeke scoffs.

The satisfied smile on his lips jolts me to my feet. "I won't settle down."

The bum rolls his eyes. "Oh, you think she's so great, huh? Well, maybe you should try to fuck her. Maybe she needs a little fire in her cunt. Your renowned, almighty cock might spark her engine to life or something—"

Thwack.

I shake off my knuckles, the impact of my fist on Zeke's face followed by a spray of blood.

He covers his nose with both hands. "You broke my nose!"

Loud gossip buzzes across the beach, and I can't make out the words, but I know they're talking about us. I draw in a shaky breath, trying to ground myself. The stares of my peers tingle across my spine, unrelenting. *By the Flame. What have I done?*

Zeke still clutches his nose, his shock morphing into rage as he wipes the blood from his face. "You'll pay for this, Summers."

"Try me."

Zeke pushes me backward toward the fire, and I stagger to keep upright, lost in the haze of my own actions for a moment before he sends a lash of shadows my way, cutting my leg. I sidestep to avoid his incoming right hook, but he shakes off the failed attack and sharpens his magic into a dagger at his side.

Is he serious?

The fire behind me stretches to meet my own, and I block Zeke's weapon with my bare hands, my flames spreading across the blade and then latching onto his clothes. He yells in a mix of surprise and pain and runs off toward the sea.

By now, everyone has stopped drinking and talking to watch, and my pulse spikes as I lock eyes with Beth. Her wide-eyed gaze reflects shock—and something more dangerous: murderous fury. Her lips are parted in disbelief, and I can almost see the wheels turning in her head, calculating the fallout of my actions.

Heat churns in my blood. I've crossed a line I can't uncross. I'm not defending her honor—I'm putting everything at risk.

Her expression hardens, and I know I've messed up. Badly.

CHAPTER 14
PROPAGANDA
SONGBIRD

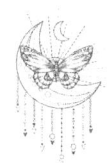

The salty air kisses my lips as I teeter on the last stone step leading down to Saffron Cove, wishing I had stayed in my room after all. I stand at the edge of the gathering, all eyes suddenly upon me. The glow of the flames illuminates the faces of my peers, their expressions a mix of horror and fascination. Clouds obscure the moon while the flickering firelight dances erratically, casting long shadows that twist and contort like phantoms on the sand.

A couple of students run to Zeke's aid, but most of them are drinking in the fallout, ravenous for more. Willow marches over to punch her brother's chest. "Blessed Flame! What was *that*?"

They argue among themselves, drawing a bit of attention away from me, and I take advantage of the reprieve to walk around them, giving the fire—and Aidan—a wide berth.

In the water, Johan and Diana are helping Zeke to his feet. Black and red marks mar his naked chest, a few scraps of fabric embedded in the burns. Tears streak down the Shadow Prince's face as he stumbles out of the ocean, his skin extinguished but his gaze burning with the fire of the seven hells.

"I'll take you to the healer—" I start, feeling responsible for what happened.

If I hadn't kissed Aidan this morning, or answered his flirty notes with my own, none of this would have happened.

Zeke pushes right past me with an enraged grunt, his hand leaving a print of water and ash on my shirt, and points a finger at Aidan. "I don't care who you are. You're going to pay for this, Summers."

Aidan holds both palms in front of him. "Let's stop here before you get really hurt."

"I'll show you hurt, you fucker."

Aidan backs away, but the flames burning along his skin intensify.

A scream tears out of my throat. "Stop!"

An unexpected burst of ice erupts from my fingertips and toes, freezing the entire beach. Gasps echo across the cove, and a couple of students tumble to the ground, taken by surprise by the suddenly slippery surface. Unabashed stares crawl along my skin—each gaze a dagger, each whisper a taunt.

Diana clicks her tongue loud enough to cut the awed, petrified silence. "You should leave. I'll take Zeke to the healer myself."

My fists ball at my sides, my heart about to fall out as I march out of Saffron Cove with my back hunched.

What I didn't expect was for Aidan to chase after me. I'm almost back under the breezeway when he picks up speed to actually catch up, and with each step he takes, the ground shifts beneath my feet. I can't meet his gaze—not when the acrid scent of burnt flesh hangs in the air between us, suffocating and bitter. I push forward, desperate for escape. "Leave me alone, Aidan."

"Let me explain, *please.*"

I shake my head, but he gains ground on me. The anger in my blood takes on a life of its own as I dig the balls of my feet in the sand. I spin around to face him and cross my arms around my chest. "Alright then. Explain."

Coming to an abrupt stop not to bump into me, he scratches the back of his neck. "You have to know... I was trying so hard to stay out of it, but you should have heard the horrible things he said about you. How badly he disrespected you—"

"So you *immolated* him? Of all the things you could have done, you figured picking a fight with my fiancé and setting him on fire in front of everyone was the one thing you just had to do tonight?" I say, my voice way too high for my taste.

"Immolated is a strong word. I burned him a little, in self-defense. Ask anyone, he used his magic first."

I clear my throat and lower my pitch. "Because you punched him," I enunciate slowly.

"He treats you like you're unworthy. Like you don't belong here."

"You did the same."

He shakes his head from side to side. "Never."

"Yes, you did. That night in the labyrinth, you didn't think I could make it out alone."

He tilts his head to the side, his lips parting. "That's not—I'd just met you then."

"And you were right. I wouldn't have made it out alone. I don't belong here. You turned me into a liar and a cheat, and the more time we spend together, the more I'm reminded of it." I force a breath through my tight jaw. "And now everyone will wonder why the great Aidan Summers lost his temper over me and beat up my fiancé. They'll start asking questions again."

"You *do* belong here, Beth. If only you knew how much... I don't know how to deal with this." He motions to the space between us. "You spend plenty of time with Elio, and no one bats an eye. I want to get to know you, I—"

"Elio is my *friend*."

"Let me be your friend, then."

A dumbfounded scoff grates my throat. "You don't want to be my *friend*. I had a moment of weakness before, but I'm telling you for the last time. Back off. I'm engaged."

"Engaged to a guy who's spent the whole night making out with someone else? That's rich."

"Zeke and I have a deal. I'm fine with it."

Aidan's expression twists, a mixture of disbelief and frustration. "You really think that makes it okay? Why settle for a ridiculous arrangement and pretend everything is fine, when you could have so much more?"

I cross my arms again, trying to shield myself from his piercing gaze. "It's not your place to judge my choices."

"You deserve more than this, Beth. More than him."

"Stop acting like you know what's best for me!" I snap, but the edge in my voice falters.

"I just... I care about you." He steps closer. "You told me yourself you don't even like the guy."

"Hence the reason for him to do whatever the hell he wants before we actually have to marry."

"Then why can't you and I do the same? You use your engagement as a shield, but the way you look at me... it makes me *burn*."

The word liquifies my gut. I wish I could wrap my arms around his neck and discover just how scorching his embrace could be. My pulse flutters, uneven and rash, but I steel myself against the lure of the flames.

"Do you really have to ask? Let's say I was dying to kiss you again, do you think Zeke would let me get away with it? That he would look the other way when he found out? You saw what he did this morning. He would pout and huff and puff and force me to stop. I would bring up his grossly unfair double-standards, but if I insisted for our arrangement to go both ways, he'd either demand that I sleep with him or break off the engagement altogether. For you, this is a game. A hunt. For me, it's my whole life."

"You felt it in the gardens. You feel it now. This thing between us —we can't help it. I don't want you for one night or to prove a point. You have no idea how greedy I feel when I'm with you." He cradles my head in his hands. "I've fallen for you, Beth. From the first moment I saw you."

My heart gives a giant squeeze at how confident and genuine he sounds, yet I can't let myself believe him. When a moth catches fire, nothing is left behind but ashes.

"Love at first sight doesn't exist. Not for us. Love arrows aren't strong enough to pierce a Fae's heart."

"Your denial doesn't make it less true."

"Oh, I'm sorry. I must have missed the archer standing beside us in the labyrinth."

"No archer. I'm talking about *true love*. A *Coup de Foudre*."

The possibility that we've been struck by the goddess of love herself is a dangerous promise of passion and ruin intertwined, but darklings know better than to trust in fate. Or love. Not when our lives hang in the balance.

Aidan's confidence makes me want to douse myself in oil and light the fire myself. But soon, I'd be nothing but dust in the wind. Aidan Summers will marry a princess; no question about it. Why should I let him destroy me first?

If I let myself fall for him, I doubt I could recover when he eventually tires of me.

"Coup de Foudre are legends... Faen stories."

His jaw clenches. "I know my own heart. I wake up thinking about you. I go to bed picturing your smile—"

"I can't listen to this." I spin around to leave, but Aidan slips in front of me, blocking my path.

"Well, you have to. You have to know how I truly feel. I won't let you write this off as a silly infatuation that'll blow over in a week, because that would be an atrocious lie. I *know* we're meant to be together, and deep down, you know it too."

I want to say that I understand exactly what he's talking about, because I feel it too. But I can't. I won't give anyone, even Aidan Summers, the means to ruin me.

"The only thing I know for sure is that you're a cocky bastard who can't take no for an answer." The ice in my tone chills his confidence, and he sucks in air.

"That's it? I bare my heart to you, and that's all you have to say?"

It physically hurts not to respond, but I keep my fists firmly planted at my sides and bite my tongue until it bleeds.

Aidan flashes me a smile that's all thorns and teeth before rubbing his face with a tired hand. "Alright. My mistake. Pardon me, Miss Elizabeth. I have clearly been afflicted by a fever that affects me and me alone. I won't bother you again."

CHAPTER 15
BY THE FLAME
BETH

Summerlands, Faerie, Present Day

The Summer royal envoy leads me directly from my hotel room in Los Angeles to the Royal Academy's bibliotheca. The air vibrates as I step out of the mirror, and a languid ache grips me. Even though it's been decades since I last felt the tremors of Aidan's bite of power, the atmosphere still becomes charged with electricity whenever he's close. I wonder if he feels it, too, or if it's a ghost that only haunts me.

The warm glow of the brass desk lamps casts dancing shadows across the leather-bound books, making me feel as though I've actually stepped back in time.

"I always figured the Crown Prince would get married in Eterna," I remark to my guide, Hector, a stern sprite with gray skin and wrinkled white ears.

"His Highness is particularly fond of the Royal Academy. He teaches here now."

Wow... Master Aidan.

The bibliotheca is empty, which tells me the students were probably sent on some new world field trip to allow for the wedding to take place without too many outsiders.

Hector gestures for me to sit on the ornate gold-and-white sofa, which offers a jaw-dropping view of the ocean, but I freeze in place. Dusk casts a golden glow across the sky that deepens into shades of amber and violet, the sea beneath it scintillating. My vision blurs with unshed tears as I drag a shaky hand along the trim of the back cushions. A familiar burgundy stain half-hidden in the wood grain of the coffee table catches my eye—an old mark that predates my arrival at the academy. I stare at it for a moment, the strange detail a reminder that no matter how hard we try to brush off our mistakes, the past can never be fully erased. I open my eyes wider not to cry.

"Do you want something to drink?" Hector asks.

I shake my head no, and he bows respectfully at my refusal.

"I'll fetch the bride," he says before flying off.

I walk around the edge of the sofa to sit. *Get it together, Snow.*

I didn't come here to make a complete fool of myself in front of my ex boyfriend, but I hadn't anticipated how familiar it would all seem. Almost nothing here has changed. Not the coffered ceilings, the hand-woven rugs, or the empty marble fireplace.

Two people inch out of the stacks, and the foggy haze of nostalgia lifts. The prospect of my imminent face-to-face with Aidan sends a fresh burst of adrenaline through my veins, and I jolt to my feet.

Thankfully, it's not the groom heading my way, but one of my oldest friends. Elio, the Winter King, raises a questioning brow at me, and the tension that had just thickened in my blood ebbs away.

"Elio! Lori!" I stammer. "What are you two doing here?"

The newlyweds exchange a glance, and Elio blushes. Only then do I notice his disheveled hair and the unbuttoned gap in Lori's black silk blouse. "Nothing— I was showing Lori around when we heard you and Hector chatting..."

I grin, amused by their obvious embarrassment to be caught fondling in public. "I meant here. At the academy."

Elio's gaze flies to the ground, his sheepish grimace deepening, and he clasps Lori's hand tighter. "Aidan invited us to his wedding. We're petitioning for the release of Lori's brother from Murkwood prison, and Aidan insisted on our presence. He wants to reaffirm our alliance so we can present a united front against the rebels."

I quickly tell myself that he's not betraying me by being here. That, as a Fae king, he had to accept Aidan's invitation. But a part of me feels scorned. We saw each other only a few days ago, and he didn't mention anything about it.

Lori pokes his side hard. "See? You should have told her."

The Winter Queen looks fierce in her fighting leathers, her disdain for more classic garbs a delightful quirk that gives her a bad-ass vibe. Her long dark hair is braided into an elaborate up-do, but one strand near her forehead is now all white, as though a tiny part of her froze beyond recognition after her coronation. Her high peep-toe heels reveal black nail polish that matches the shade on her hands, and a cluster of silver and diamond earrings gleams around the shell of her round ear.

I bite my lips at the sight of her perfect, artful smokey eyes. Is the shard of Iris's soul now residing inside her influencing her fashion choices, allowing her to wield Spring magic? Or is Lori simply adjusting to her role as queen?

"Lori's right. I should have told you about the wedding—" Elio pauses abruptly, and his brows bunch together. "Why are *you* here, Beth?"

"The bride—" I roll my shoulders back and force myself to say her name out loud. "*Heather* asked me to sing Never to Be tomorrow night, like I did at your wedding."

Elio's features slowly decompose into an expression of ghastly, wide-eyed shock. "By Thanatos. She has no idea, does she?"

I shake my head.

"And you said yes?" Elio seems to be trying very hard to rein in the wild emotions on his face, and a needle of remorse pierces my heart.

Why did I accept Heather's invitation? Did I think Aidan might cancel his wedding at the last minute if I showed up? Did I hope to punish him for the fact that I never moved on by crashing his wedding? I don't think I had any ill-intent, but the ugly truth is I still love him.

What I told myself to make the trip sound less irrational was that I had to see the bride and groom with my own eyes. That I needed to see Aidan happy with someone else, so I could finally move on. I thought I might realize I had built our romance up in my head.

But Elio's sharp gaze reminds me in no uncertain terms that I should have stayed in the new world.

"I was curious, and her letter sounded more like a summons, so I figured—" A painful breath escapes my clenched jaw. "You're right. I shouldn't have come."

"It's too late now. *The bride* is heading our way," Lori whispers, discreetly motioning to the entrance of the bibliotheca.

I spin around to greet Heather, and my lips part in surprise. She's tall, even taller than me, with tanned legs that never end and a perfect hourglass silhouette. Absolutely stunning.

I expected nothing less from a Spring princess, of course, but the warmth of her genuine smile fills me with dread. Luscious waves curl on both sides of her face, her brown skin almost golden in the twilight.

Heather Heart, the next Summer Queen, introduces herself with starstruck eyes, an excited smile, and a blatant disregard for personal space. "Elizabeth Snow! Oh my goodness, I'm so elated that you accepted my invitation." She pecks my cheeks with a nervous laugh and hugs me so hard, she knocks the breath out of me.

A heavy boulder settles in my chest. I'm not quite sure why I came at all—aside from the twinge at the pit of my stomach that begged me to. But this is self-imposed *torture...*

Dark thoughts flood my brain, filling me with a dreary sense of emptiness. I sink into a graveyard of past regrets, a mud pit crawling with the corpses of my festering hopes.

The should-haves, the would-haves, and the what-might-have-beens are all gathered to punish me for my folly.

"Congratulations on the wedding," I breathe, feeling outside myself.

"Thank you. I'm glad you could come. I wanted to discuss the ceremony and reception and see if you were open to sing—" Her face lights up, and she motions to someone behind me. "Aidan, come here!"

I black out for a moment as Aidan joins his fiancée's side.

"Elizabeth, This is my soon-to-be husband, Aidan Summers."

He's the same, and yet not. His face doesn't show much wear, his handsome jaw still as clean-shaven as ever. The vines of his family's embroideries snake along the collar of his crisp, white shirt and along his cufflinks. I remember tracing those lines back and forth between kisses, and how impatient he was for me to peel the fabric away...

His hair is slightly darker and shorter, but only his eyes are truly different. They betray the century that has passed since our last meeting, and my entire being quakes as our gazes cross.

Holy fuck.

I expect him to pause, or stop, or show any sign of recognition at all, but he grins at me with his arm slung around another woman's waist like he's...eager to meet me.

"It's an honor to meet you, Miss Elizabeth."

I blink at him, unable to say a word.

His smile widens, and his gaze darts to his fiancée. "Honestly, I think my lovely bride is more ecstatic for your performance than for the wedding at this point."

"Shush." Heather elbows his side, and his genuine laughter wrecks me.

How dare he laugh like that for someone else in front of me? my heart cries out.

I worked through a thousand scenarios when I envisioned this meeting, and Aidan's array of possible reactions ranged from quiet shock to effusive embarrassment to blinding rage.

I considered the possibility of a very public, explosive fight, cold words exchanged as he threw me out of his kingdom forever. Daydreamed about heated arguments that escalated to more intimate debates, the both of us entwined in royal sheets. Cherished silly fantasies that he would somehow call off the wedding.

I imagined it all, and then some.

A few scenarios even included his denial that we'd ever met, but I could never have conceived that he would introduce himself with that blank-slate look on his face. Like he has no idea who I am.

CHAPTER 16
WEDDING SINGER
AIDAN

The scents of aged paper and fresh lilacs hit my nose as I enter the bibliotheca, and I pause in the doorway, taken aback by the eerie bite of power vibrating through the air. Goosebumps raise along my arms, and my eyes narrow, searching for the source of the magic.

Elio and his new queen have arrived, which might explain the strange undercurrent of energy in the room, but the Winter King quickly fades from my mind. A darkling is standing with her back to me, her silhouette framed by the stained glass of the windows.

"Aidan, come here!" Heather motions me forward.

I watch my fiancée's lips move, her smile wide and unrestrained, but I can't hear anything.

The world around me fades into silence, my ears buzzing as I stare at the renowned singer Heather has been raving about for years. Elizabeth Snow is unlike anyone I've ever seen, and yet there's something achingly familiar about her.

Long dark waves cascade down her back, shining under the twilight as she spins toward me. The delicate slant of her nose compliments her high cheekbones, her face so striking that it steals my breath, but it's her eyes that make my heart stop, then race all at once. They're large, deep, and endless. A luminous blue.

A midnight-blue gown hugs her curves, her skin pale as freshly-fallen snow. Dusk licks the edges of the dress like a waning fire that yearns to be obliterated by her frost, and my mouth dries up.

She's the most beautiful woman I've ever seen. Simple as that.

I can hardly wait for Heather to introduce me and almost beat my fiancée to the punch before she says, "Elizabeth, this is my soon-to-be husband, Aidan Summers."

"It's an honor to meet you, Miss Elizabeth."

Promises of unbridled passion and indelible heartbreak burn inside her astute gaze—reminiscent of the Dark Sea I love so much—but the spark within it flickers and dies as it meets mine.

With a discreet bend in her brow, she stares at me like she expected more of the Crown Prince of the Summerlands than what I have to offer. Blood rises to my cheeks, the disappointed curve of her parted lips like a quill ready to impart a failing grade. With one look, the gorgeous stranger pits me against all the stories she's bound to have heard about me and finds me lacking in every measure of manhood.

I switch my weight from one foot to the other, unable to cope with the sudden ache in my gut, and concentrate on Heather instead. "Honestly, I think my lovely bride is more excited for your performance than for the wedding at this point."

Heather rams her elbow in my side. "Shush."

After a moment of awkward silence, my fiancée tugs her brown hair behind her ears and shakes off her obvious nerves. "I went to see you in concert once, back when you first assumed your new identity. I found it so heartbreaking that you can no longer perform "Never to Be" in the new world." Heather turns to me, adding context for my benefit. "Since Elizabeth wrote Never to Be back when she was singing as Liz Walden, she can no longer perform her most well-known song for the mortals anymore."

I nod in understanding.

"Alas, I can't risk it," Elizabeth laments.

I can't tear my gaze away as she speaks, her voice a soft melody that drums through the air. The way her fingers grip the fabric of her dress indicates some sort of frustration, but her face remains perfectly amiable.

"Even if I only claimed to cover the song, the similarities between the performances might draw too much attention, and allow the mortals to connect the dots," she adds.

Heather clasps her hands together. "I'm so glad you're finally using your real face and name, though."

"Yes, it's a relief. I'll age myself up with a glamor until I have to start over again. Plenty of the new world's most revered female singers can have a career until they're eighty, these days."

As Elizabeth delights Heather with details about her life in the new world, the strange knot at the pit of my stomach pulses and swells. The more this woman talks, the more convinced I become that I've met her before, as if she stepped out of a dream I can't quite remember.

She looks familiar because she's the most famous Fae alive, you dummy.

But the obvious explanation for the eerie sensation of déjà vu falls flat, like a more truthful, better answer is just hanging at the tip of my tongue.

"Will you sing 'Never to Be' tomorrow? I'd be eternally grateful," Heather begs.

A crimson, adorable blush taints our guest's cheeks. "I-I guess I just have to now? Right?"

"Oh thank you!" Heather jumps up and down, oblivious to the embarrassment on her idol's face. "What can we offer in return?"

Elizabeth holds the question off with both hands held in front of her as though the mere thought of getting paid for her performance sickens her. "Oh no, I wouldn't dream of asking for anything in return. It's only fitting that a bride gets what she wants at her wedding. Especially the future Summer Queen."

Heather squeals. "Oh my goodness! You're an angel, I love you!"

She wraps her arms around Elizabeth, and the new Winter Queen, Lori, whispers something that sounds an awful lot like "oh, my fucking gods," below her breath.

I know very little about her other than the fact that she's a Shadow huntress, and a perfect copy of Iris Lovatt, the Spring Queen's dead niece.

Elio's lips are twisted in a grimace, but when Elizabeth glances in my direction again, and our eyes meet for a brief second, something profound stirs within me. I can't focus on anything but her, the electric current of energy that spooked me when I entered the room is almost tangible now.

"Will you join us for the rehearsal dinner?" Heather asks quickly, like Elizabeth might *poof* into dust at any moment.

"Oh no, I wouldn't want to impose—"

"Nonsense! We can squeeze you in at Elio's table."

The singer puts on a brave smile, clearly holding something back. "Alright."

Heather hooks her elbow around Elizabeth's and leads her toward the ballroom, where tables have been set for the seven-course meal that awaits us. Elio and Lori fall into step behind them, but Hector accosts me on my way out the door, holding me back for a private word.

"Your Highness, Her Majesty the Queen says she'd rather save her energies for tomorrow. She sends her excuses," he says sternly.

"Thank you, Hector."

My lips curl down, and the strange heat in my blood vanishes. With Mother growing weaker and weaker, the wedding can't come soon enough.

Royal weddings are not much more fun than birthing ceremonies or official holidays. Uncles, aunts, cousins, and strangers all want to congratulate me, and many take the opportunity to wedge in an intrusive comment. From the insincere "A country wedding, how nice!" to the annoying "So little time between the engagement and the wedding... should we expect a wee babe soon?"

I try to remain patient, but the tense conversations between Elio and Elizabeth on the opposite side of the ballroom keep piquing my curiosity. They appear to be disagreeing about something, but with so many royal acquaintances and extended family members to satisfy, dessert has already been served by the time I manage to approach Elizabeth again.

Tons of guests asked her for an autograph, but none of them managed to hold her attention.

I slide into the empty chair next to her, the seat abandoned at the moment as Elio and his new wife take to the dance floor. "You're quite the celebrity. Everyone is dying to hear you sing," I say, unable to think of a more clever conversation opener.

She squares her shoulders and gulps down a sip of Nether cider before angling her body to me. "Everyone?"

She looks at me through her long, black lashes, daring me to include myself in that statement, and my lips quirk, a sizzling warmth nestling beneath my ribs. "Everyone."

She finally averts her gaze and motions to the tall, intricate white orchids and golden thread centerpieces. "Is this the wedding you've always dreamed of?"

"As a rule, I can't say I'm a big fan of weddings."

"Why not?"

I clear my throat awkwardly, my eyes darting to my lap. I can't tell her the whole truth, but I can find an innocuous answer. "It's all a bit too...flashy for me."

"I thought nothing was too flashy for someone as *ardent* as the Crown Prince of the Summerlands." She smiles to herself like she's privy to some dark, inside joke that I can't quite make sense of.

"I know my birthmark makes people talk, but I'm not half as garish as they say."

"Are you sure about that?" Her attention shifts to the spot where the Mark of the Gods is situated on my hip.

I swallow hard.

By the Flame. How does she know where it is? And moreover, is she flirting?

Am *I* flirting?

What the—

"Have we met?" I blurt out, flustered by the intensity of her ocean-blue gaze.

"What?" she breathes. Her creamy skin loses even more color, like the blood in her cheeks drained out entirely. "Are you serious?"

There's an unmistakable edge in her voice, and I begin to wonder if I misread our initial encounter, when I thought she found me so disappointing. Maybe she feels as oddly drawn to me as I am to her, but the thought is equally thrilling and absurd.

"I can't shake the feeling that we've met before," I say, inching forward ever so slightly.

She rubs the chill from her arms and tightens the shawl around her shoulders, her fingers gripping the fabric so firmly that her knuckles whiten. "I thought—" her mouth hangs agape for a moment before she squeezes her eyes shut. "Perhaps you've heard me sing?" She reaches for her glass of water and gulps down half of it, as if in a hurry to wash away the entire conversation.

The motion causes her delectable scent—hints of pines and abyssal violas—to fill my nose, and my mouth waters, the urge to reach out and brush her creamy skin almost impossible to quell.

"Heather listens to your songs almost every day," I admit.

"That must be it, then." She puts down her glass and returns her attention to me, her blunt, direct stare making my heart pound.

Fuck, with her looking at me like that, I can't concentrate. I'm getting married tomorrow. I can't be seen flirting with the most famous woman in Faerie, but I lean in without meaning to. "How do you know where my mark is?"

"Isn't that common knowledge?"

"No." I shake my head, and the corners of my mouth twitch. "And you've answered all my questions with questions."

"Did I?" a secret smile passes over her lips, and the teasing edge of her voice sparks a fire in my blood.

"Answer me. Please."

She opens and closes her mouth. "I'm not sure how."

A heavy silence falls between us. "Try."

"To tell you the truth, I feel like I'm about to faint." She braces her hand on my arm to steady herself, and I suck in air.

Her skin is cool, smooth, and perfect. My fire bristles at the simple touch, my magic thrashing within me, desperate to engulf her.

Elizabeth bites her bottom lip, her cheeks flushed, and her gaze drifts to my hip again, right where my birthmark lies. Her index finger moves in her lap, as though tracing invisible lines. The sight is arousing as fuck. Blood rushes to my groin as I shift awkwardly, well-aware that I'm trapped here at this table until I manage to simmer down.

I feel hot and cold, more certain than ever that something is amiss, but Elio and his wife Lori return to the table, forcing my attention away from Elizabeth.

"Aidan. Quick question. Will the King of Light be here tomorrow? I was pleasantly surprised to see he wasn't around tonight," he asks, sitting beside me.

I blink away the fog of desire. "He should attend, in theory, but ever since my father died, he hasn't set foot in Augustus."

Elio despises his father, and the feeling is mutual. The whole subject is sore between us, considering how close I was with his brother before he vanished, but some things are better left unmentioned.

In a few days, I'll be the only member of my family left standing, and the thought is sobering to say the least. Father, Willow, and now Mother...

"Do you expect any further trouble with the Tidecallers?" Elio asks grimly, aware of the queen's dreadful poisoning at the hands of the rebels.

"We've heard loud rumblings about the Lord of the Tides' incursions into the continent. According to our intel, he's particularly active at our borders with the Red Forest, the Solar Cliffs, and Wintermere, recruiting new members and gaining support among the population."

The Winter King and Queen exchange an anxious glance.

"Do you know who he is?" I say quickly.

Elio presses his lips together. "Maybe. We suspect that the man who led the attacks on the Frost Peaks is actually the Storm King's youngest son."

"Seth?" My fists curl at my side as I recall Seth Devine's rebellious antics and complete disregard for traditions. "I knew that treacherous weed had ignored my invitation for a reason."

"Not Seth," Lori explains with a wince. "Seth actually went missing trying to reason with his younger brother." I open my mouth to argue, but she adds, "Thorald Storm has a third son, one he's been keeping secret."

Lori might be a darkling, and a mortal at that, but I trust Elio, and my brows raise. "Why? What could have been so wrong about him that he was denied the opportunity to enroll in the academy?"

"He vanished before he could enroll. We're still piecing out the story, but Luther Storm was manipulated—or seduced—by Morrigan Quinn, and Seth has been looking for him for a couple of years," Elio says.

"But then, he's too young to be Lord of the Tides. Mentions of the title date back a decade at least, and this young Fae prince couldn't be older than twenty."

Lori takes a long sip of cider before she asks, "Are we sure the Lord of the Tides is not Morrigan herself?"

I deny her hypothesis with a confident shake of my head. "My sources assure me it's a man. He's often been seen around the seediest taverns and brothels, riling up the common folks."

I glance at the busy room around us, full of High Fae and royals, and congratulate myself for holding the wedding here, and not at the capital. Eterna would have been a good place to stage a coup. Augustus is safer, but considering everything that happened, I feel increasingly uneasy.

"I might be able to learn more if you allowed me access to my brother," Lori says with a stiff nod.

"Your brother is my only lead to the rebels that perpetrated the attack on the queen," I whisper. "Why shouldn't he be made to confess his sins?"

A sad smile plays at the corners of Lori's mouth. "Respectfully, Your Highness, I believe I will constrain him into talking more efficiently than you could."

"Why?"

"Do you have any siblings?"

My jaw clenches at a sudden burst of emotion, and I avert my gaze. "I did. But she died."

"Then ask yourself this: who would have been better equipped to make her crack under pressure in an interrogation? You, or a perfect stranger?"

A deep breath rushes out of my lungs. "Alright, I'll relinquish the prisoner to your care, but he must not be allowed to go free until the rebellion is extinguished. And if he's found guilty of my mother's condition, he'll be put on trial and sentenced here, in Summer."

Elio agrees to my terms with a quick incline of the head and squeezes his wife's hand. "You have my word, Aidan. I swear it."

Magic crackles through the air at his formal promise.

As I stare at their laced fingers, a twinge of jealousy cramps my gut. I relinquish my seat, squeezing the back of the chair for a moment before turning back to Elizabeth. I shouldn't have discussed matters of the realm in front of her, really, and open my mouth to ask for her discretion only to find her seat empty.

Elizabeth is gone. I search for her in the crowd, but she seems to have slipped out of the ballroom altogether.

"Aidan. Don't linger near Death, my darling, or he'll freeze the life right out of you!" Freya Heart, the Spring Queen, shouts. She approaches the table with her usual poise, her long black nails clawing at her golden fan.

Elio bares his teeth at the jab. "Freya. Never a dull moment with you."

"I wish I could say the same." The black woman's attention shifts to Lori, the Winter Queen, a perfect copy of her dead niece but for her round, human ears. "Come along, Aidan. I have a bone to pick with you."

I school my expression in one of polite interest and let the monarch usher me away.

"Your mother is not here tonight," she remarks.

"Yes. Sadly, she couldn't make it."

Freya arches her perfectly-shaped brow. "Tidecaller trouble?"

"Perhaps," I answer, keeping my tone aloof.

The Tidecallers are to blame for the queen's absence because their wicked schemes condemned her to a slow, untimely death, but I keep that part to myself.

Mother did not wish to spark up outrage across the realm by disclosing her current condition. News of her poisoning would have forced us into a quick, half-assed, retaliatory conflict. Sending out our troops blindly into the Breach would be like eating out of the palms of the rebels hands, for that's certainly what they intended to happen with their cowardly move. Hell, I'd wanted to jump onto the first available boat myself when I'd found out about the source of her sickness, but Heather had talked me off the ledge.

Still... I'll kill the ones that orchestrated the attack if it's the last thing I do.

Freya pulls me to her table full of High Fae, where I try my best to assuage their worries about the rebels and the war that's coming. There's nothing that makes a High Fae more thirsty for wine and hungry for gossip than the prospect of an armed, deadly conflict.

I get roped into endless political rambles and try to push Elizabeth from my mind.

As we're about to go to bed, Heather sinks onto the mattress beside me, one hand busy unhooking her ruby ear cuffs. "Elizabeth was a welcomed distraction from all the gruesome political talk tonight. The guests were very curious about her." She presses her lips together before adding, "And no wonder... She's the most beautiful woman alive."

"Agreed."

"Hey!"

I duck to avoid the pillow coming for my head and chuckle, "You said it first."

"It's a big weekend for us. We can't afford to...proposition our wedding singer, not when she's as gorgeous as that."

I point my index finger at her nose, no stranger to the sheepish grimace on her lips. "Oh, I can see it on your face. You've thought about it."

"Shut up!" She slaps my hand away, turning red. "I caught her stealing glances at you and remembered you're objectively attractive, for a guy, and the thought *briefly* crossed my mind. Before I dismissed it completely."

I bring a hand to my chest, falsely insulted. "Ouch!"

Heather and I are best friends, and even though we're not in love, I intend to take our new commitment seriously. I imagine we'll both have lovers at some point, but on the surface, we'll have to act like any married king and queen are expected to. And we actually like each other enough that it won't be too taxing.

"Didn't you feel like something was weighing on her, though?" I ask.

"Like what?"

"No clue. I just found her a little more...withdrawn than I would have expected."

"She probably felt out of place. You know Winter Fae are often uncomfortable in the Summerlands. She was probably just thinking back to her year at the academy—"

I prop myself up on my elbow. "Wait a minute. She attended this school?"

"Yes, for a year. I'm sure I mentioned it before. You never listen to me." She tucks a pillow between us like she always does. "Goodnight, pearl of my eyes."

"Sweet slumber, urchin of my soul."

We both snort at the familiar phrases, and I twist around to face the wall, my mind still boiling with half-formed questions. Elizabeth's haunted gaze lingers beneath my closed lids. I find myself obsessed with the notion of what might have happened tonight, if I had been in a position to ask that gorgeous darkling to dance.

I toss and turn in the king-sized bed until I can't take it anymore. This bizarre pressure between my ribs won't relent, and sweat pearls above my brows.

Unable to sleep, I sneak out of bed and head back to the bibliotheca. All the lights are closed except for a few bronze lamps lined up over the long desks. The enormous moon glares at me from the window. Craters and shadows move upon its surface, drawing shapes and patterns in a language I almost understand, a secret just out of reach, hidden in the scars of its crust.

If Elizabeth only spent one year here, it means she never graduated, so I'll have to look in the admittance records. Those are rarely used and kept on top of the built-in shelf, and I stretch to reach the right volume, one foot secured on the solid mahogany ladder. An accumulation of dust and ensuing friction slows my movements as I slide the padded cover out of the stack. I tuck the ledger open on the last step of the ladder, the tepid urgency that lured me out of my room sharpening into focus.

I drag my finger over the aged paper, across columns and rows of names written out in a neat calligraphy by the school's record clerk. My stomach flip-flops as it reaches Elizabeth's name, and I blink at the year underlined above with disbelief.

Wait.

She was here the same year I was? How is that possible? Must be a mistake.

But Hephaistos knows our temperamental record clerk and historian extraordinaire, Jillian, would not allow a blunder of this magnitude to spoil her precious archives. No, it's right here in indelible ink. Elizabeth Snow attended this school at the same time I did, and the name written two lines below hers sends acid to my throat.

Not only was Elizabeth a first-year during my time at the academy, but she knew Willow. *Blessed Flame...* Why can't I remember her at all?

CHAPTER 17
PAPER RINGS
BETH

The morning light spills through the stained glass of the bibliotheca's windows, casting fragmented colors across the floor. The sunlight seeps into me, but it does little to thaw the chill lodged deep in my chest. Despite what I promised Elio, my heart stutters on the way to the dining hall, and I slip between two bookcases instead.

I should skip brunch entirely and seek refuge deep within the stacks until the ceremony, as desperate as I am to avoid Heather's beauty, Elio's frown, and Aidan's complete lack of recollection of our past.

After our initial meeting, I toyed with the idea that he was pretending not to recognize me to protect his fiancée, but our conversation dispelled any suspicions that he was merely acting for her sake.

His memories of me are gone. *Poof.*

Just like that.

I can't fathom how. His father would have been first in line to erase me, one way or another, but I can't believe he would have enchanted his own son. We were kids, playing against the wills of kings.

I always thought, even though it hurt like hell, that Aidan had simply come to his senses. Under duress, maybe, but not without reason.

Decades went by without a word. Not one letter.

After ten years in the new world, around the time I gained enough confidence to sing and became famous, I expected him to finally visit. Finally write. Even call. Anything.

If only to get closure.

I wrote to him when his father died, but he only sent back a polite thank you for my well wishes. The impersonal, somewhat cold response wrecked me for *months*. I'd always thought it had been his way of telling me that our past was better left unmentioned. Thanatos knows I've tried to forget him, though I failed.

It always cut me to the bone that he didn't chase after me once the heat died down, but what if he just…didn't remember?

I bite my nails, desperate to soothe the anguish twisting my heart, unable to walk out of my hiding place and into the dining hall to face Aidan again.

Elio finds me a minute later, sniffing out my cowardice as if he had a special radar for Winter Fae who chicken out of following their king's orders.

"Good morning," I say, playing coy.

"Beth," he sighs. "You promised."

I hide my face in my hands. "I can't."

"We have to tell him. It's not right," he pleads again, his opinion unchanged since last night. "If his memories have been altered, he deserves to know."

"He's getting married in a few hours." I don't have it in me to rush into a difficult conversation that might ruin his current relationship. "It's too late."

What Aidan doesn't remember can't hurt him anymore. I can't let myself be tempted to put my own selfish need to make him remember above the new life he's built for himself. However awful it feels to know we might have been cheated out of a life together, his present happiness needs to be safeguarded.

"I disagree. Marriage is a forever business where we're concerned, and you can't tell *me* of all people that marrying the wrong person isn't a big deal," Elio says.

A needle of doubt stings my heart, and I turn away from him. I pick an aisle at random and peruse the books, skimming the edges with my fingers. "Fuck, Elio. How could I even begin to tell him? Why would he even believe me?"

"We'll find a way. Together."

"You stayed at the academy after I left. You ought to have noticed well before now if Aidan didn't remember me."

"Lots of stuff happened that year. Ezra left school right after you, and Aidan and I were not close. It's not impossible that a sudden memory lapse would have gone unnoticed."

A few guests stream across the room to reach the dining hall, and a confident set of footsteps approaches. I stiffen, knowing who it is before he even turns the corner, his presence filling the air with a disarming warmth.

"Good morning. Elio, can I have a moment alone with Miss Elizabeth?" Aidan asks quietly, his voice lower than usual.

"I'll leave you two to talk." Ice shines in Elio's sharp gaze, the King of Death mightily intimidating when he means to be, and the underlying message is quite clear. *You better tell him, or I will.*

Aidan flattens himself to one of the bookcases to let Elio pass, and joins me deep in the shadows of the towering furniture. "It is *Miss*, isn't it?"

The air grows sparse, but I keep my expression as neutral as possible. "Yes."

Aidan is not the only man who's asked for my hand in marriage, but he is the only one I've ever said yes to. For him to ask if I'm married feels like a knife scraping against bone.

"I have a question for you." He steps closer, his gaze searching mine. "I checked the archives last night, and I saw you attended the academy the year I was a guardian."

"That's right."

His eyes narrow slightly, as if he's trying to piece together a puzzle. "We must have met, then? Seems silly to think we didn't cross paths for an entire year. Go ahead and call me out on it if I forgot."

The smile he offers is meant to be disarming, but I glimpse at the tension beneath it. There's something in his tone, a hint of worry—or perhaps guilt.

By Thanatos...

"We did meet," I confirm, my throat tightening around the words.

He chuckles softly and runs a hand through his hair. "By the Flame, I thought I was going crazy. I bet you thought I was a pompous tool and didn't give me the time of day."

I should laugh, or smile, anything to put him at ease, but the words are stuck. How can I explain? How can I skirt around the truth when it's a blade twisting in my chest? Too heavy, too complicated, too painful.

"I can see it on your face. We did know each other. Speak your mind, please."

He's close enough now that I have to tip my chin up to look at him, and for a moment, I can almost believe he's going to lean in and kiss me, as he did so many times that year.

Where do I even begin?

You were the love of my life, and I hated you for not chasing after me.

Too abrupt.

Someone is playing with your memories.

Too cryptic.

I still love you, and even though it's selfish as hell, I need you to remember.

Too honest.

None of these options work, and before I know it, tears well up in my eyes, hot and heavy. I blink, trying to push them back, but they spill over my lids in fat, treacherous droplets that slide down my cheeks. I'm horrified by my lack of control, by how easily my composure shatters in front of him.

I move to clasp the glass ring he gave me, twisting it around my finger, wishing I had never put it on in the first place. I waited for him. That's the truth. I waited for him for *decades*, wishing and hoping, but as it turns out, the man I waited on doesn't exist anymore.

And I can't even fault him for it.

He catches my movements, and his brows pull together.

"That ring..." he grabs my hand and holds it up to the light.

"Don't," I jerk away, my voice breaking, desperate to escape before I crumble completely. "Excuse me." I try to squeeze past him, but he curls an arm around my waist.

His hold is gentle, yet firm, and so *Aidan* that my heart somersaults.

"Who gave you that ring?" he chucks out.

Fire licks the shape of his shoulders. The familiar pull of his heat mollifies my bones, our chests rising and falling harder with each breath. His amber gaze flicks to my lips, my heart racing in spite of all measures of decency.

"You did," I finally breathe.

Aidan stiffens from head to toe, frozen in place. "How can that be?" His hold on my waist slacks. "I'm about to get married." The cracks in his voice are deeper and wider than the biggest chasms up on the Frost Peaks, and I'm not sure if he's reminding himself that he's about to walk down the aisle, or apologizing for it.

"I know."

His jaw clenches, and he takes a small step back. "Why are you here, really? Why did you come?"

The unspoken accusation in his tone wrecks me.

"I-I shouldn't have. I see that now."

With the wedding being as rushed as it is, Heather is probably already pregnant. The thought strips away what's left of my composure, and I slip out of reach, barreling down the aisle toward the exit.

"Elizabeth! Wait!" Aidan calls after me, and for a moment, I'm tempted to look back, to see if there's any flicker of recognition in his eyes, any sign that his memories are not gone forever. But I can't bear the emptiness I know I'll find.

Tears blur my vision as I flee the bibliotheca. The door closes behind me with a soft thud, but the echo of his voice, the way he shouted my name, plagues my mind.

I can't believe it's almost time to change, so I can watch him get married to another woman.

CHAPTER 18
DEATH BED
AIDAN

Potent waves roll over the sandy shore of the Saffron Cove in a rhythm that mirrors the chaos in my mind. A powerful salty breeze washes over me as I step onto the beach, and I inhale deeply. Despite the storm clouds gathering over the horizon, each gulp of ocean air calms my nerves.

I've tried to work out my emotions in the forge, beating a fresh sword to submission, to no use. Sweat sticks to my forehead, the anguish I saw on Elizabeth's face burned into my memory.

I should be wary of a gorgeous, inexplicably familiar darkling crashing my wedding, but I need answers. And there's one other name on the list I found last night that could give them.

Elio is standing a few paces away, looking out at the horizon. He's lost in thought, contemplating something deeper than the crashing waves.

"Elio," I shout over the wind, trying to gauge his mood. The King of Death controls one of the most powerful and volatile wells of magic in existence, and I'd rather not taunt his dark side. "Can we talk?"

"I guess we have to," he replies, his voice steady but guarded.

The serious bend of his brows and the tick of his jaw serve as a warning that what he has to say will not be easy to hear. He hesitates, glancing over at the shoreline where Lori collects seashells along the water's edge.

"I need to know about Elizabeth."

"You never used to call her that," Elio finally says, the stretch of his tired voice giving the impression that our conversation would be better suited for a different moment—perhaps a different life.

"You were in her class at the academy, right? Did I— Did we ever —" I scratch the back of my skull, searching for the right way to phrase it, but each half-formed sentence drains my mind further and further down the rabbit hole. Finding no way to explain this tornado swirling inside me, I settle for a dry chuckle. "Blessed Flame, I'm losing my mind."

Elio runs a hand through his platinum-blonde hair. "You truly don't remember her at all?"

My eyes snap up to meet his, and the mirroring doubts and confusion I read on his features lift a weight off my shoulders. Elizabeth was not lying, earlier, and I'm not going crazy.

Elio's gaze finds Lori, who is now examining a shell, her delicate fingers tracing its contours. "I want the best for you both, but you should really talk to Beth."

"I tried. She had this ring, and I just knew I'd seen it before, and then she said I gave it to her—"

"It's true."

I shake my head from side to side. "No. You must be confusing me with Ezra. There's no way I forgot a woman I had sex with. And definitely not someone who went on to become even more famous than me."

"Aidan... It was much more than that. You and Beth were in love."

He thinks he's speaking the truth, but I know this to be untrue because I have never been in love. I've always been fascinated by the idea, but alas...

I love my mother.

I loved my sister.

I love Heather.

But I've never been *in love*, and not for a lack of trying. It's just a fact of life.

"Someone has altered your memories," he says with a deep frown. "If I were you, I'd start asking questions."

A heavy silence falls between us.

"But why?" I ask quietly. "Why would anyone want to erase that?"

"Love can be dangerous. Your connection with Beth was powerful, and your parents didn't want that bond to be a threat to their own plans. It might have been easier for them to erase your memories than to face the chaos that love can bring." The King of Death sounds more alive than he has in decades. "I've tried and failed to live a life of duty. I don't know what your relationship with Heather is like, and I was happy for you when I thought you'd moved on, but this isn't right. You deserve to know the truth."

His words hit me like a sharp wind, cutting through the fog in my mind. A sense of urgency rises in my blood, all the implications of his revelation hitting me all at once. "I'm getting married in an hour." The words are angry, even though it's not his fault. "There's no time—"

I'd finally found peace about my decision, and now this...

"Ignoring your past won't make it disappear. It will only fester. Trust me, I've learned that lesson the hard way."

The endless expanse of the sea swells in the distance. I can't shake the feeling that something deep within me is yearning to resurface.

I take my leave of the Winter King and his queen and head for my mother's apartments at the top of the academy's main building.

A mix of herbs and decay embalm the air of her bedroom, and the grayish tint of her skin contrasts with the vibrant earthly patterns of the wallpaper. Healers in burgundy robes are gathered around her, murmuring in low tones. My heart sinks.

"Mother..." I tiptoe over to her bedside, trying to keep my voice steady.

"Oh, my precious phoenix." Her eyes, though clouded with illness, light up when they find me. "Is everything ready?"

I swallow hard, forcing a smile as I reach for her hand, gently squeezing it. "Yes."

"I'm so glad I'll get to see you wed before the end. Heather is a strong, clever woman. She will make a fantastic queen." Her lips curl into a fragile smile, but it falters as she glances at the healers. "I wish I could have joined you last night. But I made them promise to let me out of here for the ceremony, at least." She grazes my cheek. "I can't believe I have to leave you, especially now with those rebels banging at our doors... I'm so sorry I can't help you deal with your new responsibilities."

"I'll protect our kingdom and its people," I say, my voice cracking at the end. "I'll make you proud."

"You already have, my phoenix."

Marrying Heather before Mother dies will secure my reign and discourage the political unrest running rampant across the realms. As King and Queen of Summer, we'll lead Faerie to war against the Tidecallers, with the combined strength of the Summerlands and Secret Springs armies. I'm looking forward to hunting those who mean to destroy thousands and thousands of lives only to assuage their own thirst for power. That should remain my priority, whatever comes, but now that I suspect parts of my life have been erased, I can't help but wonder.

Could my mother have manipulated my memories to secure my crown? The dark thought swirls in my mind.

"Mother, do you—" I begin, but the words die in my throat.

How can I confront her about the possibility that she's enchanted me? I can't bring myself to voice the accusation. She's dying. I can't risk our last few days together being clouded by anger and betrayal, but the answers I crave might die with her.

"Is everything all right, dear?" she asks, her brows furrowing.

I force a smile. "Wedding jitters, I suppose."

After all the grief I've endured and the one still to come, I wonder what it would feel like to marry for love instead of duty—to look forward to the ceremony as a way to celebrate my union with someone I'm crazy about, rather than merely tying up bows for the sake of the realm.

The possibility is both exhilarating and foreign. I've thought long and hard about this wedding, convinced it was the right choice.

"Mother," I say softly, searching for a way to get the answers I need without breaking her spirit. "Do you find it strange that I never thought of marrying for love?"

She studies me for a moment, a glimmer of worry passing through her gaze. "Love and duty don't often walk hand in hand. It's essential to find a balance. I think it's wonderful that you're willing to marry Heather for the good of the realm and put others before yourself. For that, I admire you."

"But I've never really known true love," I press on, watching her reaction.

If she enchanted me, I should glimpse at the stubborn, opinionated woman that raised me and see traces of guilt, fear, or at the very least understanding.

"Oh, my boy." She pats my hand with a patient smile. "You've had your share of love affairs."

"Meaningless infatuations. Crushes that flickered out faster than a candle flame. Never love."

"I just want you to be happy," she whispers, her voice frail. "That's all I've ever wanted for you." Her love shines bright, unwavering even in her last days, but she doesn't seem fazed at all by my questions. "I had something special made as a wedding present that will help you and Heather in these first few years of marriage."

"What gift?"

"It's a surprise. I'll show you after the wedding."

"Alright," I say, the weight of her expectations resting heavy on my shoulders.

"I'm leaving the kingdom in good hands. Just remember, ruling is about more than power or politics. Never turn your back on difficult choices, and you'll make a magnificent king, my phoenix. I'm just sorry I won't be around to see it." She kisses my knuckles the way she did when I was little. "Now, leave, so your old, dying mother can get ready for the ceremony."

Her flame is almost extinguished, really. A few days at most before Elio pays her one final visit.

I take a deep breath, trying to steady my racing heart.

It's too late.

My father was definitely the driving force behind any sort of magic-induced manipulation, and he's dead now. Soon, she will be too.

If I'm under some kind of spell, it doesn't negate my duties, and to postpone the wedding in search of lost, forgotten memories would only put everyone's safety in jeopardy. An enchantment as strong as that could not be unraveled before I have to stand at the altar in an hour. I owe it to Heather, to our families, and to the kingdom to move forward, to let go of the past, even if it means living with this... black hole.

For now, at least, that will have to be enough.

CHAPTER 19
NIGHT ON BALD MOUNTAIN
SONGBIRD

Summerlands, Faerie, 100 years ago

Our small classroom on the fourth floor of the academy's main building has six desks and chairs, one for each of the initiates. All lectures are held here, while the more practical lessons take us all over the academy and sometimes even into the new world. Since we often have to work in pairs and are encouraged to branch out and not always pick the same partner, we've become a tightly knit group in spite of all the...difficulties.

Too bad my fiancé still sets my teeth on edge.

Sean is the last to arrive to class on the final day before the first semester's exams. The tall, brown-haired boy takes his seat up front and braces an arm to glance at Willow, sitting behind him. "Hey, Will! I saw Aidan in the dining hall this morning."

My ears perk up, blood flushing my cheeks at the mere mention of his name. Despite his prolonged absence, he's been on my mind non-stop. During my visit to the new world, my sleep was filled with dreams for the first time in my life. And Aidan had been a prominent fixture in those dreams.

"Yes, he just got back," Willow replies without looking up from her book.

"Is it true that he and Devi got engaged in the new world?"

She scoffs. "Never. Who told you such a ridiculous tale?"

Sean grins from ear to ear but doesn't answer, and I twitch in my seat, my mouth going dry. The academy's rumor mill is always spinning, mixing as many truths with wild stories, but in this instance, I hope Sean is mistaken. It's bad enough my head is filled with thoughts of Aidan. With exams looming, I'd rather not face news of his engagement.

Thankfully, the long break between the two semesters is coming soon, right after exams and the summer solstice celebration. My heart has been longing for a taste of home and a reprieve from all the grueling study sessions needed to get me up to speed.

The fear of being exposed for what I did—of dragging down my family's name in disgrace—died down after a few weeks. The unease that had spiced up my blood during that first month has dulled into a lingering pang of imposter syndrome, but I no longer look over my shoulder everywhere I go, expecting a faculty member to kick me to the curb.

In all appearances, Aidan and I got away with cheating on the trials, but I won't let my guard down. I can't.

"Is your father coming or not?" Zeke asks with a huff from his usual seat next to Sean.

Willow waves dismissively at the Shadow Prince. "Don't fret. My father is always late."

Though it's not her father who walks through the door, but Aidan.

The bane of my existence steps into the classroom with the same confidence I remember, his appearance fresh out of the new world. His gray trousers are cut sharp, high on his waist, held up by dark suspenders that somehow make him look effortlessly put together. A checked waistcoat peeks beneath his slightly unbuttoned jacket, and the collar of his shirt stands crisp and clean.

Though he's been plaguing my mind with his haunting voice and his godly looks, I'd forgotten how enticing his bite of power felt. The tension in the room cranks up by a mile, and Zeke's spine straightens. The two brawlers haven't seen each other since the incident on the beach, everyone convinced Aidan had been forced to accept an off-world assignment to atone for his fiery assault. According to Willow, the Crown Prince had never been away from the Summerlands for so long.

It's been months since I discouraged his advances, but if I'm honest, a part of me still mourns what could have been. He respected his promise to leave me alone, but his hurried departure robbed me of the chance to apologize for the harsh words I'd spoken on that horrible night. I wish I'd shut him down more gently, but I'd been too angry and scared to nuance my emotions.

When he speaks, his voice raises every hair on the back of my neck, and my heart throbs as if awakened from a long slumber. "I know you were all looking forward to my dad's take on the Summerlands traditions," Aidan says, barely veiling his snark. "Alas, our King had to step out this afternoon. He asked me to go over the basics of the summer solstice with you."

He inspects the ebony chalkboard for a moment before turning away from it and hopping right up on the desk, his legs dangling casually from the ledge. "Alright. Who here knows the true meaning of St. John's Eve?"

Zeke curls his fists, Sean and Iris drinking in his reaction as if they're hoping for round two.

"No one? Really?" Aidan cracks. "I find that impossible to believe." His astute gaze darts to his sister, and he motions for her to stand up. "Willow. Please enlighten them."

The legs of Willow's chair creak along the hardwood as she stands up and clears her throat. "Way back when, the Summer King fell in love with a mortal, but she was already married. Adultery was seen as this terrible, unforgivable sin, so his beloved would not bend, afraid of being caught. But he burned for her so much that he cast a spell over her entire village and released all the evil spirits on St. John's Eve to create a diversion so they could sneak out and spend one night together without consequences." She quiets down, her voice tinged with sadness. "This sparked a tradition among Summer Fae. The night of the solstice—the shortest night of the year—you can be with whoever you want, no matter the circumstances."

I don't know why exactly, but the way she breathes the words quickens my heartbeat, and I steal a glance at Aidan.

Whoever you want.

"The spirits ended up killing hundreds of villagers. They were selfish and dumb," Elio chimes in.

Iris nods in agreement. "Elio is right. As if anyone needs an excuse for infidelity. What a bore. It's an ancient way of going about relationships."

Elio blushes deep red at that, still grappling with his unrequited crush.

"Everyone cheats. We should just embrace it and stop being so judgemental about it," Iris adds.

"But that's the point of St. John's Eve. Better to have one night set aside for everyone to give in to their hearts' desires than actually betray their vows," Willow grumbles unhappily at her roommate. "It relieves the pressure of our *centuries*-long commitments by allowing for one night of freedom each year. The trade-off is worth it."

The unease at the pit of my stomach grows as I stare out at the bright sky. I shake my head and bite my tongue. Moths take marriage and commitment more seriously than dandelion fluffs and fireflies, clearly. I can't believe we're the ones that get a bad rep, when the Summerlands official holiday is actually a shag-whoever-you-want night. I knew this already, of course, but I'd never confronted the emotions that rise in me at the thought of being allowed, even encouraged, to step outside of a *marriage*. The winter solstice actually does something incredibly beautiful and needed, and it makes me feel even more homesick.

Aidan raps his fingers on the desk. "What about you, Miss Elizabeth? Do you have something to share with the class?"

The overly formal way he addresses me feels like a slap in the face. *Miss Elizabeth.* Like I'm some young schoolgirl he's never met.

My eyes narrow. "Marriage should be built on more than just efforts to hang onto meaningless crowns. If people married for love, then St. John's Eve wouldn't be needed at all," I ground out.

"Hear, hear," Elio cheers behind me.

A red, incandescent blush sears my cheeks. *By the spindle...* where did that come from?

Zeke narrows his eyes, and I don't dare to sneak a glance at Aidan, pretty sure that I'll spontaneously combust if our gazes meet.

"Do as I say and not as I do, right, Beth?" Iris quips.

I hide my face in my palms at her jab. She's right, and my own hypocrisy threatens to choke me.

"I thought you were a fan of the ballad of St. John Eve. You sang it during your admission trials," Aidan says like he's discussing something as trivial as what he plans to eat for dinner.

"Wait. Beth sang in the labyrinth?" Willow gasps.

"A little," I admit.

Elio's voice booms behind me. "Beth is just being humble. She's a fantastic singer."

Aidan's brows furrow, his jaw clenching at the praise, his gaze searching mine for the first time since he entered the room. His amber depths ask too many questions for me to keep track of, and my heart pounds at my temples.

"Oh, Beth. You have to sing for the solstice gala. Elio can accompany you on the piano," Willow squeals.

The gala is apparently a very important tradition for the Augustus villagers, and she leads the planning committee. I'd managed to steer clear of participating until now, but I can't focus on anything but Aidan's inquisitive stare as I answer, "Err— Alright."

Shadows drape over his face, and he breaks eye contact, moving ahead with the rest of the lesson. I wonder if I've imagined the embers of jealousy I saw flicker in his irises when Elio spoke, and if it means that, against all odds, he thought of me while he was gone.

The scorching humidity I have yet to get accustomed to assaults me as soon as Willow and I step out of the main building. The horizon is quickly fading from pink to midnight-blue, the sun's departure making the stuffy air a little more bearable. Since so many of the fourth-years and graduate students have spent the last few weeks off-world, their return commands a party.

Willow guides me down the stony path that leads to Saffron Cove, her elbow hooked around my arm. "You've studied every waking hour of every day. You deserve one last night of fun before you entomb yourself in your room for the next three days."

"I agreed to come, didn't I?" I say with a smile.

An adorable pout twists her features. "I can't believe the exams are coming so quickly."

"Cheer up, Will. You're the best student in the class."

"Only because of you. You keep me honest. Sixty percent of the first-year students fail at least one exam. That means extra work next semester, and we're already crumbling under pressure…"

Despite her birthright to attend the academy, Willow isn't neglecting her school work, and I love her all the more for it.

"Is everything alright?" I ask. "You sounded emotional when you spoke of St. John's Eve."

"It's sad that Fae royals are only allowed to follow their hearts for one night per year," she sighs. "I wish someone was brave enough to enact true change, but once a Fae gets a crown, they become too scared of losing it to change the way things are done."

"Why change a ladder when you've already reached the top?" I muse.

She drags her feet along the stone steps leading down to the beach. "It's weird, you know. All my life, I've been told Aidan will be the next Summer King. My father never even took me seriously because of Aidan's mark. I wonder sometimes if it's a blessing or a curse for everyone to know, beyond the shadow of a doubt, that I won't inherit my family's throne. They all expect me to become a queen through marriage, but that means I won't get to be happy."

"Don't say that. You might fall for your betrothed."

She raises a brow. "The way you fell for Zeke?"

My gaze darts down to the red-orange sand. "Iris was right. I'm a hypocrite."

"No, it's not your fault. You're stuck because of stupid rules made up by stupid people. We're both doomed to be unhappy because of what old, crumbling kings decided was right. I swear, if I ever get to be queen..."

Her certainty that she's bound to live a life of duty prompts me to tell her the truth about my intentions with Zeke and admit I plan to get out of marrying him altogether, but the bonfire appears in the distance. It's not safe to discuss this here.

"Blessed Flame. Let's have fun tonight, and forget about real life," she tugs on my arm, hurrying me along.

She's bee-lining for the spot where Aidan and his friends are playing cards, and I stagger in the sand.

"Aidan! Come here for a second. I have something for you." She sets her over-the-shoulder bag on a tall nearby rock and rummages through it.

Aidan folds his cards on the makeshift table before heading toward us.

"Hi," I greet him, a nervous hiccup threatening to pop out of my throat.

"Hey," he answers casually, taking a sip of his cider and quickly looking away.

"Welcome back."

"How are you?" he asks.

"Good."

"Good."

We both nod. It's not only awkward, but downright painful to endure such a stilted, dishonest conversation with the man that has been plaguing my thoughts and dreams.

His fire warms the air between us, enticing and yet forbidden, the bite of his magic beckoning me closer.

I open my mouth to say something, anything, to encompass how his return makes me feel, but Willow wrenches a sealed letter out of her bag. "Here."

"What's that? Fan mail?" I joke.

"A love letter, actually." Willow chimes, and my stomach plummets until she grins mischievously and adds, "From our grandmother. After all these years, she still doesn't trust the sprites with her mail." Willow throws a knowing wink to her big brother, but the prince remains stoic, and she eyes him up and down. "What happened to you? You look...different. Quiet."

"The new world is changing, but their social rules are still pretty strict. I had to tame my impulses quite a bit to fit in." His eyes flick to me as he says the last part, and I shiver all over.

Willow pats his arm in a soothing manner. "Well, you're back in Faerie, now. Stop frowning, or I'll start to think something's wrong with you."

"Should I deal you in, then?" he asks.

"You bet."

They walk arm in arm to join the others, but I remain rooted in place. Sitting around the fire, Zeke is fooling around with Diana of all people. He's grown complacent of our non-relationship, and I draw in a deep breath, heading off toward the ocean.

The sea breeze soothes my nerves. The waves lap gently at my ankles, washing away my worries as I wade forward until they reach my knees.

Ezra's head pops out of the water up ahead, the blonde Prince of

Light wiping his wet hair from his face while the rest of his body remains submerged.

"Looking gorgeous as always, Lady Snow," he greets me. "Still betrothed, I hear?"

He swims closer and stands, water streaming down his bare chest as he leans in to peck my cheeks. Droplets spray my shoulders at his closeness.

"Ugh," I grunt. "How was your trip to the new world?"

"Enlightening, I'd say. No matter how much we read about mortals and their customs, living among them is an entirely different affair. Was it very boring without me here?"

"Oh yes, quite."

The corners of his mouth quirk. "The mortal world is changing so fast. If they keep it up, they'll shoot right past us, and we'll be the ones living in the dark ages."

From what I've glimpsed of the new world, he might be right. "I thought Winter Fae were anchored in traditions because of our close connection to death, but I've realized here that all Fae are adverse to change."

"Irrevocably so." His irises reflect the silvery orb of the moon over the sea. It feels like his soul is shining through, quietly surfacing. "Do you ever wish you could...disappear? Start over somewhere new, where no one knows who you are?"

"That's sort-of what I did when I came here."

A soft chuckle quakes his body. "Yeah. Good for you, Lady Snow." With a sad smile, Ezra glances over my shoulder before a heavy sigh heaves his lungs. "Here he comes. I'll leave you two to talk."

I open my mouth to ask him to stay, to mitigate the impression that Aidan and I want privacy, but the words get caught in my throat. Ezra spins around and sinks back into the gentle waves, floating on his back with his arms extended like he's some religious martyr.

Aidan's fiery bite of power contrasts with the coastal wind, and goosebumps tighten my skin. I rub the chill off my arms, the current suddenly tugging at my knees as if swallowed by his gravity.

He keeps himself at a safe, almost awkward distance. "I want to apologize. For how I acted that night. I'm sorry that I pushed you and made things more difficult," he whispers, his soft words almost lost to the salty breeze.

"Nothing came of it, really. After you left, everyone sort of latched on to the newest scandal." I draw absent-minded patterns on the seafloor with my big toe. "I was glad to see you, earlier."

He draws closer. "Yeah?"

"Yes," I tuck my hair behind my ears. "I'm sorry, too. For being so hard on you. Willow's become my lifeline here, and I'd love it if you and I could be friends going forward."

I meant it as an olive branch, but Aidan grimaces, suddenly widening the gap between us by several inches. "Because of Willow?"

I offer him a nod, then immediately get the impression it wasn't the answer he wanted. He combs a hand through his shorter hair, a sad smile curling his lips. "You were right before. I don't think I'd be a very good friend to you."

An ache stings deep at the pit of my belly, my tongue parched. "Right. Of course."

I move to leave, but he stops my escape, his hand hot on my shoulder. My lips part in a gasp at the smoldering heat crackling at the surface of my bare skin, and my gaze falls to his long fingers, wondering how such a small touch could feel so intense.

Aidan tucks both hands at his back, biting his bottom lip. "Don't misunderstand me, Songbird. I wish I could be your friend, but my heart went wild the second I saw you... I can't help it."

"Were the new world women not to your liking?" I ask, thinking about the rumors I've heard. Aidan is a legend around here, and it's hard to separate fact from fiction.

"To be clear, and only because you asked, I haven't so much as looked at another woman since we've met. I want *you*, Songbird." He reaches for my shoulder again, his hand sliding down my arm and leaving a trail of fire in its wake.

For a moment, I can't see anything beyond the hope in his amber gaze, the magnetic pull of his magic, or the shape of his full, tense lips. The sea itself rises up at the chemistry between us, propelling me forward, and a splash of water wets my skirt.

When Aidan looks at me like that, I want to offer myself up as a sacrifice and head straight into his flames, consequences be damned. Peel the fabric off his sculpted shoulders and kiss every inch of his skin. Burn at the stake of his pyre for the ever-growing, dangerous pull he has on me, despite all my bravado. Because when he's close, the thought of marrying, loving, or even touching any other man is heresy. Everything else feels *less real* than him.

And it scares me to my core. "I-I can't." Without looking back, I skip out of reach and jog up the beach to the stone path heading back to the Abbey, never looking back.

I can't, but I'm dying to.

Aidan and I could never be together, not in any official capacity, but I would love to know what it feels like to give into the fantasy. To indulge in the maddeningly detailed scenarios that have plagued my dreams, and lose myself to the flames. I'd be free to *burn*, even if it charred my heart forever. But a fire as bright as Aidan would certainly leave its trace. Zeke would be bound to find out. If I broke it off with him first, Willow would promise to lend me money, but she's not of age, and I'm sure her father would find a way to prevent her from doing it. Even Elio couldn't help me without his father's approval, and from what I understand, Ethan Lightbringer is pretty tight with Aidan's father.

Nothing has changed. Giving in to my attraction to Aidan will jeopardize my future, but now that the initial fear has dwindled, now that I can't dismiss his attention for something that'll blow over in a few days, I'm reeling.

It's getting harder and harder to say no.

CHAPTER 20
DAME SNOW
SONGBIRD

I tickle the piano keys as I wait for Elio to meet me for our rehearsal session, the absent-minded notes echoing across the white wood panels of the music room. Glossy hardwood floors and a myriad of leather cases and music stands furnish the room, but it's empty at this hour. Elio's been teaching me a few easy tunes, but while I have a keen ear for music, my hands are apparently made of five thumbs.

The huge mirror next to the door ripples, and my spine stiffens as two silhouettes stalk out of the sceaware.

"Hey Beth. Sorry I'm late. I lost track of time," Elio apologizes. He blinks his eyes open, the chill of the sceaware frosted over his cheeks.

He's barely a minute late, but that's Elio, and I arch a brow at his masked companion.

Damian and I have never spoken, the Crow too busy glaring at me when we crossed paths for me to work up the courage to introduce myself.

"Hi. I'm Beth."

Damian's onyx and broken glass mask enhances his stern, dark looks, and goosebumps riddle my arms as he cocks his head to the side. "I know who you are."

Elio rummages through the music sheets lying on a nearby table. "Thank you, Damian."

"I'll see you next week." The Shadow Lord spins on his heel and vanishes through the mirror without another word.

I arch a brow at my friend. "Elio Lightbringer. What in the seven hells were you doing with *him*?"

If the last few months have taught me anything, it's that Damian isn't exactly popular with the Light Fae crowd—and the mistrust goes both ways.

Elio chuckles. "Damian's not so bad. He offered to tutor me."

"But you're a Light Fae from the Sun Court. What could he possibly teach you?"

Elio scratches the back of his neck. "Light and shadows aren't so different, really. I've been... exploring my options."

My breath hitches. "You have dual magic?"

Dual wielders are proficient in more than one school of magic, but it's rare for a Fae to wield both light and dark magic.

"Shh. You don't have to shout." He slides onto the bench beside me, leaning closer as he spreads his music sheets across the rack. "I've actually been practicing with ice. And since there's no graduate student from Wintermere, Damian is taking me to the new world a few times a week to help me practice. I'm still struggling to summon it out of thin air—it's a hard feat here in the Summerlands."

The revelation that Elio's been keeping his ice magic from me—a magic we share—both thrills and annoys me. I nudge him with my elbow. "Being a dual wielder is not something to be ashamed of. You should be proud—"

He cuts me off with a quick, almost fearful shake of his head. "My father would go spare. You have to keep it secret." His lips press into a thin line before he adds, "Promise you won't tell Ezra. He'd swear to keep it quiet, but it'd still bubble up at the worst possible moment."

"I promise." I tickle the ivories again, aware that Elio's just let me in on a momentous secret. He's talented, but his Light magic doesn't hold a candle to Ezra's. "I know what the rumors say about the Winter King being near death, but Thanatos doesn't care about pedigree, and he's never picked a Light Fae. Never."

Elio disperses my suspicions with a defeated sigh. "Oh, I wouldn't dream of becoming king. Unlike most of the students here, I'm not after a crown. I just want an escape. I know it's unorthodox, but if I joined the reaper army, I think the life would suit me."

"You mean to become a reaper? Isn't that… drastic? There's no going back from that." I rise to my feet and draw in a few deep, diaphragmatic breaths, sustaining the exhalations to warm up my voice.

"Drastic sounds heavenly, believe me. If I ever leave the Sun Court, there can be no half-measures." His tone softens, and his expression twists into that familiar grimace—the one that reminds me his father most likely argues with his fists.

I hum, unwilling to push him further, and we move on with our rehearsal. Willow is adamant that we should close the gala tomorrow.

Near the end of our session, Ezra sneaks into the music room just as I finish the last verse, and my cheeks turn red. His ice-blue eyes dance under the soft light of the chandeliers while he makes his way over, hands tucked inside his pockets.

Elio slams the piano cover shut with a loud *thud*, the melody cutting off abruptly. "What do you want?"

"I was actually looking for Lady Snow." Ezra slinks closer, an elusive smile playing at the corners of his lips. "Your voice could topple empires, milady."

Elio crams his music sheets together. "See you tomorrow, Beth. Goodnight."

Elio leaves with his jaw tight and his eyes narrowed, and I throw his brother a tired look. "What did you do?"

"Who said I did something?" Ezra muses.

"Hrmph."

He leans on the piano lid with his chin propped in his hand. "They're tallying up the points of the initiation challenge for the results to be presented tomorrow. I heard that you're dead last."

I slap my thighs and climb to my feet. "I don't care."

Not in the mood for one of his enigmatic, dubious pieces of advice, I head to the bibliotheca, but Ezra falls into step with me.

"You know the loser has to suffer the whims of the fourth-years for the rest of the year, right?" he says.

"Yes, but it was rigged from the start." I wave dismissively. "My very first challenge was impossible, so I made my peace with it."

"What did Diana give you?"

"She wanted me to find out Aidan's full initials."

Ezra stops walking. "An almost impossible task, indeed. Aidan himself wouldn't share his full initials, but his handsome best friend who's got a crush on you... that's another story."

I turn around, the prince looking perfectly evil in the dimly lit corridor. "You're Aidan's best friend?" I say in jest.

Ezra gives me a genuine laugh, something rare and elusive as we enter the bibliotheca through the back door, the tall mahogany stacks towering above our heads.

Even though I've got my hands full with my fiancé and an Aidan-shaped hole in my heart, it's hard not to feel anything at all when a man like Ezra lets you glimpse at the real person hiding behind his thick Fae prince veneer.

"Now, why do you snicker and snort when your real laugh is so much better?" I ask.

His gaze darts to the ceiling as he slides past me along the narrow path between the stacks and spins around, walking backwards. "Keep stroking my ego like that, and I might give you what you want."

I pry the book I started earlier off the shelf. "Be nicer to Elio, and I might just start thinking of you as a friend."

"Haven't you heard? I don't have any female friends. I have groupies. And lovers. And lover-groupies."

I reach out to pinch his arm, but he slips out of reach, laughing.

"Do you have any brothers or sisters?"

I shake my head.

Ezra sinks to the ground, his back propped against the heavy books near the floor. "Then you don't know what it's like. I love Elio to death, but he and I have to quarrel. It's how it's always been."

He looks so defeated and remorseful that I slide down next to him, pressing my butt down to prevent my tartan skirt from riding up. "How do you know Aidan's initials?"

The wicked glint in his eyes flickers to life once more. "I caught a glimpse of them while I was skulking around our dorm, back when he didn't know I could become invisible."

I barely hold in a gasp. "You can become invisible?"

"Elio and I have trained ourselves to disappear with a glow as feeble as a candle flame. It's a life skill we developed pretty early. Evelyn said she's never seen such a flawless iteration of that power. I'm not supposed to use it inside the academy walls unless I have her permission."

"Flawless, eh?" I arch a teasing, skeptic brow. "Can you do it now?"

The man flat-out vanishes into thin air, and a hiccup quakes my throat. "By the spindle!" A mix of awe, jealousy, and unease mingle in my blood as my shaky hand inches closer to the space he just occupied. My hand reaches a solid form and slowly wraps over the soft fabric of Ezra's white button-down shirt and over the shape of his shoulder.

"Show off!" I grin.

"Imagine what secrets I could find out. Much more important than Aidan's full initials..." his breath stirs the sensitive hairs behind my neck.

I reach for him only to find empty air, then shift to my knees. A soft nudge on my back spooks me, and I let out a nervous, throaty laugh. "Alright, I'm thoroughly impressed. And jealous. You can stop now."

I paw at the space around me, searching for him and trying to sense his bite of power, but it's no use. "Can you make someone else invisible?"

"No, just me."

The warm light filtering through the stacks turns to shadows for a second, Iris's small frame suddenly obscuring the path. "What are you doing?" she asks as she takes in the sight of me propped on my knees.

"Don't tell her I'm here," Ezra breathes against my ear.

"Nothing."

Iris narrows her eyes. "Have you seen Ezra? Elio told me he was with you."

"I have not *seen* Ezra, no. Not for a little while," I answer, immediately biting down on my bottom lip not to smile.

Ezra's full-bellied laugh vibrates along my back, and I lose all semblance of composure, burying my face in my hands to muffle the ensuing giggles.

Iris inspects her nails, her mouth twisted in a pout. "You're so weird, moth."

"Err—thank you."

She rolls her eyes as she leaves.

"She thinks I should be nicer to her because we're about to be betrothed," Ezra whispers.

My brows raise. "Are you?"

"Um," he takes a pause. "Maybe."

"Is that why Elio—" I stop, now captive in the invisible prince's embrace, the weight of his arm settling in my lap. I stiffen, and not so much because he's encroaching on my personal space, but for what he might imply if I let him. "Ezra."

"Settle down. I'm comfy."

"Ezra..."

He hides his face in the crook of my neck. "I know, I know. Pure as snow until marriage. Betrothed to your dull Shadow Prince and playing with the fires of Summer." His warmth leaves me as he blinks into view and shuffles to his knees. "You know what? I can solve this. I will knight you as my friend, Lady Snow. Get on one knee." He rises to his feet and summons a long, light sword to his side.

I arch a brow but shift to one knee in front of him, playing along, the glow of the weapon giving a hilarious, over-the-top religious vibe to the scene.

"I, Ezra Lightbringer, officially name you my knight friend."

"Shouldn't I be dubbed a dame, though?" I whisper quickly.

"Be quiet. I'm bestowing a huge honor upon you." He lays his sword upon my right shoulder, then my left, with a mischievous glint in his eyes. "As I was saying. I, Ezra Lightbringer, name you, Lady Snow, as my one and only knight friend." A wolfish smile blooms on his lips. "And as your platonic prince, I will hug you whenever I please."

"And I will strive to be worthy of your benevolence, my prince," I say using my best fake, ceremonious voice.

Ezra holds out a hand to help me up. "Alright, *friend*. I have a question, and I need you to honor our new friendship by not making a fuss about it. Are you into my boy Aidan at all?" He tilts his head forward with a blunt, intimate look.

I grimace, and a quiet, "Yeah," escapes me.

"The poor guy has been tearing his hair out for months now, balling unfinished letters and tossing them into the trash. He seemed to think you didn't want him to write, so if you like him, why do you keep shutting him down? Is it only because of the engagement, or is there something else?"

I avert my gaze. "It's complicated."

"Isn't it always?" he sighs, nodding as if he's making up his mind about something. "Very well. I will tell you Aidan's precious initials, but you have to promise in return to make his life hell about it."

My brows furrow at his peculiar turn of phrase. "I swear it."

He licks his lips in a machiavellian manner. "It's A. S. S."

My jaw drops. "Are you telling me Aidan's initials are actually *ass*?"

He nods emphatically. "I bet his mother—on account of his big head of course—had a hard delivery and was feeling snarky when she named him."

I lean into him, and we laugh together until tears stream from our eyes. Whatever sexual tension or unspoken attraction had existed between us dissolves, his allure fading. For the first time, I see his offer of friendship as genuine.

"Are you performing tomorrow?" I ask.

"In a way. I have to be up before dawn for the royal hunt, and Ethan, my father, expects me to bring my A-game. But I'll be back in time to hear you sing," he adds with a wink.

Willow was right about him. Deep down, Ezra is a big softie. Still, a part of me can't help but wonder about the implications of his power, the endless possibilities it presents. If only I could become invisible, too, I might finally live the life I want—free from the fear of being spied on and thrown out of school.

Free to love without fear of losing everything.

CHAPTER 21
HEY, JEALOUSY
WONDER BOY

Devi's lips part in surprise, the two of us trailing at the rear of the hunting party. The deer we've been tracking for hours steps into the clearing ahead, my heart pounding in my temples. Drawn by its appetite for the white windflowers, it grazes closer and closer to my hiding spot.

The royal hunt isn't about feeding ourselves or protecting our lands from monsters. It's a display of power. Golden-horned deer are sacred, their incredible healing capabilities making them nearly impossible to kill. We hunt only one during the solstice each year. Mounting a set of golden antlers on your wall is a symbol of triumph over your peers—a tradition in which one of the reigning monarchs almost always prevails.

The others have already crossed the river. This is our chance. The Spring Fae lowers her bow with a sad smile, a thick bush of rustberries blocking her line of sight. She tosses me a glance, equal parts eye-roll and encouragement, and motions for me to take my best shot.

My fire arrow is poised to fly true, the creak of the bowstring soft enough not to alert my prey. The deer's gilded antlers glimmer under the orange glow of dusk, and a hot thrill surges through me.

Just as I'm about to let the arrow fly, accounting for the speed of the wind, a branch snaps off the tree beside me and falls to the ground. The deer lets out a loud, anguished grunt, then leaps out of the arrow's path, the projectile missing it by inches.

Flaming hell.

I narrow my eyes at the tree for its ill-fated timing, the beast's escape path taking it directly toward the river.

"What happened?" Devi scolds.

I grumble, "A stupid branch fell off," and sling the bow over my back.

By the time we reach the rocky banks of the river on the opposite side of the meadow, voices boom through the vegetation, and we zigzag through the trees to rejoin the hunting party.

A clod of mud collides with my face as the deer thrashes on the ground under Ethan Lightbringer's foot. The arrow sticking out of the beast's hide has reached its heart, and yet the sacred animal is not dead. Left to its own devices, it might even recover.

"Well done, Ethan," my father praises his friend. "That was a long one."

"Not at all. It was almost too easy, Jayden." Ethan serves us a wide, self-satisfied smile.

The sting of defeat sears down my spine. *Too easy my ass.* We've been at this since dawn.

Blood pools on the ground, and I look anywhere but at the majestic animal, hoping the King of Light will stop gloating and put the poor beast out of its misery. His long blond hair catches in the breeze, his hooded blue eyes almost black and difficult to read.

My father passes him a rowan blade. The ceremonial weapon is made out of our court's special iron and silver alloy and rowan wood. This blade could finish off any Faerie-born creature in one strike and kill even the most powerful king.

If we were to only nick ourselves on the sharp edge, it would poison any of us to death, and I instinctively recoil from it, trying to smooth out my reaction with an awkward stretch. Only a few daggers of the sort exist, and we only use them in special circumstances.

Considering the damage they can do, I believe they should be melted down and destroyed, but no monarch would willingly obliterate its own murder-all weapon. Not without the certainty that his allies would do the same. Since only the most talented blacksmiths of Summer can forge new ones, they are also extremely valuable.

Ethan passes the lethal blade to his son. "Finish it off, Ezra."

My best friend looks perfectly at ease and doesn't even flinch away from the deadly blade as he picks it up and bends down to slice the beast's throat, but I know him well-enough to spot the tick of his jaw. Ezra despises his father and would have given anything for him not to win the hunt.

Devi clips a short, breathless curse behind me. "The whole thing was rigged. That branch didn't fall by accident," she whispers only to my benefit, and I keep a straight face, considering the possibility.

My father is the only one who could have made that branch fall from such a distance, and I don't see why he would have robbed me from the win. The summer solstice celebration brings along a flock of royal visitors. Me winning the hunt would have made for a great story at dinner tonight.

Thorald Storm rubs down his tensed mouth to hide a sneer, the Storm King barely able to mask his disdain for us Light Fae. "Well, some of us have to hurry back to prepare for the ritual."

My father grumbles under his breath. He's not part of the *some of us* who have to get ready. The seven Faerie monarchs are expected to reunite in Eterna's throne room tonight to perform a mysterious ritual, but that doesn't include their spouses. Even my father isn't allowed to know the details of what goes on in that octagonal room after the doors close. Being a king consort is hard on his ego, because no matter how much he likes to pretend otherwise, my mother is the true head of the family.

"Ezra, I leave you in charge of my trophy," Ethan orders.

Ezra gives his father a tight nod. "Yes, Sir."

I can hardly recognize my goofy roommate, his serious pout, stiff spine, and overall gloomy attitude a total contrast to his usual self, but that's always the case when his father is around.

The crowd disperses, and Ezra begins skinning the dead deer. Its meat will be smoked and salted for the palace healers, its hooves used for ointments, and only the antlers will be surrendered to the winner.

My father leans closer. "The Winter King could barely walk all the way up here, did you notice?"

"At least he came. Oberon Eros didn't even bother to try."

"Yes. And didn't you think Ferdinand Nocturna looked quite winded after the hike? That certainly doesn't bode well for Morheim."

The mention of Zeke's father sours what's left of my good mood. "When are you ever optimistic about Morheim?"

With a wry grin, my father motions for us to walk through the mirror the servants brought along. We leave a bloody, quiet Ezra to his disagreeable task, and return to Eterna through the sceawere. We enter directly through our private apartments, the glittering runes drawn around the mirror preventing anyone but us from entering.

The adrenaline ebbs out of my blood as my father serves us both a glass of cider to take the edge off our unfruitful hunt.

"After this morning, who do you think should marry Willow?" my father muses. "Given that only Spring, Winter, and Shadow should see a new monarch in this century?"

I go through the list of influential men we spoke to this morning that have a good shot at being king. The game my father is playing is similar to a game of chess, if the pieces moved at an incredibly slow pace. Decades could pass before any of the current kings and queens die. "There's Maddox Storm. He did well today."

"An interesting choice. His father is still in his prime, but Maddox is the heir apparent. Only, he's already betrothed." He purses his lips. "Is Ezekiel still living up to his underwhelming potential?"

"Worse."

"That settles it. The old Winter King will die before his new wife, so he's out of the running, too."

I can't believe he even considered the Winter crown for Willow, given the old king's reputation. Thankfully, my sister was too young to be presented at the last Yule pageant.

I take a deep breath, ready to broach a difficult subject. "Now, don't get mad. But what would happen if Willow was allowed to marry into the Spring Court?"

"Don't be ridiculous. Violet Eros is Oberon's obvious successor."

"I'm just saying—" I have no idea if Devi likes girls, but I've heard rumors, and she'll be queen for sure. Willow would certainly be interested in the idea of marrying her. Fascinated in fact.

"Violet can do whatever she wants in her spare time, but she has to marry a man, Aidan. Well-born children are the pillar of any reign."

He's acting as though it's never been done. Sure, it's been centuries, but I'm not entirely insane to suggest it. The Spring Court once had two queens—they're more open to such matters than we are.

"If not Zeke, Maddox, or Damian, then the only other viable choice is—" I cut myself off, the obvious answer to my father's wicked riddle finally staring me in the face. "You mean to marry Willow and Ezra?"

"Ethan Lightbringer will be in a gleeful mood tonight because of the hunt. It's the perfect time to work out such arrangements. Freya's been petitioning for her niece, but who is she kidding? Idris Lovatt's girl is hardly a proper princess."

An emotion between relief and anxiety, both liberating and worrisome, settles in my chest. "You sabotaged me on purpose to let him win."

"His little brother is not going to surprise us, is he?" my father asks, glossing over my comment.

"Doubtful. Elio is powerful, but the limelight doesn't suit him."

"Then Ezra it is. You should be glad, son. You two are already great friends, and now, you'll be family."

I stare down into my cider, the greenish liquid swirling in the bronze cup. Ezra and Willow... If my father is bent on marrying her before she comes of age, it's not the worst idea.

"Ezra might not accept. I think he suspects that he's not exactly... Willow's type."

The King waves away my concerns. "Ezra will do whatever his father tells him to do."

A shiver quakes my spine at the certainty in his tone. The terror I see on Ezra's face when he knows his father is angry at him is unequaled. And the stories I managed to piece together over the years tell me Ethan Lightbringer disciplines his sons with cruel, unusual punishments.

I do not want Will to be under that man's influence in any way whatsoever, but I trust Ezra to protect her.

My father's valet knocks on the door before inching it open. "I'm sorry to disturb you, My King." The forest-green coat of moss growing over the sprite's skull has been neatly trimmed for the occasion. "The royal ball is about to begin."

"I'll meet you in my room in a minute."

I check the clock on the wall. If I want to make it back to the academy in time for Beth's performance, I have to leave now. "Am I dismissed, sir?"

He removes his jacket and shakes out his wrists, quickly unfastening the cufflinks of his hunting clothes. "Why are you so eager to leave the capital on such a momentous night?"

"Willow made me promise to attend the solstice gala. She's organizing this year."

He doesn't bother to conceal his eye roll, his feelings about my love for the academy and its less glamorous traditions perfectly clear. "Oh, very well. Enjoy your night, Aidan."

Parents seldom want their children around for the only party of the year when they can fool around with anyone but their spouses, and he doesn't have to tell me twice. I slip out of Eterna through the mirror, the icy kiss of the sceawere leaving a trail of snowflakes on my neck, and return to the Abbey.

Ezra is fresh out of the shower and out of his bloody clothes when I get home.

"Hey," I whisper quietly, wondering how to break the news.

He walks past me to the sofa, rubbing a white towel into his wet hair. "Blessed Flame. From the looks of you, I guess I'm about to be betrothed."

"How?" I ask, taking a seat in front of him, flabbergasted by his insight.

Looking at the ceiling, he sinks into the cushions. "Why else would your father have sabotaged you like that, right as you were about to let your fire arrow fly, if he didn't intend for Ethan to win?"

"But how did you bridge the gap between letting him win and being betrothed?"

Ezra springs to his feet, clearly agitated, and snatches a bottle of cider from the cooling pantry, pouring himself a cup. "Why else would he give him the win? It's fine. I know my father was eager to get me settled. I thought Iris might be his choice, but as stunning as she is, Will and I will make a fine match, too."

It hits me then—Ezra has never hoped to marry someone of his own choosing. If I've let myself forget it, it's only because of the privilege the Mark of the Gods affords me. And now, I can't ignore the discomfort gnawing at me as my best friend plans a life with my sister, all without the faintest clue of what's really going on.

I peel myself off the sofa and head into my room to change. The tension in my chest increases with each breath until I return to the common room. "You should have a chat with Will before it's announced in any formal fashion," I muse.

I can't tell him the truth, but he needs to know. And given the opportunity, I believe Willow will tell him herself. If only to try and get out of it.

Ezra adjusts his gold vest over his bare chest, leaving it unbuttoned, the swirl of clouds from the Sun Court's crest sewn onto the folded lapels. "I know about Will, Aidan. That's why I said I wasn't her type. I'm fine with it. After the wedding, we can both come to a discreet arrangement. I'll keep doing what I do best, and she can find herself a nice mistress that we'll call her lady's maid, and voilà—the perfect marriage."

My shoulders hunch. "I know it's not what you wanted."

Ezra talks a big game, but he's like me. He's desperate to be loved for who he is, and not the throne he's being groomed for.

"Not what I wanted? What are you talking about? We'll be brothers." He serves me a cup of Nether cider and passes it over. "To family!"

I plaster a smile on my face, not wanting to make him feel worse about his predicament, truly glad for him to join the family if someone has to. "To family!"

We gulp down the entire thing, the frosty aftertaste numbing the ache between my ribs.

With a wistful smile, Ezra pats my back forcefully, ushering me toward the door. "Let's go. I need another drink."

"Can you tell Willow? When it's a good time?" I plead.

He pauses over the doorway, clearly taken aback. "Why?"

"My father made me swear not to tell, and used his magic to seal my promise."

"Oh, alright. But not tonight. I'll wait for Ethan to confirm it, first. No need to freak her out unnecessarily."

I nod, and we head off toward the village.

Augustus is a special town where common Fae coexist with the wealthy. Every year, the academy students host a gala for the solstice. Most of the villagers are eager to pay a small fee to see us try our hands at anything from poetry to jazz, and my mother doubles their contribution. The proceeds go directly to charity, funding the healers who maintain a permanent sanctuary in the heart of the village.

The small stage in the middle of the square is mostly used for plays or recitals, a highlight along the route for the occasional traveling troupe passing through the Summerlands.

All the villagers come out for the occasion, wearing either gold or green to signal their intentions. Gold signifies a desire to partake in the night's activities while those in green should not be accosted.

It's customary for unmarried Fae to wear gold, so Ezra and I don matching black and gold vests. While he chose not to wear anything underneath his, I opted for a light, long-sleeved black shirt.

Ezra makes a beeline for the cantina. The small stand is selling fire candy and flameroot wine—a cider that loosens one's grip on their heart's desires. It may not be as potent as Feyfire wine, but it's cheap to make and gives a warm, comforting glow inside. Something we're both desperate for at the moment.

Most of the other students are standing near the front of the stage, but I can't spot Beth among them. Zeke's dark aura is unmistakable, and I grimace, struggling to keep my nonchalant exterior intact. My only consolation is that Beth is nowhere near him. As usual, the Shadow Prince is cozying up to Diana and her friends.

"You're almost late. The gala's about to start," Willow scolds me from behind, and I spin around to greet her.

"You did great, sis." I head over to peck her cheek. "Well done."

Her eyes dim. "How did the oh-so-special royal hunt go?"

"It was wretched, if you must know."

Willow and I love each other, but we're also stuck in this strange, never-ending loop of sibling rivalry. She resents me for the Mark of the Gods and all the privileges that come with it. I begrudge that resentment and often wish she could get a taste of the pressure I'm under. It's not all rosy in my shoes either, but tonight, I have to admit that I prefer not being forced into a marriage I don't want at such a young age.

It hurts that I can't warn her myself, but maybe Ezra will find a gentler way to break the news. He'll certainly empathize with her predicament more than I ever could.

My lips press together as my eyes finally find Beth. She's wearing a green dress that flows to the ground. The bodice is made of vines crawling along her stomach and over her shoulders to cover her breasts, leaving her back bare. The pattern is so masterfully done that I'd believe it's been sewn by Ceres herself, the Fae goddess of nature and plants.

Ezra hands her an extra cup of wine. *By the Flame... How did he get over there so fast?*

My jaw clenches as she giggles and takes a sip, apparently pleased by the gesture.

Diana comes up to me with her clipboard, erasing them from my vision. "I know the moth failed at getting your initials. Hell, she probably didn't even try, but I need to ask anyway."

"Wait!" Beth runs over to me, the skirt of her dress flowing on either side.

I gape as she slips her hand over my arm and stands on her tiptoes. "I called you a bastard before, but I was wrong." She whispers in my ear, and my entire nervous system goes haywire. "You're an *ass*, actually." She raises a pointed brow at the word, and I half-choke on a ball of saliva.

Her hand leaves my arm, and I blink one too many times, my abs clenching at the knee-jerk fear that my true name might become common knowledge. It's so ingrained in our traditions to keep our initials safe that a cold trickle of nausea slithers into my gut.

Ezra tucks his hands deep in his pockets. The fucker has never stood so straight in his entire life, and I bite the insides of my cheeks not to call him out for his betrayal. He sold me out.

Diana frowns. "It's too late—"

Ezra checks the sky. "It's not midnight yet. Not even close."

"But—"

"The moth completed the challenge, Di. Get over it," he clips.

"Whatever. She's still not in first place." Diana leaves on a frustrated huff, shoving him hard with her shoulder, but Ezra dusts himself off with a smirk, unaffected.

"Oh, she really hates you, Lady Snow."

Beth fails to mask a grin with the heel of her hand. "Now, if you'll excuse me, I have to get ready for my performance."

Ezra raises his cup in cheer. "Knock 'em dead."

The playful smile Beth sends his way as she skips onto the stage before disappearing between the black tarps goes directly to the pit of my stomach.

"Why did you tell her my initials?" I ask through my teeth.

"Oh, don't give me that look. Diana was going to eat your girl alive. I figured you wouldn't mind so much, given how you feel about her."

"Is that truly the reason?"

He doesn't answer, and I force my fist to uncurl, a sickly warmth blazing through my body. "You want her," I croak.

He swallows a mouthful of wine, then lowers his voice. "Beth is my friend. And you know I'd never move against you."

"Could have fooled me. You two were giggling like schoolgirls."

"We were only chatting about the song she's going to sing. It's no big deal." He holds out his cup to share, but I stare down at the crimson tint of the flameroot wine and give him an impatient shake of the head.

The last thing I need tonight is to give in to my emotions or artificially pacify my turmoil. Beth isn't interested. She's told me twice now. And yet she's getting awfully comfortable with both Ezra and his brother.

Maybe blue eyes and blonde hair are more to her taste.

"I'll leave you two to your secrets, then," I grumble. "I wouldn't want to stand in the way of true love."

"Aidan!"

I leave Ezra behind, the stuffy sting of rejection and jealousy ringing in my ears. Just the thought of hearing Beth sing tonight fills me with misery. She'll be glorious, but out of reach. I've never wanted anything more. I'd cut off my right arm for her to smile at me with the same ease she displayed for Ezra earlier.

I'm a creep. She said no—twice. Why can't I just move on already? Why does she haunt my thoughts, night after night?

I can't let this sickness rule my life anymore. I need a proper cure.

CHAPTER 22
VERTIGO
SONGBIRD

Elio and I will be closing the gala with an upbeat tune, but as I'm setting up the mic, Devi strolls onto the stage. The satisfied curl of her damn perfect mouth spell trouble. Her gold, semi-translucent dress reveals the shape of her breasts, and the sight is almost too erotic and distracting for me to notice the long matching bow propped over her back, or the crystalline arrow in her grip.

The intoxicated crowd quiets down. If even the strongest of us turn into bumbling idiots in her presence, I can't imagine what the villagers must feel like, considering some of them are mortal.

"Before the last musical number, I have a surprise of my own to share." She licks her purple-painted lips. "Dear cousins and citizens of Augustus, I present to you a love arrow sharp enough to pierce a Fae's heart."

My pulse swirls at the news.

Wry laughs and dubious exclamations buzz through the crowd.

"Look at her..."

"What did she say?"

"It's impossible."

"Is this a joke?"

"Shut up and listen," Aidan roars over the rowdy chatter. His arms are crossed over his chest, his entire posture rigid and uncharacteristic.

He's been in a sour mood since he got here. I almost thought he was going to faint, earlier, when I whispered his full initials. His skin was warm, and I couldn't resist the urge to brush my lips to his ear. I figured he might be upset that Ezra had shared such an intimate and personal secret with me, but I also expected him to be proud of my success, in a way. For it to tie us together tighter. Instead, he just looks... hollow.

"I need two volunteers," Devi announces. "One will write down their full name, in discreet calligraphy, along the shaft of the arrow. Then, I will shoot someone else, and until dawn, my target will feel genuine romantic love for them—the same way it works for a mortal."

My heart plunges past my feet when Aidan climbs onto the stage. "Shoot me." He's so close, barely two feet away, yet I've never felt a wider chasm between us.

The devil of Spring raises her perfectly plucked brows. "Aren't you afraid to endanger your precious...jewels?"

"You can play with my jewels anytime, Devi," he jokes with his back to me, and my mouth dries up.

"Remove your shirt, then. I don't want to miss."

Howls and cat calls erupt from the crowd as Aidan unbuttons his vest and shirt and dumps them over the edge of the stage. A heavy lump settles in my throat as I stare at the smooth expanse of his back. Why did he choose to wear gold tonight? Any of the women here would be all too eager to sleep with him. And I'm not naive enough to believe he would turn them down.

"There's a catch, though," Devi adds.

Aidan chuckles, shaking his head. "Isn't there always?"

"Are you in love, Aidan? Because if you've already fallen for someone else, it would be dangerous for me to shoot you." Devi grins from ear to ear. "I'm not speaking in jest."

Aidan's smirk falters, and he scratches the back of his head before jumping off stage and picking up his clothes from the ground. "Choose someone else, then."

"Sounds like Aidan found himself a nice mortal girl in the new world," Johan booms over the gossip.

I catch Ezra's gaze across the square, the Prince of Light looking quite glum, too.

A feline smile stretches Devi's lips before she turns to Iris. "Will you do the honors, Little Flower? You're not in love with anyone, right?"

"My heart is free as a bird."

"She's your friend. How are we to know she's not pretending?" Aidan asks Devi with his eyes narrowed.

"Make her fall for Elio, and I'll believe it," Ezra cracks.

Blood drains from Elio's face, my friend already sitting on the piano bench. "Please don't."

But Ezra doubles down on his suggestion, the wicked shard of his soul rising to the occasion. "We all know my brother would never press his advantage, and this way, we'll be sure it's real."

"Come on, Elio. I'm game for a kiss, if it works," Iris adds with a wink.

Blood flushes Elio's neck, and he gives a small incline of the head, clearly unwilling to argue this further in front of everyone.

"Perfect. We have consent on both parts. Let's see." Devi hands over the arrow and a pen to Elio.

He quickly writes down his name along the shaft and rises to his feet to hand it over.

Iris raises her arms to the sky, her lips pursed in a daring, seductive pout. "Alright, I'm ready."

Devi nocks the arrow, her fingers steady on the string. It springs forward, whistling through the air, and bursts upon impact instead of sinking into Iris's flesh. A warm red glow spreads over her heart, fading after a moment.

Iris glances down at her chest and pats the spot where the glow had shined the brightest. "Well?" she asks, her tone expectant.

"How about that kiss now, Iris?" Devi quips.

I hold my breath as Iris struts over to Elio in her gold heels and plants a kiss on his mouth. My friend reaches for her arms, his hand curling around her wrists like he means to hold her off, but he thinks better of it and kisses her back instead. A throng of applause echoes across the square.

I can't bring myself to clap along and plaster a fake smile on my lips instead. Elio didn't want this, not really. It's going to mess with his head.

After a very heated, very public make out session, Elio tears himself away, angling his face away from the crowd. "Alright, enough."

Iris covers her mouth with her hand, looking positively shocked. Devi gives the crowd an impish curtsy before collecting her test subject and dragging her off stage.

Willow cups her hands around her mouth to amplify her voice. "Woo-hoo. Beth! Elio!" She sways from side to side even though we haven't even started, drunk on flameroot wine. I'm partly to blame since I gave her my share, and a chuckle escapes me.

Iris whispers something in her ear, but instead of dialing it down, Willow shakes her roommate's arms until the Spring Fae is dancing and laughing, too. The way Iris stares at Elio is pretty telling that Devi indeed managed to craft a love arrow sharp enough to pierce a Fae's heart. It was staged, but she wasn't faking it.

Ezra claps in his signature over-the-top attitude in the front row. "Beth. Beth. Beth." My breath stutters as the villagers join in.

And then there's Aidan sulking in the background, leaning on the old church's fence, his gaze as vivid as a trail of fire ghosting along my shoulders.

"Err— Good evening." My voice trembles, so I draw in a deep breath and adjust the height of the mic. "Elio and I bounced ideas around about what we wanted to play. This song by Irving Berlin just soared up the charts in the new world, and it got stuck in my head during our visit."

The original song itself is pretty fast and upbeat, but since it's just the two of us, Elio and I worked through the kinks of slowing it down.

I catch Aidan's gaze and hold it for a moment, and a question flickers in his gaze, asking, *What are you planning, Songbird?*

Oh, he's in for a treat.

I lick my lips. "I hope you enjoy it."

I look over at Elio, and give him the go-ahead. I'm a mess of nerves, but as soon as the first lyrics come, a comforting certainty takes over me. I'm not used to singing in front of Fae royals, but in this moment, I have absolutely no second-guesses or fears that my voice is not good enough.

If one part of me is worthy of greatness, it's my voice. And to sing is my ultimate release.

> Listen to me, honey dear
> Something's wrong with you I fear
> It's getting harder to please you
> Harder and harder each year
> I don't want to make you blue
> But you need a talking to
> Like a lot of people I know
> Here's what's wrong with you

Aidan squints, his arms braced on the fence behind him like he's holding himself off from forging closer to the stage.

That's right, Wonder boy. This one's for you.

The chorus comes, and I unleash a buttload of sass.

After you get what you want, you don't want it
If I gave you the moon, you'd grow tired of it soon
You're like a baby
You want what you want when you want it
But after you are presented
With what you want, you're discontented

You're always wishing and wanting for something
When you get what you want
You don't want what you get
And if I sit upon your knee
You'll grow tired of me
'cause after you get what you want
You don't want what you wanted at all

The only thing I can see is Aidan, as if all the torch lights have suddenly shifted to him. His back is hunched, masking his true height, his jaw set in a hard line. I only meant to tease him, but he looks...destroyed by the song, and my heart races.

There's a longing in your eye
That is hard to satisfy
You're unhappy most of the time
Here's the reason why

— ADAPTED FROM LYRICS BY IRVING BERLIN

The chorus comes again, and I'm pleasantly surprised at all the people singing along. Devi even raises her cup in my direction, a glint of curiosity widening her silver gaze. When I circle back to the chorus, Aidan pushes off the fence and approaches her. Tonight is a fuck whoever the hell you want without consequences night. Looks like Aidan has decided to claim the ultimate prize.

Devi grins and nods at whatever he says.

The song ends, and I plaster a fake smile on my lips, the turmoil in my soul threatening to show on my face. "Thank you." I hand off the mic to Willow, who's looking at me funny.

She shakes off the tearful look on her face and addresses the crowd to close out the gala, wishing our audience a great solstice.

Elio peels himself from his piano bench and grins from ear to ear. "Blessed Flame. What a performance!"

"Right back at you."

Students and villagers alike squeeze closer to the stage to shake my hand, and Iris is among them, her attention solely focused on Elio.

The jazz band takes over the stage to set up for the dance, and I slip to the ground, elbowing my way past Iris and following the curve of the platform, smiling gently at my new fans. What did they put in the flameroot wine for them to be so enamored with me after just one song? I humbly accept praises left and right, shaking hands as I make my way toward the cantina—until I bump into Zeke.

"Moth... you were hot up there," he slurs, invading my personal space.

"Err—thanks." I push him off me, taking advantage of his slow reflexes to lose him, racing between the dancers only to find Aidan gone. The boulder in my stomach pulses. I climb on the bottom part of the fence to peek over the crowd, but he's vanished. And so has Devi.

Ezra catches up to me. "That was— You're a star, Beth."

I stand stock-still in front of him, tears welling up in my eyes. I don't know what I expected, but I never thought my performance would drive Aidan into another woman's arms.

Ezra leans closer. "Aidan left right as you stepped off stage. He took the shortcut toward the forest."

I whisper a quick, "Thank you," and slip off my heels before heading into the dark.

If Aidan whisked Devi away to celebrate the solstice, I need to see it—to cure myself of these half-formed fantasies. But as I run down the well-beaten path to the forest and catch sight of his lonely silhouette, my heart pounds harder with each step.

His hands are tucked deep inside his pockets.

He hears me before he sees me and spins around, squinting at the darkness. A hint of fire flares in his fists, and he crouches into a fighting stance, probably thinking a wild beast is stalking him. I skid to a stop, catching my breath, and wonder why I came—why I'm so happy to find him alone. So...deliriously relieved.

You know why, that pesky inner voice quips.

A hint of moonlight streams between the clouds, and with a grunt of acknowledgment, Aidan turns his back to me and continues his trek toward the short wooden bridge crossing the creek, a couple of tall pines now encroaching on the path. "That song... You think I'm some weak-minded fool, but that's simply not true."

Across the bridge, the grassy field gives way to a soft carpet of long pine needles and cushy moss. I skip forward, gaining ground on him with the help of my perfect night vision. "I didn't write it."

"I know," he shouts, weaving carefully between the trees as the forest grows denser with every step. The rumbling creek widens and slows beyond the bridge, its waters flowing between the hills toward the ocean.

Aidan halts at the base of a massive white oak, its colossal trunk gleaming under the silvery moonlight spilling through the canopy above. The light bathes him in an otherworldly glow, and a pulse of magic hums through the air, beckoning me deeper into the forest—urgent, electric.

The scent of damp earth and crushed leaves hangs thick in the humid air, mingling with the sharp tang of pine sap and the sweetness of night-blooming jasmine. Crickets sing in a steady rhythm, their chorus accompanied by the low murmur of the wind whispering secrets only Aidan can hear.

His fingers trail over the oak's rough bark. "I'm trying to do the right thing here." He scans the path behind us with his lips pursed. "You should go. I'm waiting for someone."

I cross my arms over my chest, the need to scratch his face for his flawed logic rising in my blood. "Doing the right thing by whom?"

"You," he says as though it's obvious.

"And why in the seven hells would you sleep with Devi to please *me*?"

He doubles back, feral, bridging the distance between us. "Is that why you chased me here? I can't have you, but I can't have anyone else, either. Is that it?"

I scoff, digging the balls of my feet into the ground, recoiling from the implications of his statement. "Please, do whatever you want."

His eyes narrow, taking stock of my bare feet. "Why did you run after me if you don't care?"

"I had to see it for myself."

He grins dryly, as if this is all a cruel joke. "I can't lie, yet you don't believe me when I tell you the only woman I want is you."

"Because it doesn't make sense. Devi's more powerful, more beautiful. *And* she's a princess."

He rubs the bottom half of his face, avoiding my gaze. "Are you playing matchmaker now?"

I tip my chin up. Whatever he says, he still chose to be with someone else. Nobody forced him to proposition anyone, let alone the most sexual woman alive. "You're the one who asked her to meet you here. And it wasn't to talk or play cards."

"Stop with that wounded look." He gestures at the space between my brows. "I asked Devi to meet me here and shoot me with an arrow. To see if it could... cure me."

"Cure you of what?"

He cups one side of my face. "Of my love for you."

"You...love me?" I shudder at his touch, stretching to feel his heat, reeling from the weight of his confession.

"I thought I'd made that clear when I said I couldn't think of anyone or anything but you. Hell, I had to admit it in front of *everyone*."

"But— She said it was dangerous."

"I'm at my wits' end. After seeing you on that stage and hearing you sing... I have to try *something*." He turns away, but I tug on the golden lapels of his vest for him to look at me.

"Aidan."

"Now, when you breathe my name like that...it gives me hope. Don't give me false hope, Songbird."

"You were right. I feel it, too." I try to find a graceful and eloquent explanation, but my hands are shaking. "I wasn't kidding when I said being caught with you could ruin my whole life, so I pushed you away..." I glance at the ground between us. "But I wish I didn't have to."

A heavy sigh escapes him.

I play with my fingers, unable to meet his gaze. "Tonight's different, though."

He covers my hands with his. "Because of St. John's Eve."

He thinks he loves me, but I'd wager it's only because he's not allowed to. I'm his forbidden frost apple, so to speak—the only woman at the academy who's too far beneath him for commitment.

Lust can be satiated. Maybe if I give in to my attraction for him once, the magnetic pull of his flames will wane, so I nod. "Yes. And tomorrow, we can finally turn the page."

He rubs the back of his neck, his lips curled down as he considers my offer. "You came to me tonight because you figured it doesn't count."

"Even if someone found out... they couldn't condemn me for it. Not without insulting your traditions."

"You think one night will be enough?" He laces our fingers, slowly, reverently, like he wants to commit the sight of them entwined to memory. "I'll still want you in the morning. And every morning after that."

A sad smile glazes my lips. "We'll see."

His eyes gleam as if he's taking my doubts as a challenge. "Dance with me, Songbird." He holds out his other hand for me to take, but I glance around, nervous to see Devi appear between the trees.

"Here?" I hesitate.

"You're right. I know a place where we won't be disturbed." He twirls me around and wraps his arm around my shoulder, never letting go of my hand. "Follow me."

CHAPTER 23
EVERLONG
SONGBIRD

Aidan twists a small silver key into the lock at the center of a garden gate and holds it open for me. Overgrown vines have laid claim to the fence and trellis above the passage, grazing my hair as I pass, while Aidan dips his head to avoid being scratched by the twigs. The wrought iron gate clanks shut behind us, the metal groaning as the latch clicks back into place.

In the heart of the south-west gardens, a wild patch of silver-leafed bushes and tall willow trees conceals a small log cabin. The rustic building is tucked away on top of the hill, almost completely hidden, a real oasis in the middle of nowhere, untouched and protected from prying eyes. Aidan walks ahead of me, guiding me with quiet confidence, as if this place is a part of him. His sanctuary.

"Where are we?"

"Ezra and I built this cabin during my first year here."

"It's beautiful. For a man's den, I mean." I muse, and Aidan's lips twist in a sheepish grimace.

"It hasn't been used much, not by me, at least. And certainly not this year."

That's an acceptable answer, and my shoulders relax. The patio offers a wide-angle full view of the twinkling ocean, and a salty wind blows my hair back. I draw in a deep, soothing breath, tingles of nerves and excitement buzzing across my skin.

Aidan disappears inside the cabin for a few seconds and comes back with a pile of blankets and a bottle of wine.

A bed of fresh, soft leaves grows over the patio, twisting and entwining to create a cushy mattress.

Aidan sprawls a red and white tartan blanket over them and lies down, tucking his arms behind his head and staring up at the sky. "Seems like a waste not to watch the stars on a night like this."

I hesitate. "Shouldn't we go inside?"

"This whole meadow is enchanted. We're safe, I promise." He pats the empty space beside him.

Fireflies flicker in the night and in my stomach, my insides aglow as I sit next to him with my legs tucked beneath me.

He twists around to face me. "Tell me more about you, Songbird."

My eyes dart to the empty space between us. "My life's not so glamorous, I'm afraid. There's not much to tell."

Henri was always too glad to skip right to the sex part. Aidan appears determined to make this night last, and not only to steal my fake virginity, but my secrets, too. He shifts to a seated position, grows two horned-shape flowers and snaps them off the stems. He hands one over and fills it up with wine. It's so eerie to be here with him, in this picture-perfect environment, with the sea twinkling in the distance, the stars above, and the sexiest Fae prince alive pouring me wine as though we've got all the time in the world.

"Where did you grow up?" he asks.

An icy aftertaste of shame stings my gut. "In the underbelly of the Winter castle. My father is one of the Winter King's favorite political advisers."

"Is that how he ended up selling you off to the Shadow King's son?"

The knee-jerk impulse to defend my father rears its head. "Papa only wants the best for me."

Aidan stops pouring and sets the bottle aside, raising his brows. "Does he truly believe Zeke is the best man for you?"

"Coming here instead of the Ice City is the best life I could hope for."

He squints at me, deep lines appearing on his forehead at the mention of the Ice City. "I thought the reaper army didn't force anyone to enroll?"

"They wouldn't have *forced* me, per se. But it would have been considered my duty to train as a reaper. If I had been selected to spend my life in the Ice City, I wouldn't have brought shame to my entire family by skirting my responsibilities—" My heart hammers in my chest. "Why do you insist on this...interrogation? Did you bring me here to argue, or have sex?"

"So impatient." With a knowing grin, he dips his head down to kiss me.

I've got half a mind to pick a fight with him and chicken out of this all together, but the taste of his lips tames my temper. Pine and sandalwood mingle to form a woodsy, masculine scent with hints of charred honey. Just like the candies we roast over the fire to sweeten the coldest, harshest night of winter.

I can't get enough.

My fingers tense around the makeshift glass of wine, the flower threatening to squish in my grip as I blink my eyes open.

Aidan presses his nose to mine. "I want to make love to you, Songbird."

By the spindle... Does he want me to burn to ashes before we even start?

"Cin-cin."

We bump the rims of the flowers together, and the silky texture of the petals brushes my lips. Pollen sweetens the wine, but the weather made it a little too hot for my taste, so I ice the pistil before doing the same to Aidan's glass. "Here. The ice won't melt for hours, so don't worry about it diluting the wine."

"Nice trick."

I bite my bottom lip, the warm, loving expression on his face filling me with pride, as though what I just did was actually special. Maybe if I turn the tables on him, he'll be more inclined to skip the heart-to-heart part. It's not as if we could actually date after this.

"Who are you meant to marry? Devi?" I ask in a falsely nonchalant tone.

Aidan chuckles and shakes his head. "Never. Devi is almost sure to be her grandfather's heir."

"I thought that would only make your parents more eager for you two to marry."

"You see, if Devi was to be crowned queen while I was married to her, it would destroy my chances to inherit the Summer crown."

"Why?"

He sets his wine to the ground. "It's a well-kept secret, but the seven crowns would actually kill for two kingdoms not to fall under the control of a married couple. It would put too much power into one family's hands."

"Oh."

"You have no reason to be jealous." He caresses my bare knee.

"I'd be jealous of any woman you'd be free to marry," I deadpan, the statement crawling out of some dark, bottomless trench inside my heart.

His throat bobs. "Yeah?"

"Yes."

The rest of my defenses shatter as I slip my arms around his neck and lean forward, caressing his hairline with my free hand. "I dreamed about you—when I was in the new world. I couldn't quite make up my mind to be good and stay away from you."

"Never settle for good, Songbird. You deserve *more*." He dives in for a kiss, and the brush of our tongues is the most erotic thing I've ever felt. I spread my legs to make space for him and discard the wine to the side, his grip on my waist making my belly clench and my nipples harden.

"I dreamed about you, too. Every night. It nearly consumed me."

Aidan drags his thumb over my pointy ear. His fingertips linger on the angle of my jaw, and in this small, careful touch, I get a glimpse of the extent of his greediness. "I want to learn every detail there is to know about you. Touch every inch of your skin. Own every bit of your soul. I want to play with your body until it craves me and me alone."

I quake under the decadence of his desire, his words spreading through my body like bottled sin, my rational mind checking off completely. The chorus of *only one night* slips away, banished to some dusty dungeon at the back of my mind.

"Tell me about your heart, Songbird. What does it sing for? Do you want me to worship you, or do you prefer to be ravished? Should I make you beg for your release, or spoil you with more pleasure than you can stand?"

"All of it," I gasp. "Make me *burn*."

He smiles like my answer is even more perfect than I knew.

Fire and ice. Ice and fire.

Kissing, gripping, *clawing* each other closer. I unbutton and tug the vest off his broad shoulders, then his shirt. Running a hand down the grooves of his smooth, naked back, my heart cries out in bliss. *Finally.*

"I will drive you mad with pleasure until you agree to be mine." He combs my hair to the side and pecks the tender skin of my neck as he undoes the hook-and-eye closures at the back of my dress, one by one, until he manages to slip it over my head.

"So cocky."

"Is that doubt I hear?" He shifts on top of me. "I'll keep count, then. Past ten, you'll have to yield, right?"

Ten?

The weight of him steals a heavy groan from my lips. "Concentrate on one, alright?" I quip.

His answering gaze is so filthy and dissolute that I almost believe him, his pride clearly rising to the challenge.

Our bodies are like long-lost puzzle pieces, moving in tandem. I scrape his ass under the hem of his trousers, and he reaches behind me to unclasp my satin bra.

My breasts bounce free, and I shiver, moving to cover myself, but Aidan discards the ivory piece of fabric to the side, his nostrils flaring, his hooded eyes dipping to the heavy, sensitive flesh.

I shudder all over, feeling more beautiful than Eros herself as he traces the swell of my breast with his thumb. The pad of it is as hot as melted wax, and I hum when he drags it over the chilled, pebbled peak. My back arches, the contrast between his fire and my wintry skin almost painful, but not quite. I need more.

"If I'm too much, too rough, too *ardent*..." he says with humor. "Just tell me," he whispers against my skin.

"Duly noted." I reach for the top of his trousers, but he shakes his head.

"Not yet."

I bite my bottom lip and stroke him over the fabric, my insides hot and slick as I take in the shape of him.

A dark glint burns in his gaze, but he pins my hands above my head. "I said not yet."

Two bare vines grow out of the ground and shackle my arms in place, their rough bark scraping the underside of my wrists. I tuck my tongue behind my front teeth and offer my lover a provocative smile. "You're bossy, too. I kind of like it."

He chuckles at that, the sound soft and enchanting, as he mirrors my own words back to me. "Duly noted."

I stretch out my neck to lick the freckles under his jaw, absolutely entranced by the sight of him hovering above me as he slides a hand down my stomach, under the lace, and over my sensitive spot.

"Blessed Flame. You're already soaked. Keep your legs spread for me. Let me see all of you."

I want to drag my nose down the hollow between his pecs, trace the muscles and indentation toning his arms, and kiss the maroon birthmark peaking above the hem of his pants.

He peels off my underwear impossibly slowly, caressing my legs up and down. His hands paint a trail of fire on my skin, a warm, scarlet glow left in their wake. His lips engrave sinful praises in my skin, his hot mouth teasing, nibbling, *feasting* on me until I'm writhing. Marking my neck, my breasts, my belly, my soul.

And I feel like a goddess being worshipped by her king.

Aidan tortures me with delicate, scandalous bruises that will brand me for weeks to come, and the process spurs me on like nothing else, the sweet pressure between my thighs exploding outward as he finally grazes my entrance with his hand.

He sinks one finger inside me, then two, his other palm pressed flat to my belly, grounding my hips to the homemade mattress. I shudder as he dips his head to lick my throbbing flesh, my body ripe for an orgasm that wrecks my chances of keeping his ego his check.

"One," he grins. "And easy, too."

"You're so cocky. I should leave just to spite you."

"Maybe, but you won't."

No, I won't.

He's too good at this, and it's *infuriating*.

Aidan is not content with this first, *easy* victory and uses my orgasm as a preamble for the next, getting comfortable between my thighs. With a satisfied smirk, he kneads the smooth skin of my thighs and ass until the sensitive ache ebbs. I tuck my bottom lip between my teeth, flustered to find out I'm simply starving for more.

Aidan plays wicked games with his tongue until violent, liberating tremors melt a frozen river inside me, my pleasure gushing out around his fingers. "Two," the cocky prince hums against my core, drinking it in.

I ice the vines holding my wrists to reach for him, my nails sinking deep in his shoulder. *By the spindle.*

A surprised groan quakes my throat, and I almost apologize for the mess, but Aidan looks so damn pleased and horny, I figure he meant for it to happen. He slips out of his trousers, not wearing anything underneath, and I let out a lust-filled pant.

"I need you to touch me, Songbird," he groans quietly. His abs clench as he guides my hand to his cock. "I need to be inside you."

He's hard as steel and so, so thick.

I run my fingers from the base to the tip, and his hips jerk forward. "Fuck."

"Come here." I spread my legs in invitation, and he sinks down on top of me, our chests bumping in a delicious friction as he lines himself with my entrance.

His previous caress teased and prodded at a hollowness in my belly that's now wild and insatiable, aching for him. I hold my breath as he pushes all the way in, the delicious stretch almost holy. Our foreheads rest against one another, my body adjusting to his size.

I rock my hips, hungry for him to strive for number three, and scratch deep lines into his back, as eager to brand him as he did me, staking my claim.

"Blessed Flame, you're not making it easy for me to go slow."

One corner of my mouth lifts as I graze his chin. "I didn't ask for slow."

He exhales and darts his tongue out to touch my lips. "Your wish is my command, Songbird."

Aidan fucks me as though he's starving for me body, mind, and soul, and I love every moment of it, gazing up at him, his silhouette framed by a black, endless sky. The chafe of the blanket warms my ass in a maddening, delectable way.

His mood shifts, his control peeled away layer by layer, switching from the measured thrusts of a patient, dedicated lover to a greedy, famished beast. "You're so wet and tight." He buries himself deeper with a long, possessive thrust. "I'm going to spend *days* inside you. Paint every inch of your beautiful body with my come until you agree to be mine."

He's so turned on by what we're doing that he can't quite keep control, flirting with the spiral of a quick, abrupt climax judging by the enraptured look on his face. He holds my legs at the exact angle he craves, and I tighten my walls around him.

"Oh, flaming hell." He moans darkly, slowing down the pace and palming my ass as if he means to punish me for the intensity of his pleasure. But as he tries to hold off his climax, he hits the same secret spot, over and over again.

A string of desperate whimpers tears from my throat. I can't hold my noises in, each thrust so perfectly placed as to push me higher and higher without sending me over the edge.

"Come for me hard, Songbird. Show me how much you love my cock."

While I loved to see him so intent on pleasuring me, I think I prefer this iteration of him. Wild, demanding, and dark.

I arch off the ground and grip a fist of his hair, his name leaving my lips in prayer, blood rushing from my center to my thighs and spreading all the way down to my toes. My walls pulse in rash, powerful waves, so hard I bite down on my tongue. As if my body means to keep him there forever, or crush him, or both.

"How are you even— That's insane... Fuck-Fuck-Fuck. I can't—"

He slams his hips forward and fills me with his seed, his head falling on my chest.

He gives an almost apologetic grunt as he falls to his side next to me. "By the Flame... how did you ensnare me so tightly?"

I take it as a post-climax, rhetorical question, and abandon myself to his embrace.

With Henri, sex was almost a race to the end, meant to reach a point where we felt satisfied enough to put our clothes back on and go on with our day, but Aidan was not kidding when he said he wanted my body to become addicted to him. The self-consciousness I expected to feel now that we've given in to our most basic instincts and said a bunch of embarrassing nonsense is nowhere to be found, and I close my eyes, feeling perfectly comfortable.

With him. With my body. Safe. Satisfied. *Happy.*

Loved, even.

Aidan rubs my back up and down a few times before dipping below my waist to caress my ass, softly kneading the flesh as he places butterfly kisses on my shoulder blades. "You're perfect, Songbird. I'm simply obsessed with you."

"You're not so bad yourself, Wonder Boy."

"Say that again."

I bite my bottom lip to keep from giggling. "I kind of like you, too, *Wonder Boy*," I repeat in a sultry drawl.

He groans against the back of my ear and pulls on my knee, guiding my left leg across his body before dragging his hand between my thighs. The scents of our sweaty bodies have mixed to form a new, entirely different scent that rekindles the blaze in my belly.

"Mm," I coo, my body spent and yet incredibly pleased with his attentions, as though he activated some kind of never-ending loop. "You're being greedy, now."

"Do you want me to stop?" he grins, curling a finger to stroke my insides.

I claw his arm to keep it in place. "Nuh-uh." My body coils in a fourth, almost immediate release, soaking the blanket underneath us as I bite the back of my free hand to muffle a scream.

"Sorry," I breathe.

"Not at all. It was glorious."

"I meant the blanket."

"Forget the blanket." He pecks my lips.

"Let me see that mark." I twist around to face him and trace the phoenix mark, caressing the burns that forever etched his skin, and my brows furrow. "Did it hurt?"

"Not that I can remember," he breathes, tucking a strand of hair behind my ear. "You're so fucking beautiful."

"Look who's talking." I press my ear to his chest and listen to his heartbeat, indulging my fascination for the lines of his body until his eyelids flutter. His chest rises and falls as my hand wanders lower, and his cock stiffens almost immediately in my grip.

His eyes snap open. "I want you on your hands and knees. Is that okay?"

"I'm at your command, my prince," I tease.

His lips part in surprise. The bob of his throat betrays just how much he loved that, and a gleeful smile spreads on my lips. The tip of him points at the sky, red and glistening, *aching* for round two.

I slide off him and roll unto my stomach, the logistics of switching positions somehow lost to his pure, devout touch. He strokes my sides and ass as though it's an actual act of worship, and I claw at the blanket in anticipation. The angle puts him deeper, somehow, and my head falls forward as he enters me.

I'm already addicted to the rush.

Aidan doesn't just *make love* to me for a second time. He doesn't just fuck my brains out. He takes ownership of my body in ways that melt me from the inside out, effortlessly mixing hot, filthy commands with sweet, enamored promises, and blinding, carefree fun. I never thought sex could be all those things at once, but here I am, eager to both please my prince and make him beg. Both teasing him for his confidence and blushing at his guile.

I give him the words he craves and agree to be his. The hushed pieces of forever will no doubt be smashed to dust in the morning, but they sound so real by moonlight. Crazy thing is, even though they're not true, they're no longer a lie, either.

Another loophole in the *Fae can't lie* rule. I want to belong to Aidan, and he wants to belong to me, and for now, that's enough.

And I will remember every minute of this terribly beautiful night until the reaper comes for me.

CHAPTER 24
SEA WITCH
SONGBIRD

Waking up in Aidan's arms could spoil me for all time. His sizzling warmth and the scent we made together lulled me into a heartbreakingly sweet slumber, and I grimace as I wake up, unwilling to let go of the glow hovering in my chest. We didn't even bother to enter the cabin, so I'm still sprawled over the makeshift bed, tangled up in his embrace.

The precocious dawn that accompanies the shortest night of the year paints bloody warning signs on the horizon. Stormy clouds gather over the sea, creeping lazily toward the shore. They look like angry Red priestesses stretching their necks to judge us for our sins.

I trace Aidan's calm, serene features one last time, desperately jealous of the princess he's meant to marry. As sad and bitter as it sounds, I need to remind myself that it can't be me before I lose sight of what this night really was.

An indulgence.

A bewitching exception.

I try to slip out unnoticed, but he squeezes me to him. I twist around in his arms, his amber eyes burning under the fiery dawn, clear and full of love.

"Good morning, Songbird."

The sweet drawl of the nickname physically hurts. I might never hear it again after today. It's a complex feeling to love something so fiercely and yet be so certain of its demise. But Aidan and I were a dream only meant to last one night.

I clear my throat, muttering a muted, "Morning."

He brushes my hair away from my face, tracing the hollow of my neck down the valley between my breasts. His fire chases away the chill of the night, warm and hypnotic. I've got half a mind to bury my head in his chest and pretend we're just another couple, sharing a lazy, uncomplicated morning.

He kisses the angle of my jaw. "I wish every morning could be like this."

My stomach squeezes in response, and a breathless sigh whistles out of my lungs.

The statement stings like the tip of a double-edged sword, a unique brand of torture. It won't do us any good to spend the next few hours luxuriating in this impossible bubble, only to watch it burst the moment we step outside, listing all the promises we won't be able to keep, and the things we will never do together.

Yet, Aidan seems intent on doing just that.

"Everyone will be gone on break soon," he says with a naughty grin. "You should stay and spend one more night with me. Tomorrow morning, we could even walk down to the ocean and swim...*naked*." He bites my earlobe playfully, but the hollowness in the pit of my belly throbs at the suggestion.

"I can't stay. My father would worry."

His furrowed brows call me out for my cowardice. "You could write to him that you'll arrive tomorrow, instead. It's not like he knows the ins and outs of this place—"

The comment rubs me the wrong way, highlighting the divide between our circumstances. "And what would one more night accomplish, exactly?" I shift to a sitting position and wrap an arm around my bare breasts. "It doesn't change the fact that I have to go home."

It doesn't change the fact that you're not for me, I almost add, but the angry words get caught in my throat. It's not Aidan's fault that he's the infamous Crown Prince of the Summerlands, and that I'm just a moth. That I'm engaged to a man I despise. And even if I weren't, Aidan would never be free to court me openly. But it *hurts*.

"In two months, then?" he asks.

"Aidan..."

"Songbird."

I crawl to my knees, keeping my eyes firmly planted in my lap and playing with a loose thread of the tartan blanket. "Aidan. We said one night."

"As I recall, we said a lot of things. For example, you *begged* me never to stop licking your sweet, hot—"

I seal his mouth with my hand. "Shush!"

Our gazes lock as I slowly peel it away, and his eyes wrinkle at the corners.

"I'll miss you. Can we at least agree to revisit this one night policy next semester?"

I shake my head, turning away from him. If I let this dangerous hope take root inside me—that there'll be a next time—it'll fester.

"Five more minutes, then," he pleads with a boyish pout. "*Please.*"

He snakes his arms around me, and I relax in his embrace, resting my head on his shoulder. "Oh, alright."

I'm not as strong as I pretend to be. Certainly not enough to know what's good for me.

His breath stirs the hairs at the back of my ear. "But you have to admit, that naked swimming lesson sounds heavenly."

I can't help but chuckle, then deny him with a regretful wrinkle of the nose and a firm head-shake. "I doubt there would be much swimming involved."

"Oh, there'd be *plenty* of swimming..." His voice drops a few octaves, low and intense. "But after, I'd spread you out on the sand and drink the seawater off your skin." He gives a sharp pinch to my nipple and dips his hand down to caress the space between my legs, his cunning, talented fingers stoking the embers of my need for him.

I cry out at the friction and sink my nails into his thigh. "This is torture."

The shape of Aidan's desire swells against my lower back as he cups my breasts in turn, lifting them up and squeezing them tight. "Torture?"

I wish my voice didn't tremble as I whisper, "Because I can't have you," but my walls have crumbled around me. Gone is the girl who played the long game, using her wits to shield herself from bad choices and worse decisions.

His playful tone vanishes. "You have me, Songbird. All of me."

For now.

Sleeping with Aidan was like stepping into an avalanche. Now that I've slipped, there's nowhere to go but down. Everything but him feels cold.

Tears sting my eyes as I spin around, swinging one leg over his hips and pinning him down. I dive down to kiss him, silencing him in equal measure, desperate to hide the conflicting emotions on my face, terrified that his lovely words might shatter what's left of my resolve.

He adjusts his hold on my waist, guiding my hips. A sharp moan escapes me as I slide down the length of him to the root. I bite my lower lip, trembling with need and a hint of rage. No one else will ever fit so deeply inside me, or burn so divinely hot against my icy flesh. I'll never know such bliss again. In one night, he seduced me thoroughly, awakening desires I never knew I had, and gave me a taste of a life I can't have, a passion unmatched. The dizzying certainty settles deep in my bones—that no one else will ever compare, and that I've become addicted to something I'll forever starve for.

Something I might never find again.

He lifts me just high enough for the tip of his cock to tease my greedy flesh. "Don't give up on us before we even start. This is not our last morning together."

"But what if it is?" I choke, the heaviness in my chest making me feel like I'm drowning.

Aidan utters a pained growl. "Then let me *torture* you until you scream." He lowers me in one sharp, urgent movement, joining us together once more.

I kiss him hard, hard enough to bruise him, afraid to cut myself deeper at the altar of his love, yet terrified not to. I claw him closer, rocking over him, chasing both release and destruction. His hold on my hips is unyielding—wild. Delicious.

We reach a savage, bittersweet pleasure. The kind you only find in the eye of a storm. The type of heights you can only plummet from.

Slowly, the cabin comes back into focus. The sky and ocean are still ablaze, as if only minutes have passed, though it feels like I've lived and mourned an entire existence.

"I have to go," I croak, pulling myself off him in search of my discarded clothes.

"Then I'll go with you," he whispers back.

The protective way he holds my hand on our way over to the girls' wing wrecks me all over again, my rib cage painful and tight as I unlace our fingers. I inch up the vines, trying to keep quiet, and the vegetation plies to meet my needs, allowing for an easy climb. I don't want Willow—or Thanatos forbid, Iris—to catch me sneaking in.

Aidan follows me all the way up to my bedroom window. "Wait." He pulls me in for another delirious kiss. "Let me in."

I crawl over the cushioned bench and turn back to face him, barring his entry. "We already talked about this."

The dark, incensed look on his face melts away like snow on hot coals so quickly, I wonder if I imagined it. "Okay, okay. You've won this round. Go take a shower and wash me off of you if you must.

Grab breakfast. Head home like nothing happened. But this isn't the end, Songbird."

He sounds so sure again, he almost makes me doubt. After landing on the ground, he blows me one last kiss and spins around, burying both hands in his pockets.

I follow his silhouette until it disappears between the bushes.

"Morning." My stomach clenches at the unexpected greeting, and I jolt around to find Devi sprawled over the empty bed on the opposite side of the room. *What in the seven hells? How did I miss her, before?*

Thanatos be kind... The gleeful smile on her lips is terrifying.

"So... you and Aidan. How long has that been going on?" she muses.

I open my mouth to blurt out a defensive mention of St. John's Eve, but Devi doesn't wait for my answer. "Since he helped you in the trials, I bet."

My insides coil to a standstill, and my breath frosts in front of my face, the temperature in the room dropping below freezing.

"You know, it's been driving Damian crazy, how you—a moth with no special training—managed to cross Aidan's deadly maze in record time. But last night, as you were singing, I finally got it." She rakes her black manicured nails across the pillow propped over her lap. "Aidan helped you. The thought had crossed my mind before, but I couldn't figure out why. Aidan is a ruthless competitor. Why would he help a moth, of all people?"

"I suppose you're not actually asking?" I crack.

She slinks to her feet. "What do you know of your mother?"

My brows furrow at the sudden turn the conversation has taken, but I know better than to tell Devi Eros to mind her own business, not when she's holding me by my metaphorical balls. "Not much. She died when I was young, and she had no family."

She draws a sharp intake of breath. "So you don't know."

"Know what?"

"And your father has kept you away from the sea, of course. He never taught you how to swim," she whispers, mostly to herself.

"What are you getting at?"

"You're a siren, moth. That's why Aidan helped you in the labyrinth. He never suspected of course, because of all the silly Summer legends about love at first sight, and his own vanity. He never suspected for a moment that *you*, a nobody, could have enchanted *him*."

"Err— No chance." I shake my head, her hypothesis absolutely ridiculous. "That's impossible. Sirens kill their lovers."

"How do you explain last night, then? You basically bewitched everyone."

"No," I repeat. "If I was a siren, the whole audience would have been under my thrall. There would have been a riot and bloodshed—"

"I figure you might be half siren. A quarter? An eighth? I'm right about the trials, yes? I bet you sang your heart out in that labyrinth..."

The instinct to deny it at all cost takes a life of its own, and my fists curl at my sides. "It doesn't mean that I'm a siren, because I'm not."

Sea Fae aren't allowed to live on the continent. They're vicious and violent, luring many to their deaths.

"A man like Aidan, cheating himself of a major win against his nemesis and risking his mother's ire for a girl he's never even met? It doesn't make sense."

A small voice in my head agrees, and I swallow hard, replaying the trials in my mind. "You're wrong." I turn away from her, retreating to the foot of my bed, trying to put as much distance between us as possible.

"I'm not," she deadpans, stepping closer.

A wince escapes me. "Wrong or not, people will believe you over me, no matter what," I whisper. "So I might as well pack my bags and crawl into some hole in the wall."

Her demeanor shifts in an instant, going from dry and accusatory to amused. "Oh, you haven't been paying attention, moth. One day, this secret might become a weapon in some major battle, and I wouldn't waste it just to see you expelled." She takes a meaningful pause, then crawls over my duvet as though we're friends gossiping at a sleepover. "But I do need you to tell me about the impending nuptials I caught wind of. Did you hear anything about it?"

Cold sweat pearls above my brows. "Who's getting married?"

She squints, her stare raising goosebumps on my arms. "That's what I'd like to know. It's supposed to be a *Summer* wedding, and a *royal* one at that. I figured you'd be open to sharing secrets now that we're... better acquainted."

A *Summer* wedding? My throat tightens. Devi's obvious enthusiasm for coercion sinks like an anchor in my chest, dragging all my hopes and dreams down with it.

"Aidan?" I gasp, cold tremors rocking my body.

By Thanatos. I feared Aidan might marry someone else, but I certainly didn't expect it to happen so soon.

"Or Willow."

I scoff at the possibility. "Willow would have told me if she was getting married."

"And your boyfriend wouldn't have?" Devi lets the question dangle like a hook, a grin spreading across her red-painted lips. "No, I guess he wouldn't have. Well, I need to know today, so be a dear and ask him."

"You want me to ask Aidan if he's getting married?" I screech.

Devi shrugs in an overly nonchalant manner. "He's fond of you, and he can't lie, so it should only take a minute. Don't let him play with words, though. He's good at that. I'll be anxiously awaiting your answer."

I don't want to acquiesce to her demand, but I have no choice, not if I ever want to return to the academy. And if Aidan is getting married this summer, I'd rather know now than read about it in the news.

I've never sneaked into the boys' wing before, but today, I climb the stairs two at a time to the top floor, my hooded cape concealing my hair. My knuckles tighten around the handle of my second-hand travel bag as I reach the penthouse door. I knock softly, bracing myself for the conversation to come, and my mouth goes dry when it's not Aidan who answers, but Ezra.

He scans me from head to toe, his blonde hair slicked over his head, which is a stark change to his usual disheveled-ness. "Ooh, a traveling salesman. What are you selling, milady?" He meets my gaze, and his playfulness cranks down several notches as he opens the door for me to enter. "Aidan, you have a visitor."

I stay rooted in place, feeling eerie and hot.

"Songbird, hi."

I throw him an awkward wave, my heart bleeding at the obvious joy on his face. The fact that he's fresh out of the shower and only wearing a white towel doesn't help my concentration, but the possibility of hearing about his betrothal certainly tarnishes his appeal. A bit.

Ezra's gaze flicks between us before he tucks his hands deep into his pockets. "Well, I suddenly feel like I have urgent business elsewhere. I'll wait for you in the hall, boo. Lady Snow, I wish you a glorious break." He kisses my knuckles and slips past me with a wink.

"You too." Warmth floods my cheeks as Aidan walks to take Ezra's place by the door, his bare chest filling my line of vision. He looks so pleased as he asks, "Did you change your mind about that swimming lesson?"

"Afraid not," I say quickly, avoiding his stare. "But I had to see you before I left."

If only he knew the real reason I came. I still don't believe Devi's claim that I'm a Sea mutt, but I'm acting as her spy all the same.

Aidan holds the door wider, stepping aside. "Please, come in."

I press my lips together, and the soft thud of the door closing behind me sends a shiver through my body.

Once we're alone, he grabs my waist with an ease and confidence that makes me want to untuck his towel.

"I have to admit... that cape is incredibly sexy. I fear you might have woven me a new fantasy. And you can't imagine how many times I've pictured you in that uniform..." he trails off.

He steers me to the side, pinning me against the kitchen counter. The top edge of the marble slab presses into my back as he kisses me, and the purpose of my visit is forgotten.

"I have to leave soon," I gasp.

He drags his lips down the slope of my neck. "How soon?"

I push him off gently, palms flat to his naked chest, and wince. "Too soon for any of that."

With a chuckle, he runs his hands down my arms to lace our fingers. "I'll be good, then."

Now that we're together, I'm almost sure Devi was mistaken. This man can't be planning to marry someone else.

"I have a question. And I don't want you to spare my feelings, alright? I need to know the whole truth."

His brows furrow. "I'm all ears."

"I heard there's a summer wedding in the works... And that's it's going to be a *royal* wedding." My heartbeat pounds in my temples, dizzying me, but Aidan doesn't look as guilty as I feared. He even smiles.

"Oh, Songbird. I'm not getting married." Our fingers still entwined, he kisses the back of my hand. "Unless you're hinting for a proposal, because if you are, I'm in," he adds in jest, the off-hand comment painting my cheeks scarlet.

"So it was all just a rumor? There's no royal wedding in the works?"

He draws in a sharp breath, his jaw slightly askew. "Now, I didn't say *that*."

I wait for him to elaborate, but his uncomfortable grimace doesn't relent. "Willow?"

His relieved sigh confirms my hunch, and he nods.

"But she didn't say anything about it." I'm flabbergasted to learn this, truly.

"She doesn't know."

By Thanatos...

"What?" My mind flashes back to my best friend, the sweet pixie-like woman who's been vociferating against the rules of high society for months now. Even though I agreed with most of her arguments, it was a bit jarring at times to hear about injustice from the mouth of a privileged princess. The threat of famine that would condemn most common Fae I've grown up with to work their fingers bloody in the mines in exchange for a meager salary was more vivid to me than Willow's fear of destitution and having to live below a certain status if she chose to blaze her own path.

Sometimes, I couldn't connect to her philosophical crusades, but this is different.

"How could you not tell her?" I blurt out without thinking.

"My father forbade it and sealed my promise with his magic, but don't worry. Ezra is going to break the news better than I ever could."

"Why would Ezra—" I pause, my heart in my throat. "Wait. Willow is engaged to *Ezra*?"

"It's not official, so please keep it to yourself, but yes."

I would have *never* imagined.

"Are you...upset?" he adds quietly.

I shake off the dumbfounded look. "No, just surprised. Why would I be upset about that?"

He dips his head to kiss me again. "I'll write to you."

I open my mouth to argue, but Aidan tucks a strand of hair behind my ear.

"Don't worry. I'll use the same spell as before to conceal my handwriting. No one will be able to figure it out, I promise."

He shouldn't make such promises. Not in the world we live in.

I stop by the bibliotheca on my way out, my pen trembling over the parchment as I scrawl Devi a note with only Ezra's name on it. She's clever enough to piece together the rest. The scrap of paper weighs nothing, yet it feels like I'm writing a love letter to someone else.

I cheated my way into this school, and now I've betrayed Aidan.

CHAPTER 25
MESSAGE IN A BOTTLE
SONGBIRD

"Tell me more! Please! How were the princesses? Are they as elegant and beautiful in person as they seem in the brochures?" My cousin, Marjorie, asks me, rummaging through my travel bag like a pirate scouring for treasure.

"Not at all. They're just like us, really."

Kiro snickers from the door. "Just more spoiled and snobbish. And rich enough to do whatever they want."

"Shush," Marge scolds her twin.

"It's nice to have you back, Beth. I'll be back before sundown," Kiro says with a boyish grin.

"Lots of new friends, eh?" I quip.

He gives a dismissive shrug. "The guys from the new school are alright. Mum told me I could hang out with them if it didn't interfere with my schoolwork."

Marge's nose wrinkles. "Mum felt guilty for leaving us to our own devices. I just wish she didn't have to work in the mines all summer."

"You know she has to work while the weather's good enough to allow for safe travel on the mountains." The miners hire a ton of city moths to chisel the gems, and while it's hard work, it's a decent pay.

"But she could find a safer job here," Marge says, gnawing at her bottom lip.

With Aunt Paola's salary, along with the money I'll earn as a clerk in the Winter royal bibliotheca every summer before I graduate, the twins won't have to quit school, and maybe even go on to the Tundra university, Thanatos willing.

"Oh, this is divine," Marge holds my academy corset to her chest, her big round eyes full of admiration, her chatterbox attitude drowning the constant *ploc, ploc, ploc* of the ceiling leak in the corner of our bedroom.

I grin. "Be careful with that."

I left most of my uniforms at the academy but brought along the fanciest one. If I get expelled, I can sell it for a nice price. It won't make much of a consolation prize, but it'll be something.

After months of handling invaluable books and having my pick of round-the-clock, all-you-can-eat buffets, it's humbling to be home and dealing with the day-to-day reality of being poor again.

"Are you excited to start work tomorrow? I heard tons of lords visit the palace bibliotheca every day," Marge says.

"Sure," I mumble, my mind elsewhere.

She pokes my arm with one finger. "What's wrong with you? I thought you'd be thrilled to recount your adventures, but you've barely said a word about school. Do you miss your drop-dead-gorgeous fiancé?" She clasps her hands together and lets herself fall back onto the mattress, her brown pigtails sprawled on either side of her youthful face. "Oh, are you in love with him, Beth? Your prince? It's so romantic. I wish I had a prince."

I can't bring myself to shatter her sweet, unrealistic romantic notions. She just turned thirteen. I'd rather she remains a kid for a little while longer.

Aidan's smile pops into my mind. "My prince is very handsome," I say, skirting the truth.

"And you love him?"

Air whistles out of my lungs, and I look down at my hands. The memory of Aidan's fingers entwined with mine is vivid enough to hurt. "I do."

Marjorie crashes into my side and hugs me tight. "Oh, I'm so glad."

We cook dinner together as we have countless times and eat once Kiro gets home. Afterward, the twins retreat to their bedroom to study. We usually all share a room, but their mother relinquished her small bedroom on the other side of the thin partition wall during her absence.

The familiarity of it all forms a raw ache in my chest. I clean out the bedroom leak bucket, each of the tiny bumps and dents in its surface telling stories of the years of use. The water sloshes out into the sink, and I wipe away the droplets that cling to the sides, the old habits coming back to me in an instant.

The academy was such a different world. A different life, almost.

Aidan fills my thoughts as I tidy the minuscule kitchen. My family's entire life could fit into the little cabin he built for fun in the gardens. The contrast stings—his luxuries, our struggles, and the impossibility of my fantasies.

Despite the promises I made to myself, my planned marriage to Zeke would ensure both of my cousins a life they've only dreamed of. But at what cost?

The click of the latch pulls me out of my dark thoughts, and I press my lips together.

Papa cracks open the door, the hinges whining from the cold and humidity, and slips inside. "Welcome home, Lizzie," he says, resting his work binder on the hall table.

I scurry over to hang his jacket and peck his cheek. "Thank you, Papa." The uniform smells of oil and winter air, a familiar scent that grounds me to reality. He's munching on his bottom lip the way he does when he's stressed, and I ask, "Do you want some stew? I could reheat supper if you want."

The tensed lines of his brows soften. "Oh, it's nice to have you home. But if you don't mind, I'm going to go straight to bed. I'm exhausted."

I grimace, hesitating. After wracking my brain all day about this siren business, I don't think I can wait any longer. "There's actually something I wanted to talk to you about."

I hand him the cup of hot cider I'd prepared, the steam curling between us, and pull out a chair for him at the kitchen table.

He sits slowly, his lips curled down, and wraps his hands tightly around the cup. The warm amber glow from the kitchen lamp deepens the lines on his face. "You look worried, Lizzie. What's wrong?"

My mouth is dry, and my prepared speech isn't quite as natural as I'd hoped. "I sang last night. For the gala Willow organized."

"That's... nice." He averts his gaze. "Can you do the shopping after work tomorrow? Take Kiro and Marge with you. We need wood, flour, and a bit of witch hazel powder to keep the spiders in check."

"I sang. And people *loved* it," I continue, unsettled by his blatant attempt to switch the subject.

"Mm. I'm not surprised. Did Marge iron out your new uniform? I asked her to."

And I see it then. The avoidance. The guilt.

By Thanatos and all his reapers. Devi was right.

"Papa..." My voice cracks.

The cup shakes in his hands, and he sets it down on the table with a heavy sigh.

"Papa. A girl at school figured it out. She knows about my... song." The word feels horrible, blasphemous.

I have a siren's song. *Me.*

"But when did you even find out about this? Did something happen while you were singing?" he breathes, his voice thin and strained. "Is your song something you could... feel?"

Tears spill over my lids, hot and unrelenting. "No. I had no idea I even had one. Not until she told me."

Before I can process it, his hand curls around mine like a snow serpent guarding its eggs. His voice drops, urgent and sharp. "Promise me you'll never sing again. As long as you don't, there's no way for them to tell you're one of them—at least, none that's widely known. If you never sing again, you'll be fine."

"Fine?" I croak.

The words crush me, each syllable laced with a contempt that twists in my chest. I want to cry, to scream. The idea of never singing again feels like a death sentence. I'd rather cut off my own arm than make that promise.

Papa sighs. "Oh, I'm so sorry, my Lizzie. But not singing is a small price to pay compared to being exiled, shunned, or worse—locked away forever."

The air between us feels too thick to breathe.

"Why didn't you tell me?"

He looks away, his lips pressing into a thin line. For a moment, I think he won't answer, but then his shoulders slump. "Your mother asked me not to. She didn't want you to think ill of her—not if it could be avoided."

"Who was she, really?"

"She was as I've always told you. Brave, strong, and absolutely lovely."

He rubs a hand down his face, the gesture tired and worn, before he stands. His chair creaks against the wood, the sound echoing in the quiet kitchen.

I stay silent, my mind racing as he crosses the room to the magical chest where he keeps his most important documents. He hesitates for a moment, his hand hovering over the lock, then presses his thumb against it and mutters the combination. The metallic click reverberates through the room.

My breath catches as he retrieves a sealed letter from the lid's flap pocket. "She gave me this for you," he says, turning it over in his hands like it's a most cherished treasure. "In case you inherited too much of her blood after all. She made me promise not to read it."

I stare at the letter, my chest tightening. "But you always said she died suddenly."

"Go to work tomorrow. Do the shopping. When I get home, we'll talk. Alright?"

I nod, almost tearing the letter from his grasp, the ball of saliva in my mouth too thick to swallow. My heart pounds as I retreat to my bedroom, close the door, and crawl under the covers.

Hands trembling, I rub my puffy eyes, desperate to hold it together, to keep the sobs clawing at my chest at bay. But as I unfold the letter, my resolve cracks. The first words blur through the tears I can no longer stop.

How fair is it that this letter, the only tangible piece of my dead mother that exists, was kept from me all this time? If not for Devi's meddling, would Papa have simply ripped it to shreds?

I never even knew her hand.

Dear Elizabeth,

I'm terribly sorry that I can't be with you on such a confusing, momentous day, but a reaper will come to me within days, I'm afraid. And your beloved Papa was always better in a crisis than I was.

Contrary to what we told the family, we didn't meet in Taiga after he survived a shipwreck in the northern skerries. I collected him from the waves and escorted him to shore. It was love at first sight, my dear, and I decided to leave my old life behind.

Don't resent him. We agreed this is the story you should be told until you are old enough to hear the truth—or until your Sea Fae blood manifests.

The light of my heart, my wonderful little girl, please know our kind isn't as wretched as you've heard. The siren's song our goddess Melpomene gave you is a gift. And like most god-given powers, it comes with great responsibility. We live in a harsh world that has forgotten how beautiful a siren's song can be. A world of quick judgments and misconstrued fears. Were you to be discovered, to be identified as a Sea mutt... It ices my blood right in my veins, just thinking about it.

Sirens are punished for the magnetic pull we have on men, but it's not something we can entirely control. You should always be able to tell the good ones from the bad, so trust your instincts, my darling. Be careful of going too close to the sea, as it would only strengthen your song. To write down any more about where I came from or the secrets of our blood would be too much of a risk, but know I love you even in death. With enough practice, I know you will find a way to use your song as a blessing to the world, not a weapon.

I only wish I could have heard you sing, my Beth. I'm sure your voice is magnificent.

Your loving mother,
Melissa

That's it, then. I'm a siren. Aidan never loved me. He never meant to cheat in the trials and lure me into his gravity. It was all a spell, an enchantment of my own making. And if anyone finds out, I won't only be expelled from the academy, but executed for seducing the Crown Prince of the Summerlands.

CHAPTER 26
ROYAL SEAL
SONGBIRD

The summer break both flies by and drags on, weeks blurring together with studies and grueling shifts at the bibliotheca. Between helping patrons and shelving books, I comb through volumes for any mention of sirens, my thoughts constantly straying to Aidan.

"Ahem." Papa clears his throat, pulling me from my reading at the breakfast table. I look up to see him holding a pile of letters, his brow raised expectantly. "I checked the mail," he says, giving the stack a small shake. "Look what I found."

He fans the letters over the table. In the middle of the pile, a folded piece of plain parchment causes my heart to skip a beat. The folded letter is sealed with a blank dot of wax, just like all the others Aidan sent me. A heavy blush taints my cheeks at the prospect of reading another of his sweet, passion-filled, and frankly erotic notes.

Guilt for not writing back creeps up my spine as I pick it up, but a high-pitched gasp shakes me out of my reverie.

"Is that a royal seal? By the spindle, that paper is so fancy. Who is it from?" Marge climbs to her knees on her chair, leaning over the table to look at another letter, this one glimmering with gold dust and adorning the royal Summer seal.

"Language, Marjorie," Papa sighs.

She grips the side of the table and offers him a sheepish grin. "Sorry, Uncle Paul."

By Thanatos. The only other time I'd received such a fancy missive was when I got my official invitation to the academy's admission trials.

What if they'd finally connected the dots? Worse, what if Aidan, tired of waiting for an answer, had done something rash?

Papa's thumb lingers on the royal seal, rubbing over it with fascination. When he finally hands it over, my stomach sinks. There's no escaping this. "Well, Lizzie? Tell us who it's from."

My fingers tremble as I tear open the seal, the crisp parchment wrinkling under my touch. My eyes dart to the signature at the bottom, and I exhale, the weight on my chest lifting. "Willow Summers," I breathe, relief washing over me.

Papa's eyes brighten at the name, and he settles back in his chair. "Well? Tell us more."

I discreetly slip Aidan's note between my thighs, hiding it from view.

"Yes, tell us," Kiro chimes in, his voice lively with curiosity.

Marge nods quickly. "Please."

I glance at the three of them, their focus unwavering, and carefully edit out a few details before reading a few curated sentences of the letter aloud.

Dearest Beth,

I have dreadful news to share. My father insists I marry before the next semester even starts.

These antiquated traditions are suffocating. I wish I had the power to simply refuse, to choose my own path, but instead, I'm bound by my father's will. He doesn't care about my happiness. All that matters to him is making the right political match and solidifying our family's influence over the continent. It's so unfair, Beth, and I feel trapped, but my parents have made it crystal clear that my emotions and feelings do not count.

If I have to suffer through this wedding, I want you to be my kindred.

Please, please, please, say yes. As my kindred, you will be my guest of honor. I'll arrange for someone to escort you to Eterna, and we can return to the academy together after the celebrations.

Anxiously awaiting your answer,
Willow
P.S. Please burn this letter after reading.

Papa sucks in a sharp breath. "It's such an honor, Lizzie. You have to go."

I carefully fold Willow's letter back, trying to ignore the sick feeling in my stomach. "Of course. Willow's my best friend."

His chair creaks as he stands, the motion abrupt. "I'll get some paper so you can write your answer. I'll send it through the royal courier to avoid any unnecessary delays."

I force a smile, nodding, and wait for him to return with a pen and some of our finest paper. As I begin to write my response to Willow's missive, affirming my support and pledging to be there for her, my cheeks flush with an uncomfortable heat. Papa's right. I can't tell anyone about my Sea Fae blood. I have to act as though nothing is wrong. No one else can know but Devi. And I will never sing again.

I'm in too deep to back out.

Once the trip is arranged, I retreat to my room and shut the door behind me, the wood cool against my back. Alone at last, I unfold Aidan's letter.

> DEAREST SONGBIRD,
> I CAN'T EXPRESS IN WORDS HOW MUCH I MISS YOU, OR HOW DESPERATELY I LONG FOR A RESPONSE. BUT I CHOOSE TO BELIEVE THAT YOU ARE NOT YET FREE TO SEND A LETTER. I HOPE YOU FIND SOME SMALL COMFORT IN RECEIVING MINE, AND IF I AM WRONG IN THAT BELIEF, PLEASE ACCEPT MY SINCEREST APOLOGIES.
> EZRA'S AND WILLOW'S WEDDING IS ALL SET FOR THE END OF THE WEEK. THE SERVANTS HAVE ALREADY BEGUN DECORATING THE ETERNAL HALLS. IT'S SHAPING UP TO BE THE WEDDING OF THE CENTURY.
> I WISH WITH ALL MY HEART THAT YOU COULD ATTEND. I BURN FOR YOU.
> WONDER BOY

Not real.

Deep wrinkles form on the letter as I press it to my chest, my heart hammering. I miss him, too, more than I care to admit, but I can't be with him anymore—not after what I've learned. He doesn't truly love me; he's trapped under my spell, ensnared by an enchantment I never meant to weave.

I stole his right to choose, violated his consent, and it's killing me.

I feared the whole kindred business might be a ploy to lure me there, using Willow as a cover. I thought Aidan might have confided in her about us, but from the sound of it, he doesn't even know I'll be attending. A Summer royal wedding might seem romantic, but it's the worst possible place to try to convince him that we should walk away from each other.

How can I face him—or explain why we can't be together—without spilling my most dangerous secret yet?

CHAPTER 27
STARLIGHT
WONDER BOY

Willow folds her cards with a huff. "Well played. I'm heading to bed."

"It's early," I argue, eager to keep her mind on the card game and off more difficult subjects. "You could still whip my ass."

Ezra, Willow, and I have been playing in the drawing room for about an hour. Our tournaments are usually competitive and fun, but I can see Willow's heart is not in it. The soon-to-be blended family gathered for some pre-wedding strategy on the eve of the rehearsal dinner, our parents huddled at the back of the room, probably still squabbling over the guest list and the exact amount of Willow's dowry.

"Nah. I need my beauty sleep. Goodnight, light of my life." Willow pecks Ezra on the cheek, and I cover my mouth to mask a grimace.

"Sweet slumber, flame of my heart," he shoots right back, like it's normal.

"Ugh." A cold, oily shiver rocks me from head to toe. "I'll never get used to this. It's a bit much, no?"

"Why? We're getting married the day after tomorrow." Ezra pats my arm in a patronizing manner, smirking as though his new married status will somehow hold him above me, but a flicker of understanding passes in his cider-affected eyes. "It'll be alright, boo." He smacks a big, drunken kiss on my temple. "Your sister and I are going to be great friends, and that's more than most royals get."

I stare down at the dark liquid swirling at the bottom of my glass, his promise not quite as heartwarming as I'd wish it to be. The unease I've been wrestling with ever since I caught wind of this engagement is somehow magnified by the cider.

Hephaistos knows how emotionally draining family affairs can be.

"Will you stand with me, as my kindred witness?" Ezra blurts out.

My brow furrows. "I thought your brother—"

"Ethan wanted me to pick Elio to alleviate any rumors that our family is not as tightly-knit as it should be, but it's my decision. The kid offered to play for the ceremony instead. He can't do both, so that'll smooth out appearances."

Royal wedding ceremonies are flashy public affairs, where the bride and groom each select someone they trust to witness their union.

"I'm honored," I whisper.

He purses his lips in a humorous pout. "Now, boo, don't cry."

"I love you, mate."

"Love you, too." His gaze flicks to the ground for a split second. "Willow is keeping it secret, but she asked Beth to be her kindred."

My melancholic thoughts screech to a halt, my heart already racing in my chest at the mere mention of her name. "Wait. Beth is coming *here* for the wedding?"

He shuffles the cards, taking his sweet time to answer. "Yes. She's supposed to arrive tomorrow, and in only two days, you two lovebirds will be standing on an altar together. In case you wanted to make this a double wedding," he says in jest.

"Who's officiating?"

"I asked for my grandmother. She should be here soon."

I arch a brow. "The Old Queen?"

"The one and only."

Mabel lives in the new world. She's the legendary widow of the Mist King, revered for her role in ending the war and stopping her monstrous husband from seizing power over the entire continent—yet feared nonetheless.

She's a witch, one of the last remnants of the Red Forest's ancient roots, predating the realm's rebuilding. Reds now harbor a profound disdain for the old ways, favoring brute strength over mystical rituals. Old Queen Mabel had three daughters with her second husband, one of whom is Ezra's mother. But ever since Siobhan Lightbringer's death, the powerful matriarch hasn't been keen on public appearances. "She'd never agree to do it."

"Blessed Flame. I was joking," Ezra scoffs.

"I know you were, but humor me. Would Mabel go for it, given the chance?"

"I have no idea. Probably. Mab's a maverick, and she's not loyal to your father. Or mine."

I shake my head from side to side, slowly coming back to my senses. "Beth still hasn't answered my letters."

Ezra gulps down the rest of his wine. "Concentrate on getting the girl, yes? You can marry her later."

"What are you two whispering about?" A smooth, velvety voice teases.

Mabel enters, her weathered eyes gleaming with mischief, the witch looking smaller than I remembered.

Ezra's face lights up, and he leaps to his feet. "Grandmab!"

Her presence fills the room, a bite of power that spreads like spicy honey—potent, yet oddly comforting.

"My starlight. You look even more handsome than the last time I saw you," she beams, her long white hair twisted into a bun at the nape of her neck.

Ezra crushes her into his embrace. "Now, you're just stroking my ego," he chuckles.

Mabel shifts her weight, both hands resting on the pommel of her cane, and turns her attention to me. "Aidan. You've grown up, too, young phoenix."

I offer her a respectful bow. "It's an honor, as always, Mabel."

"Aunt Kerri!" Ezra exclaims, pulling the woman trailing behind Mabel into a hug next.

"You remember my eldest daughter, Kerrigan?" Mabel says for my benefit.

I hesitate, my mind racing. "I'm sorry to say, but I don't think I've had the pleasure."

"Last I saw you, Kerri, I was eye-level with your belly button, I'd say," Ezra interjects, laughter ringing in his voice.

"That's right," Kerrigan replies, a smile tugging at the corners of her mouth.

"Is it true that you and my father were engaged before he married your sister?" he asks.

"Yes, I was the eldest," Kerrigan acknowledges with a wince. "But your mother was a much stronger Fae, and terribly beautiful, so your father preferred her to me."

"Siobhan would have loved to be here," Mabel breathes, her gaze flickering to her eldest daughter, the two women silently united in grief.

"Oh, I don't know about that," Ezra croaks, his voice thick with the weight of a pain I can't fully understand.

The circumstances surrounding his mother's suicide remain a mystery to me, Ezra clamming up whenever I've tried to broach the subject.

Mabel and Kerrigan exchange a heavy glance. Family reunions always pick at scabs that aren't quite healed, and I shift uncomfortably, feeling as though I've overstayed my welcome. If only I could slip away unnoticed…

Kerrigan's eyes fill with tears as she braces a hand on Ezra's shoulder. "Your mother loved you, Ezra. She only did what she did because she was sick."

"Sick, right." Ezra snorts, his voice dripping with sarcasm as he raises his wine glass to her. "You dodged a bullet, Kerri. And we all know that's the truth."

Ethan slides off his seat at the back of the room, heading toward us.

I offer the three women a loose grin and wrap an arm around Ezra's shoulders. "The groom's a little nervous, I'm afraid." I squeeze his upper arm, trying to instill some much-needed sense into him. His father might hear, for Hephaistos' sake. "You've got to ease up on the cider, mate," I breathe in his ear.

"Aidan takes his kindred duties very seriously." He shrugs me off, but Mabel steps in before I can react and stands on her tiptoes to cup his cheeks.

"Don't worry, my starlight. One day, the time will come for you to shine."

"But not soon enough to stop this wedding," Ezra grumbles.

"Alas, no." Mabel wraps her bony arm around Ezra, ushering him toward the exit and away from Ethan. "Now, let's take a tour of this castle, so you can tell me everything that's on your mind."

They walk down the length of the room, thick as thieves, and I'm glad he's got someone else in his corner. Hephaistos knows, when shit hits the fan with his father, which is bound to happen at some point, he's going to need as many allies as he can get.

CHAPTER 28

SMALL FAVORS

SONGBIRD

The sprite that fetched me from home shows me into a single guest room thrice as big as my family's apartments. The soft taupe of the walls compliments a spotless white marble floor, lavish art works integrating splashes of color and romance to the decor. A painting of a young man sketching his beloved by a twinkling blue lake, both of them naked and aroused, sends a rush of heat to my cheeks.

The last rays of sunlight spill through large windows, illuminating a bouquet of fresh lavender on the dresser. The bed is piled high with cushions, each adorned with intricate vine patterns that form the Summer's royal crest. I draw back the drapes to reveal a stunning view of the waterfall streaming down to the Eternal River below, its silhouette snaking away in the distance.

Despite having seen countless paintings of these gardens, the beauty feels alien, making me acutely aware of the faint scuff marks in the soles of my shoes or the loose threads in the button holes of my jacket.

The tall, free-standing mirror in the corner has been warded off, unsuitable for travel, the runes covering the corners of the glass blending with the wood moldings of the frame.

"This is your room for the wedding, Miss Snow. Please change, and when you're ready, follow this firefly to the chapel. The royal family is already there, working out the kinks of the reception. They're expecting you in half an hour for the rehearsal."

I set my travel bag on the bed, awestruck by the opulence of it all. I thought the academy was luxurious, but this is something else.

"Miss Snow?" the sprite repeats.

"Yes." I clear my throat, feeling self-conscious about how frayed and unkempt I must appear. "I'll be there. Thank you."

A shuddering breath escapes me, and I quickly slip into the black dress I brought with me, acutely aware that it's inappropriate for the setting. Here in the Summerlands, it's probably more suited for a funeral than a wedding.

Almost as soon as I'm done changing, Devi slips into my room.

She's not wearing a dress, exactly, but a shimmering, hand-beaded gold bodysuit. The criss-cross design creates a striking, lattice-like effect across her body, leaving her navel and hips bare while revealing the shape of her breasts, with the nipple area covered by a solid gold underlay. The delicate freckles on her collarbone add a flair of mystique to her presence, and I blush all over.

"By the spindle. What are you doing here?" I breathe.

She presses the door closed quietly behind her. "They told me you would be here. Is that what you're wearing for the rehearsal?" She wrinkles her nose at my plain black cocktail dress.

"It's all I have. Isn't the bride supposed to be the center of attention anyway?" I say in a scalding tone, my jaw slightly askew at the sheer sensuality rolling off of her.

No one should have such a flawless body. I'm especially annoyed by the heat in my gut, once again caught in the snare of her powers, once again a lame black duck forced into a line of golden Fae ducklings.

"Moth, this is a royal wedding. It's meant to be a spectacle. We're not expected to go to bed before dawn tonight. Why do you think tomorrow's ceremony is set for dusk?"

I turn away from her, my hand clutching the skirt of my dress. "I have no clue what I'm doing here, honestly. Or why you're in my room. Or how anyone thought it was a good idea for me to come—"

"Breathe. Here." She barrels to the window and grabs a fist of one of the lavender silk curtains.

The whole thing starts to unspool under my awestruck gaze and levitates toward me, replacing my current dress, which flakes away into nothingness. The threads weave into a floor-length evening gown with a twisted, scandalous strapless bustier. I draw in a deep breath. The fabric is so light in my grip that it might as well be liquid, the lavender hue twinkling with hints of silver.

Devi nods proudly at her own work. "That'll do nicely."

"What are you doing here, Devi?"

Her mouth opens slightly, and the corners twist into a devilish grin. "I need another favor."

"Bite me," I bark, one hand tugging at the top of the dress to see if I can cover myself up a little more, terrified the neckline might slip straight past my breasts.

"So spirited today. Aren't you enjoying the beauty of the Summer Court? I thought you were into warm, long, *hard* Summer nights," she adds, wiggling her brows.

"Stop it."

"I can't help it. You're crimson, and I've barely said anything." With a sigh, she spins my hair into an elaborate up-do, the strands all but sighing at her touch. "I don't blame you. We all have a weak spot. Dark, broody, and emotionally unavailable men is mine." Her gaze falls to my hand, and she clicks her tongue. "Stop fidgeting. The dress will not fail you. Oh, I forgot the shoes." She crouches down and motions for me to sit down on the velvet bench at the foot of the bed, but I refuse to budge.

"Why do you even care?"

"We're partners now. Whether you like it or not." She weaves a pair of silver stilettos that wrap around my ankles and make the arches of my feet scream in discomfort.

"We're not *partners*. You're blackmailing me."

"Details." She waves my comment away. "Look, this weekend is not just about a wedding. The news that my grandsire is dying has breached the confines of the Secret Springs. The healers gave him a month to live, at best, and everybody is whispering about it. My step-mother, Freya, is making a play to succeed him instead of me."

My eyes narrow at the onslaught of information. "And how could I possibly help you?"

"I need you to slip this"—she says, reaching inside her bra to retrieve a small, oval flask—"into her drink."

"Are you nuts? No!"

"Relax, it's harmless. Just a little something to loosen her tongue. She's probably trying to line up her next husband and secure alliances over the weekend. This potion will just make her more... honest."

My fingers shake around the small translucent flask. "Your grandfather is not even dead, yet. Is she so eager to remarry that she can't even wait for him to die?"

"You think that'll stop her?" she scoffs. "Freya is not powerful enough to win the throne in a challenge, but she's a beloved queen consort and excels at politics. She's going to try to convince a handful of royals that I'm too young for the task, and that she should be made queen until I'm older. She'll even promise to abdicate when the time comes, but the exact timeline will be pushed and pushed indefinitely."

"Is that something a Spring royal can do? Abdicate?"

She rolls her eyes as though my ignorance of such things annoys her to no end. "Rarely, but yes. The Winter crown can't be survived, so you've assumed it's the same for us, but Winter is actually an exception."

"I heard the Red circlet prefers to be claimed in bloodshed, cut right off the head of its predecessor," I mumble.

She gives a sharp incline of the head. "Yes. Reds don't like to mess around. If only it was so simple in Spring."

And she's not kidding.

A shadow passes over her beautiful face, her cleverness and cunning lurking beneath the freckled, polished veneer. "Most royals are terrified of change. None of them truly want me on the throne, even though I've earned it. I'm too outspoken, too rash, too modern. They see my power as a threat to their boring old traditions. The Eternal Chalice allows the reigning monarchs a say in who gets to rule over Spring next, and I just want to prevent Freya from getting too much of a head start."

I try to hand the flask back, the glass slippery in my grip. "Anyone could do this. Why don't you ask Iris?"

"Iris doesn't know how to keep her mouth shut, and she's Freya's niece. I need someone with enough wit to keep track of it all, and yet not enough skin in the game to jeopardize my plans. Someone with enough access to matter, but who will mostly blend with the crowd and not attract too much attention. That's you, my little mermaid."

"You need a sucker who can't say no or rat you out, you mean."

"That too."

"And how many favors am I supposed to grant for you to be satisfied?" I ask in a fake sugary tone.

"As many as I need."

My teeth grit together. "You think yourself above them, but you're blackmailing me into doing your bidding, just as desperate to be queen."

She begins walking away, still nonchalant about it all. "Are you done whining? It's only a small favor. I'll swing by your room later. Until then, we shouldn't be seen in public together."

"No problem here," I shout at her retreating back, tucking the flask into my cleavage, a little pocket of its exact size fashioned right into the underlining of my dress.

How am I supposed to get rid of her?

If she tells on me, I'm done.

I draw in a deep breath and follow the firefly meant to guide me to the wedding chapel, adjusting my posture and strides to account for the ridiculously high heels Devi made me.

My steps grow shorter and shorter as I enter the ballroom through one of the many side entrances. The firefly darts across the room to the chapel on the other side, faltering as it reaches its final destination. The two doors stand ajar, marked by white columns entwined with vines, mosaics on either side depicting the Flame of Fate. Dozens of tables are elegantly set with white orchid centerpieces, crisp white cloths, and gold cutlery—but my gaze is drawn to the ceiling.

My skin tingles. One of the most famous art pieces in history, Fall of the Mist King, is here, stretching high above me. There's one such mural in each of the first kingdoms, though the Summerlands version is larger and more beautiful than I'd ever imagined. I've studied many of the scenes depicted up there, but seeing it all at once is breathtaking. It doesn't even feel real.

I spin to take it all in, my heart beating in my throat, and come to an abrupt stop.

A precious stone wall scintillates at the very back of the ballroom, composed of squares of emerald, onyx, amethyst, ruby, opal, diamond, and garnet—one jewel for each of the eight kingdoms—even the former rainbow moonstones of the Mist, now outlawed everywhere but here. The double doors are shut, held in place with a long piece of iron.

The Hall of Eternity lies behind that wall, the eight thrones of Faerie contained within its halls, the chalice of power at their center.

A soft tap on my shoulder sends my already racing heart into a frenzy, and I gasp.

"Lady Snow. Oh, how I've missed you," Ezra says, leaning in to peck my cheeks.

"Ezra!" I grip his arm out of instinct, nearly toppling over from the jump scare and the heels. "You snuck up on me."

His soft laugh warms the space between us. "I didn't mean to, I swear. You looked...bewitched by the sight of the Eternal Halls." He points to the back wall. "Ask Aidan for a peek, later. It's worth it." He ushers me toward the entrance of the chapel, his hand resting on my shoulder blade for an instant. "You look absolutely divine. We should have asked you to sing for the ceremony."

My eyes widen and my gut cramps at the mere possibility of singing—perhaps even being mobbed and arrested—in the *oh-so-grand* Summerlands palace. "Please don't."

"Are you ready to meet the Summer Queen?"

"As ready as I'll ever be."

He elbows my side just as we cross the threshold. "Your future mother-in-law."

I slap his arm. "Shush."

Inside the chapel, rows and rows of golden pews are arranged in the same fashion as they are in the academy's chapel, though in a much grander setting. Bouquets of white orchids cascade to the ground at the end of each row.

A glass dome opens to the sky above, while the checkered windows reveal the vast scope of the Lunar Cascades—white terraces made of minerals that make them appear as though covered in fresh snow. They spill down the hillside in tiers, stretching far beyond the castle walls. The half-moon-shaped pools glow against the rugged landscape in strange, milky hues. Each terrace blends softly from blue to white, as if sculpted from clouds and ice.

A few bright stars pierce the veil of twilight, the sky slowly darkening to a deep, midnight blue.

My breath stutters. I can't imagine what it must feel like to get married in such a place, let alone own it, and Ezra's cheeky comment echoes in my brain.

One day, Aidan will get married here too. To a *real* princess. And he'll reign over all of this with his queen. They'll take moonlit strolls hand in hand along the Eternal River, gasping for breath as he traces the lines of her body in the basins. Every day will be spent at the top of the Fae food chain, feasting on the riches of our world while the Wintermere commoners barely survive another freezing winter.

No matter how addictive the fantasy is, the lucky, oblivious woman won't be me. It couldn't be.

"Come on, Lady Snow," Ezra warns quietly. "You'll have ample time to admire the view later."

I force my eyes away from the windows, where the Summer Queen, Willow, and a rugged sprite with green moss growing in the creases of his skin and lichen-filled wings wait for us at the front of the chapel.

"Beth!" Willow saunters closer to greet me, her long brown hair braided into a crown atop her head, her form-fitting white satin dress hugging her curves. "I'm so glad you're here." She hooks her arm through mine and tugs me up the aisle. "This is my mother, Queen Thera Summers."

"Your Majesty." I curtsy as low as I can manage in my heels, my tongue parched and dry.

"Welcome, Elizabeth. My daughter's told me so much about you," she replies quickly, her affable smile catching me by surprise.

The warm greeting chokes me, leaving only the heavy, pasty aftertaste of my secrets on my tongue.

Against all odds, she doesn't mind that you're a moth.

But she'd have you arrested if she knew you were a siren.

And she definitely has no idea you're secretly fucking her son.

Willow's eyes dart down to my cleavage. "By the Flame, who weaved that dress?"

I look down at the gown. "Devi Eros."

"Why? Are you two friends now?" Willow asks, clearly dumbfounded.

"It's a long story." I force a polite smile on my face and widen my eyes at Willow, trying to convey a loud *I'll tell you about it later* with just my eyes.

"Ah, Mabel. Welcome," Thera says, walking toward the entrance to greet a short, old woman.

The infamous Mabel Bloodsinger tiptoes over to us, grand despite her small stature. "Thera." She acknowledges the Summer Queen with a small head tilt, gripping the carved raven forming the tip of her cane with both hands. "You, young bride. Let me see you." She angles her body toward Willow.

"My grandson is a handful, but you look poised for the challenge." She throws a playful wink at Ezra before patting Willow's arm with her small hand. "The shortest women make the most interesting queens, my dear. Remember that." She chuckles, clearly including herself in that assessment, and Willow grins.

"Yes, we do."

Mabel's cunning gaze finally lands on me, and I shudder. With just one look, her bite of power lulls me into a waking dream. I dig my nails into my palms, desperate to anchor myself against her magic. It feels as though she's clawing inside my skull, prying away all my secrets.

"And who are you?" Her hazelnut eyes gleam with a crimson spark.

"Elizabeth Snow. I'm Willow's kindred."

She smiles at me—not the same smile she gave Thera or Willow. This one reaches the corners of her eyes, brimming with both joy and curiosity. "I have a feeling you and I will get along perfectly."

I press my tongue to the roof of my mouth.

She knows. I don't know how, but in one glance, this woman sees the truths of my blood and lineage—and appears thrilled by it. Yet, when her attention shifts back to the Summer Queen, a strange calm washes over me. It's as if her gaze carried both an unspoken acknowledgment of my true nature and a silent promise to keep it hidden.

"Mabel, can I discuss something with you in private?" Thera asks.

The two women step aside for a private chat while the rest of us huddle closer together.

"Who's that?" I ask Ezra, pointing to the young girl who sneaked into the chapel behind Mabel.

He rolls his eyes. "Don't look at her. She's so boring, and she's going to want to come over—hey, Brit. This is Elizabeth Snow, Willow's kindred."

"Are you a relative of Mabel?" I ask.

"No, I'm Aidan's date, actually."

Wonderful. Being in Aidan's home, it was inevitable that we'd run into each other sooner or later. Still, my body warms at the mere mention of him.

Even though I know he couldn't have asked me, it still stings that he chose some snobbish, beautiful blonde to accompany him to Willow's wedding. His last letter implied he was unaware of his sister's plan to name me as her kindred, but surely he knows by now.

Willow shifts restlessly beside us. "And my dear brother left you to your own devices. Typical," she laments.

Why is she even here? No one else's date is here; only the wedding party.

Thera and Mabel rejoin our circle, and we spend a few minutes discussing the cascades, rivers, gardens, and waterfalls—the royal equivalent of small talk.

"We should really get started," Mabel announces.

"Yes, but we're still one short for the rehearsal." Thera presses her lips together, clearly annoyed.

"Are we waiting for the Summer King?" I ask quietly.

Willow shakes her head. "Oh no, my father doesn't bother with these things. We need Ezra's kindred."

"Aidan," Ezra supplies with a discreet wink.

"Not Elio?" I remark, struggling to catch up.

"Elio's playing music during the ceremony," Willow explains.

Loud footsteps draw our attention to the entrance of the chapel, Aidan half-running through the door, and my heart gives a giant, debilitating squeeze.

He's dressed in all the bells and whistles of a Fae prince, two rows of gold buttons running down the front of his waistcoat, clashing against the midnight-black velvet that emphasizes his large shoulders.

A sharp throb pulses through my belly.

"You're late." Willow huffs, hands braced on her hips, turning away from her brother just as he opens his mouth to justify his tardiness.

"I know, I know. I was just—" His gaze lands on me, enveloping me in his attention better than a blanket, as if everyone else faded from the room—or perhaps the world itself. "Beth. You're already here."

Surprise flickers across his face before he blinks it away, his apologetic, lopsided grin stretching into a smile that's smooth and rich as butter, yet subdued. Secret. Just for me.

Without meaning to, I tilt forward on my treacherous heels, my body yearning for his warmth even as my mind steels itself to stay away.

"Let's do this thing," Willow snaps, her usual cheerful tone cracking at the end, as though the ceremony—the thing—repulses her. Ezra's face falls, but the groom faithfully steps up to the altar.

Mabel gives us quick instructions on where to stand and how to behave. I follow along carefully—until the worst possible interruption yanks me out of my reverie, shattering the waking dream of standing opposite Aidan at the altar.

"They told me you were in here, darling." Zeke is dressed in the dark glamour of his court, shadows curling along his shoulders as he smiles at me like we're not only betrothed but thrilled to be so. He salutes the Summer Queen with a gracious bow. "It's such an honor for my precious Lizzie and me to be part of the wedding party, Your Majesty."

CHAPTER 29
CARDHOLDERS
SONGBIRD

Zeke's arms curl around my shoulders as the wedding rehearsal comes to an end, ushering me away from the Summer royal family and into his dark, smokey embrace.

"You look gorgeous, moth," he whispers in my ear.

"My name is Elizabeth," I grit through my teeth, the weight of his hand on my bare shoulder so bothersome that I have to concentrate hard not to shrug it off.

His eyes narrow at my obvious unease. "My father was pleased to hear you're Willow's kindred, so he decided to send me in his stead, since we're engaged and all." He offers me his arm. "Let me show you to our table."

Our table.

The warning in his voice is thick. I glare at his outstretched arm but finally take it, knowing better than to make a scene in front of Thera.

I'm well aware that our engagement isn't some creepy nightmare I made up, but it feels even more wretched and false than it did that first night in the labyrinth. My heart rebels louder and louder against the idea that I could ever vow to stand by this man's side forever.

While we were cooped up in the chapel, guests began filtering into the ballroom—at least a hundred patrons clinking glasses in cheers and sampling the finest appetizers from trays floating gracefully around the room.

The grand Summer Court ballroom is poised to receive hundreds more tomorrow, only a select few apparently invited to attend the rehearsal. Zeke guides me straight past what I can only describe as a mountain of gifts to *our* table.

"Ezekiel, dear." A bosomed woman dressed in the most outrageous dress I have ever seen fans herself as she makes her way to us. Her ebony skin glistens under the light of the chandeliers. "It's a pity your father decided not to attend. I don't mean to pry, only—he did seem a little worn down at the solstice celebration."

"Your Majesty, this is Elizabeth Snow, my fiancée," Zeke offers politely, smoothly bringing me into the conversation despite the rather abrupt way she accosted us.

Zeke might have many, many flaws, but he knows how to conduct himself at a royal dinner party.

I offer Freya Heart a quick curtsy, but she waves her fan in the space between us like she couldn't be bothered to learn my inconsequential name.

"Your father is well, I hope? With Foghar just around the corner, it's only natural for us to wonder," she says.

"Very well indeed. He sent me in his stead because my gorgeous fiancée here is the bride's kindred."

Zeke's hand rests on the small of my back, his shadows clogging my lungs. Just being this close to him irks me, the feel of his thumb running up and down my bare spine crawling under my skin.

Freya finally spares me a full glance. "Are you really? What an honor. I'm afraid I don't recall meeting you before, Miss Snow, was it?"

"Elizabeth."

"I'm Freya Heart, the Spring Queen."

Queen Consort, I add in my head, but curtsy again all the same. "It's an honor to meet you."

"Now, I'd love to have a chat with you later, Ezekiel. I'd rather hope to speak to your father in person before the week is over."

"And he'll be honored by your visit, Your Majesty," Zeke says, his gaze following Freya as she slips away, moving on to other guests, her figure blending into the crowd.

Our table seats six and is right next to the head table, which also has six seats.

Our names are written on little white folded cards, side by side, and the sight twists my stomach as the sprite of ceremony announces the arrival of the royal family. All eyes turn to the chapel entrance, and the queen enters, followed by her husband and the bride and groom.

Everyone takes their place and waits for them to sit first before taking their own seats.

Aidan and Elio sit with us in an alternating man-woman configuration: Zeke to my left, and Elio to my right. Though, I don't know the woman sitting beside him.

"I met your grandmother," I say quietly.

Elio's eyes dim. "Mabel used to visit when my mother was alive, but she stopped after... Truth is, I was so young that I barely remember her."

Ezra quickly abandons his seat to squeeze in between his brother and me, crouching down to speak to him. "Are you seeing this?" He downs Elio's untouched glass of wine. "Looks like daddy dearest is about to get remarried."

My gaze snaps to the woman sitting next to Ezra at the head table. Ezra's mother is dead, so this woman must be the King of Light's plus-one. She looks young and stunning, one of the most beautiful women I've ever seen, with white-blonde hair and endless green eyes.

But then I spot the man beside her.

Ethan Lightbringer is as handsome as his two sons, but also

dangerous. One look at him tells me that. The upturned corners of his eyes give him a feline flair, and his aristocratic bearing makes him seem like the kind of man who could both kiss your knuckles to charm you or break them to see you squirm.

I quickly avert my gaze, trying to avoid his notice as Ezra returns to his seat.

The rustling of fine fabrics and murmurs of polite conversation echo through the ballroom, while flutes of Feyfire wine are placed at every seat.

The Summer King takes his flute in hand and rises to his feet. He thanks the guests for their attendance, his voice smooth and commanding, filling the room with authority. Thera follows with a heartfelt address about young love and devotion, her words so genuine and full of warmth that, for a moment, I'm tempted to forget the reality of this wedding.

The warmth of her words lingers, but it's quickly replaced by the cold formality of the evening as the long, seven-course dinner is served. The abundance of food feels almost incongruent with my current mood, and I can't help but feel disconnected from the lavish spread before me.

"You brought a date?" I mouth quietly to Aidan when I'm confident Zeke is too busy eating to notice.

"Sorry," he mouths back with a sheepish grimace.

Elio's company isn't enough to distract me from the way Aidan glowers at Zeke every chance he gets until it's time to get up and dance, the stilted torture of dinner finally over. Elio asks his date to dance, and she gives him a timid smile, clearly enchanted by his offer.

Zeke's hand rests on the small of my back as we stand on the edge of the dance floor, me praying that he won't ask me to do the same, and him probably picking up on my silent wish. Ezra and Willow move to join us.

Ethan Lightbringer follows behind them, and the hope to avoid meeting him altogether quickly goes up in flames, his gaze riveted on me as he joins our circle.

"So, this is the moth that has everyone under her cold spell," he enunciates slowly. His chilly tone has a powerful ring to it, yet it's eerily quiet.

I offer the man a polite curtsy. "It's an honor to meet you, Your Majesty."

"Yes. It would be."

Again, so quiet, yet terrifying.

I dart my eyes up to him, and my knuckles turn white against the skirt of my dress.

Not unlike Ezra did during our first meeting, the King of Light undresses me with his eyes, but the moment feels anything but lighthearted. Ethan Lightbringer's intense gaze leaves prints in its wake, each of them heavy and soiled, like his darkest desire is to play with me for a night and leave me trampled forever.

I've seen that look in a man's eyes before, in the back alleys of Tundra, and my blood turns cold. I doubt I could blast the King of Light with ice strong enough to buy me freedom if he forced himself on me. Thanatos knows there are many, many empty hallways in this castle where no one could hear me scream for help.

I grip the skirt of my dress even tighter, trying to dispel the fear in my gut, but I can see it in his eyes. Dark as sin and bright as a promise. This man would hurt me, given the chance.

Zeke clears his throat. "Please excuse us, Your Majesty. I'm eager to dance with my beautiful fiancée." With a firm hand wrapped around my shoulder, he guides me to the dance floor in time for a romantic waltz.

"Wh—"

"One dance won't kill you. I had to get away from that man. He's vicious."

A sigh heaves out of my lungs. "For once, I agree with you."

I hang onto him, unsure where to put my hands.

"You're not a very good dancer, are you?" he cracks.

"This is my first ball."

I practiced with Marjorie, but I was always the man.

It's awkward to be standing so close to Zeke, but it's nothing compared to the King of Light's scrutiny. Or Aidan's fiery stare following along with every step. I'm practically smoldering by the time the song ends, and my fiancé leads me back to our table, oblivious.

I catch a stranger smiling at us. "You two make a fine couple."

She walks away before I can find enough air to respond, and a sudden bout of dizziness turns my head. "I need to sit," I announce gravely.

Zeke holds out the chair for me in a perfectly rehearsed picture of gallantry. "There's someone I want to have a quick chat with. I'll be back in a minute." He heads off toward the gardens.

Bile rises to my mouth.

Devi said everyone here was playing a part, and I'm no exception. I thought I could escape this marriage, but now I'm not so sure. I take a few swigs of wine to wash away the bitter taste of my own shame.

The Spring Queen sits not far from me, dancing with one gorgeous man after another, a line of high-born suitors gathered by the dance floor to admire her—and if Devi is right, to scheme for the chance to become the next Spring King. The flask Devi gave me is still tucked into my corset, and I pour it into my own drink, planning to swap the matching cups later as I wait for the right moment.

I take advantage of the start of a slow waltz, with Freya's suitors all vying to be her partner, and slip behind the wall of men to switch the cups. Keeping a measured pace, I walk to the restroom and back after I'm done, careful not to linger near the scene of the crime.

On my return to the table, a teenage girl with limbs too long for her body and big hazelnut eyes accosts me. "You switched drinks with the Spring Queen." She tilts her head to the side. "Why?"

Busted.

"I'm Rye. Who are you?" she demands. I scan the surroundings for her chaperone, but no one else seems to be within earshot.

"Beth."

"Beth who?"

"Beth Snow."

Her sharp, clever eyes sparkle. "You're the moth who got into the academy. I'm only half-Fae, but I'd do anything to get in if they'd give me the chance to apply." She sways from her heels to the balls of her feet a few times. "That's against the rules for now, but they've bent the rules for you, so they might do it again, right?"

She adds the last part as though goading me to disagree, but she's mostly right.

"Oh, absolutely. I'm sure the pure-blood nonsense is just another way to keep undesirables out, and the rules will bend the second a powerful king sires a half-Fae prince."

Her eyes bulge at my language. "You're fun, so I'll keep your secret. For now."

I swallow a sip of wine to dispel the nerves as Elio joins us.

"Hello, Rye. I see you've met my friend, Beth."

"Yes, she's nice."

Elio raises his brows at the praise. "That's a big compliment coming from her. What did you do?"

"You don't want to know."

Damian squeezes between Elio and me, looking even darker than usual. "I can't believe you talked me into coming," he grunts to Elio. "Only to abandon me to my fate for the longest dinner in the history of time."

Elio takes a careful sip of cider. "Well, you can thank me later. Everyone needs to see you here, or they won't believe you're a true contender for the throne."

"Ahem." Rye clears her throat. "It's rude to ignore a lady. Who are you?" She hands Damian her knuckles for him to kiss.

"Damian Sombra, and you are?" Damian answers with humor.

"Morrigan. Morrigan Quinn, Your Highness," she does a quick curtsy, a bright flush rising to her cheeks, clearly enamoured with the tall, dark, and broody Fae.

"Damian's not a prince, Rye. Not even close," Elio corrects her.

"But I will be king," Damian adds with a wink. "Someday."

Rye smiles at his confidence. "Then I shall serve you faithfully."

"You're a Shadow seed?" Damian asks.

"Yes. I wield both blood and shadow magic, but the former is not a path open to mortals these days. I'm glad of it, if it means I get to have *you* as my king." She rakes her eyes across his body.

Damian clears his throat in an awkward fashion, clearly unsure how to deal with the teenager's brazenness. "Then we'll meet again when you're of age, I'm sure."

Aidan's hot hand lands on my shoulder, erasing everyone else from view. "A dance, fellow kindred? It's customary for us to open the ball tomorrow. We should practice," he says loudly enough for everyone in a ten feet radius to hear.

I can't possibly. Not now, and not tomorrow.

But he made it so I couldn't say no, and I give him a stiff nod, letting him guide me to the dance floor.

The pressure of his hand on the small of my back is a little heavier than necessary, as though he means to erase Zeke's handprint there.

"I've missed you bitterly, Songbird. Especially tonight."

"Brittany's nice," I say quickly, trying and failing to conceal my annoyance.

Aidan sets the pace of the slow, languorous dance, and the union of our hands shivers through me. "My father wouldn't let me come by myself. I had to improvise."

"You improvised a tall, buxom blonde, huh?"

The dance is easy and yet elegant, crushing us together then apart. *1, 2, 3, 4 step forward and pivot, 5, 6, 7, 8, step back and he gives chase.* The story of our lives.

His gaze softens. "You're cute when you're jealous."

My mouth hangs open at his guile. "I'm *not* jealous."

"Yes, you are, but don't be. Brittany is my cousin."

I barely catch a bright smile from surfacing at the news, but my relief is short lived.

Aidan molds his body to mine, his congenial tone faltering, replaced by the hushed, intense tone of the man who made love to me for hours on end. He grips the curve of my hip. "I can't stop thinking of you. Your skin... your lips... I'm a ghost without you. One night was never going to be enough." He leans in way too close for it to be proper, his nose ghosting along the shell of my ear. "Did you get my letters?"

I draw back a few inches, missing a step, and my hand shakes along his shoulder blade. "I did."

He squeezes my fingers. "Why didn't you write back?"

"I know how this works, Aidan," I reply, my voice tinged with more bitterness than I intended. "Soon, your turn will come, and you'll marry the person your parents have chosen for you, just like Willow."

"What's going on? You haven't held my gaze since you arrived."

"We said one night. I don't see why we would torture ourselves further with some *fling* when nothing can come of it."

He presses his lips to my ear. "Don't give me that. I'm not going to let you dismiss this, not after the night we had. It's real between us, Beth." He aces our fingers, and the motion tugs and tears at my wild, throbbing heart. "I *love* you."

"Careful. People will see."

"No one's looking."

I quickly scan the crowd. "Ezra's looking."

"Ezra already knows about us."

The way he says "us," like we're actually an item, weakens my knees.

I cross Ethan's gaze as the music stops and let go of Aidan's hand with a start. "Thank you for the dance, Your Highness. I think that's enough practice for one lifetime." I offer him a quick curtsy to keep up appearances and slip into the crowd, trying—and failing—not to let the dark slant of his mouth wreck my soul.

CHAPTER 30
BROKEN GLASS
SONGBIRD

It's well past four in the morning by the time I put a drunk Willow to bed. I remained glued to her side for the rest of the evening, focussed on my kindred duties at the great annoyance of my fiancé—and my lover.

"Blessed Flame, I don't want to do this," she whispers for the third time in a row. "Eight out of ten Fae women bleed the first time."

I give her a quick, embarrassed nod as I help her out of her heels. "I did."

I expect her to notice my admission and call me out for not revealing it sooner, but she's too absorbed in her own despair to notice.

"Does it hurt a lot?" she asks quickly, her amber eyes so big it's hard to see past them.

"It didn't for me. Just a pinch."

"At least it's Ezra. He'll know what to do. I mean—he's got to be good at it, right?" She nods again, obviously trying to talk herself off the ledge of a panic attack. "Of course. He's probably been with virgins before. He'll know what to do."

I unclasp the little hook holding her dress and unzip it, her docile, needy mood making it easy. "Of course he will."

"I love him, I do. He's the hottest man I've ever met, and he's always been nice to me. But I can't fathom having sex with any man." She draws in a sharp intake of breath, the secret that had been at the tip of her tongue for months now finally flowing out. "I like girls, you see? I shouldn't be marrying a *boy*." She pouts in a drunken, exaggerated fashion. "Do you hate me now?"

My heart melts. "I love you just as you are. Thank you for telling me, Will. You can trust me."

"I wanted to tell you before, but I was afraid you wouldn't want to be friends with me." She climbs over the bed and hides her face in the pillows, and I lie down next to her, giving her a minute to catch up with her intoxicated confession.

She cries, muffling her high-pitched sniffles with her hands.

"Shh. It's okay." I try to soothe her and stroke her back up and down.

The princess's bedroom is larger than the guest suite, but she looks small and fragile, curled up on the lavish lavender duvet of her baldaquin bed, her eyes glassy. In that moment, she reminds me so much of Marjorie that my instincts flare to protect her from the monsters under her bed.

Only tonight, the monster is the man she has to marry—or rather, his cock.

"Are you angry with me?" she whines. "You were quieter than usual all night."

"Angry? Why would I be angry?"

She tucks her hands into her lap, shifting to a cross-legged position. "I thought, back on the solstice, when you and Ezra disappeared... I thought maybe you spent the night together. That perhaps you resented me for marrying him, when clearly, he should be with you instead."

A patient smile appears on my lips as I give her hands a gentle squeeze. "Ezra's my friend. Nothing more."

"Really?"

"Yes!"

"So, it doesn't bother you that we're going to marry?"

I tilt my head, wondering how she could worry about me at a time like this. "It bothers me that you're sad."

She dries her tears and straightens her spine. "Zeke was so annoying tonight. I hope he didn't say anything too egregious. I'm sorry you had to suffer through that, and again tomorrow, because I'm too chicken to do this alone."

"You're here for me, and I'm here for you. That's what best friends are for."

She throws herself in my arms and hugs me tight. "Goodnight, my sweet Beth."

"Goodnight, Will."

"Thank you for being a true friend."

With a final glance, I step into the hallway, the soft click of the door behind me marking the end of this quiet moment. The long, gilded corridors blur together, and my heart races as I take turn after turn. I briefly wonder what it would be like if I ended up crossing paths with Aidan or somehow found his room first, but the fantasy quickly disappears in favor of a real fear of losing my way in this labyrinthine castle.

Relief washes over me when I finally find my room, grateful for my decent sense of direction despite the disorienting twists—and only slightly disappointed that Aidan is not there, waiting for me, as I thought he might be.

I kick off my heels, the marble floor cool and slightly damp beneath my feet, the open window letting in the morning dew. A deep sigh quakes my chest as I start inspecting the seams of my custom-made dress for a way out. My fingers fumble until they find the little clasp, and I unhook it with a soft snap.

But an eerie sensation slithers across the back of my neck, sending a chill through me. I squint at the empty room.

"Ezra?" I call, dragging my eyes to the gentle sway of the

curtains, the warm summer breeze whistling softly through the window. "Ezra, are you in here? Don't play games with me. I'm not in the mood."

Extending my arms, I search the shadows, each step making the floor seem colder, the silence heavier. What kind of mood must Ezra be in to sneak into my bedroom at this hour without a word?

When my hand finally collides with something solid—an invisible wall—I growl in frustration. "Ezra! Come on!"

"Now, why would my son be sneaking into your bed on the eve of his wedding, Miss Snow?"

I jolt away from the apparition, ice spreading all over the marble floor.

"You and Aidan make a cute couple. Does your fiancé know about your very high-profile lover, or is he as blind to it as he's inattentive to the poor state of his kingdom?" Ethan Lightbringer says slowly, drinking in my reaction.

I sink my nails in my palms, unsure of what to say, if anything. I've heard the rumors, and if this king is not above beating his sons bloody, Thanatos knows what he'll do to me.

He sits on the edge of the bed as though he means to get himself comfortable. "Relax, your secret will be safe with me, Miss Snow. I'm sure, between us, we can come to a quick agreement. By the Flame, if you make it worth my while, I might agree to support you financially when this whole thing explodes in your face."

"Worth your while?" I stammer.

His wicked eyes shine in the dark. "Tonight, I mean." He sinks back on the mattress, arms braced behind his head. "Strip for me, Miss Snow. I want to admire your body without all that useless fabric obstructing it."

Bile rises to my mouth as I lift my hands in denial. "I— No, Sir. Respectfully." I tack on the last part, hoping it softens the edge in my voice and masks the rising panic.

His brows bunch together, though his smile widens in contrast as if he knows something I don't. "Are you the kind of girl who will destroy her future for nothing?"

I bite my tongue not to answer.

I can't afford to anger him, not when we're alone in a bedroom in the middle of the night, but he must read the determination on my face, because he adds, "If you deny me, I will expose your silly romance, and you will lose everything."

"Then I'll live with the consequences, Your Majesty."

He jumps out of bed so fast, I barely follow his movements. "You think a moth like you can say no to a king like me?"

I inch toward the door, but he corners me between the sofa and the tall mirror hung on the wall.

Out of instinct, I summon an ice dagger and aim it at his incoming form, but he wraps a hand around my wrist, and the weapon crumbles to dust in my grip.

"I'm the King of Light." He flattens me to the reflective glass, and his nails sink painfully into my skin, his hold strong enough to bruise. "And when I tell you to strip for me, the only acceptable answer is *yes, Sir.*"

I push my ice forward, but it bounces off his body and spreads across my skin instead, the impact shattering the mirror. Frost coats my arms, shoulders, and chest until I feel like nothing more than a frozen statue, immobile and docile as the King of Light tears the dress off my frame, leaving me in nothing but two flimsy pieces of underwear.

A gut-wrenching sob grinds between my lips.

"Now, shall we try that again?" he asks.

The loud creak of the door is barely audible over the sound of my frazzled heartbeats, and my gaze darts up to see Devi enter the room, barefoot and wrapped in fighting leathers instead of her golden dress.

"It's late, Your Majesty," Devi enunciates slowly, her voice as even and congenial as ever as she inches my bedroom door open all the way.

"Violet," Ethan gasps.

I keep my eyes down, my arms firmly planted at my sides, shaking all over.

"I think we should all get to bed. Don't you agree?"

Ethan snarls under his breath and slicks his long hair back. "Oh, why do I care if some silly girl is too stupid to grab the chance of a lifetime. I would have paid you tenfold, moth. And now you'll be left with nothing."

He storms out of the room, and Devi presses the door shut behind him.

"Wh— How?" my body quakes, wave after wave of cold sweat dripping between my shoulder blades, overwhelmed with all that just happened.

And what *almost* happened.

She swallows hard. "He might resent you forever for turning him down, but he shouldn't try to force himself on you again, not for a while."

I sit on the sofa and wrap a spare blanket around my frame, my legs too weak to hold me up anymore, and wait for the trembles to subside. Devi waits patiently, silent as I try to fix together the pieces of the night and how they led me here, puzzled by what gave this king the idea to wait for me in my bedroom. Why he would even bother, when his partner was so much more beautiful? *What did I do?*

After a while, Devi sighs. "You did nothing wrong, Beth. Imagine what it's like to be him. The King of Light, able to walk anywhere unseen, unchecked, and slip into anyone's bed... and that's not even the worst of it. I bet most women acquiesce to his demand, terrified of his reprisal, and then it's not rape, is it? It never is when powerful men are concerned. When I'm queen, they'll all have to change their tune. Especially a demon like Ethan Lucifer Lightbringer."

"But why?" I ask quietly, the tears in my voice somehow not reaching my eyes.

"We're more similar than you think. Spring princesses and sirens, I mean. Men blame us for their appetites, putting the burden of not being so beautiful and enticing upon us instead of taking responsibility for their flawed characters. Do you know how many married men pursue me, at times for months on end, sometimes even succeeding in their seduction, only to curse my magic and me come morning?

Once they got what their egos craved, they blamed me, a teenager, for their sins."

My mind flashes to the way Ethan looked at her. "What do you have on him? Why did he leave?"

"It doesn't matter." She hands me my flannel pajamas. "Let's get you to bed."

I take the fabric and hold it close to my chest. "Thank you."

"You did well tonight. Being there for Willow, dealing with Zeke while following through on what I asked, and holding Aidan at arms' length. It must not have been easy," she says soothingly.

"Did it work? Did she drink the wine?" I ask, desperate to distract myself from the memory of Ethan's razor-sharp nails scratching my neck.

"Yes."

"Did you find out who she means to marry?"

"Not yet."

I climb to my wobbly feet and put on the two-piece pajama set. Once I'm covered, Devi places a soft hand on my shoulder and gently guides me toward the bed.

"Lie down. I'll stay here, in the chair, until you fall asleep, alright?"

Standing guard. Because Ethan might return. Despite her earlier reassurance that he would not try again, Devi's actions seem to imply she doesn't know what he might do.

"Why are you being so nice? You hate me," I croak.

"I don't hate you, moth. I think you're dangerously unprepared for what's coming. You're just like me, cursed to attract all sorts of creeps, and yet you blush at the first mention of sex and pretend you're as plain looking as the other moths you grew up with. And frankly, the studious virgin facade irks me." A heavy sigh whistles out of her lungs. "But I wouldn't wish what happened tonight on my worst enemy."

"You're kinder than I thought."

"Am not."

"Are too."

"Don't you dare tell anyone that I'm *kind*." A disgusted grimace twists her lips, a full-bodied shiver shaking her down from head to toe. "Ugh."

The silly argument brings back colors to my cheeks and warmth to my chest. I glare at the cold bed, the imprint of Ethan's body still ruffling the duvet, and shake my head. "Do you know this castle well?"

"Well enough."

"I need you to do me a favor, too."

She arches a brow, her careful, pacifying tone melting in favor of her usual snark. "Another one?"

"I-I need to find Aidan's room."

Her gaze softens. "You really love him."

I take offense at the surprise in her tone. "Is that so hard to believe?"

"Yes. I can read people's feelings pretty well, but I can't read yours, and distrusted you from the start because of it." She opens the door for me, and guides me through the hallways. "Maybe your siren blood was blocking my radar or something."

"But you don't approve."

A wistful pout overpowers her face. "Aidan is just like the rest of them. When the time comes, he'll choose his birthright and duties over his heart."

I bite my bottom lip. "Maybe."

"I'll take you to him."

We weave through a series of long hallways and cross a mezzanine. Devi motions me forward to a set of double-doors with gilded frames and amber knobs. "Here he is."

I give the panel a soft knock, and almost immediately, Aidan cracks open the door, his hair disheveled. The sight of him in his bedroom fills me with a mix of heat and dread, and I wish I could have come here under different circumstances.

A bright smile stretches across his full lips as our gazes meet. "Songbird."

I turn to acknowledge Devi and thank her for her help, but she's gone—evaporated, just like that. Poof. I squint at the empty corridor, my guts in knots.

Aidan opens the door wider. "I'm so glad. I was dying to come and see you."

"I don't want to be alone tonight, but I can't— Will you just hold me?" I whisper.

He nods solemnly, as if he can see every emotional scar etched across my face, and drapes his arm around me. "Always."

Out there in Wintermere, the only thought that kept me going was how much I missed him. How different his touch feels—how it registers in a way no one else's does. Deep down, I believe Aidan would protect me from even the most vicious of kings.

He wraps his arms around me as we settle onto his mattress, spooning me, but I accidentally bump my ass against his crotch. My lids flutter at the notion that he's already that hard, even though we haven't even kissed. I don't want to escalate this any further, but his warmth and scent lull the horror of the night away, my neck flushed. I bite my bottom lip, resisting the temptation to grind against him.

"Now *this* is torture," he pants, squeezing me closer but keeping his hands in a safe, innocent spot.

I sleep better in Aidan's royal bed than I did the entire break.

The shadow of my siren heritage looms over us, threatening to steal another night like this, so I hold him tighter, savoring every moment. I won't have sex with him—not when his free will is in question—but it feels so good to hold him.

Because, in spite of my best efforts, I'm desperately in love with him.

CHAPTER 31
FAIRYTALES
SONGBIRD

Ezra's voice jolts me out of a delightfully peaceful sleep. "Wakey, wakey." Spider fingers climb up my spine and nudge me to consciousness as I stir awake, nestled in Aidan's arms.

His solid chest is pressed to my cheek, and an annoyed grunt falls from his lips as he swats Ezra's hand away from us. "By the Flame, mate. Don't you knock?"

"You two should be grateful I'm not the bride, or there would be some explaining to do." Ezra pulls the blinds wide open, the blaring light assaulting my retinas, the sun already high in the sky.

"Willow would never sneak into my room without knocking," Aidan grumbles.

"Well, in a few hours, we'll be brothers, and that's what brothers do. Get used to it."

Aidan rubs down his face, his other arm not giving me an inch to spare. "Why are you here, Ezra?"

"I'm getting married today, or have you forgotten? It's time to get ready."

I glance at the clock on the dresser—I was supposed to meet

Willow in her room half an hour ago. I slip from Aidan's grasp. "By the spindle! I'm late!"

"Don't worry, I covered for you. I need to speak with you before you go," Ezra says quickly, his gaze darting from me to Aidan. "Can I have a word in private with your girl? I need to ask her something."

"Are you pushing me out of my own room?"

"*Please*," Ezra adds with a throaty laugh, and from Aidan's reaction, I figure it's not a word he uses often.

The groom closes the door behind his pissed off friend and averts his gaze. "Willow looked wretched this morning. She says it's just a hangover from all the cider she had last night, but I almost thought she was about to run away. Did she mention anything to you?"

"You don't look much better," I say instead of answering the question.

Dark circles drag down Ezra's ice-blue eyes, the glow of his skin mute in comparison to his usual luminous complexion.

"I know I'm not her choice, and it's killing me," he chucks out, pulling at his platinum-blonde hair. The lapels of his dress shirt are half-opened and skewed to one side. "What should I do?"

"Oh, Ezra." I wince, unsure if I should encourage him to put a stop to this or not.

I understand better than ever how evil his father truly is. If Ezra went along with the wedding up until now, he clearly thinks he doesn't have a choice. He wouldn't have let it get this far if he had another option, so I probably should assuage his worries, knowing the worst can't be avoided.

I wrap him up in a hug and stroke his back, and he hides his face in my tangled hair.

"Willow will never love me," he grimaces, "and we both know why. Any commitment between us is purely for politics. I was glad to get both our fathers off our backs when I thought she was alright with it, but after what she said last night..."

The mention of his father drains the blood right from my face, but I try to stay on subject. I'm not naive enough to think Willow would be allowed to disclose her sexuality and live the life she wants without burning all her bridges, not in the world we live in.

"It's not fair to her. Or you. I'm so sorry."

It's not like with me and Zeke. If the Shadow Prince was a decent man, I could learn to love him, and maybe even enjoy intimacy with him, but Ezra and Willow's sham marriage is doomed from the start.

He chokes out a tensed breath, eyes glazing with unshed tears. "I can't believe I have to fuck her in front of all these people."

I straighten the lapels of his shirt and button up the collar. "Then let me say this. If I had to have sex with someone I wasn't in love with, in front of a crowd, it would be you."

"Really?"

"No question." I nudge his side playfully. "Come on, you're Ezra Lightbringer."

"That's true," he says with a bit of sass.

"Having sex with a friend is probably the best option after true love, and Willow trusts you. She said so last night."

"She did?"

"Yes."

"Thank you. That helps."

I smooth out the intensity of the moment with a gentle chuckle. "When my turn comes with Zeke, I hope you'll be there to give me a pep talk."

Ezra rolls his eyes. "Be real, Lady Snow. Aidan will never let that happen."

I give him a sad smile, knowing in my heart that he's probably right. I can't fathom what he must be feeling right now, about to give a part of himself to someone he didn't choose.

"Don't you dare send me off to war without a kiss, my lady." He presses a quick kiss to my mouth.

A jolt of electricity raises all my hairs to attention as he lingers into the faint touch, but his lips quickly twitch in a sad, fleeting motion. He sidesteps, and I stare at his retreating back until he disappears from view.

Aidan reenters the room almost immediately. A forlorn pout pulls at his mouth. "What did he want?"

I shake off the strange aftershocks of Ezra's chaste, almost fearful kiss. "Um, he needed a little encouragement, that's all."

Aidan wraps me up in his arms, but I recoil from his embrace. It's all so clear in the daylight. If I can't tell Aidan the truth about me, I can't continue to lean on him. I have to choose between the fear of losing him forever and the fear of being outed for what I am.

"You're pulling away from me," he breathes, his arms falling at his sides. "Is it because of Ezra?"

By the spindle... Willow first, and now Aidan? "Not at all."

He cups my cheek and angles my face toward his, his thumb hot on the corner of my mouth, tempting me to push aside my dilemma and give in to the magnetic pull of his kiss. But I dig my nails into the underside of his wrist.

"Tell me if something's going on between you two. I beg you."

I press my cheek to his palm, holding his inquisitive gaze. "Nothing is going on between me and Ezra. I swear."

The clear-cut answer seems to put him at ease, and his shoulders relax. "Sorry. I'm acting like a jealous creep. I'll do better, I promise."

I tear myself away. "Nonetheless, I have to go."

"Beth. Talk to me. What are you hiding?"

"I have to go," I repeat, the ice from last night returning full force.

If I don't hurry, I'll be late to the ceremony, and when Willow asks where in the seven hells I've been, I can't admit to spending the night in her brother's arms.

I take a deep breath, trying to push aside the guilt that coils in my chest. But I can't afford to let the truth slip now—not when everything is so fragile, not when one wrong word could shatter it all.

Willow's wedding dress, though delicate and elegant, carries an unexpected strength in its design. Metallic accents glimmer in the twilight, strategically placed across her bodice and waist, resembling the armor of a soldier heading into battle. The rubies in her tiara mirror the sheen of polished weapons, and the metallic threads woven through the gown's layers hint at an unspoken resilience.

Ezra traded his wings in favor of a white, pristine cloak that drapes around him like a living thing. The fabric shimmers with an opalescent glow, its delicate folds soft like clouds but carrying the weight of something much stronger underneath. His matching waistcoat and pants are adorned with golden accents, reminiscent of the Solar Cliffs' hawthorn.

Officiating the ceremony, Mabel recites her lines in a voice that raises goosebumps on my neck. "Mortal love wanes, but Fae love burns to the bone."

The wedding ceremony is similar to the ones we hold in Wintermere, with a few key differences, starting with the ruby-encrusted blade being purified over a pyre symbolizing the Flame of Fate.

The Summerlands are still using a version of the vows that accounts for their old religion, and I find the difference enthralling. Tears well up in Thera's eyes, everyone so consumed by the ceremony that they don't notice how Aidan only has eyes for me.

I'm about to melt into nothingness, leaving behind only a ruined puddle of unfulfilled dreams and gnawing hunger on the marble, as he digs his gaze into every inch of bare skin exposed by my studded, fire-and-amber dress—an ensemble that perfectly matches his suit.

By Thanatos, my cheeks must be red as flames.

I need a dip in freezing water—or a slap in the face.

The most striking and surreal view in all the realms has filled my head with fairy tales that are harder to shake than the most powerful of enchantments. From the other side of the altar, Aidan's eyes drift to me every so often as Mabel recites lines that speak of passion, love, and giving yourself fully to another by the mutual spilling of blood. Ezra and Willow conceal their nervousness to a T, and if I didn't know them, I could almost believe they were in love.

The pointy end of the Summer's ruby dagger shines, more enticing than a spindle atop a cursed spinning wheel.

Aidan's chest rises and falls faster as he unfurls his fingers, his hands trembling slightly. The impossible, seductive fantasy of us standing together in much the same way at *our* wedding takes a life of its own. His amber irises thin, the black fire burning behind them all-consuming, starving for more than just *one more* night.

I would gladly forget my tainted Sea Fae blood, my humble past, and all matters of logic if it meant I could claim Aidan as my own forever. I'd cut myself deep and never look back. From the dark, hungry gaze he gives me, I know he's contemplating the same thing.

CHAPTER 32
CONSUMMATION
SONGBIRD

The marital bed is set squarely in the middle of the ballroom, two layers of fabric separating the newlyweds from the guests' avid curiosity. The semi-translucent tarps cast shadows for their benefit, but Mabel, Aidan, and I are meant to stay between the two tarps until consummation is confirmed.

Contrary to yesterday's stuffy, ceremonial dinner, the wedding party is loud and scandalous, cider and Feyfire wine flowing as the guests revel in the thrill of witnessing something usually kept private.

Without consummation, the magic that is meant to bind their powers forever would fizzle away come midnight, so these traditions are meant to insure the validity of their union.

"Words can be spoken in vain, so actions must always follow promises. The union of your bodies will ensure the gods of your commitment to each other. May their blessing seal your marriage forever." Mabel says, motioning the newlyweds beyond the second tarp. "For better or worse."

The old woman brushes the long black feathers of her

masquerade mask. We're all wearing one, save for the newlyweds, but the mask gives the white-haired witch a mysterious flair.

Ezra squeezes her frail arm. "Thank you, Grandmother."

Something passes between them. "I will say this to you, just as I've said it to all the young people I've married. Marriage is a long, permanent affair for us Fae. *Until death* can't be cheated by waning affections or grander passions, for your magics will be irrevocably linked. This is your last chance to turn back."

Willow frowns at that. "Do people actually change their minds at the last minute?"

The corners of Mabel's eyes wrinkle. "More than you'd think."

Will grasps Ezra's hand in hers with more confidence than expected. "We're ready, I think."

Mabel nods. "Then with your kindreds as witnesses, you will now share blood and magic, just as the gods intended."

Willow meets my gaze, and I give her a small smile, trying to push past the discomfort in my stomach. "You've got this," I whisper.

They slide between the two diaphanous seams. Ezra tips Willow's chin up and bends down to kiss her, a kiss that holds all the heat the one they shared after their vows lacked. Willow gasps, apparently swept away by the moment. The crowd goes wild as Ezra expertly tugs at the threads of her corset, unfastening the criss-crosses one by one, and Willow slips off his cloak.

I angle my gaze away as the heavy skirt of her dress falls at her feet.

"You're beautiful, flame of my heart," Ezra says warmly, cupping her cheek.

Willow steps out of her dress, her voice brimming with unshed tears, but also a hint of her usual sass. "And you're the most attractive man on this continent."

It's objectively true, of course.

Here we go.

The ritual is a hundred times worse than watching a couple from far away, as we do in Wintermere. Moreover, the sinful fascination of watching others in such a vulnerable state fades when you know them well enough to understand how fucking terrified they really are.

"Close your eyes," Ezra whispers to his bride, the words barely audible. "Don't think. Just feel." He guides her toward the mattress and climbs on top of her, still almost fully clothed.

"I think two witnesses is enough, eh, lovebirds?" Mabel says, stealing my focus away from the scene beyond the tarp. "I'll give you some privacy." She slips between the tarps to rejoin the party with a knowing smile.

Aidan reaches for my hand now that we're alone, holding on tight.

"When Will asked me to be her kindred witness, and I accepted, I don't think either of us thought it all the way through," I whisper.

"You think?" Aidan answers with his eyes screwed shut.

I try to concentrate on the mural of the Fall of the Mist King sprawled above our heads, but Willow's breathless moans slowly grow into a high-pitched choir.

I've seen worse. Done worse. But this is Willow and *Ezra*. Somehow, my body is both incredibly cold and hot at the same time. The flush in my cheeks spreads to my temples and blurs their hushed conversation, Aidan's grip tightening as Willow's groans get louder.

Yet, I'm a Winter Fae. I can't help but steal another peek.

When the time comes for them to take this further, my insides curl.

"Ow," Willow rasps, and the crowd beyond the tarps howls in cheer, the white linen walls shuddering under their boastful taps.

"Sorry," Ezra croaks.

"It's not so bad, actually. Just a sting." I can hear the sorrow crackling in her voice, and my stomach lurches.

"What a compliment," Ezra chuckles darkly.

I hear the ruffle of fabric and crack one eye open when Ezra gasps. Willow is on top of him now, taking control, and a golden glow pierces the tarps, wrapping them in sunshine.

It's done.

My breath hitches, and I hide my face in Aidan's chest. "This is so strange."

After today, I no longer find this *tradition* harmless. Maybe when two people are crazy for each other, it's easier to zone out the witnesses, but how many Fae royals marry for love, really, when power is valued above all else? When marriage is a way to amplify that power?

Aidan squeezes my hand in his. "Let's get out of here."

"Please."

The crowd is roaring with applause as we slither out of the tent, and I let go of Aidan's hand with a start.

"You can't want that for yourself," he says quickly, wrapping a hand around my waist and guiding me through the raucous crowd.

"A Summer wedding?" I croak, patching my unease with dark humor.

"Songbird. I'm serious."

It used to be a vague, abstract idea, but now I can too easily picture myself in a similar situation, my family cheering me on as I bed Zeke in front of them. Adrenaline rushes through my blood. I'm disgusted by the idea of linking my body and soul to him forever, when I'm simply *aching* for someone else.

I lean into Aidan's embrace without meaning to, yearning for his heat to melt the ice in my blood. Marriage means being linked to someone *forever*. What happened between Ezra and Willow can *never* be undone, and the concept is both thrilling and suffocating.

If I ever speak those vows out loud in front of everyone I've ever known, I want it to be to Aidan. Just the idea of us sharing something so profound and permanent wrecks my brain.

Aidan ushers me away toward the gardens, taking charge as if he senses the depths of my anguish. "Come on. Walk with me. Please."

Tall vines with orange, white, and pink flowers grow around the trellis and arches leading to the shoreline of the Lunar Cascades where the stone path ends right at the edge of the sand. The shore is made of the whitest, most delicate sand I've ever felt. My heels sink into it, so I slip them off and hold them by the straps—just like I did the night of the solstice—and fall into step beside him, a few inches of trauma still keeping me from bridging the gap between us.

I glance back at the castle, its golden turrets glowing behind us. Now that we've cleared the canopy of vines, anyone could see us, and I shiver at the thought, eager to reclaim the privacy of the gardens. But Aidan tugs on my arm, leading me farther still, away from the ballroom and toward a secluded area near the base of the castle. Here, where the castle walls leave a narrow gap, overgrown vegetation hides the entrance to a well-trodden path.

"Come with me. I want to show you something," he says, squeezing my hand. But I can't bring myself to speak—not now, not here, in the gardens of the capital. *His* gardens. *His* castle.

He's so far above me, I can't believe I ever let myself think this could end in anything but disaster.

I cross my arms over my chest, "We should really get back."

A couple walks out of the very same path, heading straight toward us, and Aidan pushes me deep into the bushes. "In here, quick."

My heels dig into the white sand, thorns scratching at my arms until Aidan's magic allows us to hide comfortably within the branches, the vegetation rearranging to form a cocoon around us.

The Spring Queen takes a late-night stroll with a tall, white-haired man, the jackal tattoo on his neck marking him as the Storm King.

"I don't want you to remarry, Frey. We can petition for you to become queen on your own," he says.

Freya fans herself in response. "Don't be ridiculous. The others wouldn't support me if I didn't marry."

"I can't stand the thought of you with someone else."

"Oberon never bothered you."

"Oberon is old and dying. Ferdinand will expect you to bear him more children. If you can't get the others to back you without a husband, then leave your crown to the girl, and come to Storm's End with me."

The Spring Queen and the Storm King are lovers—yet another couple thwarted by politics, by the sound of it. Aidan's hands are solid and warm on my hips, and I rest my head on his chest.

"I could never be *just* your mistress, Thor. That's out of the question."

They walk past us and disappear beyond the hedges. We wait for a minute before moving or talking, and I revel in the feel of Aidan's solid frame at my back, my lids fluttering.

"Sounds like Freya plans to marry Zeke's father," he finally says, enlacing our fingers once more.

"Why did they come here?"

"For the same reason we did, I expect, though I can't understand how they would know about this place. It's a family secret." He uses his magic to clear a way out of our hiding nook, and we rejoin the main trail. "We can't head back until we're sure they've gone, so I might as well show you why we came."

The small entrance to the cylindrical tunnel is freckled with polished glass, embedded seamlessly into the ancient stones. It looks as though the passage was carved by molten lava, its edges smooth and gleaming with an unnatural sheen. The stones catch and reflect the moonlight, sending faint ripples of silver along the tube. Aidan lets a spark of his fire flicker to life in his hand, illuminating the way ahead. The light dances along the glass, casting flickering shadows and bursts of amber in its wake.

My blood pounds at my temples as we reach the end of the tunnel. Aidan pushes open a heavy stone door, the muscles in his shoulders and arms bunching with the effort.

"We're in—" I gasp.

"The throne room."

The Eternal Chalice sits right there, perched on a mound of black ashes. The cup—from which every Fae monarch has drunk—is shaped like an hourglass, the top ready to receive the blood of others so a new king can be anointed and access the magic of his lands. It was forged as a failsafe against the dangerous whims of the divine. But, as Devi described, the chalice also allows Fae Kings to circumvent the will of the gods—an instrument that makes them able to name a king of their choosing, one who doesn't bear the Mark of the Gods.

Its presence is both a symbol of power and a shadow of defiance. The air around it is thick with centuries of history, and a subtle hum of magic pulses from the powdery coals beneath it. It's a temptation, a promise of freedom from the gods' unyielding influence. And in this room, where the fate of the Fae hangs in the balance, it feels both like a gift and a curse.

My fingers tingle as I reach to touch it. The black metal from which it's been forged glows opalescent under the flickering light of Aidan's fire.

"The chalice balances the powers of the gods and keeps the current of our magics steady."

I press my lips together. "It's also an instrument that favors the most shrewd politicians."

"That, too."

I extend my hand to touch the rim but pull back at the last second, weary of yearning for something that will never be mine. I already crave Aidan in spite of my best judgment—there's no need to add a crown to the list.

"There will never be a throne for me, Aidan," I say softly.

He stands tall in front of me. "I would give it up, you know? The throne, the amber crown, and even the power that comes with it."

"You don't mean that."

"I would rather not have to, but I would. You are worth more to me."

"I'm not worth *anything*." I slip back behind the tapestry, beyond the hidden door, and head down the tunnel on my own. Aidan doesn't bother to close the door behind him and runs after me in the shifting sand.

He clasps my hand and forces me to a standstill, and I turn to face him, my ragged breath and unshed tears blurring my senses.

"Everything that happened tonight only reaffirmed my desire not to marry for duty." He caresses my knuckles with his thumb, his movements gentle despite how breathless we both are. "Let me *love* you, Songbird. I'd be pretty good at it. Break it off with Zeke. Break it off and be with me instead."

I shake my head, terrified of being swept away by the same madness. "If I end it, I won't be able to afford next year's tuition. I'll be forced to train as a reaper, and my father will be heartbroken."

"If your father wants you to be engaged to a prince, then so be it." Aidan gets on one knee and gathers a fistful of sand in his grip, and my heart implodes from the sight alone.

There he is, my Summer Prince on his knees, not desperate to keep me by his side for *one* more night, but for *all* of them. Not hungry for my body, but for me. Forever.

His fist turns red and orange, and he dusts off a feminine, perfectly transparent glass ring and holds it in the dim streak of moonlight that penetrates the glass tunnel.

"Marry me, Songbird."

My lips part, my head spinning with the weight of everything he's offering. He's there on one knee as though it's as simple as that. As though a proposal from him is something he can give out in the spur of the moment. It solidifies my worst fear—that I enchanted him. That he's not quite right in his mind.

"I'm a moth. Your mother would never approve. By the spindle, your father would probably kick me out of the Summerlands forever if he knew we were even considering this."

He opens his mouth to argue, but hesitates. "Then we'll just see each other in secret until you're ready to elope with me. I'm not a patient man, but I can be patient for you."

"Aidan..."

"I saw your expression on that altar. You're as hungry for this as I am."

I don't have it in me to fight anymore, not when he's right on all counts. I pat down the lapels of his jacket, praying that he'll understand, or at least not destroy me for my honesty. This might be the last time he looks at me this way. As if he'd cut off his own heart to heal mine.

"We can't marry because I'm a siren."

His expression darkens, his brows pulling together. "What?"

"When we first met, I had no idea, but I accidentally enchanted you," I blurt out. "That's why you broke the rules to help me. I found out very recently that I have siren blood, so when I sang, you felt *compelled* to help me."

"Siren blood—That's impossible."

"I couldn't believe it either, at first, but my father confirmed it. I'm a siren, Aidan. A Sea mutt. A soiled, hybrid creature that belongs far away from the continent. From *you*."

And I cry. I cry like I did the night I read my mother's letter and realized Aidan might not actually love me. I let it all go and fall at his feet, toppled over by the weight of my own shame.

"Hey, hey. It's alright." He falls to his knees, too, and wraps me up in his arms.

"I promise you I had no idea. I would never have violated your free will like that. Never."

"I know you wouldn't."

I rub my eyes and inch away from him. "But don't you see? It was my fault you cheated. And maybe it's still affecting you." My chin trembles. "When I sang, it made you fall for me, but it's not real. None of it is."

"Shh. It's alright." He envelops me in his arms once more while I weep and weep on his shoulder, the stress and doubts that overshadowed the last few months condensing into heavy, torrential pain.

"You don't believe me," I say on a sniffle, thinking he's acting way too affectionate to have heard me right.

"I do, truly. It makes sense."

"How?"

"I threw a contest for you after hearing you sing, I can connect the dots. But it doesn't matter."

"How can you say that? I enchanted you; manipulated you."

"Songbird. It's not your fault if you didn't know."

"How can you be so calm about this?" I squeak.

A smile tugs at the corners of his mouth. "I'd love you if you were a harpy, Beth Snow. Haven't you figured it out by now?" He cups my cheeks and presses a kiss to my nose. "A siren's song never lingers past a good night's sleep, and I count hundreds of cold, lonely mornings since we've met. I love you, Songbird. And not because you can bewitch men with a song."

I shake my head. There are so few reliable references about the Sea Fae. I can't bring myself to believe the 'cured by dawn' folklore is as simple as that. "But how can you be sure?"

"Feel my heartbeat." He presses my palm to his chest. "This isn't the result of some siren song. I've studied the legends. I've read the stories of sailors rushing to their deaths. The ones who survive wake groggy in the morning, but by lunchtime, they're ready to reach for their harpoons—not shop for centerpieces and matching rings. If your song inspired me to help you in the labyrinth, I'm glad, because it brought us together."

Hot tears spill over my lashes, his reaction so unexpected, his certainty and understanding trampling the walls I've built to protect myself from the truth of my lineage and the destructive consequences I was sure would come with it.

My fingers tremble over his face as I graze the soft arch of his brow, struck once more by his beauty and kindness.

He kisses the underside of my wrist, just as he did that first, fateful night. "I love you because you're clever and funny, with a sharp tongue that rivals my charming prince-ness. You study harder than anyone else, yet you still care about people. You're a great listener, but you also have the confidence to speak your truths, even when they challenge the status quo. You don't accept the current laws and rules as gospel—you take them as the foundation for a better world to come. You see past the princely mask I've forged for myself, and you blush when you think of me—right here."

He traces the angle of my jaw, caressing the tender skin underneath. "I see you, Beth Snow, and I stand by my offer. We'll go home for now, back to the academy, but I'll be counting the days until you agree to become my wife."

We're both panting despite staying still. Sand digs into my knees, the high slit of my dress allowing the fabric to splay on either side as Aidan slides closer. "I want to love you freely, both under the moonlight and in the sunshine. Forever."

"I love you, too." There it is. The *other* truth I was so afraid to tell.

His lips claim mine in a fierce, urgent kiss, and I gasp at the force of his hold, his hands caressing my hips up and down.

"One night was never going to be enough. I need to be inside you, Songbird."

Last time, he wanted it to be slow. Tonight, we're both too desperate for slow and crash against each other in a flurry of heated moans and hungry tugs as he climbs over me, spreading me down on the sand.

He peels the silk of my dress aside and tears off my underwear.

I unfasten the knot of his trousers.

He fills my hand, hot and ravenous, and I wrap my legs around him, beckoning him closer. I do not want to wait, or talk, or even breathe for another minute without the feel of him tucked deep inside me.

He shares my impatience and gives in to the urgency of the moment, lining himself up with my entrance without qualms.

I've been craving this ever since our gut-wrenching conversation in his apartments, where he was wearing nothing but a towel. I was so sure we were done then, so certain I could never be with him again, never touch him again. I thought I would never spend another night in his arms or learn to love as fiercely as he does.

My skin heats up at his touch, hot enough to burn, but I abandon myself completely to the flames.

My flames.

My Aidan.

He knows the truth, and he still loves me. A huge, giddy smile stretches my lips as he fucks me hard and fast, just how I need it tonight. The sand grinds against the skin of my buttocks in a delicious and unexpected way, setting each nerve ending ablaze. I twist my hand in his hair, my nails embedded in his scalp, clutching him closer.

We collide like falling stars, shattering on impact. I'm left shuddering and vulnerable in Aidan's arms as a quick, almost destructive climax turns the world beyond him to stardust, erasing the tunnels from my vision.

We catch our breath, and my cheeks flush crimson at how desperate we both were to lose ourselves to each other. To our incredible, reckless connection.

Aidan traces the shape of my collarbone. "Marry me."

"You have to stop saying that."

"Why?"

Because I'm dying to say yes.

I bite my bottom lip, what seemed impossible just this morning sounding more and more reasonable in the afterglow of our tryst. "We need to wait until Morheim at the very least, so I can get my Shadow mask."

Aidan pouts at that, dragging his lips along the curve of my jaw. "But that's *weeks* away."

"We'll revisit this nonsense—"

"—proposal," he corrects me with a grin.

"Alright, we'll revisit this *proposal* after Morheim." I raise one finger between us and try to look as fierce as I can. "But it's not a yes."

His hand tangled in my hair, he pulls me to him, swallowing my doubts with a hot, dizzying kiss. "It's not a no, either," he murmurs against my lips.

CHAPTER 33
AFTER THE VOWS
BETH

Summerlands, Faerie, Present Day

I'm supposed to sing *after* the vows, for the first dance.

My hands are clammy as I smooth down the front of my silver, glittering dress. It's a call-back to the one I used to wear on the new world's stages in the 1950s, with a thigh-high slit and glass slippers. Cinderella was all the rage back then, and it's fitting considering I'm daydreaming about a hurried, dramatic exit.

The first few rows on either side of the wedding aisle are usually reserved for family and royals, and I'm sitting on Elio's left in the third row as we wait for the ceremony to begin. His father is nowhere to be found, which leaves my friend in a somewhat better mood, but I'm dying to leave.

I can't watch Aidan marry someone else. It'll kill me.

But you must. You came here expecting closure and tore open that wound instead. You made your bed, and now you have to lie in it.

I'm going to watch the ceremony, sing my part, and sneak out as soon as it's over. I'm not sticking around for the creepy consummation part, that's for sure.

Aidan and Thera enter from the side, and the groom escorts his mother to her reserved seat in the front row. My stomach somersaults. *Fuck.*

He looks even better in his formal wedding coat.

The dark fabric shimmers with a dynamic, ever-shifting intensity, both captivating and unpredictable. Amber vines twist over the collar and cuffs as though they mean to spark them ablaze. The threads are warm and inviting, yet with an edge of something untamed, and I am struck by a beauty that isn't mine to hold.

The gardens fill the window behind him—the same ones I used to gaze at while waiting for him to knock on my window late at night.

The wide, boyish smile I couldn't resist. Our giggles as we would sneak out together, whispering secrets along the creek to reach our oasis of privacy, the world shrinking down to just the two of us. Those memories are so vivid in my mind, it kills me to know there's no one else to share them with. Even if it's over between us, I always figured the memories stitched us together forever.

But no "forever" can be taken for granted.

Bile rises to my mouth, and I gulp it all back down, my arms shaking.

I force my gaze back to Thera, wondering if she's the one who erased his memories. My eyes narrow as I take in her appearance. From a distance, she just looks tired, but I've never known Thera to wear an inch thick of makeup, even at her daughter's wedding. Her groomer is one of the most talented in Faerie, but she failed to completely conceal the gray tint of the queen's skin.

"Is Thera alright?" I whisper to Elio.

His lips press together, a dark glint flickering in his gaze as he plays with the cufflinks of his double-breasted, white tuxedo. "No."

I swallow hard. I know that look of his. As Winter King, Elio is often called to collect the souls of Fae royals, and regards the dying with a mix of pity, sadness, and acceptance.

The Summer Queen is sick.

Terminally so.

My head swims, the rushed timeline of this wedding taking on a whole new meaning.

The sprite of ceremonies flies to the front, and the live music starts. The band plays a soft rendition of another one of my songs as everyone stands to welcome the bride.

"Oh my—" Thera exclaims loudly. The affable smile on her face has been wiped out in favor of a terrified, wide-eyed gaze directed at me.

For a few long, odd seconds, the Summer Queen glares like I'm her own personal nightmare.

Aidan catches her reaction, his eyes darting from his mother to me before she turns away and fans herself. Most of the guests probably haven't noticed the interlude, too busy clapping and cheering for the bride's arrival, but Aidan's gaze meets mine again, and his lips move like he just cursed under his breath.

The queen tugs on the wide, standing collar of her dress as though she means to erase me from her vision.

Heather glides down the aisle in her nude, sleeveless ball gown and takes her place beside Aidan at the altar, oblivious to what just happened, and all the blood drains from my body. The claps and cheers of the crowd blur together as I sit down and grip the edge of the pew, my knuckles white over the glossy wood, the other guests also shifting to a seat.

Bitter, heavy tears roll over my cheeks, but I keep my spine straight. Everyone cries at weddings.

"Mortal love wanes. Fae love burns to the bone," the sprite starts, the words severe and dry, like a warning.

Fuck. I'm going to be sick.

I brace my shaky hands on my thighs, biting the insides of my cheeks. Elio covers my hand with his and gives it a gentle squeeze.

Everything plays out impossibly slowly, Heather's vows carving out my heart, one eloquent word at the time.

"Aidan Summers. We've been through so much together. From a

fast friendship during which you proved yourself the best confidante a woman could ask for, you claimed a permanent piece of my heart and became so much more. Often my partner in crime, at times my savior, but always in my corner, you showed me the light in my darkest days. I couldn't have found someone more passionate or kind as you, and I thank the Flame that our paths crossed when they did. As your wife and future queen, I promise to stand by your side through every challenge life might bring."

She passes Aidan the familiar ruby-encrusted dagger, and my stomach clenches as he fails to take it. His gaze darts to the ground for a second before it veers to the side, toward the crowd.

Searching for something. Or someone.

I sink my nails into my palms as he steps off the altar with a worried frown.

"Mother!" He suddenly leaps toward the front row.

Under the paralyzed stares of the Summer Court, Thera collapses to the floor of the Abbey, her regal tulle gown sprawled out over the white marble, red as blood.

CHAPTER 34
A THOUSAND CUTS
AIDAN

After tucking Mother into bed with the healers at her side, I find Heather standing on the royal balcony that overlooks the gardens. The expansive apartments my father used back when he ruled over the academy have been remodeled to allow the queen a much needed reprieve from the scrutiny she suffered in the capital.

The sun is high in the sky and casts a warm golden glow over the sprawling hedges of bleeding hearts and meticulously arranged flower beds. The scent of blooming roses drifts up on the afternoon breeze, mingling with the salt of the stormy sea. Heather's long brown hair catches the light, shimmering as it cascades down her back. She's a vision of elegance in her wedding dress.

"This is a disaster. I told her she should have been transparent about her condition from the start. Now, people are going to talk even more," my bride laments, hands clenched around the wrought-iron railing of the balcony.

"Fae royals better function at full power or six feet under. Anything in between sparks pockets of unrest."

It was my mother's decision not to let anyone know she's sick, to avoid the uncertainty and anguish that would inevitably shake the kingdom at the news of her impending death.

Even though I've been marked as her heir since the womb, people would draw up every crazy scenario in the books, wondering about possible challengers. "And she didn't want to cast a shadow over the wedding," I add.

"That worked well," Heather huffs with a sarcastic smile. "If her sickness was a widely spread fact, it would be easier to smooth out what happened. What are we supposed to tell people, now?"

"I don't know."

"Some luck, eh?" She turns to face me as I approach, her brown eyes meeting mine with a warmth that's as familiar as it is comforting. I've known Heather for most of my adult life—she's been my best friend, my confidante, and now, the woman I'm meant to spend the rest of my life with. But as I look at her, a pang of uncertainty stabs at my chest.

She cups my cheek. "Are you having cold feet? It's perfectly normal. Our lives are about to change, and it's not always going to be easy. To make us work, I mean."

"You're the best partner I could hope for."

"But we're not in love. You know that has been an issue for me ever since we made the decision."

"Remember last month, when you refused my proposal because you didn't think it was fair to me?"

"Yes?" She tilts her head slightly, studying me with a curious expression.

"What changed?"

She pauses, her gaze drifting out over the gardens. The silence stretches between us, filled with the distant chirping of birds and the rustle of leaves.

"Your mother told me she was sick, of course," she finally replies, her voice soft. "But that's not all. She also told me about that girl from your past..."

My brow furrows in confusion, and my muscles turn to stone, as though I've been dipped into some melted alloy and left somewhere cold to dry, about to chip off into a million pieces. "What girl?"

"The one who cursed you of course," she whispers, her voice brittle and sad and so unlike Heather that it quickens my pulse.

I shake my head. "I have no idea what you're talking about."

She turns to me fully, her eyes wide. "Thera said that a woman from your past had tried to steal your heart and cursed you never to love another. She said I needed to know if I was to accept your proposal, that I could be certain that marrying me wouldn't keep you from finding happiness elsewhere. She also made me promise not to mention it to you." She tucks a strand of hair behind her ear as though she's struggling with having to break that promise.

"What?" I bark in protest, but the words feel hollow as they leave my lips. The shadow of something forgotten, something important crawls like a line of ants at the back of my skull.

Her gaze falls to the ground between us. "Nobody likes to dredge up the past. I thought you didn't want it mentioned."

I shake my head. "I truly don't know who you're talking about. I think someone—or something—messed with my brain and erased my memories. Elio mentioned something about that girl, earlier, and I swear I can't recall anything about her."

Her nose wrinkles. "Erased your memories?"

"Yes."

"The woman who cursed you is gone now. For good. Your mother swore to this the night she told me about your past."

Her words hang in the air between us. The story my mother told her is at such a stark contrast to the one Elio and Elizabeth let me catch glimpses of. I'm not sure what to believe. Was I in love with her, or did she curse me to live a loveless life? Because I can't fathom how those two things can be true at once, yet both of them were true enough to be spoken out by a full-blooded Fae.

The nagging voice in my brain won't stop yapping. It clings to the edges of my thoughts, whispering that there's more to the story, something I can't remember but desperately need to.

As I look at my best friend standing beside me with unwavering support and kindness shining in her patient gaze, I wonder if I'm not about to smash to pieces my future—and the fate of the whole realm—for nothing.

I wrap my hands around hers. "I can't marry you today."

The moment the words leave my mouth, I know they're right.

"What—are you serious?"

"I need answers. The woman you speak of isn't gone. It's Elizabeth."

"She's the girl? The one you—" Her eyes widen, and the tears that gloss over them catch me off guard. "Elizabeth Snow?"

"I think so. It doesn't make much sense, but... there's just something achingly familiar about her."

Heather wraps her arms around herself, her breath shaky. A sniffle rocks her chest, and she presses her knuckles to her nose to stifle another. "By Eros... I can't believe I invited her here."

"I'm so sorry. I had no idea this would happen," I whisper.

The corners of her mouth quirk. "It's my fault. By the Flame, I even thought it would cheer your mother up to hear her sing. Be careful, Aidan. If that woman cursed you and crashed our wedding, who knows what she's willing to do next."

I rub her arms up and down, feeling guilty and more than a little reckless for my decision. "I'll get to the bottom of this, I swear. And then we can decide what's best."

Heather presses her lips together. "Alright. I'll hold the line with the guests and tell them your mother is sick, and that we are postponing the wedding. Hopefully, they'll infer that we're hoping for her to get better."

"Hopefully." I give her a quick, comforting nod, knowing better than to pray for a miracle. There's no use pretending the choice I just made means my mother will not live to see me wed, after all.

CHAPTER 35
ONE KISS
BETH

"Elizabeth. Are you in there?" A powerful knock at the door sends a jolt through me.

I've been standing by the window, crying, wondering how the hell I'm supposed to suffer through a second ceremony and planning an ungraceful escape. I hurriedly dry the salt trails on my face and turn to the door in time to see Aidan barrel into the room.

There he is—the groom, looking as though he's about to head off to war.

"Aidan," I croak. "Is your mother alright?"

He slows down, his gaze riveted to my packed suitcase, my Shadow mask tucked on top of the rose gold leather. "You're leaving," he replies, his voice filled with an uncertainty I've rarely heard from him.

For a moment, neither of us speaks. The silence thickens and expands, heavy with all the things I haven't said and the memories he can't reach. His gaze drifts past me, out the window, to the gardens below.

To the place where our love flourished.

"The queen is resting," he begins, his voice tight and formal. "But she wants the wedding to go along without her." He runs a hand through his hair, leaving it even more disheveled than it was when he entered, before his gaze snaps back to me. "She recognized you. I saw it."

"Yes," I say.

His brows pull together. "I can't remember."

"I know," I reply softly, the pain of it anchored deep in my chest.

"We were together, yes?" he asks quickly.

I answer with a nod.

"Did you truly love me?"

"Yes!"

For a moment, I'm back there with him, young and in love, the world full of possibilities.

"And I loved you?" he holds his breath, like my answer could shift his world on its axis.

I swallow hard. "Yes. Even though you ended it."

"Are you alright, my prince?" A male voice asks from the corridor, popping our bubble.

Aidan's gaze never leaves me as he doubles back to close the door. "Stand down, Peter. Just wait for me to come out."

"At your command, Your Highness."

My eyes narrow. "You brought guards with you?"

Aidan rubs the back of his skull, the gesture betraying his frustration. "I came in here to interrogate you."

"Interrogate me?" I inch backward, but he stalks closer, as if my subtle retreat taunts him.

Dark embers flicker in his amber eyes. "My mother told Heather that you'd cursed me."

The accusation tingles across my cheeks like a physical blow, and my arms fall at my sides. Thera believes this, or she wouldn't have been able to say it. I bump against the wall, and my back hunches, my heart in tatters.

A hundred years haven't eroded the royals' distrust toward my kin. The hatred that follows them—and me—wherever we go.

"Why did you come to the wedding?" Aidan breathes.

I play with my fingers, eyes cast down. "I had to see you. It was incredibly selfish, but I couldn't help myself."

"I'm not in love with Heather, and as far as I know, I've never loved anyone else." He raises my chin with his index finger. "Is that because you cursed me?"

My heart booms so hard, I fear it might leap out of my chest. "No. I swear it."

Aidan doesn't love his bride, and the knowledge fills me with a hot, molten heat.

"Or enchanted me. Or cast any kind of spell over me whatsoever?" he adds.

"No. I'm not playing on words, here."

"I'm not sure what to believe. If you're even truly Fae." He curls a hand around my shoulder, slowly raising it to my neck in a meticulous, trial-and-error manner, until his thumb traces the shell of my pointy ear. "I should have you arrested, really."

If he's testing my reaction, or his, I wouldn't know, but my lids flutter at the warm caress. I lean deeper into it, the years I spent fantasizing about his touch nullifying any survival instinct I still possess. No matter what he's saying, my body can't process that Aidan would ever hurt me, and it's reacting accordingly.

"The drum of my heart when I'm with you...the tremors of your magic... It's intoxicating. I've never felt anything like it." His eyes flick to my lips. "Kiss me." He breathes the words as though he's afraid to say them out loud.

No. I'm older and wiser now.

I look away, taken aback by his demand. "And what would a kiss accomplish, exactly?" I chuckle darkly.

"You know what fairytales say about true love's kiss... It might dispel whatever curse or enchantment erased my memories," he says. His voice remains eerily nonchalant, but his eyes gleam with mischief as he prevents me from widening the gap between us further.

Oh, how I've missed this impish side of him.

A smile pierces through my anguish, and I rest a hand over his breastbone. "Silly Faen stories." My fingers shake as I trace the v-shape of his wedding waistcoat. "But it's so *you* to suggest such a thing."

"Is it?" he murmurs. "I've always thought of myself as a skeptic."

"Then they've altered more than your memories."

He rests his forehead on mine. "I can't believe my parents went to such lengths to erase you because they didn't want me to marry a commoner. It sounds far-fetched, even for them. Especially my mother..." His eyes close for a moment.

A hiccup rakes my throat. *Here we go again.* "There's something you should know. Your parents didn't try to erase me because I was a moth."

His gaze hardens, a little more calculating than it was before, his hold on my neck a little heavier, but not to the point of becoming uncomfortable. By Thanatos, the way I'm feeling, I'd let him choke me to death if it earned me back his trust.

"I'm part siren. A Sea mutt." I hold my breath, entirely focussed on his reaction, proud that I mustered the courage to say it without being cornered into it. "That's why your parents never trusted your feelings for me. That and the fact that it made me completely unsuitable as a potential queen."

Aidan's nose wrinkles in the cutest way, but he doesn't draw back. "But siren songs don't last more than a day."

Tears mist in my eyes, his reaction so similar despite the drastically different circumstances. "You said the same thing back then." I stand on my tip-toes without meaning to, my nails skimming the side of his face.

He angles my lips to his. A flicker of something joyful and fragile —perhaps hope—illuminating his face. If it hadn't nearly killed me to see him with a ruby dagger in his hands, ready to swear his life and future to another woman, I'd turn him away. But this is my last chance.

There's nothing quite like a second first kiss.

Aidan presses his mouth to mine with caution, the way he'd approach a wild, untamed beast. It's not a dive, but a careful exploration. An investigation full of riddles, his tongue serving as a final question mark as it slips past my defenses.

And the answer to all of them is, *fuck yes!*

He's no longer the man who broke my heart.

I'm not the stranger who crashed his wedding.

In that kiss, we're more than just the sum of all parts, more than old lovers separated by space and time and the oh-so-annoying bout of amnesia. We're *us*. Aidan's body apparently remembers details his mind has forgotten as he takes hold of my waist, flattening me to the wall with just the right pressure to set my body ablaze.

I force my eyes open, shying away from him. "Anything?"

His chest rises and falls. "Blessed Flame. Are you sure this isn't our first kiss? Because I don't fathom how I could have been made to forget *that*."

A heavy sigh drags down the elation that had built up in my chest. "Quite sure."

He caresses the side of my face with his thumb. "I wish I could remember."

"But you don't. That's okay." I tuck my chin down to hide my face. So he doesn't see me crumble.

"No, it's not." He leans in again, but I press one finger to his mouth.

"You said one kiss."

"I feel...greedy when I'm with you," he chucks out, the words rough and quiet, brimming with actual pain.

If I had any doubt this was *my* Aidan, this sentence disperses the very last one of them.

I sink my nails in his hairline, and he hums in approval, devouring me. His mistrust acts as gasoline on the flames, spicing up the first intimate moment we've shared in a century with a pinch of desperation, and a sprinkle of violence.

Any false hope that I might have blown our chemistry out of proportions during our time apart is absolutely dead, my heart hammering in my chest.

A loud knock on the door coaxes a snarl out of him, and he finally breaks the kiss.

"Your Highness, we need to know you're alright."

Aidan's arms shake, his fist curling and uncurling before he tears himself away. "I told you to *just wait*." He strides over to ease the door open. "You're all dismissed."

"Sir?"

"Leave us. I won't ask again," he barks before closing it again and clicking the lock.

Aidan walks down the length of the room and back, his features draped in shadows. "Was it always like this?"

"Always." I hide my hands behind my back, the sweet leftover sting of his kisses on my lips throbbing under his scrutiny.

I smother a heated moan as he shrugs off his waistcoat. He throws it over the foot of the bed and unbuttons his cufflinks, looking ready to *pounce*.

"Maybe we should—" I start, but he storms back over to me and swallows the rest of my sentence with a bruising kiss.

Aidan pins me to the wall with his knee, one hand exploring the thigh-high slit of my silk dress until he reaches the lace of my underwear, his fingertips digging into the flesh of my hip. I pull the shirt off his back, peeling one sleeve off at a time. The muscles in his shoulders are broader and more defined than they were, and I rake my nails over the grooves and ridges.

His nostrils flare. "Fuck. I want you."

His touch grows intently precise, as if he found his old *How to Drive Beth Crazy* playbook. He brushes the curve of my buttocks to the tender skin of my inner thigh back and forth, and I wrap one leg around his midriff, my center rubbing against the enticing shape of his erection.

His head falls forward. "I want you more than I ever thought possible, which isn't a good sign considering the accusations made against you," he chucks out, his voice unsteady. "But my body remembers you, even though I can't, and it's irresistible."

His big hand stretches the lace of my underwear as it travels back to my front, creeping dangerously close to my pulsing heat.

"Are you going to arrest me?"

"Maybe. But I kind of want to see you come, first."

My breasts strain against the low neckline of my dress. "Don't play with me. Please."

"Too bad, because that's exactly what I mean to do, Miss Elizabeth." He slips the silk down below my hard, painful nipples, and licks his lips at the sight. "Tell me about us. Where did we meet?"

"In the labyrinth."

He dips his head down to taste each breast, sucking them into his mouth and teasing the peaks until I'm panting.

"And where did I taste you for the first time?"

He means more than just a kiss and slides down to his knees, turning my brain to mush.

I grip his shoulders. "Wait. Are you still going through with the wedding?"

"Tell me not to," he breathes against my inner thigh, the husky demand rippling across my sensitive flesh. "Tell me this is real, and not just some curse or spell."

"It's real."

"Where did I taste you for the first time?" he repeats.

I quake all over, tugging on his hair. "At the cabin. On St. John's Eve."

"How hard did you come, then?"

"Harder than I'd ever come before."

He grins wickedly. "Not as hard as you'll come now. Do you want me to touch you, Miss Elizabeth?"

"Yes!"

Aidan pushes the lace of my underwear aside. He sinks one finger inside me, then two, and alternates between hard strokes and slow circles as though he feels jealous of his past self, competing with a version of himself he feels too distant from.

My belly cramps at how beautiful he is. If he flicked his tongue across the aching bundle of nerves, I'd simply die.

"Look at me. I need to make sure you mean it."

The eye contact feels scandalous as Aidan drags his thumb across my sensitive flesh. The friction between the soaked lace and the hard pad of his thumb coaxes a gasp out of me with a heavy, delightful stroke. He darts his tongue out to touch his bottom lip, his amber eyes darker and more impatient than I remember.

He licks me over the lace, the rub of his tongue hot and soft. My head falls to the wall at my back as he dives for a deeper taste.

Aidan pins me in place with both hands as he feasts on me, drawing out long, breathless praises out of my lungs.

I curl my hands in his hair, my lips parting in shock as I come hard, grinding myself against his hungry tongue without shame.

I shake all over, squeezing my lids shut.

"That was fucking beautiful. I want to see it again," he says on a low growl.

I claw at his shoulders. "Stand up. I need you inside me."

"I can't. Not until I vet your story further." He arches a brow. "Isn't this better than a prison cell?"

"Depends if you're in there with me," I deadpan.

The corners of his mouth quirk. "I like how you think, Miss Elizabeth."

"Call me Beth, please. Like you used to."

He leans in for a long, intense kiss, before finally saying, "Alright. *Beth.*"

I cup a hand over his hot, hard cock and start to lower to my knees, but he squeezes my hips to keep me standing. "Don't."

"Are you sure?" I tease. "You used to love my mouth."

A dark chuckle grates his throat. "Ah, hells. I don't doubt that at all. But I can't right now; I have to keep some semblance of control over this clusterfuck." His eyes burn into me tenfold as he growls, hungry for more and yet denying himself the release he needs. "But mark my words. Once your story checks out, I will spend an entire day inside your mouth."

I raise my brows, surprised by his restraint. "You're more patient than you used to be."

"Argh." He stumbles backward with a grimace of pain, curling onto himself.

"What's happening?" I ask quickly. "Are you hurt?" My eyes scan him from head to toe, trying to figure out what went wrong.

Fire burns through the top of his trousers, and the fabric covering the Mark of the Gods blackens and flakes to ashes.

"Aidan..." I gasp, shocked.

Our gazes meet for a fleeting, disastrous second. The guilt I read in his amber depths wrecks me.

"The queen..." he breathes.

He barrels out of my room, and Thanatos forgive me, I run after him.

CHAPTER 36

MORHEIM

WONDER BOY

Summerlands, Faerie, 100 years ago

"Oh." Beth rests her head on the wall at her back, the midday sun filtering through her bedroom window. "We're going to be late," she scolds half-heartedly, tugging on my hair.

I push aside her underwear and drag my fingers across her drenched folds, happy to find her wet and wanton. "It's just a ball game."

A hushed breath escapes her. "But you're playing."

"I'd rather do this."

I massage her sweet core until her hips buck, then sink two fingers inside, dragging in and out of her a few times, teasing her just the way she likes it. I crave the sounds she makes when she's right there on the edge and swallow them with a kiss, our foreheads resting against one another as I drink in the sight of her.

Her nails sink into my shoulder blade. "More. Please."

I increase the pressure but keep the same rhythm, eager to see her come apart slowly and completely. I take my time, making her mad for that next, deep stroke. Her back arches, the gush of her pleasure dripping along my fingers as she screams, and I smother her loudest cries with my free hand.

When she's done shuddering in my arms, I lick her arousal off my fingers and pull her in for a bruising kiss. "Meet me in the gardens afterwards. To celebrate my victory."

"And what if you lose?" she teases with a false grimace of worry, linking her arms around my neck, preventing me from pulling away.

I grin from ear to ear. "Don't you have faith in your man, Songbird? I wouldn't let a bunch of weak-minded darklings beat me."

"I'm a darkling," she muses, pressing her hand to my erection.

I groan at the pressure and stop moving, unable to walk away.

She palms me back and forth over the fabric, destroying my chances to calm down, before slipping her small hand inside my trousers and rubbing the wet tip with her thumb.

"Ah, flaming hells."

"If I kept you here, the game would be forfeit, would it not?"

I close my eyes, her hard strokes driving me wild. "Don't stop."

She falls to her knees in front of me, her long black braid tucked at her back, her hooded eyes still thick with pleasure. "I want you in my mouth, *now*."

It's the hottest thing I've ever seen.

I wrap my hand in her braid and control the pace, her talented mouth wreaking havoc on my body as she traces the shape of my tattoo.

"That's cheating," I groan, my cock throbbing so hard, I'm ready to come balls deep inside her beautiful mouth, her tongue doing wicked, wicked things to the tip.

From the way she uses both hands to drive me wild, her caresses urgent and delicious, I figure she doesn't really mean to disqualify me from the match.

She bobs her head up and down, and I can't take it anymore, undone like a horny virgin every damn time she uses her mouth. I empty myself at the back of her throat, and she swallows it all, the lustful look on her face morphing into a naughty grin.

I help her to her feet and peck her lips. "I love you. Please meet me at the cabin after the match."

"Love you too, but hurry up, or there won't be a game to win."

I reluctantly tear myself away and climb through her window. My heart tightens as I exit the gardens, smoothing down my hair. Out there on the field, I'll have to slip back into my prince mask and pretend Beth is merely my sister's best friend. She won't cheer for me, and I won't kiss her at the end of the match.

Because, no matter how many mind-blowing orgasms and warm nights we share together, she's not mine. Not yet. But I swat the unwanted twinge of fear away. I have to give her time to process this, and reassure her at every turn that I'm not going to change my mind.

After a while, she'll see that breaking off her engagement is the first step to the rest of our lives together. Besides, I can't complain… sneaking around can be tremendous fun.

"You're late, boo," Ezra greets me on the field, his lips pressed into a grim line.

"I know."

"We almost had to forfeit." He tosses me a matching white vest, and I slip it over my head before grabbing the ball from the ground.

"I'm here now."

Sean and the other members of the team glower at me for my tardiness, but I'm too happy to care.

Ezra raises an eyebrow. "Plenty of people noticed Beth's absence, too. You two will get caught soon if you're not more careful."

"Let's play ball, eh? You can lecture me later." I tap his breastbone with the ball to nudge him off.

Ezra rolls his eyes. "I reserve the right to say I told you so."

The match starts, and adrenaline surges through me with the claps and cheers of the villagers and students in the crowd filling the bleachers. Soon, I spot Beth among them, sitting right beside Willow, and I fight the urge to wave at her.

We're almost at halftime, the darklings trailing behind by three points, when the sky darkens in a very sudden and unexpected manner.

I slow to a jog and angle my gaze upward, but the sun hasn't been obscured by storm clouds. Instead, a thick, shapeless shadow blocks its light. The phenomenon moves at the edges, shimmering like a mirage, and sends a bout of dizziness through my blood.

"Flaming hell, what is that?" Ezra shouts over the gasps and clamor of the other players. "Morheim isn't supposed to start for another week."

Morheim, when it arrives, keeps the sun from rising in our sky for up to ten days and allows nightmares to prowl our lands, but it's never come early before.

Damian freezes, and the ball topples from his hands. "By Morpheus... It's a flock of crows."

I squint at the strange shadow once more, and sure enough, as the shifting darkness sharpens into focus, I can make out the shapes of black wings and yellow eyes. Hundreds—no, thousands—of crows form a dense wall of sleek feathers and long beaks, heading straight toward us.

"Under the trees. Now!" Ezra commands.

A chorus of panicked cries rise from the spectators, who quickly abandon the bleachers, rushing for the cover of the trees. The Prince of Light leaves my side, joining the frantic retreat.

I search for Beth in the chaos and make a beeline for her. The ground is overrun with pine needles, and long shadows stretch beneath the trees as the *caws* and *kraas* of the crows grow louder and louder.

Everyone takes refuge under the nearest canopy of trees—everyone but Damian.

The Shadow Lord stands alone in the middle of the field.

"What is he doing?" Zeke grunts, his voice tinged with disbelief.

Willow's eyes glaze over, and she speaks in the eerie, far-off tone she uses whenever she has a premonition. "Four crows nest on top of the Shadow tree. They'll be crowned before the next dawn."

The living cloud of birds picks up speed as they dive, plunging directly at him, but Damian doesn't raise a hand to protect himself—he doesn't move an inch, only grinning at the incoming flock.

Under our awestruck stares, the crows plummet to their deaths around him in a terrifying blur, their frail necks snapping from the force of the impact. Despite the violence of the blows, Damian himself only takes one direct hit, a ripple of magic slicing through the air as the very last crow crashes into the side of his head.

Blood drips down the side of his face, and I'm the first to rush to him, slowly processing what just happened. "Blessed Flame. You're—"

Damian touches his bloody neck, and I notice the swirl of circles and lines now adorning the back of his ear, black as night.

"The Mark of the Gods," Ezra breathes, his voice barely a whisper next to me.

"The Shadow King is dead." I beat my chest with a closed fist, the panicked glares of the villagers and students prompting me to restore order. "Morpheus has made his will known. Damian Sombra has been called to rule."

"The gods have spoken," Ezra says quickly, and the others follow.

"The gods have spoken."

"The gods have spoken."

Damian blinks, as though waking from a long, heavy sleep. He clenches and unclenches his fists and meets Zeke's horrified glare head on.

I clear my throat and address the Shadow Prince in a muted tone. "My condolences, Zeke. Your father was a fine king."

Despite all our differences, this is a momentous occasion, and I will not dishonor the gods—or my mother. As the highest-ranking impartial royal present, it's my duty to lead by example.

The only thing worse than learning of your father's death in front of the entire school is discovering, at the very same moment, that you're not destined to take his place on the throne. It must sting beyond belief, a humiliation that cuts deeper than any blade.

"Yes. Sorrows. Prayers," Ezra snips, feral.

I throw him a warning glare, but Zeke ignores us both.

His focus is locked entirely on Damian as he barrels closer, fists clenched at his sides. "I should kill you here and now."

"I worked my whole life for this. My sympathies for your father, but you'd make a pitiful king," Damian replies with unshakable poise, his calm delivery raising goosebumps on my arms.

I shudder as his eyes swirl with liquid gold, shadows twisting over his shoulders and arms, alive with the power imbued by the Mark of the Gods. It's as though Morpheus himself is lending Damian his cloak of night ahead of his coronation, the God's choice clear and undeniable.

His time to rule has come far sooner than any of us anticipated, and while he's outshined me yet again, I wouldn't trade places with him for anything in the worlds. Not if it meant living a life of duty so young.

"I challenge you!" Zeke roars, shoving Damian hard enough to send him stumbling backward. But the Crow regains his footing quickly, his dark eyes narrowing in warning.

"Zeke, take a minute—" I begin, my voice low but urgent.

The Shadow Prince slices his arms through the air, puffing out his chest with reckless bravado. "I won't let you steal my crown! I challenge you, Damian Sombra, and in ten days, you'll be dead."

His words ring out, sharp and deliberate, the official challenge crackling with magic that lingers in the air like an aftertaste of smoke and steel. Every witness tenses, the weight of the ancient ritual settling over us, as the reality of what Zeke has set in motion becomes impossible to ignore.

Beth gasps, my Songbird standing barely a few feet away. Her ocean-blue eyes are wide, and frost glazes her cheeks, a chilling testament to the shock coursing through her veins. Every instinct in me screams to comfort her, to brush away the ice and pull her close, but I can't. Not here. Not with everyone watching. The secrecy of our relationship chains me in place, forcing me to do nothing when all I want is to warm her with my touch.

We exchange a fleeting glance, a silent understanding passing between us. The students stand more rigid and silent than usual, their posturing and bravado stripped away by what they've just witnessed. We play games, we taunt, we posture—but this? What Zeke has done will have egregious consequences.

In ten days, the new Shadow King will be crowned, with either Damian or Zeke poised to claim the throne. And if the past is any indication, as the High Fae of the Shadowlands provinces cheer for their new king, the corpse of the loser will be lowered six feet under.

CHAPTER 37
WEDDING PLANS
SONGBIRD

The smell of dead crows—of blood and feathers and entrails—lingers in my nose. Acidic. Pungent.

An hour ago, I was sneaking around with my secret boyfriend, having the time of my life. Now, I'm petrified.

Willow keeps a firm hold on my arm, guiding me away from the bleachers and into the gardens toward our apartments. The scene we just witnessed weighed heavily on us both. What should have been a lighthearted, unceremonious ballgame turned into an impromptu gathering to mourn the fallen Shadow King, with the promise of more death looming ahead.

"Ninety-seven percent of crown challenges end in death," she whispers.

"Yes."

Her large amber eyes, red and glassy with tears, meet mine. "Are you okay?"

"I don't know."

It's no secret that I don't want to marry Zeke, but him dying before the end of the year had never crossed my mind as a solution to my predicament. A wave of nausea washes over me as we reach the shade of the breezeway, my rendezvous with Aidan obviously canceled.

"Elizabeth!" Zeke's voice booms behind us, barely recognizable, and my eyes widen.

Since when does he call me by my name? I freeze on the marble slab and give Willow's hand a tight squeeze. "Go ahead. I'll catch up."

Zeke slows down as he draws near, no longer running, but pacing, never settling down in one spot. "I need to speak with you." His chest rises and falls, his movements all over the place as though he's been pumped raw with fear and adrenaline. Seeing him this way dizzies me, and I wrap my arms around my frame.

"Your father— It's terrible. I'm sorry you had to find out in this way."

He nods to himself a few times. "You and I have to get married *now*. Before the challenge."

My heart somersaults. "What?"

I must not have heard him right.

"Well, not *now*, but tomorrow. If I'm to beat Sombra, I need all the magic I can get, but this has to stay between us. Meet me in the main hall at dawn, and I'll take you with me to Nocturna."

My voice feels brittle as I say, "I have my Shadow mask ceremony tomorrow."

"The Shadow King oversees every Shadow mask ceremony, so that's postponed until his successor is crowned."

"Oh." My jaw drops in a mix of icy dread and panicked disbelief. I've been waiting for this for months—for that forever instrument of freedom—and it was right there within my reach.

"Everything will be arranged, and you can teach me how to handle your ice magic for a few days so I can take Damian by surprise at the challenge."

The cocky, boastful prince is gone. The Zeke standing before me looks dead serious—bereft, and frankly, terrified.

He lifts his gaze to meet mine. "Chin up, moth. In ten days, you'll either be my queen or my widow, free to live the life you want."

There's no suspicion in his eyes, no fear that I might back out—not now that his father is dead and a Faerie crown is actually within reach. Most students at the academy would kill for a chance to rule, and as Zeke shrewdly pointed out, I will either be his widow or his queen.

He doesn't think anyone would be so foolish as to let such an opportunity slip away. Especially not a moth.

I climb the stairs to my room in a haze, playing absentmindedly with the ring Aidan gave me. I wear it on a chain around my neck, hidden from view most of the time, but so precious to me.

Willow is pouring us both a glass of wine when I enter the room, and I close the door quietly behind me.

"He wants you to marry him, doesn't he?" she asks, not looking up from her task.

"Yes."

She walks over and hands me a glass, her sharp eyes scanning my face. "And will you?"

"I'm not sure."

Willow sighs, giving me a small nod. "I'll stand by you every step of the way, Beth Snow," she says, her voice warm but steady. She squeezes my arm briefly before slipping past me to sit on the sofa. "But let's be honest. Zeke doesn't have the brains to win that challenge. Even with your combined magic, Damian will eat him alive. I'd give him less than a five percent chance."

Her bluntness stings, but she's right. I sink into the armchair across from her, staring down at the wineglass in my hands. The weight of Aidan's ring on its chain feels unbearable around my neck.

"And I don't think even my father would risk the outrage of driving a young widow out of school. Once you two are married, you'll inherit his status, even in death. No one will dare call you a moth again."

I have been presented with the opportunity to both fulfill my promise to Zeke's father and be free, but I don't feel any relief at all.

"I don't want to be a widow," I say softly, the words cracking as they leave my mouth.

Willow's expression shifts. "Better a widow than stuck in a loveless marriage," she murmurs.

I don't respond right away. Her smile is dim but brave, her eyes full of resignation. She never said it out loud, but I know how much her wedding night cost her.

The possibility gnaws at something raw inside me, and I bite my bottom lip, trying to suppress the guilt rising in my chest. Willow thinks Zeke is the problem; that I'm hesitating because I don't love him and want to avoid the sex altogether. She doesn't know the truth about Aidan.

"It's not that simple," I whisper, clutching the glass ring tighter.

Willow leans forward, resting her elbows on her knees. "Zeke's chances against Damian are slim, but he *could* make it out against all odds. Is that what's stopping you?"

When I don't answer, she tilts her head, studying me. "Beth, what's going on? Is there something you're not telling me?"

My breath catches, and for a fleeting moment, I consider telling her everything—about Aidan, about the nights we've stolen, about the way he makes me feel. But the words are too slow to come. I can't seem to force them out to Willow who's trusted me with her own secrets and struggles. Before I gather the courage to explain, Iris storms through the door and slams her bag onto the kitchen counter, her hair more disheveled than I've ever seen it, her eyes red and blotchy.

"Hey, are you alright?" Willow asks, her spine stiffening at our roommate's eerie appearance.

"How do you *dare* ask me that question?" Iris deadpans, her voice quiet and hollow. "After what happened last night."

Willow grimaces, her fingers rapping against her knee as she turns back around to face me. "Iris is furious with me," she whispers under her breath. "Her father was convinced that he would get Ezra to marry her instead, and now that it's not to be, I can't do anything right."

Iris's face wrinkles in fury, the slender woman looking twice as tall as she marches into the living room area, fists balled at her sides. "It should have been me! You don't give a damn about him. You like *girls*."

Willow's eyes widen in shock. "Iris!"

"Oh, come on. It's hardly a secret," Iris says dismissively. "I thought that with me around, you two newlyweds might find some common ground, but you stood me up without so much as a heads-up."

"I should go." I rise and tiptoe toward my bedroom, hoping to give the two women some space.

"Ezra changed his mind," Willow says quietly. "I can't help that. With Elio being head over heels for you, it's not so surprising he had scruples about accepting your offer."

"Please, Ezra couldn't care less about his brother's pathetic obsession with me. He chickened out because of her." Iris points at me, freezing me mid-retreat.

My hand clenches around the doorknob. "What do you mean?"

Iris creates a very small gap between her index finger and thumb. "He came this close to giving in, but he said he couldn't bear how you'd look at him if you found out about us. He wasn't afraid to hurt Elio's feelings. Not scared of Willow's reaction—his damn wife. But *you*."

"I-I'll talk to you both later, alright?" I slip inside my bedroom and lock the door behind me, the argument picking up where I left it, Iris's heart and pride wounded enough for the Spring Fae to abandon all pretenses.

I zone out their conversation, but a dark silhouette at my window makes me jump. Aidan is here, waiting for me, and I bring a shaky head to my forehead. *Oh, hells!*

I crack open the window, the eerie darkness of Morheim spilling into the room. Even in the middle of the day, it feels like midnight, the sun banished from the sky for the holiday's duration. "You can't be in here—Willow and Iris will hear," I whisper, glancing over my shoulder to the door.

"Let me in," Aidan says, his voice low but urgent.

I push the window open wider, and he climbs inside with practiced ease, his bite of power filling the room. His brows pull together at the loud argument going on beyond the door, but he doesn't mention it.

"Please don't marry him." His head tilts slightly, desperation bleeding into every syllable. "I beg you."

I blink a few times, shocked by his insight. "How did you know?"

"When you didn't meet me at the cabin, I came to meet you and heard you two talking." He steps closer, his jaw tight. "He needs your magic, but you can't marry him, Songbird. He probably won't win the challenge, with or without your magic, but I can't bear the thought of the two of you together. Even for one night."

I clutch the foot of the bed for support, finally making up my mind about it. "I don't want to marry him," I whisper. "I want you. Only you."

The ring Aidan gave me grows hot between my breasts as he draws near, and his breath hitches. "Songbird. Are you saying—"

I cut him off, shaking my head. "No one would marry us, Aidan. They'd be terrified of reprisal."

"Mabel lives in the new world. With the Shadow King dead, I can get us there without fear of being followed. Ezra said she'd marry us for a price."

The knowledge that Ezra and Aidan discussed this sends my head spinning, and I look down at the ring hanging around my neck. "She's a witch."

"I don't care. Once it's done, no one—not even the gods themselves—will be able to undo it. And we can finally be together in broad daylight."

"But we're so young. Your feelings might change."

I'm arguing against my own desires, here, but if we're about to link our destinies permanently and anger his very *royal* family, he needs to be sure. Otherwise, regrets would just fester between us.

Aidan seems to understand where I'm coming from, and his voice softens. "My feelings for you will never change. They're as permanent as this mark," he says, pressing his hand to his tattoo.

A rushed breath whistles out of my lungs. "What if someone figures out I'm part siren?"

"Then we'll leave...settle in the new world for a while. Plenty of sirens have fled there over the years."

My heart stumbles as each fear rolls off Aidan's back, his confidence dissolving my doubts, one wild hypothesis at a time. "You'd truly choose exile to be with me?" I whisper, awed and shocked by the depths of his devotion.

"Without a doubt."

I sink my hand into his hair until our noses bump. "What about your family? Your future?" I breathe.

"My mother is still in her prime. It could be centuries before the crown calls for a new king, and by then, things will have blown over, you'll see. I refuse to believe our world will still be so...backwards then." He gives me a smile that's secret and masculine and so *Aidan* that I'd give anything to see it everyday. Every night.

Every morning.

As my husband.

"Alright, we should make plans." My voice trembles. "But we have to be *extremely* careful until we figure this out."

"Is that a yes?" Aidan chucks out.

I press my lips together, the enormity of what we're about to do sending my heart into a frenzy. "Yes, but you can't stay here."

He cups my face, staring at me as though I've lost my mind—but in a way that pleases him immensely. "You can't tell me you're ready to become my wife and expect me to leave," he says, his voice thick with longing. He rests his forehead on mine, his steady grip grounding me. "We'll escape to the new world, get married, and after that... they'll just have to come around. Mortal love wanes, but Fae love burns to the bone. Once we're married, even the gods themselves won't be able to keep us apart."

He moves to kiss me, but I deny him.

"Wait! I need to make sure beyond the shadow of a doubt that you're all mine, no magic involved." I meet his gaze despite the crimson blush on my cheeks.

His brow furrows. "What are you talking about?"

I cross the room to my desk, pull out my notebook, and flip to the right page. "A spell," I explain, my tone firm. "To ensure my song is not still influencing you. I found it in the archives, and if you want us to get married, it's non-negotiable."

"Beth," he says softly, shaking his head. "I don't care about your siren blood. I love you."

"I love you too, but—"

"No buts. We're past that. I love you." He catches my hand in his, his expression a mixture of tenderness and determination. "Blessed Flame," he breathes, his smile breaking through the last shreds of doubt in my heart. "I'm so incredibly happy right now." His lips brush mine, but I press my hands to his chest again.

"Aidan, if my siren blood—" A nervous gasp pops out of my mouth. "I need this. If we're going to get married, it has to be real. No magic. No doubt." Tears spill over, sliding down my cheeks.

The elation on his face dims slightly, settling into something quieter but no less steadfast. He nods. "Alright. What do you need for the spell?"

I glance down at the list I compiled, the culmination of weeks of research. "Here."

Aidan pulls me to him for one last kiss before he heads back for the opened window. "I'll get the supplies together. Meet me by the Eros fountain in the gardens at midnight, and we'll go to the new world first, then seek out Mabel once the spell is done. Don't tell anyone you're leaving—not even Willow." He sounds like an officer heading off to war, confident of his victory, and the fire in his amber gaze takes my breath away.

I'd follow him to the ends of the Dark Sea, through the Breach and beyond the edges of our world.

The prince who stole my heart with his first fiery kiss, back when I feared he was merely a fever dream—a perfect construct of the labyrinth fashioned to my exact fantasies. An ideal tailor-made to my preferences, yet forever out of reach.

He'd taken charge in much the same way that night, eager to lead me where I yearned to go. Confident, mischievous, and devoted to my cause, ready to cheat, lie and scheme just so he could keep me by his side.

I catch up with him before he crosses the windowsill, in awe that I, an insignificant moth with barely two pieces of silver to her name, can incite such passion in the most bewitching and powerful Fae heir on the continent.

Before now, I never truly believed we could make it. It sounded too good to be true, empty promises whispered in the throes of passion. The sentiment behind them was true enough for our silly dreams to be spoken out, but not acted upon.

Yet, Aidan truly *craves* for me to become his wife. He's ready to put our love first, above the demands of his birth and the crown he's supposed to inherit. I've argued against it for months—often contrary to my own desires—but he still chooses *me*.

My heart races in my chest, too wide and hot for the ice in my veins not to melt.

By the spindle. We're really doing this.

Aidan and I are going to elope.

CHAPTER 38
LESSONS
WONDER BOY

The restless energy in my chest would set me ablaze if I let it, the fire that lives inside me sizzling right under the skin. I'm a ball of nerves, planning out everything I need for the enchantment Beth plans to weave.

I can only commend her for her desire to test that I'm not under some kind of influence from her siren song. If it's something she needs to feel more comfortable, I'm all for it, but from the looks of the ingredients and instruction, the spell might take a few hours to complete. It's a talisman-type of enchantment that wards sailors against the effects of the Sea folks' voices. A powerful spell that was locked away in the archives of the academy and meant for our eyes only—not the type of enchantment you'd find in any glorified witch shop. It probably hasn't been used since the Mist wars, when the Summerlands armies had to venture out through the Breach, but it's a tried and true way to dispel any siren song and protect the wearer from any further harm or influence.

I dry off my hands on the front of my shirt, my skin growing hotter by the second. By this time tomorrow, Beth and I will be married, and once it's done, we can find a gentle way to break the news to our parents. Even my father will have to accept my decision, given no alternative.

No one has to know that she's part siren, and people will have plenty of time to get used to the idea of me marrying a moth before I'm called to rule.

The thought fills me with equal parts giddiness and apprehension.

I catch a glimpse of Ezra entering our kitchen from the corner of my eye as I double-check the list Beth gave me. "Hey. I need you to run interference for me. My father is probably going to swing by tomorrow morning to talk about the challenge, and I need you to tell him I'm running a quick errand, and that I'll be back soon."

"Alright." Ezra peruses the gear on the counter in front of me, frown lines wrinkling his forehead. "What's that for?"

"A spell."

"Are you going somewhere?" he asks quietly, looking more glum than usual.

My lips quirk. "Yes, but I can't tell you the details."

Ezra has been struggling to adjust to married life, distancing himself from most, if not all, of the women he used to have fun with. He's hell-bent on doing right by Willow, at least in appearances, but his newfound misery is at such a stark contrast to my current happiness that he's been keeping me at arm's length, too.

"Oh, come on, boo. You know you can trust your best friend. What's going on?" His voice borders on sugary, and his eyes bore into me in a very blunt, intimate way.

Even though Ezra knows about Beth and me, I suspect he's still hot for her, so I've spared him the details of our relationship.

"When I come back, after the Shadowlands challenge is settled, you and I should go somewhere together. Pick a place we've never been before and visit, just for fun." I slip on my jacket, my Shadow mask safely tucked in my pocket.

"Damian has to win that challenge, right?"

I scoff at the trace of uncertainty in his tone. "Are you serious? There's no doubt about it."

His pale brows pull together. "You mean since your girlfriend won't marry him?" he says in a dry, almost sarcastic quip. "Because logic dictates he'd stand a chance if she did."

"Beth is obviously not marrying Zeke. What's gotten into you?"

Ezra wrinkles his nose at the last of the ingredients lying across the counter. "What kind of spell calls for something as foul as myrtle seaweed? Are you planning to hunt a siren?"

I grimace at the word. "Of course not."

"What does it have to do with your little whore of a moth, unless..."

A tingle of warning sizzles up my spine as I spread my arms on each side and let fire rise to my fists. "Flaming hell, you're not Ezra."

The man in front of me isn't my best friend. The realization lands like a physical blow, hollowing out the air between us. I read it in the void of his eyes, the cruel twist of his mouth as his disguise fades. I've been played. Ezra melts into something sharper, colder—the King of Light.

"Quite a plan you've got there, Aidan," he drawls, his tone a study in condescension. "I'm impressed. It takes a real man to elope with a siren."

I flinch, but his smirk only deepens. He takes a step closer, hands clasped behind his back like he's taking a stroll through the palace grounds. "I admit, I'm not often taken off guard. I came here to make sure you'd tell her to marry Zeke, to keep Damian from the throne. But I see now that your little Sea whore wouldn't make a suitable Shadow Queen."

"Beth doesn't belong with the Sea folk. She's mine."

"Oh, you're so naïve." His eyes gleam, malicious delight dripping from every word. "You figured that once you were married, everything would be fine, right?"

I raise my chin. "Nothing can nullify a Fae marriage. Not even kings."

He inclines his body to me, hands still braced behind his back, his grin razor-sharp. "Nothing but death."

My blood chills in my veins. *Is he saying—*

"You're meant to become *king*, Aidan. Don't you think your father would *kill* to make that happen? Even before I tell him about you two, he'll be relieved to see the moth arrested, and once she's in his custody, it'll be all too easy to get rid of her permanently."

Bile rises to my throat.

"He wouldn't kill her himself, of course," Ethan drawls out. "He'd ask, let's say, a good friend to do it. Someone who doesn't shy away from violence. Someone with enough power to make it seem like an accident." He melts into a perfect copy of Beth, the vicious curl of her mouth shivering through me. "Or better yet, a suicide."

"It won't take a lot of work or imagination to justify the poor girls' actions, given her soiled blood. We'll say that she was about to stand trial and took the easy way out... Nothing too hard to fake."

"You're a monster," I say, my voice sharp, cutting through the scorching air between us.

Ethan smirks, unfazed. "And yet, you know I'm right."

My mind races, shame and rage and bitterness settling in my cramped muscles, my heart like a vulgar piece of metal held in a vice grip and beaten against a forger's anvil. Ethan Lightbringer could easily disguise Beth's murder as a suicide, and if I was anyone else, he'd get away with it. While it disgusts me to barter with a man that should have been arrested for his crimes against his family a lifetime ago, I might have to play along for now and make him believe he's won.

"What do you want?" I ask, letting out an exaggerated sigh of defeat.

He straightens, misreading the slump in my shoulders and the frown on my face as signs of surrender. "Break her heart. Abandon your foolish plans, and I will let her live. This is my best offer, and I warn you, it's final."

"How can I be sure you won't find her in the new world? That you won't double-cross me and get rid of her anyway?"

The hatred that coats his every word makes me doubt he would let her live her life at all, even if I did everything he asks. I can't risk him hurting Beth while I figure out a way out of this.

"If you want me to break it off with her tonight," I say, stepping closer, "I need your solemn promise that you—nor my father or anyone within your influence—won't hurt her."

His astute gaze slides to the side for a split second. "That's unnecessary—"

"Swear it," I interrupt, my tone hardening. "Or I'll take my chances with fire."

Ethan studies me, his expression unreadable. Finally, he sighs, his voice losing some of its mocking edge. "Alright, I swear. If she leaves Faerie, and you stay here, I won't hurt her. But let me be clear—I won't let you out of my sight until it's done." I glare at him, my fists clenched, but he doesn't stop. "And while she's running away crying, you and I will head directly to Eterna to speak to your father."

I can't fully grasp the scope of Ethan's plan, but he certainly has one. My father might escalate these threats, but my mother would never allow her son and heir to be blackmailed by another Fae king. She'll stand with me on this, at least, if not on the marriage.

Does Ethan think me so young and fickle that I would just grit my teeth and not fight back? That I'll just be a good boy and stay away from Beth for the rest of time?

But again... he's used to his sons' obedience, and he's probably thinking he can control me with the same schemes. But I'm not his to control, and unlike Ezra, I don't depend on him for anything.

Ethan smirks. "We should go. I wouldn't want us to be late for a date with a girl as beautiful as your Beth."

He blocks my path before we head outside, one hand braced against my chest. The touch sends a wave of disgust through me, and I fight the urge to shove him away. "On second thought," he says, leaning in closer, his tone laced with malice, "I'll have a little chat with her first. And when she inevitably asks for you, make sure she leaves right away. Break her heart so I don't have to slit her throat. Deal?"

"Deal," I grit through my teeth, the word stinging like poison on my tongue.

I bite my bottom lip hard enough to bleed, fire searing my shoulders as we head for the gardens.

Hephaistos willing, I will find a way to destroy that man and make him regret he ever stuck his nose in my affairs.

I'll play by his rules for now, but he won't be glued to my hip forever. As soon as he thinks he's won, after the volatile situation with Zeke and Damian is resolved and things have died down, I'll find Beth and we can disappear in the new world, never to be found again.

CHAPTER 39
BLACK, BLACK HEART
SONGBIRD

The moon hangs low in the sky by the time I make it to the gardens. Somewhere far off, a fountain burbles, its song blending with the rustle of leaves swaying in the night breeze. My pulse quickens as I make my way toward the secluded corner where Aidan and I agreed to meet, my steps muffled against the moss-covered stones. The air is cool, crisp, and charged with a nervous energy that makes my skin prickle. The rendezvous point is quiet but for the crickets and the occasional lazy hoot of a white-bearded owl.

Aidan beelines directly for me, the spell ingredients he promised to bring nowhere in sight.

A strange light flickers in his eyes as he wordlessly leans in. I wrap my arms around his neck out of instinct, but his kiss is not soft or sweet or even passionate, but vicious.

Aidan grips both sides of my face, his nails digging into my neck as his tongue spears itself inside my mouth. He tastes of tears and roses, overly sweet and yet with a tang of steely, dry iron. It's all wrong, and my blood freezes right in the veins.

I tear myself away, gripping the man's shoulders as strongly as I can to hold him off. "Stop! You're not Aidan."

The edges of my lover blur into someone else, into the form of the only man I know to be wicked enough to deceive me in this way. Long strands of platinum blonde hair shine in the dark, and my heart drops past my feet, my mouth full of ash.

"Where is he?" I search the garden behind Ethan for an answer.

The King of Light grins from ear to ear. "Aidan is terribly sorry, but he sent me in his place. He came around to my point of view, in the end, that your silly infatuation for each other wasn't the most important thing in the worlds."

Fae can't lie, but I won't trust a word coming out of this man's mouth.

A branch snaps under the balls of my feet as I step backward. "I don't believe you."

"I know your dirty little secret." He holds his hand to his chest in a show of fake outrage. "Jayden would never forgive himself that a woman of your sort was able to soil his precious academy, slipping in right under his nose and seducing his son. The poor man will faint when he learns of how you planned to cheat your way to his crown." He raises a delighted brow, all smiles. "Imagine my surprise when I realized we're not so different, you and me—both using our magic to smooth things over with our most reluctant lovers..."

"I didn't enchant Aidan. I love him, and he loves me. That's all," I answer with more conviction than I possess.

If Ethan Lightbringer knows about my siren heritage, I'm finished. I dig my heels into the ground, unwilling to turn my back on a predator as powerful as the King of Light when every muscle in my body urges me to run.

Ethan shrugs as if the truth holds no significance, one way or the other. "In matters of crowns and marriages, love is rarely all there is to it, sweetheart. And it's never enough, regardless of what anyone says." He veers to the side, examining a bush of white anemone flowers. "Do you know what will happen if Aidan marries you? Do you really think his parents will just...welcome you into the family?" He snaps one flower off its stem. "That he'll live up to his potential with a Sea mutt like you forever attached to his name? Is that what you want for him?" Ethan crushes the flower inside his fist. Wrinkled white petals fall to the ground as he opens his hand again, the flower falling to pieces at his feet.

"He's old enough to make his own choice, and he chose me."

"Did he? You're not married yet, are you? What if he came to his senses?"

"I'd have to hear it from his lips."

Ethan nods happily at that, as though it was part of his plan from the start. "Good thing I brought him along, then. Aidan. You can come out now."

My stomach twists in pain, and the betrayal of knowing Aidan allowed this wretched man within two feet of me stings beyond belief.

He stalks out of the nearest path, the crestfallen grimace on his face spelling out the end of our love.

"Give us a bit of space," he grinds through his clenched teeth.

Ethan smirks but doesn't move an inch, and Aidan's fists ball at his sides. His gaze flies to the ground and up to my cheeks, before settling on the chain around my neck. "I'm so sorry, Songbird. I have to let you go."

"Let me go?" I repeat, so full of shock and disbelief that I can barely believe this is real life. "Is that what he asked you to do?"

"Yes." Aidan grips the side of my arm. "Now that he knows the truth about you being a siren, you're in danger. You wouldn't have passed the academy trials if not for your siren's song. If Ethan reveals what you are, what you've done, you'll be arrested. Being a Sea mutt is one thing, but using your song to cheat your way into the Royal Academy—into my heart—could mean death."

"Are you saying you only love me because of my song?" I squeak.

Sometimes, when fear is too raw, it becomes an unshakable ghost.

Aidan's jaw ticks. "The optics aren't good, Beth. People would never believe me if I vouched for you. You have to leave Faerie. I'll make sure Ethan and my father keep your secret."

"Why would they do that?" I ask, my voice hollow.

"My father would agree to it just to save the academy from scandal," he answers quietly, his new plan apparently all figured out.

"Speak louder, please," Ethan orders. "I don't want to miss anything."

"You need to leave tonight, or they'll arrest you," Aidan says louder, a mere puppet to the monster standing behind him, and my heart breaks into a million pieces.

"Leave Faerie, little mutt. Aidan understands the stakes. He won't come after you," Ethan adds, twisting the knife where it hurts most.

This is the end of us. We've stretched the fantasy as far as we could, but it ends tonight in a cloud of ash. There's no *but* or *maybe* about it. Aidan is saying goodbye. For good.

CHAPTER 40
BRAVE NEW WORLD
SONGBIRD

The towering bookshelves of the bibliotheca offer me some cover, my heart pounding, bleeding, *aching* with all the horror of my secret midnight rendezvous. Ethan's vile kiss still chafes my lips, the hollow look on Aidan's face imprinted in my retinas.

"Ezra?" I call out, my throaty, uneven voice echoing through the silent halls.

Ethan ordered for me to leave Faerie at once, and I tremble at the thought of what he might do if I dared to disobey him. Somehow, I fear death wouldn't be his first choice of punishment.

"Lady Snow, what's the matter?" Ezra answers from the heart of the stacks, his voice filled with concern.

Shadows and light move on the ground, the glow of his powers casting patterns on marble as he weaves a path out of the maze to meet me.

The Prince of Light has spent many evenings here of late. He hasn't said so out loud, but he's clearly been burying himself in work to distract himself from the trauma of his wedding, as though he's searching for a way to erase the indelible mark left in his bones within the ancient books.

"I need your help. You have your Shadow mask on you?" I ask quickly.

"Yes." He scans me from head to toe, his frown deepening. "Beth, you're scaring me. What's happening?"

"I was supposed to meet Aidan in the gardens. We were about to—we planned to go to the new world together, but he ended things instead."

Ezra clasps my hand in his. "Breathe, Lady Snow. You're not making sense."

My eyes flick to his face, the shadow swirling in his ice-blue irises mirroring my unease. "Your father was there, too."

"Ethan was in the gardens?" Ezra's eyes widen, and he rests both hands on my shoulders. "Did he hurt you?"

I wrap my arms around my frame. "No. But he will. Unless I leave Faerie for good."

Ezra combs his hair back, giving me a bit of space. "What did Aidan say?"

"He told me to go," I squeak.

"What? He's giving up on you?"

"I'm not meant to be his queen, Ezra. I'm not meant to be anyone's queen," I rephrase for clarity.

He grows quiet at that—a little *too* quiet. "Why not?"

"If I stay here, your father will destroy me. You have to take me to the new world, now."

Ezra doesn't hesitate. "Come." He clasps my hand in his and pulls me to the closest mirror. "Close your eyes and hold on tight."

A cold wave washes over us as he guides me through the sceawere—the space between worlds where only those in possession of a Shadow mask thrive. I was *so* close to getting one, too. I screw my lids shut, because if I dared open them, nightmares might follow me wherever I went.

Ezra stops abruptly, and the momentum of our trip causes me to collide into his side. "Alright. We're here. You can open your eyes now."

I blink, taking in my surroundings.

We've emerged from the sceawere into a quaint Scottish cottage. The voyage left a trail of frozen tears on my cheeks, and I scratch them off my skin with my nails.

"Where are we?" I ask, still disoriented from Aidan's brutal dismissal and the rushed trip through the in-between.

A heavy mahogany desk, cluttered with antique inkwells, quills, and stacks of yellowed letters, dominates the study. A glass curio cabinet, filled with delicate porcelain figurines and antique teacups stands in the corner, catching the daylight streaming through the bay window.

A plush, velvet sofa flaunts a deep, inviting purple. Its cushions, firm and plump, are covered in a subtle floral pattern. It looks brand new, a stark contrast to the antique charm of the rest of our surroundings.

It's so eerie to see the sun here, still shining as though my whole world hasn't been swallowed by darkness in the span of a few hours.

Ezra grabs a purple wool throw from the sofa and wraps it up around my frame, rubbing some life back into me. "Scotland, in the new world. My grandmother lives here. She's the best person to ask for help in a crisis. She's used to dealing with exiles and the like. She can help you."

"Ahem," a stern voice interrupts. "Don't speak for me, my starlight. It's rude."

"Beth needs your help," Ezra explains with a sheepish grin.

"Yes, I see that." She motions to the next room with her cane. "Why don't you both sit in the kitchen? I'll make us some tea."

Ezra moves to sit at the head of the table in the next room, but I grab his arm. "Thank you for taking me here, but you should go."

"No, I'm staying with you for the night. You're shaken." He moves to touch me, but I slip away.

"You have to go." I give his chest a gentle but determined push.

He frowns, his gaze flying down to my hands. "Why?"

"Your father might have tracked us through the sceawere. And if he catches you helping me, he'll punish you, I'm sure."

Ezra's brows knit together, his face ashen. "I did what he asked. That better have bought me some leeway."

My gaze drops to the floor as I confess, "Ezra... Iris told me. She told me you had feelings for me."

He runs a hand through his hair. "For Helios' sake, Beth, I'm so sorry about Aidan. I knew how you felt about each other, so I figured... I knew as long as he was around, you wouldn't be able to really see me. And I'm glad to be your friend—truly. Since the wedding happened, I've been drinking a little more than is good for me, and I slipped up and said too much. Please don't think... I mean, it's not exactly..."

"Flaming hell. I never meant to tell you tonight. I'm in love with you, and I know you're not in the same place, but I can't hold you in my arms while you cry and try to twist my words out of this. I love you, Lady Snow, and I don't care who comes for me, I will not abandon you in this world, all alone."

I shake my head. "Ezra. You know how much I care about you..."

"Shh. Don't do that. I don't need to be coddled. Let me be there for you knowing damn well you don't love me back. You love Aidan. I get that, really, I do. But he's proven today that he doesn't deserve you."

"I'm sure he didn't have a choice."

"Nonsense. If he let you go, it's because he's a scared idiot."

I chuckle bitterly. "How do you know you're not simply under my spell, too?"

One prince falling for me was strange enough. How am I supposed to live with that damn siren blood knowing it can influence emotions in ways I don't totally understand?

He offers a sad smile. "Lady Snow... no offense, but my heart is a fucking fortress."

"Listen to the girl. She needs a warm drink and a good night's sleep. Not romance," Mabel interjects.

He caresses my spine up and down in a soothing motion. "Okay, then I'll meet you back here in a few days, and we'll think of a plan."

I'm too overwhelmed to reply. He presses his mouth to mine for a quick second, and the gesture is so tender and natural... it scares me to my core.

"I'll see you soon, Lady Snow."

I offer a small nod, and he disappears through the mirror, leaving me alone with Mabel.

"He's a passionate kid. It usually gets him into trouble," Mabel comments. "You've never trained your song, have you?"

"How did you know? The first time you saw me, you knew."

"Plenty of Sea folk lived on the coast of the Islantide, in my day. I can tell the difference."

"It's almost funny how this worked out. Aidan planned to ask you to marry us tonight."

"If it helps, I wouldn't have agreed."

"Why?" I ask, lowering my gaze. "Because of what I am?"

Her kind eyes soften, her bite of power washing over me like a warm blanket. "No, because of who he's meant to become."

A raven lands on the windowsill and taps on the glass, spooking me. Mabel peels herself from her seat and inches the window open. The bird deposits a rolled piece of parchment in the cup of her hand before flying off to its perch in the corner.

I watch the sleek black bird for a moment before asking, "Who is Aidan meant to become?"

"Never mind that now. Most prophecies end up being incorrect, especially those about the end of the world." She unrolls the message. "My grandson was right. I'm used to smuggling all sorts of troubled folks out of Faerie. And the world hasn't been particularly kind to your lot, not since the fall of my first husband."

The scope of her life hits me all at once. This woman has lived through all the wars and battles and history I've been studying.

"Was the Eye of the Mists as beautiful as the legends say?"

Her eyes glaze over. "It was all they say and *more*." She takes a meaningful pause, staring off at the emptiness in front of her as if it's a gilded and glorious past. After a minute, she clears her throat. "I know someone who can help you. She's in America now, but she's trained stranded sirens before."

I consider her offer.

Unless I learn how to control the siren in me, I will never be sure of a man's heart again. And in spite of what he said, Ezra can't make the trip back and forth from Faerie without being followed. Ethan would probably beat his son to death before allowing him to cavort in the new world with me—or loving anyone he isn't told to.

Besides, I love Aidan. And I will love Aidan until my last breath.

Ezra is better off without me in his life altogether. He might have been forced into an arranged marriage, but he doesn't deserve to pine over someone who doesn't love him back.

Mabel sips on her tea, pulling me out of my dark thoughts. "Mélusine is getting old, but I'd say she wouldn't pass up the chance to help someone as brave as you."

"Brave? I'm not brave," I scoff.

Mabel tips her cup of tea toward me. "You stood without a shred of fear on that altar at Ezra's wedding, under the scrutiny of the most powerful beings in the worlds, while secretly planning to elope with the Crown Prince of the Summerlands. I'd say that's pretty courageous."

"Naive and dumb is more like it."

"Don't do that. Don't sell yourself short for dreaming up a better world, young Beth. When you've lived as long as I have, you might find some dreams end up stretching farther than we ever thought possible."

"Dreams and nightmares, too," I say quickly, thinking of her life before she came here.

Mabel Bloodsinger, the Mist Queen, ruler of a kingdom that was destroyed for the sins of its last reigning king, her adopted land burned to ashes, her subjects slaughtered just for existing. She probably knows more about nightmares than any other Fae alive.

The cup of tea trembles in her grip. "I can't deny that."

"I should go and meet your friend. As soon as possible."

Mabel nods. "That's a wise decision. Do stay away from mirrors on your journey. I wouldn't put it past Ethan Lucifer Lightbringer to hunt you down just for sport. You caught his eye, yes?"

"Unfortunately."

Her hazelnut eyes darken. "Then you should leave at sunrise. Come now, I'll show you where to rest for the night."

I'm leaving Faerie, Aidan, Ezra, and my entire world behind. I write letters to Papa and Marjorie, hoping I'll get to see them again one day. I'm heading to a new continent—a place that has forgotten about Fae kings and sirens. A world that disavowed magic altogether. A land where I don't belong, but also hold an advantage.

It'll be easier to hide in a place where people believe I don't exist. I'll be exiled and heartbroken, but in some ways, freer than I've ever been.

And irrevocably alone.

CHAPTER 41
TWIN FLAMES
BETH

Summerlands, Faerie, Present Day

"Flaming hell. Where did the healers go?" Aidan remarks out loud as we reach the top floor of the main building.

The Summer Queen's apartments smell of death and rare herbs. I screech to a halt on the sleek wood floor, coming to an abrupt stop behind Aidan, the royal apartments eerily quiet. A hint of moonlight pierces through the curtains, the long flaps of nude fabric billowing softly in the late evening breeze. A large balcony is visible beyond the opened double doors connecting the living room area to the outside.

I would have expected Thera to be surrounded by a flock of healers, but there's no one in sight, no commotion at all.

Just silence.

As though Aidan's mother simply slipped away, unnoticed.

Disheveled from the intensity of our kiss, I grip the train of my dress even tighter to prevent the bothersome garment from scraping the floor, wondering if I should have let him come alone. I might not be part of Aidan's life anymore, but it kills me to leave him at a time like this.

The unnerving silence ties a tight knot in my stomach as he tiptoes closer to her bedroom. I follow into the doorway, the sight in front of me lowering my body temperature by several degrees, a hint of ice settling inside my bones.

Thera's laying down on the bed, unmoving, the grayish tint of her cheeks even more pronounced than it was during the ceremony. Her eyes are open, angled at the sky, staring into the worlds beyond.

Her chest does not rise or fall. A white sheet has been pulled over her body and tucked under her chin, the usual way for healers to lay down a hollowed-out corpse, one from which the soul has already been collected. My heart squeezes at the sight, but there would have been no other reason for Aidan's mark to catch fire the way it did, not if Thera was still alive.

"Mother..." he breathes.

I see a part of him still hoped, still yearned, for it not to be true despite the evidence branding his flesh.

His brows knit together, his gaze searching the room. "The healers are gone. The guards. Heather. Why is there nobody here?" he asks the blank wall before turning to me for an answer.

"I'm so sorry, Aidan," I murmur, unsure whether to leave him to his grief or stride forward to stand by his side.

He shakes his head, a high, trembling edge to his voice. "No, something's not right. She shouldn't have been left alone, not before the sacred rites were performed."

"I sent everyone away," a deep, masculine voice murmurs. The sound is hoarse and choppy, as though coming straight from the grave, crawling out of some deep, forgotten abyss. "Don't worry, Elio already came to collect her soul."

A shadow shimmers into view next to the bed, slowly sharpening from a blurry shape to one of a ghost I'm all too familiar with. I inch backward, spooked, and goosebumps tighten my arms as fire rises up to the surface of Aidan's skin, bathing the entire scene with warm light.

The man holding the lifeless queen's hand looks identical to the one in front of me.

Two men. Two Aidans.

The second Aidan angles his body away from the dead queen. "By all means, come in, Beth."

This Aidan remembers me, but there's no amity in his tone, no warmth. And definitely no love. And while I'm not a hundred percent sure, I'm almost positive the Aidan I came in with, the one who looks about to burst out into a supernova of flames, is the real one, meaning the one holding the queen's hand must be the impostor.

Only Light Fae royalty has the power to disguise their appearances to such a degree, so the man in front of us might be Ethan Lightbringer. But his voice is a little off compared to the cruel, hollow tone I remember.

"Fancy seeing you two here, together…" The trickster adds. "No wonder your bride was crying when I found her." The man whispers in a very deliberate and rehearsed manner, as though to hide his true pitch.

Aidan curls his fists, marching to the empty side of the bed to clasp his mother's wrist. "What did you do to my mother?" he croaks, letting Thera's arm fall as quickly as he picked it up.

"Nothing. Thera's time had come." Faux-Aidan rises to his feet. "I wanted to be here for the end and came to deliver your wedding gift." He reaches into his green cloak and retrieves a long, narrow wooden box. "The queen had ordered a special present for the occasion."

He flicks open the lid of the carved ornamental box and showcases the contents. Tucked over the white silk lining of the box, two crystalline forbidden arrows shine, their pointy tips reflecting the fury of Aidan's fire.

"She didn't want to condemn her precious phoenix to a loveless marriage." Faux-Aidan's voice is laced with a sharp edge of bitterness. "You should thank me, really. Who knows what that arrow would have done to you, given your current state."

"My mother had love arrows made for me and Heather?" Aidan asks.

The impostor nods. "Yes, two love arrows, custom made just for you newlyweds, meant to smooth out the adverse effects of her botched memory-altering enchantment. Do you think she cared that there might not be anything left of the real you after all that meddling? Or was she so far gone that she truly believed it was for your own good?"

A gasp pops out of my mouth. "Thera was the one who erased his memories?"

"Yes. She wanted to make sure her son—her heir—forgot all about his first love. Little did she know it would also prevent him from moving on—or loving anyone else." An exaggerated grimace twists the imposter's face, followed by a hollow smirk. "Whoops."

He tosses one of the arrows at Aidan, who catches it in his fist.

"Who are you?" Aidan asks.

The impostor chuckles, shaking his head. "I'm the Lord of the Tides. The leader of the *rebels*, as you call us."

A second shadow appears at my back and shoves me deeper inside the room. I struggle to keep my balance, scrambling to stay upright. Before I can react, the newcomer bands one arm across my neck, the bulge of his forearm settling over my throat, immobilizing me in a bear hug.

He's tall and lean, but with some serious muscles in his unforgiving hold, and I feel as though I've been swallowed by a dark, expansive void. My assailant is dressed in black from head to toe, along with the blackest hair I've ever seen. A geodesic mask covers his eyes, not as light or functional as most Shadow masks, but definitely magic. His bite of power feels like the crack of a whip across my back, the scents of blackfyre oil and charcoal entering my nose at his proximity.

His other hand is wrapped around the hilt of a rowan and silver blade, a weapon that could either kill me in seconds, or condemn me to a slow, agonizing death with just a scratch. I grip the arm holding me captive and try to ice it through, but my captor grits his teeth and endures the pain, not letting go. "Stop moving, woman, or I'll nick you with my blade," he hisses in my ear, pressing me down harder against his hard frame.

A whimper pops out of my lungs as I let the magic flake off into white, powdery snow.

Electricity crackles in the air, nefarious shadows creeping out of the walls and transforming the moonlit room into the eye of a dark, forsaken storm.

Aidan spreads his arms out to both sides. "Release her at once!" He moves to attack my captor, but his doppelgänger wags his finger.

"Tut-tut. One false move, and Beth dies." The impostor holds his hands up. "Don't burn the academy down for nothing. I just want to chat."

"Where is Heather?" Aidan barks. The shock and grief that had settled over his face has lifted, replaced by a menacing scowl.

"Safe, for now." The Lord of the Tides answers, "But that could change if you decide to make a scene."

"What do you want?" I chime in, sinking my nails into my assailant's arm to keep him from choking me. The dark man presses harder and harder on my windpipe, his arm apparently made of stone, the feel of them sturdier than skin ought to feel.

The copycat winks at the dark-haired man. "We're here to save Aidan from a sham marriage...and take his place on the Summer throne. For the tides."

"For the tides," the man behind me whispers lovingly.

"The time has come for Fae royals to answer for their crimes." The Lord of the Tides pries the second arrow from the box and retrieves a small, red vial hidden underneath the silk. "Drink this." He tosses the red vial over to Aidan. "Drink it now, or Beth will suffer the same fate as the Summer Queen."

Aidan grips the vial, his lips pressed into a firm line. "I won't let you destroy my kingdom."

The doppelgänger's gaze slides over to my captor. "Make her bleed, Luther."

I can hear the answering smile in Luther's voice as the cold edge of the blade touches my throat. "With pleasure."

"No! Wait!" Aidan tilts his head back and gulps down the vial's contents. Within moments, his eyes roll inward, and he collapses to the ground with a loud *thud*.

I thrash against Luther's hold, panic rising in my chest.

"What are you going to do with him?" I shout out.

The way the impostor kneels to check Aidan's pulse sends my heart into a frenzy. Faux-Aidan rises, his movements calm and deliberate as he pries a second vial out of the box. "Your turn now, Beth. Open your mouth."

A hot sting spreads across my chest as the rowan and silver blade is laid flat across my neck, the mere contact of the blade on my skin burning like a bee sting. "She wasn't part of the plan. We should get rid of her—" Luther begins.

The impostor moves to stand right in front of me. "Elio's fond of Beth. We might be able to trade her for Morrigan later."

A low growl reverberates across my back as Luther clasps my mouth to pry it open.

The Lord of the Tides quickly pours the red liquid into my mouth, his amber eyes burning with as much fire as the real Aidan could muster—if not more.

The shadows already edging my vision smother me from all sides, dark and thick until they swallow me whole.

CHAPTER 42

SHACKLED

BETH

Cold spikes dig into my wrists as I emerge from my drug-induced slumber, and I let out a low, confused groan. I'm tied to a metal ring by a pair of fancy shackles and a long chain, in a cramped, dark space. Faint light filters through the cracks in the wooden beams above my head, my night vision allowing me a good view of the barrels and crates that litter the...cargo hold?

A surge of fear and alarm scatters goosebumps along my rigid, painful spine as I try and fail to call forth my magic to ice the chains.

My left cheek is cold and wet, indented by the patterns of the wood plank I was dumped on. Knots of hair stick to my neck, a few strands entangled in the terrifying needle-like spikes that cover the inside of the shackles. The needles penetrated my skin deep enough to draw blood, painting red lines along my lower arms. The dull throb radiating across my cramped muscles indicates the spikes are made of rowan wood.

Fright ices my ribs, my magic entombed inside the confines of my body, unable to get out.

I wince as I sit up, still too groggy to make sense of it all. The loud splashes of waves slamming against a smooth, powerful surface confirms my hunch that I'm in the cargo hold of a small ship. A semi-constant groaning and creaking accompanies the rumble of the sea.

Despite the dizziness and overall muscle weakness that has taken hold of my body, I shift to my knees, and the spikes wrapped around my ankles dig into my flesh at the movement. A second, shorter set of shackles and chain prevent me from moving my legs by more than a few inches.

"Elizabeth?" a soft voice rasps behind me.

"Aidan?" My body gives a heave of nausea and pain as I crane my neck around to look at him.

The rattle of his chains intensifies as he tries and fails to bridge the narrow gap between us. "Are you alright?" His restraints look tighter and more restrictive than mine.

A nervous chuckle bubbles out of my lungs. "I'm alive. You?"

"Same."

The length of the chain holding my wrists allows for a bit of wiggle room so I can stand, and I brace my hand on the ceiling, barely inches from the top of my head. The train of my dress rips at the movement, catching on the nail bolting the metal ring to the wood planks.

The silk bustier slides down my front-buckle bralette. The edgy two-piece lingerie I put on to look my best for Aidan's damn wedding does little to shield me from the damp air of the hold. It's not cold, per se, but I feel completely exposed, the lace of my underwear visible at my hip.

"You know, when I first caught a glimpse of my copycat, I feared you might have been working with him from the start. That you had been sent to distract me while he finished my mother."

"I wasn't."

His amber eyes shine in the dark, the fire within piercing through the darkness. "I hope not."

"Aren't the shackles and chains enough to convince you?" I huff.

"They help. A bit," he answers with a mix of worry and humor. "Seth also vouched for you."

Last time I saw Seth Devine, the illegitimate prince of Spring and Storms, it was during the winter solstice, when he disappeared trying to stop his brother's escape. We were watching the Tide-caller's attack that night to intervene at the right time, but Seth had vanished without a trace before I could even make it out to the lake.

"Seth?" I call out loudly. "Are you here?"

"And here I thought you didn't like me, Betty Snow," a smooth, familiar voice answers from the other side of the pyramid of crates.

My lips quirk. While his promiscuous attitude irks me, I'm still relieved to know for sure that he survived the attack on Wintermere. "Have you been here all this time?"

It's been *weeks* since he went missing, and even Elio and Damian couldn't track him with their powers combined.

"Afraid so. A ship makes a brilliant prison. It's almost impossible for anyone to track," Seth laments. "But it's been a little more fun around here since Aidan recovered this morning."

The occasional stretch or snap of ropes tightening or loosening with the movement of the sails and rigging, along with the faint footsteps of our captors on the deck, echo through the air.

I squint at the light filtering through the crack. "I count only two sets of footsteps. Do you think there's more of them?"

"So far, I've only heard Luther and his pal Imogen, but she never comes down here. Luther comes alone when it's time to feed me, which is usually once a day, but he never gets close enough for me to try anything," Seth explains. "Dinner will be soon, though. It's almost sunset."

"What are his powers?" Aidan asks.

"He was born a talented Storm Fae with a keen affinity for Shadow magic, but he's embedded Mist jewels inside his skin, so he's all juiced up."

"What do they plan to do with us?"

"Me, I think I just got unlucky, but the Lord of the Tides has plans for you both. I've heard them talking. He plans to take Aidan's place at the coronation."

Take Aidan's place... If the Lord of the Tides manages to fool every other royal, he could steal Aidan's crown and access the magic of his lands. He could even assume his identity for good considering most of Aidan's family is dead. And I doubt he'll want the real Aidan around for much longer if that's what he intends to do.

"They have to wait ten days before crowning a successor, right?" I ask.

Aidan shakes his head, looking a little green. "Not necessarily. I've been the heir from the start."

I swallow hard. The possibilities for chaos and violence are endless if the leader of the rebels manages to steal the Summerlands' magic and become its one true king. "Who is the Lord of the Tides? What do we know for sure?"

"My younger brother appears to be his number two, but I have no clue who he is," Seth answers.

I bite my bottom lip, trying to piece together our quick exchange. "He knew me, and there's not a lot of Fae on this continent who do." I search Aidan's gaze. "Whoever this Lord of the Tides is, he was at the academy at the same time we were."

He nods, understanding my logic. "Yes, and that narrows it down quite a bit."

"Couldn't it be someone from your past?" Seth argues.

"No. I'm a moth. I don't know any High Fae but for the ones I met at school."

"A Fae with Light magic both powerful and refined enough to reflect my exact image... It's got to be Ezra," Aidan says. "It makes sense. No one has seen him in decades, and with everything that happened before he vanished, it wouldn't be so surprising."

Seth's voice booms from the dark. "Don't jump to conclusions. Mist jewels are stronger than we knew, and it only makes sense that their leader would be the most juiced up."

"He's the only one who knows me well enough to emulate me so perfectly, and it would explain why we're not dead," Aidan adds with a pointed look.

"How did Willow die? Was it Ethan?" I ask quietly.

We exchange a heavy glance, and the corners of his mouth fall.

"Maybe. Officially, it was a suicide, but I wouldn't put it past Ethan Lightbringer to have manipulated the investigation to conceal her murder."

"I wrote to you, when she died. You never answered," I say with my eyes downcast.

His jaw hangs slightly askew as he rubs his chin with a tired hand. "I'm afraid I didn't read many of the letters I got that year. Especially the ones sent by strangers."

"I'm not a stranger," I croak, the emotions in my gut threatening to choke me.

"You know what I mean. I wouldn't have recognized your handwriting—or even your name. You were a stranger to me, then."

I inhale deeply, willing away the tears that threaten to spill over my lids. It's so unfair, so cruel, that Thera erased something sacred to me. That she dared to mess with the very essence of Aidan, if the Lord of the Tides is to be believed.

"I can get us out of here, but I'll have to sing," I declare, quickly making up my mind about it.

"Sing?" Seth interjects.

"I'm part siren," I grumble.

It's a damning secret for a young Fae attending the Royal Academy and hoping for a place at court—or to become queen—but it's not as problematic for an eccentric, self-exiled artist. Just the thought that I used to feel so much shame about my very blood and once considered never singing again dries my mouth.

"That's...drastic," Aidan grounds out.

"Do either of you have a better idea?" I ask the two men, but our bindings prevent us from using our usual powers.

If I ever hope to find a way to reverse Aidan's memory lapse, we have to stop the Lord of the Tides before he finalizes his plan. The need to regain control over our fates—to fight back—burns like acid at the back of my throat.

"Didn't you sing at Elio's wedding?" Seth asks. "How come the crowd didn't go all crazy, then?"

"I've trained myself not to induce unhealthy obsessions and mindless lust in my audience. A siren's song is not always used as a weapon. It can be quite beautiful and healing. But just as I can leave that part out, I can also crank it up by design." I smooth out my torn dress, feeling nauseous.

Unease creeps into my chest at the prospect of using my song as the dreaded instrument of violence most people believe it to be. And I'm not sure how Aidan and Seth will react, because if I aim to make a strong, lasting impression on our kidnapper, they're going to be affected, too.

"If I get him to free me, would that be enough?" I muse.

"Could you steal the keys to the shackles? He keeps them in the top pocket of his cloak."

Aidan nods emphatically at Seth's suggestion. "Yes, the keys. This way, we can free ourselves while you distract him."

"Alright, but if we're going to do this, find something to plug your ears. Loose threads, or dust bunnies. Anything to lessen the thrall of the song. I've never sang to bewitch a Fae, especially not at sea, so I'm not sure how powerful the spell will be."

Aidan moves behind me, taking the advice seriously as he crams small pieces of lint in his ears.

"How can you even be sure your song will work on my brother?" Seth asks. "He's very powerful."

I press my lips together. The hard lessons I learned after I left Faerie for the new world, taught by my dear Mélusine, still live in me. "The more powerful the Fae, the harder the fall."

The hatch on top of the ladder leading to the upper deck rattles on its hinges, a stream of light illuminating the opposite end of the cargo hold.

"Here he comes. Quick!" Seth whispers loud enough for me to hear.

Luther climbs down the ladder, his eyes no longer covered by a thick mask. He's young, I realize, younger than I'd expected. Barely out of puberty by the shape of his plump cheekbones. Dark curls fall over his forehead, his eyes gray but for the purple flecks shared by the Storm family.

He's holding a food tray in his hand, his shiny black boots gleaming in the faint glow of twilight. "Oh, you're all awake." He squints at Aidan, then me, pausing at the bottom. "Don't get any ideas. I'm just here to feed Seth."

"What about us?" Aidan asks.

Luther titters, grinning at him the way you grin at a naughty child. "I think you can survive one day without food, Fancy."

I open my mouth and let all the confusion, anger, and heartbreak I've been carrying with me condense into the vibrations of my vocal chords. A high note tears from my lungs, reaching into the depths of my soul and reverberating through my bones.

All my years of training, learning how *not* to hurt or enchant or even influence people with my voice, used in reverse.

The decades spent in exile, all alone, before I could sing safely in front of others are tangible in the murky cargo hold. The time spent separated from all the people I loved, away from Aidan, pining over a man who didn't even remember I existed.

If I mess this up, it'll be my last performance, so I better make it count. I lay it all out on the line for one more song.

> I never knew a love
> Quite so rare as yours
> Never knew a gaze
> Quite so entrancing
> You held out your hand
> By the river bank
> And asked me for a dance

"What are you—" Luther stops abruptly, his eyes glazing over as the tray slips from his hands. The bread and fruit he meant to give his brother tumble to the ground, and Seth mutters a begrudging curse.

> Just one night; in lieu of forever
> One chance; it was now or never
> As luck had it, my star-crossed lover
> I was promised to another
> But I only wanted you

Aidan lets out a low whimper behind me, and Luther inches closer.

His gaze clears, as though the sun itself has just peeked through the clouds, revealing an endless sky after the storm. His pupils contract into pinholes. "May the tides have mercy. You're a siren."

> I never knew a name
> Quite so forbidden
> Never knew a love
> Quite as doomed from the start
> We were oil and water
> Sweet and sour
> It was never to be
> Never to be
> But I only wanted you

Our captor stumbles closer, navigating over a barrage of barrels, now within arm's reach. The inside pockets of his dark hooded cloak should be just below the holes meant for his arms.

> Yours was a crown of gold
> Mine only a shard of cold
> A piece of coal
> Safe from my cruel shadow
> I risked it all to hold you

And lost it all in one go
It was never to be
Never to be
But I only wanted you

"I never thought—I should have killed you when I had the chance," Luther whispers, now standing barely an inch away.

"But you won't kill me now," I answer, my tone soothing, beckoning him closer with a beguiling smile.

"Never." He reaches for a loose strand of my hair, tucking it behind my pointy ear with a strange, almost tender affection. "You're the most precious jewel I've ever owned."

CHAPTER 43
NEVER LET ME GO
BETH

The man that argued in favor of murdering me back at the academy cups my face in the most gentle manner, tipping my chin up for a kiss that'll seal his fate. I keep my eyes open as our lips meet, his kiss both impatient and delicate, as if I'm something to be treasured.

He tastes even darker than I imagined, a blend of loneliness and misery that clings to him. Beneath the bite of his shadows, there's something fresh and salty, like afternoon rain beating relentlessly over the surface of the sea.

I steady myself against his chest, one hand creeping subtly toward the inside of his cloak, toward his pocket, where the keychain waits.

Deepening the kiss to keep him distracted, I toss the golden ring and keys toward Aidan, who swiftly works to free himself, the shackles snapping open. Tears streak down his face, but he's lucid enough to ensure our makeshift escape plan works.

Luther Storm cradles my face in his hands, oblivious to everything else around us. I hear the sharp cracks of wood as Aidan works to free Seth, but I'm too deep in this twisted game to pay any attention. A sinister fragment of my soul rises to the surface—this dark, aching void within me throbs, desperate to be filled with the love of a man, begging me to find prey, eager to be consumed, chewed up, and spit out.

Sirens heed the call of their goddess, feeding not just for themselves, but to please her. And Melpomene is starving, desperate to seduce this man through me.

I scrape my nails along the back of Luther's neck, and he exhales sharply, a quiet gasp escaping him. "Mm, you're a talented sorceress. Let's leave these two behind and visit my private cabin." He presses his erection to my hip, his hands stroking my sides amorously.

"Won't your girlfriend be jealous?" I murmur against his lips.

"She's not my girlfriend, but you're right. I should sneak you in there before she notices I'm gone."

"Do you have your rowan and silver blade on you?" I whisper.

"No, but I've got the keys to your cuffs—" Luther reaches for his cloak, his hand patting at the empty pocket, his focus wavering as the haze of my song begins to lift. But it's too late.

Aidan delivers a brutal sucker-punch to Luther's jaw, his fist glowing a bright, furious orange, sending the man flying through the air. Luther's head slams into the wall with a sickening *crack*, and he collapses to the floor face-first with a resounding *thud*.

Seth is already there, swift and efficient, his hands quick to snare Luther's ankles with the rowan shackles he used on us.

Luther thrashes on the ground and attempts to crawl away. He punches his brother's nose to keep him from shackling his wrists. Seth howls in pain, but doesn't flinch, continuing his work, determined to restrain his brother. With Aidan's help, he overpowers Luther, gradually cutting him off from his magic, one limb at a time. Aidan tightens the spikes on the rowan shackles with a grim determination, while Seth stuffs a torn piece of fabric in Luther's mouth and ties his belt around his head, gagging him before he can cry out for help.

Luther roars in agony, his eyes bulging from the strain. Blood streams down his hands as he desperately tugs at the chains anchoring him to the ship, his body trembling with effort, but it's all in vain. "Rhh um rh!" he mumbles.

A sad, almost pitying smile crosses Seth's face. "Sorry, kid, but you've earned it."

Aidan unlocks my restraints and pulls me free.

In an uncharacteristic show of care, Seth wraps his heavy green cloak around me, fastening it securely at my neck. "Here, darling. You look cold." He rubs down my arms, a ripple of Spring magic caressing my neck and making me blush. He's standing awfully close, especially given my obvious state of undress. His eerily gentle and non-sarcastic tone makes me pause.

Ah, hells.

Aidan pulls me into his embrace, his arms circling me, red-hot embers radiating from his body. "Here, I'll warm her up," he murmurs, his voice rough.

I first dismiss his obvious jealousy as a fluke, a byproduct of the spell that ensnared the men who heard my performance.

But Seth isn't having it. He tugs on my arm, a firm grip that pulls me in the opposite direction. "No need. I've got her."

The two of them stand at odds, glaring at each other. They each look ready to tear the other apart over who gets to escort me to the deck.

"Get off her, she's mine," Seth orders.

Aidan, not one to back down, moves to shove his opponent aside. But in an instant, Seth dissipates into a cloud, only to reappear behind Aidan with a snarl. The side effects of my song boil over, pushing their rivalry to the brink of violence.

Before the situation can escalate any further, I raise my hands. "Guys, stop!"

They both freeze, eyes locking on me, the aggression in their stances evident even in their sudden stillness. They're waiting for my command, hanging on my every word.

A twinge of regret twists my gut. I wish I could dispel the song's effects now that Luther has been dealt with, but only a good night's sleep will return them to normal. And we don't have the luxury of rest right now.

Aidan presses my back to his chest, his warmth seeping through the fabric of my cloak. His breath skims my earlobe, hot and heavy. "Let me kill the rebel for what he did to you."

"We're not killing Luther," Seth argues. A storm cloud, black as night, churns above his head, crackling with deadly energy.

I brace myself on his arm, dizzy from his heat. "No one is killing anyone, not while you two are still under my spell," I command, my voice trembling as I fight against the call of the sea.

Seth balls his fists at his sides, and the swirling storm above us spreads to the entire cargo hold. "I'd die for you, Betty Snow," he mutters, his words rough and possessive. "But your friend here needs to be taught a lesson."

Full-blown flames lick the surface of Aidan's skin, the fiery orange glow cutting through the dim, damp room. But beneath the raw power, I catch a glimpse of something more—something that wasn't there before. The love, the hurt, the unspeakable heartbreak that has haunted me for years now mirrors in his gaze. The decades that dug an insurmountable chasm between us, too deep to heal in a single moment.

"Shut up, Seth," he barks.

A heavy set of footsteps resonates above our heads, and a confident, feminine voice echoes through the cargo hold. "Luther? What's happening?"

"Stand down, both of you," I hiss under my breath.

The cloud rains down to the ground in a heavy mist, Seth's thunder tapering off in a flare of static electricity that covers me in goosebumps.

"Or I'll tie you back up," I add.

"Fuck. You look so fierce when you're angry," Aidan declares, and my entire body quakes as he spins me around in his embrace.

A hot, molten heat explodes from the pit of my belly and spreads to the tips of my toes as he swallows my next threat with a kiss.

It's not like it was when he met me after his botched wedding. It's been a century since I've been kissed with such passion. Aidan breathes in my whimpers, his strong grip crushing me to him.

He caresses the side of my face with his thumb, looking ready to eat me alive. "By the Flame, Songbird," he growls against my swollen lips. "I'm going to burn my name into your flesh, peel those tatters from your skin, and make you mine again if it kills me."

My heart pounds in my chest.

He remembers.

Seth observes the hatch with his bottom lip tucked between his teeth, his need to confront Aidan gradually fading. "Imogen was Luther's childhood friend back at the Storm Court. I know her well enough. I might be able to convince her to stand down. She's a run-of-the-mill Storm Fae, so unless she's covered in Mist jewels, she shouldn't pose a threat."

Aidan motions him forward. "You go first then, but you have one minute. If you haven't called for us after that, I'll cook her through."

"Now, don't go burning the ship, or we'll sink," I whisper.

"Don't tell me you never learned how to swim," he teases with an edge of danger.

Seth shakes his head. "I'm not leaving you two alone, not even for a minute. Beth is too good for you. Weren't you supposed to get married today?"

I push Seth away from me and up the ladder. "Go. We have no time to waste."

He grumbles but obeys, quickly climbing the ladder and stepping onto the upper deck, leaving it open. The night breeze swirls down to brush my cheeks, the hot, humid air of the Summerlands replaced by a crisp autumn wind. Judging by the stark change in temperature, we're nowhere near the academy.

I place my foot on the bottom step, ready to rush to Seth's aid, but Aidan braces his arms on both sides of me. "Say something, Songbird."

"You remember," I croak, keeping my eyes glued to the hatch, listening for any signs of trouble.

Seth's voice booms from the deck above, but his exact words are swallowed by the loud beats of my heart.

Aidan rests his chin on my shoulder and inhales deep. "I can't believe I was ever made to forget you." He pauses. "I'm so ashamed."

"It wasn't your fault," I whisper, desperate to tame the tsunami of emotions swirling inside me. "But let's not talk about it now."

"Seth is still affected by your song," Aidan says.

I arch a brow. "And you're not?"

He nuzzles my neck, the gesture so foreign yet so right. "I've been cheated out of a hundred years by your side. It's going to take a lot for me to let go of you."

My knuckles turn white against the side of the ladder. "It's been a minute. Let's go."

There's a lot to do before I can figure out exactly what this means for us. We have to survive the night first, and I can't afford to drift into a waking dream.

I press upward and emerge onto the upper deck. The ship is made of wood, but its design reminds me of a modern sailing boat, with metal guardrails and ropes keeping the sailors from falling overboard. A forceful, unnatural wind beats against my cheeks, and the sky above is obscured by a twisting vortex of clouds.

A single mast and boom hold the tall mainsail. Its fabric twists back and forth under the uneven wind while Seth argues with a woman near the wheel.

She looks petite but deadly, her short black hair tied down with a bandana. Golden rings adorn her pointy ears, and she holds a set of magic daggers, the blades rumbling with energy.

Her knuckles clench when she sees us coming, thunder rumbling overhead. "Stand back, or I'll sink the ship."

"Be reasonable, Imogen! You can't win a fight against me, let alone all three of us," Seth growls over the screech of the gale. "Surrender, and I won't have to hurt you!"

"I'd like to see you try!" she shouts, pirouetting under the railing of the cockpit to reach the boom. She uses it as a stepping stone to leap over the cockpit and attack Seth just as a violent gust tips the boat to the side.

My stomach clenches, and I grip the railing, trying to keep my balance as the ship thrashes on its axis and begins to swirl around in a circle. Dark waves crash over the bow, leaving a fresh, salty kiss on my cheeks.

Aidan moves to steady me, but I lose my footing, tumbling toward the angry sea. The momentum of my fall propels me headfirst over the side of the ship, and I crash into the waves, the saltwater embracing me like an old friend.

I hold my breath out of instinct, the force of the fall dizzying me for a moment. It's cold, but not for a Winter Fae, and even less for a daughter of the Sea.

The storm that rages over the surface makes the sea murkier and darker than it ought to be, but also calmer and less chaotic than the world above. It's so quiet underneath, the agitation on the surface giving way to a vast ocean that spreads hundreds of miles down to the seabed.

The ripples of magic tightening my skin tell me that I'm home. A home I'm estranged from, but a home nonetheless. I unfasten the button of Seth's cloak and let it float away, liberated from the cumbersome attire.

The arms of the ocean could never hurt me.

But the respite is short-lived, replaced by a sudden, terrible fear.

A second body hits the surface. Aidan is wrapped in flames, but even the strongest fire can be smothered by the sea. He looks frantic as he searches the waves and swims deeper and deeper. He freezes when he finally spots me, suspended upside-down for a moment, his arm finally reaching down to touch my hand.

Bubbles of precious air escape his mouth as I pull him to me, letting my powers envelop him. It's a magic I don't often practice, but Mélusine didn't only teach me how to master my song, but all the powers of a Sea Fae.

CHAPTER 44
MERMAIDS
AIDAN

The siren's kiss infuses me with a sense of peace I've only read about in legends. I don't need anything but her, and my muscles relax as I entangle my hands in her hair, ravenous for another gulp of Beth.

I'd plunged into the sea to save her from the storm only to be swept away by the current. By the time I'd managed to tell left from right or top from bottom, my lungs had become tight and painful, but not anymore.

My Songbird's magic tingles across my shoulders, arms, and down to my core. My fire lights the water around us. Her lips are cool. Smooth. Their touch eases the pressure in my chest.

I can't believe I ever thought she was a common Fae.

Seth's hideous cloak is gone, the shreds of the dress that still clung to her lost to the waves, leaving her bare to me but for the black lingerie covering her breasts.

Hundreds of teal and green scales transformed her legs into a striking mermaid tail, a glorious masterpiece woven from the ocean's magic. Each flick of her fins sent ripples of light dancing through the depths. Her hair fans around her face, dark and alive, but it's her eyes, bright and blue and bewitching, that hold the mysteries of the deep. She isn't just beautiful, but otherworldly—a being forged from currents and tides, a force of nature. The water hums with her essence, a quiet melody that calls to every part of me, and I know that she is my destiny, my anchor in this boundless world beneath the waves—and above.

The whiplash of my memories returning lulls into a dull ache, and the urgency to recoup the last decades and somehow make up for all the time lost takes a backseat to this kiss.

There's no need for air when you've found the love of your life, and I groan when she pulls away—I would have been content to stay there forever. She gives my lips one last peck before pointing to the surface.

The ship has steadied itself against the current, the black void above our heads now forming a silvery horizon.

Beth braces her arms under mine and swims us to the surface. The power that was protecting me from the cold water breaks like a bubble being popped as we emerge, and I wipe the water from my face with a gasp.

The sky is full of stars, with no trace of the storm.

"You look..."

She blushes as she looks down at her tail. "It's jarring, isn't it?"

"It's beautiful. You're beautiful."

Seth throws me a long rope, interrupting our tête-à-tête, most likely on purpose. "That's quite a rescue mission you've got going on there, Aidan."

I reluctantly grab onto the rope. "Where's your friend?"

"Out of service. We'll just tie her up in the hold with the kid, and we'll be golden." Seth offers me his hand to help me over the railing, but I grab the wire rope and jump inside, spinning around to help Beth. In the blink of an eye, her mermaid tail vanishes, replaced by her long, incredible legs...and her bare ass.

Heat creeps up my ears as my body betrays me, blood pooling in my groin, low and sudden. I strip off my undershirt and hand it to her without a word.

Beth sighs softly, tying the sleeves around her waist to shield herself from our unrelenting stares. The spell she's cast over me hasn't faded—it's maddening, an ache that makes it hard not to lunge at Seth for daring to look at her.

She taps my forehead with a teasing grin. "Still jealous, I see." Her hand falls to my bare stomach, and I cover it with mine.

"Don't scold me." I offer her a sheepish grin. "If I listened to my instincts, I'd do a lot worse."

I remember everything from her unraveled braid in the labyrinth and our reckless escapades to our bitter goodbye. I recall how lost I felt the night Ethan and my parents enchanted me to forget, but I also remember everything else. All the loneliness, the loss, the grief that plagued the years in between. All the emptiness suffered.

Seth motions us to the cabin. "Imogen managed to shatter all the mirrors before I knocked her unconscious. We're stuck on this boat now." A knowing grin stretches his lips. "Hope you two enjoyed your skinny dipping session, but we should set sail now if we ever hope of making it back to the Summerlands in time for your coronation."

I clear my throat and wrap my arms around my chest. "Where are we?"

"I'd say fifty miles north of the Red Forest. Even with my wind at full speed, it'll be almost a day before we reach the shores of the Summerlands."

"How soon can we get to the Royal Academy?" Beth asks.

"I can get us there by tomorrow night."

I chew on my bottom lip, my hands firmly wrapped around Beth's waist. "Anything closer in between?"

Not that I don't like the idea of being trapped with her on a boat for the next twenty-four hours, but I still have a crown to save.

Seth shakes his head. "Wintermere's coast is covered in ice. I wouldn't step a toe in the Red Forest to save my life, and we'd need a plane, not a boat, to reach the Solar Cliffs. No, your turf is the closest and safest anchorage on this side of the continent."

"Let's go, then."

The white sail changes direction as suddenly as it did when Seth and Imogen were fighting.

Beth frowns at the mainsail. "Seth?"

"I'm not doing it," Seth grunts under his breath, his fists clenching at his sides.

We all look at Imogen's unconscious form, but she's still out cold.

Seth backtracks toward the hatch. "I'll check on Luther."

A low hum becomes audible in the night. "Wait!"

Fog creeps over the ship's bow, extending its long white claws toward us, encroaching over the railings on all sides, and a silhouette appears at the back of the stern.

I shield Beth with my body, positioning myself between her and the phenomenon just as a tall, naked woman stalks out of the mists. Long red hair covers her breasts and falls below her waist, her posture full of confidence despite her lack of clothes. "I'm Melisandra, leader of the North Sea clan. You're holding one of my blood against her will, and you'll pay for it with your life."

Her voice is hauntingly beautiful. Faint tattooed lines in her bronze skin draw my attention to her belly button, guiding my sight down to the place between her thighs, but I blink away the haze of her magic, steeling myself against its influence and tearing my gaze away from her enticing form.

Seth gulps beside me, his pupils wide and dark, clearly bewitched.

Another siren climbs over the bow. "We heard your song and answered your call, sister."

Beth grips my upper arm and sinks her nails in my flesh to keep me by her side, though I have no intention to move. "Wait. They're with me."

Melisandra shifts her weight from her toes to her heels and

braces her hands on her hips. She squints at Beth as if the slits of her eyes could somehow see directly inside her soul. "What's your name?"

"Elizabeth Snow." My Songbird tips her chin up, unintimidated by the siren, and my heart swells at how confident and commanding she is. The years since our last meeting have chiseled her into an even more formidable woman, the insecurities of her youth gone.

The siren's full red lips curl in a grimace. "Not your earthling name. Your song would not answer to that name."

Beth licks her lips. "Giving you my full name will only give you more power over me."

Melisandra cocks her hip to the side. "Your refusal to answer will only make *me* more violent."

"I'm Melia," Beth says on a shaky breath.

Melisandra remains unmoved. "And your mother's name?"

"Melissa."

"Sisters, meet Melia, daughter of Melissa"—she purses her lips to the side in a smirk—"and her earthling men."

The mermaids laugh, and the sound is absolutely chilling.

A dry chortle draws my attention to our rear, where another redheaded siren squats over the top of the cabin as she extends her arm toward Seth. "The men of Storm's End are always eager to meet a siren, I hear," she says.

"You bet," Seth drawls in a trance, licking his lips.

"What about the one tied up in the hold?" a blonde one asks. She peers down the opened hatch, her wavy locks brushing the floor as she moves.

Yet another siren, identical to the one who spotted Luther, nudges her sister's side. "He's cute. I'd share him."

The women are all flawless and naked, and their combined magic sinks into my pores. The most irrational and inconvenient erection pulses inside the confines of my trousers, as though I'm a teenager having sex for the first time, and I stifle a groan.

"Please, can we talk about this?" Beth negotiates.

"You can keep one, if you like. We're sisters. But it's always polite to share."

Beth sinks her nails even deeper into my arm. "I'm not in a sharing mood. And to be frank I need this one, too, to sail home," Beth says as she points to Seth.

The redheaded siren behind Seth leaps to the ground and inches closer. She looks very similar to Melisandra, her breasts round and full, her nipples dark and taut. Despite similarities, she looks a tad younger, and her hair is more fiery than dark red. "Earthling men are incredibly fickle. He still stands there by your side, but one song, and he'd swear his life to me, instead."

My spine stiffens at her hungry gaze. "I would never," I chuck out.

"Easy, Malon." Melisandra warns. "He's powerful."

"Do you care for a wager, sister?" The siren climbs up my chest with spider fingers, filling me up without a shred of shame as she addresses Beth. "If this one stays with you in spite of my performance, you can keep your men. If he follows me to the deep, we'll take them *all*." She smacks her lips together, clearly pleased with herself.

I squeeze Beth's hand for her to let me answer for myself. "I'd never go with you."

"Is that a yes, then?"

My lids flutter as she traces at the top of my mark, her green eyes shining with curiosity, her hand so close to my cock, I can't exactly pretend her powers aren't affecting me. "Yes."

I swallow hard. What have I done? There's no doubt in my mind these sirens could convince all the men on this boat to slice their own throats in exchange for a kiss, and to be honest, a part of me really craves the death they offer. Down there, in the deep, exhausted and dizzy with pleasure.

Malon grins up at me and opens her mouth to sing.

I once saw a sailor with gorgeous eyes,

A strong jaw and a charming smile,
Wore a crown of night,
And a sword of might.
I'd never met a man like him,
He'd never heard a song like mine.

He followed me to the deep,
Said he wanted me for a wife,
Clinging to me even in his sleep.
I thought I'd found a lover to keep.

But dawn came, and he remembered his life,
The children and queen he already had.
He could have just taken his leave,
But tried to erase his mistake with a cleave,
Called me a villain, a temptress, a freak—
Oh, how the waves take care of the weak.

The others start to sing along, their voices merging together, their choir rippling through the air as though hundreds of sirens—and not just a handful—are actually in the water, surrounding us.

I know we're all in terrible danger, but my body doesn't care. I'm losing my grip.

Something about their magic fills me with a raw, primal need. All my thoughts narrow on the heat building in my body, focused on how to alleviate the ache that floods through me. I feel rather inclined to strip and claim Beth right here—in front of everyone.

Pre-cum leaks from the tip of my cock, and the throb is so intense it hurts. My head is spinning. I hesitate, debating whether to give in to the temptation to stroke myself, but I know one touch might shatter what's left of my self-control.

Seth leaps toward the blonde standing in front of the hatch, and she lets out a delighted chuckle as he drags her into his embrace, kissing her passionately, lost to his lust.

His men came to our home with weapons and hooks,
Mistaking us for some warm-water snooks.
They tried to needle our bodies with spears,
Overcome by their silly earthling fears.

They hunted us night after night,
Driven by some silly vengeful plight.
We sank their boats to the deep sea bed,
And kept the best of them for ransom instead.
This is how things have to be.
When your blood is from the sea.

I peer over the bow but see no more of them. Was the throng of voices real, or merely a figment of my imagination?

Malon's eyes gleam in the night, shimmering with bottomless lust and a flicker of envy. "Come with me, Summer Fae."

I step forward without meaning to, my rational mind retreating to a dark, dusty attic inside me.

"See? Fickle," Malon goads Beth.

Despite my instinct to obey, I stay in control. I seize her invitation, leaning in as though to kiss her neck, only to twist at the last moment—wrapping her in a rear chokehold, my fire flaring to life, my hand flat against her throat. "Not as fickle as you imagined," I growl. "Let us go."

Loud hisses rise from the waves as the women on the boat draw their weapons. The handmade blades, crafted from the jagged teeth of sea monsters, glint in the moonlight. A shiver of self-loathing dissects me from the inside out as Malon presses against me, her ass grinding provocatively on the ridge of my erection. "Come on, you want me, handsome. The high is worth your life, I promise."

"I'll kill you if you don't honor our wager," I respond flatly, my voice steady despite the rush of conflicting emotions.

"Enough." Melisandra's arm slices through the air in a halting motion. "No one is killing anyone." She clicks her tongue at Malon.

"The man won the bet. His heart is true to his beloved." She dismisses the others with a wave. "Let them go."

I release Malon's throat, my grip slackening, and rush back to Beth's side.

Seth lets out a frustrated whimper as the blonde who had been toying with him pushes him off, the Storm Prince landing hard on the deck.

"Thank you," Beth says, tipping her chin in gratitude toward Melisandra. "For honoring your word."

"I'm not quite done with you yet." Melisandra waits as her sirens leap from the ship, each hitting the water with a chorus of splashes, all except for Malon, who stays by her side.

"Sing, child," the leader commands. "I want to know your soul."

CHAPTER 45
HORIZON
BETH

I bite my bottom lip as I finish the song. My cheeks tingle as though Melisandra could hear my entire life story—past, present, and future—in the lyrics.

"You were taught the ways of the kingdom under the horizon by Mélusine, daughter of Melpomene herself. You are indeed one of us." Melisandra turns to Aidan and smiles , showing all her teeth. "And you, handsome, I knew you were special, but I didn't know how much." She titters, amused. "Malon, this is Aidan Summers, the Crown Prince of the Summerlands."

Malon's resentful pout morphs into a full-blown sneer. "Bet or no bet, we're not letting that fucker slip through our fins," she growls.

Melisandra's eyes gleam with mischief. "Shush, daughter. He might be our enemy, but he's in love with one of us."

"We can't let him go, for tides' sake. And she's *not* one of us," Malon says begrudgingly, rubbing down her burnt throat.

"The salt of the sea runs in her veins." Melisandra's tone softens. "A sister on the throne of Summer... I never thought I'd see the day. With her as queen, we might finally end this vicious cycle of violence and death. We might finally be allowed to walk the beaches of the continent again."

Tears mist the corners of her eyes.

"The Lord of the Tides said—" the younger siren argues, but her mother cuts her off almost immediately.

"The Lord of the Tides is an earthling. I don't care what he promised us, he will never know what it's like to be hunted for his song."

"But who's to say that man will marry her, in the end? That he won't simply change his mind? Why should we trust him?" Malon adds.

Aidan links our fingers, his sharp tone cutting through the tension between the two women. "You don't have to trust me or take my word for it. I'll marry her now."

A delighted gasp whistles out of Melisandra. "You will?"

He holds her baring gaze. "Yes. It's all I've ever wanted."

"What do you say, daughter of the sea? Will you take him?" she asks me.

My head spins. "Err— Now?"

"Will you let us ensure that we're not passing up on the opportunity to kill the next Summer King for nothing?" Melisandra says with a pointed look, clearly hinting for me to take her up on her generous offer.

My gaze flicks from Melisandra to Malon, the younger siren looking disgusted by the idea, and to Aidan, who gazes down at me expectantly, his bottom lip tucked between his teeth.

I squeeze his hand with a profound, almost visceral determination. "I will. Yes."

THE CAPTAIN'S CABIN NEAR THE BOW IS STIFLING, THE AIR THICK WITH THE smell of damp wood and the faint, sharp tang of the sea that clings to the walls. The low groan of the ship's timbers beneath us is a constant reminder of our precarious situation, but there's something almost comforting in it, too.

I play with my fingers, my heart racing. "We don't have to do this, not if you don't want to. I could still talk to Melisandra. Maybe—"

I had asked to speak privately with Aidan while Melisandra summoned the rest of her clan, insisting on a proper Sea wedding.

Aidan covers my hands, forcing them to a standstill. "Songbird. I want to marry you."

My gaze flies up to meet his. "Yes?"

"I would have done so a long time ago," he says, his eyes darkening, "if not for Ethan and my parents thinking they could blatantly overwrite my free will."

We always talked about getting married, about finding a way to make it work, but this—this feels like a dream twisted into something darker. There's a quiet thrill between us. We're finally going to do this, but it's shrouded by the knowledge that it's not for us, at least not in the way we wanted. It's an obligation, a fulfillment of a murderous stranger's agenda, and a sharp edge of unease cuts through me.

"What about Heather?" I ask, unable to leave well-enough alone.

"Heather arrived at the academy the year after you left. She became Will's friend and spent tons of time with her at the castle."

"And you two grew close. I get it," I say, crestfallen.

Aidan kisses my knuckles, one at a time. "Heather was Will's lover, Beth. Not mine. After Will died, she became my best friend. I figured, since I had never been able to fall in love, Heather would make the finest queen I could hope for and proposed."

"Oh."

I can't deny the flutter in my chest when Aidan catches my gaze, his hand resting on mine like it's meant to be this way. We've wanted this, wanted each other, for so long. Is it foolish—or even dangerous—for me to go along with these crazy circumstances?

The ship rocks beneath us, but in this small, suffocating cabin, it's just us—and for once, I feel a fragile sense of peace.

Until Seth marches inside the cabin. "Now, don't think I'm not enjoying the company of all these gorgeous, naked women, but your other bride is on this ship," he announces.

Aidan's body tenses at the revelation. "What? Where?" he asks, his voice tight.

Seth smirks, his impatience growing. "She's tied up in the other cabin, but I can't find the keys to the cuffs. I went through the books and notes lying around the room, and I'm pretty sure the Lord of the Tides lives on this boat, along with my brother."

"I need to speak with her—" Aidan begins, but Seth cuts him off.

"You can catch up with your ex-fiancée later. She's a little shaken, but I checked, and she's all for getting rid of the murderous fish before we go and rescue her."

"Have you told her about the wedding?" Aidan asks, his voice betraying a flicker of guilt.

"She was supposed to marry you today," Seth replies with a shrug. "I think you should tell her yourself."

My throat tightens as I glance at Aidan. "You can go to her," I say, forcing the words out, even though it feels like sandpaper scraping my insides. "I understand."

Aidan shakes his head firmly. "No," he says, his voice steady now. "Seth is right. We've already delayed long enough."

The salty air wraps around us as we make our way back to the deck, the wind whipping through our hair, carrying with it the distant hum of the sirens' song. The sea is rougher now, dark waves crashing against the sides of the ship, yet it feels like the calm before the storm. As we step onto the deck, a school of sirens circles the ship, their voices rising in harmony, creating an eerie, haunting melody that ripples through the breeze.

"Ah, finally. Our bride and groom," Melisandra calls, her voice dripping with amusement.

She steps forward to take her place as the officiant. Her dark red hair falls in soft waves around her shoulders, and she wears a necklace of shells that drapes across her chest, the polished pieces covering her breasts. Seaweed bracelets adorn her ankles, and her bronze skin catches the faint light, glimmering under the stars. Her green eyes lock onto mine as she begins the ritual, her voice clear and commanding despite the quiet of the night.

The ocean breeze tugs gently at her hair as she says, "Sirens love the hardest. Our song demands nothing less than unfailing loyalty. Will you engrave your bones with the promise to cherish your beloved, to rise above temptation in every form, and remain faithful to her forever?" she asks Aidan.

"I will," Aidan answers, his voice unwavering.

"And you, daughter of Melpomene, will you claim this man as your own and protect him from the waves?" the siren continues, her voice smooth as silk, and yet it carries a sharp edge.

The wind dies down, as though the sea itself is listening.

"I will," I say, the words leaving my mouth more easily than I expected. The promise feels raw, crawling out from the depths of my soul despite the strange circumstances—despite my fears, and everything that's still swirling in my mind.

The siren nods in approval. "Your marriage will last even beyond death, and your female children will know the call of the sea." She pauses, glancing over at the others, a faint smile playing on her lips. "And as for the rest of the ceremony..."

I hesitate. "What about...the rest?" I ask, my voice barely more than a whisper, unsure of what I'm even asking.

"What about it?" she replies nonchalantly.

"Is there a Sea-preferred way to consummate a wedding?" Seth adds with a teasing grin. "The tail must make things awkward, I bet."

The sirens laugh in unison, the sound like a cascade of water over smooth rocks.

"Earthlings have such ridiculous traditions," Melisandra chuckles. "You have taken your vows before Melpomene herself, under the moonlight where the ocean meets the sky," she adds, her voice growing more serious. "There's no power in the worlds above or below the horizon that could prevent your union now. Besides, the groom would die if he didn't claim his bride before dawn."

I open my mouth, ready to ask if it's a figure of speech, but when my eyes meet Melisandra's, I see the glimmer of mischief there—no, it's not a metaphor.

Aidan catches my eye, and I wonder if the weight of his choice is finally catching up to him. If he's truly ready to pledge his life to me under the eyes of the sea gods—under the looming threat of whatever comes next.

He steps closer, his eyes dark and intense, and before I can even react, he scoops me up into his arms. His kiss is fierce, desperate, like he's trying to consume me, and I lose myself in it. My pulse quickens, the world around us fading into a blur. His hands are on my back, gripping me tightly as though he's afraid to let me go, his mouth claiming mine with a fervor that makes my entire body ignite.

The sirens chant in cheer, then slip back into the waves with the same stealth with which they appeared, leaving only the echoes of their song behind.

I melt into my husband's body, my fingers threading through his hair, pulling him closer, eager to feel every inch of him as he guides me back toward the cabin.

Aidan closes the door behind us and presses me to it. "You deserved better than a rushed wedding," he says with a frown.

"It's too late to turn back now." I scrape my nails down his shoulder blades, impatient for him to touch me. "You heard the sirens. You'd *die* without me," I say in jest, my heart both heavy and light at the finality of that statement.

"I've died without you for a hundred years." Aidan glances

around the room, the tiny cabin cluttered with maps and scrolls. His hands fall from my shoulders to my waist, tracing the flimsy buttons of the undershirt he lent me. "But you deserved a better wedding."

Luther's cabin is a strange place for us to celebrate our love, but I've been waiting for this moment forever, and now that it's here, nothing else matters. "Who cares about the wedding when I finally have *you*?"

Aidan bares me to him, one button at a time, his hands shaking as he slides them up my stomach to caress my breasts. He dips his head down to taste them, the areolas thick and dark under his scrutiny. "I'm never letting you out of my sight again."

I can't believe I almost watched him marry someone else, or that Malon tried to steal him away, and the thought fills me with a needy, hungry flare of rage. Jealousy spikes in my blood, the siren in me stirring to life.

I palm his erection over his trousers, and he hisses under his breath. "Oh, fuck."

From the way his cock throbs at the simplest touch, I have trouble believing he's able to function at all. "That must hurt," I breathe.

His eyes shine with bottomless greed as his hips buck forward. "You have no idea. I was ready to kill them all just to be left alone with you..."

He's still affected by my song, and my insides are slick in response, my body arching into his touch. He pulls me into a heated kiss before ridding himself of his trousers, the fabric bunching at his feet as he picks me up in his arms. His hardness rubs against my entrance, and I cry out at the friction. "Take me now. I need you inside me."

I've never indulged in the high a siren's song can bring, least of all with Aidan, my *husband*, and the rush sizzling through me is unequaled.

Magic spices up the air of the cabin. Waves rock the boat from side to side, as though the sea itself is dancing in cheer. Oxygen grows sparse, and I struggle to catch my breath, my walls pulsing, the anticipation radiating across my belly.

I shake all over. The visceral need for Aidan to fill me, to soothe the tender sting of emptiness within my body, eclipses everything else. Our eyes lock, and he muffles a heavy groan as he feeds me his cock inch by inch.

My head falls back against the door, the feel of him even better than I remembered.

Hotter.

Harder.

Ice and fire meld together as though they were always meant to collide as Aidan moves in and out of me, the moment heightened by the power of the sea and the weight of our vows. The magic that sank into our bones tingles in delight at the meeting of our flesh, drugging and raw. Aidan appears as intoxicated as I am as he places an open-mouthed kiss on my lips, fucking me slow and steady.

He's mine.

Finally.

The foolish promises we made as kids have become reality, and I can't get enough of us like this, together. Of the scent we make, and the fury of my love for him.

Every kiss, every touch, is a promise, and for a brief, blissful moment, I forget everything but him. Sirens love the hardest, indeed.

CHAPTER 46
LORD OF THE TIDES
AIDAN

The sun dips low on the horizon, casting a warm, golden light over the Augustus shore as the boat glides toward land. I hold Beth close, her body pressed against mine. The finality of our vows still lingers between us, but it's no longer a burden—it's the promise of a future side by side, no matter the storm ahead.

"It pains me to say, but you're a fine captain," I tell Seth.

He looks more at ease here than I've ever seen him, working the ropes and pulleys with an absent-minded smile. "I'm a Storm Fae. If I'm not a good sailor, I'm good at nothing."

"Thank you, Seth. I mean it," I say.

"Hey, if things work out for us, I'll be able to tell my children I captained the Summer King's honeymoon."

Heather is sitting at the bow, impatient to reach solid ground, and I untangle myself from my wife to join her melancholy. I sit with my legs dangling from the side of the bow and try to find the words to ease her sorrow. "I'm still so, so sorry, Heather."

She looks down at her lap, playing with the loose threads of the shirt she borrowed from Luther's cabin. "I'm happy for you. Truly."

"I hope you'll find someone, too, Heather. Someone you'd die for."

"Willow was that for me."

I press my lips together. "I know. I miss her bitterly still, especially on a day like this."

"She would have loved this boat. She used to dream about a life away from court, traditions, and responsibilities."

My lips quirk at the truth in those words. "And she would have made a fine sailor, too." She stifles a sob on a long, heavy breath. "The Lord of the Tides mentioned her, you know. He said that it would have broken her heart—if she were still alive—to see you and me wed. That she'd be...disgusted." Her long hair fans to hide her face as she gazes down at the sea.

I catch a wince from surfacing on my lips. "We suspect he was in school at the same time as Beth was, so it makes sense for him to know her, too."

"He was right. I think this all happened for a reason. I can't believe we ever came so close to dishonoring Will's memory like that. She always reviled arranged weddings, and yet we were about to choose one for ourselves—" The sobs she was barely holding back shake her shoulders, and I pat her gently, waiting for her sniffles to subside.

"Honestly... I think it's Ezra," I say softly, hoping she won't be too upset.

Her voice hikes up to a squeaky denial. "Ezra? No. Ezra was always sweet with me. I don't know what the Lord of the Tides planned to do or why he sequestered me in his cabin and chained me to his bedpost, but he certainly wasn't planning to cuddle. Ezra would never have done that."

"He's been gone for a long time. The years might have hardened him."

She rubs the tears off her long, wet lashes. "I understand that you'd like it to be him, to finally have some closure as to what happened to your friend, but I'm telling you it wasn't him."

"Who, then?"

"I have no idea."

"Hey, I need everyone by the stern," Seth calls out, and we join him at the back of the ship. "Alright. This is as close as I can go to shore without beaching the boat. You three will have to swim the rest of the way," he announces.

Beth frowns. "Aren't you coming with us?"

Seth shakes his head, his lips pursed in a regretful grimace. "Luther is a rebel. If I leave him in your hands to stand trial, he'll be executed."

"We could work out an arrangement—" Beth starts.

Seth cuts her off. "I can't surrender him to your care. Not after what he's done."

I understand his point of view. If his brother sets foot on dry land and is arrested in the Summerlands—after the queen's poisoning and subsequent death at the hands of the Tidecallers—I'll have to make an example out of him.

"But you can go and save your crown, and tell everyone you couldn't possibly do both since it would have required you to sail this boat without my help," he adds for my benefit.

I give him a nod. "I could do that. But I can't believe you'd still protect him."

"My brother was taken from us when he was still too young to know any better. Hell, he's not even twenty, yet. I won't let my father's mistakes destroy him."

"I respect that." I extend my hand, not for a handshake but a forearm clasp. Seth hesitates, then grips my arm, matching my hold. Our eyes lock. We're not friends, not even close, but in this moment, we understand each other.

Beth, Heather, and I leap over the side of the boat, plunging into the sea below. Beth helps Heather toward the safety of Saffron Cove, the Spring Fae uneasy about swimming alone, while I guard our rear until my feet sink into the orange sand.

Beth adjusts my shirt around herself, her shift from tail to legs leaving her bare again as she steps out of the water. I take her hand briefly, but the moment is cut short by the sound of hurried boots on the beach. A group of academy guards rushes forward, their hands resting on their weapons, but it's Evelyn who reaches us first.

She strides forward, her braided hair tied back, her sharp gaze assessing us like the academy headmaster she once was. "Aidan! Beth! What are you doing here toge—" She cuts herself off, though her expression finishes the thought plainly.

"Evelyn. You're back from retirement?" I ask.

"They needed someone to step in," she replies. "With you about to be king."

"When is the coronation?"

Her eyes narrow. "You tell me. I thought it was tonight—"

I don't wait for her to finish. "It is. We have to go. I promise I'll explain everything later."

Beth and I break away, racing up the winding path to my study.

I grab my Shadow mask, and guide Beth into the closest mirror to reach the Eternal Hall, the nearest gateway to the throne room where the coronation will take place.

We're barely out of the glass when the sound hits me—the deep grind of stone sealing the entrance to the throne room. My heart kicks hard against my ribs as I glance at Beth.

"We're not too late," she says, her voice steady but quick. "The tunnels."

There might still be time to stop the impostor from stealing my crown—if we move now.

CHAPTER 47
PHOENIX
AIDAN

A masculine voice echoes through the tunnels as Beth and I sneak closer to the secret passage allowing access to the Hall of Eternity. The Lord of the Tides is taking his vows as the new king of Summer—using my body, my voice—and my fists clench at my sides.

He's powerful enough to fool the King of Light himself, and the thought fills me with dread.

"I want you to stay here," I tell Beth.

She snorts in the most telling show of disbelief. "No chance."

"Who knows what he'll do when he sees me coming..."

"And I'll be right there beside you the whole time, Aidan. As you did for me on that boat."

She's right, but my instinct to keep her safe begs me not to put her in the presence of that monster again.

The secret door leading into the throne room has always been a well-guarded secret, though I know at least a couple of other royals are aware of it. I click the mechanism preventing the door from being opened and roll the heavy stone out of the way, the back of the tapestry concealing the door letting a faint light through.

I grip a fist of the red fabric, the tapestry flaking off into ashes and revealing our intrusion to all the monarchs at the same time.

The imposter is sitting on my mother's old throne, chatting with the others as though he belongs on it, and anger lances up my spine. Thorald Storm, Damian Sombra, and Elio Lightbringer on one side, the imposter, Freya Heart, Ethan Lightbringer, and Eliza Bloodfyre on the other. All in their finest, Ethan even wearing his wings for the occasion. They all gawk at Beth and me. The entire magic of Faerie buzzes at our arrival, sharp bites of power numbing my cheeks.

Only the empty throne of the Mist King remains unclaimed.

"Aidan. What a surprise," The Lord of the Tides says on a smirk, not at all put out by our arrival.

Elio, Damian, and Eliza jolt to their feet, exchanging alarmed looks.

"What's going on?" The Red Queen asks, a jewelled scarf covering her forehead and masking her brows.

Freya gasps. "Ethan, what is the meaning of this?"

Ethan squints at me and the Lord of the Tides in turn, clearly annoyed.

Damian sits back down, gripping the armrests of his onyx throne. "Is this another one of your schemes, Ethan?"

Elio clicks his tongue. "Enough games, Father. Which Aidan is the real one?"

"This is no place or time for parlor tricks. This is a sacred ritual, and our actions here are watched closely by the Gods—" Thorald Storm spits as he summons a long sword to his side, a dark cloud gathering above our heads. "You've gone too far this time, Ethan."

Ethan raises his hands in surrender. "Calm down, cousins. I'm not to blame for this intrusion. I do not know which of them is real, or what's happening." He squints, sliding to the edge of his seat. "But I'm curious."

The uneven flow of magic swirling through the air creates a wild draft in the small room, raising all my hairs to attention. If all of them were to use their powers at once in a space as cramped as this, it'd probably blow up the whole castle.

"Let me explain, then," the Lord of the Tides quips, finally rising to his feet.

He walks to the center of the room to the chalice and snatches it from its pedestal. "Aidan thinks I came here to steal his birthright and cheat my way to a Faerie crown, but that's actually not the case. I was intrigued, though, by the instrument which allows you all to choose between the contenders to the crown, and sometimes overrule the will of the Gods." He tips the chalice at the Spring Queen. "Freya here is a good example of such meddling. When Devi was put on trial for misplacing a couple of her forbidden arrows, you all forced her to abdicate and placed Freya on the throne."

Freya's jaw is set in a hard line, "Why are we even listening to this impostor?"

"I agree. Let's put a stop to this," the Red Queen snaps.

The Lord of the Tides rolls up his sleeves to expose the myriad of jewels embedded in his arms. There's dozens of them, the precious stones shining under the light of the torches. "Please, give me a minute. I wouldn't want to have to kill any of you before the show."

"The show?" The Red Queen scoffs.

"You're a rebel scum. Why should we listen to you?" Thorald grits through his teeth, his sword raised in warning.

The Lord of the Tides saunters closer to Ethan. "As I was saying, the chalice here was meant as a failsafe to prevent any deranged king to keep ruling if he was found unfit. To temporarily put the power in someone else's hands. But your lot used it as a way to cheat the rules of succession. And I came here not to bypass the natural order of things, but to make sure it could never be done again."

Ethan rolls his eyes at the impostor. "The chalice can't be dismantled. It's made out of the souls of the first kings and was forged by Hephaistos himself. Nothing can destroy it."

The Lord of the Tides bristles at Ethan's confidence, his smile stretching beyond unbridled joy into something sinister. "Even something as pure as a soul can be broken. You're the one who taught me that, Ethan."

Shadows, ice, blood, and light twist into vines, slithering from the thrones to ensnare the rulers of the Fae Continent. Thorald swings his blade at the tendrils creeping toward his midriff, but the sword shatters on impact. In mere moments, every Faerie monarch is bound to their throne by the Lord of the Tides' magic. Only Beth and I remain untouched, though the sight leaves us sobered and still.

The kings and queens writhe against their restraints in a futile struggle, and Ethan's eyes betray a hint of worry.

The impostor, still wearing my face, strides toward the Spring throne. "Freya stole Devi's crown because all of you let her," he scolds. With a leap, he lands behind Ethan's throne, advancing on the Red Queen. "Eliza is a rotten queen. She slaughtered so many of her kin that the Red Forest still drips with their blood."

He steps closer to Thorald, leaning down to prod the Storm King's forehead. The vines curl tighter, silencing Thorald's furious shouts. "Thorald Storm... Your queen is dead. Your sons despise you. Yet you still rule over their lives as if it's your right."

From Storms, he saunters toward the Shadow throne. "Damian Sombra. You hung to your crown with both hands, knuckles bloody, for decades, and now that you're finally back to full strength, finally happy, you hide your wife so that others in this room don't harm her."

My doppelgänger takes a pregnant pause, then doubles back to reach the Winter throne. "And Elio. You escaped your father's cruelty only to be stuck in a never-ending loop of death. All because you had to marry someone who didn't love you. How long do you think Ethan will let you keep your new wife before he destroys her too, just for the hell of it?"

"Who are you? How can you use Light magic against *me*," Ethan says on a sneer.

"Have you destroyed so many souls that you can't even remember? How many women did you blackmail into your bed? How many did you trick with your powers? How many did you rape outright because they dared to say no?" The Lord of the Tides asks in a stark, accusatory tone, his composure slowly slipping away.

Shadow vines crawl over Ethan until he's covered in them, worming their way inside his nostrils, ears, and eyes as though they mean to choke him from the inside out.

"Do you see the damage you've done to your victims, your wives, your *children*? To the realm you're sworn to protect? While you all watched and said nothing." He shifts his focus to the rest of the Fae royals, quietly scanning the room for a moment.

"Three of you never should have been crowned, and the rest have proven themselves unfit to rule." The Lord of the Tides points the chalice at every monarch in turn, ready to impart his own brand of justice. "I only hope the next kings and queens will be more worthy than you were." An impish grin curls his lips, his chest heaving as though his performance cost him quite a bit. "It's a good night for a revolution."

A smoldering heat radiates from his incandescent frame, his body shifting from orange to red to blinding white. Globs of molten metal spill over the chalice's rim as it begins to warp and melt. I meet the imposter's amber gaze—the only part of him that still resembles anything human—and realize he's no longer using magic to mirror me.

With a deafening crack, he slams the most powerful relic ever forged onto the ground. It shatters in an explosion of molten solder. But the destruction doesn't stop there. Flames erupt from the Lord of the Tides, racing outward to engulf the thrones.

Beth steps forward, her voice sharp with desperation. "Willow! Stop!"

My heart pounds as the truth snaps into focus. The Lord of the Tides has dropped her disguise. Her amber eyes—hauntingly familiar—confirm what I refuse to believe.

Willow is the fuse, the spark, and the kindling. *How could this be?*

The mark on my upper thigh ignites with searing heat, ten times stronger than before, as the Hall of Eternity is consumed in flames. The destruction of the chalice triggered my immediate crowning, the magic acting of its own will and consecrating my rise as Summer King. The divine power bestowed upon me merges with the inferno born of my sister's wrath.

Everything and everyone is swallowed by the fire, the acrid stench of burning flesh choking the air. The flares of my new magic are too strong and unfamiliar for me to know exactly how to control them, either to stop Willow from burning all the others alive, or simply tame the blaze.

Beth strides forward to grip her wrist. "Willow, please! This isn't the answer."

Each mention of her name seems to weaken her grip on the magic, and Willow staggers outright at the unexpected touch. The vines of magic vanish into smoke, freeing the monarchs.

Chaos erupts. Flames lick the hem of Freya's dress, and she screams, fleeing toward the tunnels. The Red Queen's face twists with fury as she lunges at Willow, her blade aimed at my sister's neck. But before the strike lands, the fire engulfs her, turning her into a human-shaped torch at the heart of the inferno.

Ethan's wings ignite, the sharp stench of burning feathers choking the air as he howls in agony beneath the weight of the flames. A bubble of light ripples from his skin, expanding outward—his magic strong enough to repel the inferno. With a roar, he charges toward the entrance, punching through solid stone as if it were water, leaving a jagged hole in his wake.

Willow chases after him, drawing the worst of the heat with her. The temperature drops slightly, but the flames still rage, devouring everything in their path.

Beth and Elio seize the Shadow King, dragging his unconscious, charred body toward the tunnels.

"Come with us!" Beth pleads, her voice shaking with desperation.

"I have to speak to her."

"Aidan!" she cries again.

I lean down, pressing a swift kiss to her forehead. "Get them out. I'll see you soon, Songbird."

Through the swirling smoke, I watch Beth and Elio disappear into the tunnels, struggling to carry a severely burned Damian. They're safe—for now. But I can't follow them.

I just have to see her.

I stagger forward, past the gaping hole Ethan left behind, and into the burning remnants of the ballroom. Reaching for the banister of the grand staircase, I recoil in pain as my hand grazes molten metal. The once-magnificent railing has become a twisted, warped ruin.

The heat is relentless, a living thing that presses against my skin, smothering everything else. Flames lick at the stone walls, devouring tapestries and wood beams with a crackling roar that drowns out all other sound. The air is thick with smoke, acrid and choking, a bitter mix of charred oak, burning fabric, and molten iron. My fire magic hums beneath my skin, keeping the inferno from claiming me, but even that can't dull the sharp sting of ash scraping my throat.

I dodge falling timber, the beam crashing to the ground with an ear-splitting boom, sending embers skittering like angry fireflies across the stone floor. The Eternal Halls, once so grand, a symbol of the strength of my kingdom, are crumbling around me. Every step feels precarious as the structure groans and shudders, a beast in its death throes. I push forward, my bare feet sliding on slick patches of melted varnish, the firelight casting long, flickering shadows against the walls.

"Willow!" I shout, my voice hoarse, swallowed by the roaring blaze. She has to be here. My sister is as much a part of this fire as the flames themselves, her magic feeding the destruction as though it's a living extension of her will. The thought both enrages and terrifies me. The smoke claws at my lungs as I push toward the heart of the octagonal room, its center glowing with an unearthly light. Every instinct screams at me to turn back, to let the place fall, but I can't leave without her. My family. My responsibility. Even if she's the arsonist, even if this was her doing, she's still my sister—and I'll drag her out of this hell if I have to.

I find her at the heart of the ballroom.

"Willow!"

She turns, her amber eyes almost red in the firelight. "The thrones are gone. Poof. Just like that. Isn't it curious? I always thought they were imbued with magic, too, but I guess not."

Flames lick at every surface of the room. She stands at its heart, unbothered by the heat that would have killed me, had the powers of the Summerlands not ripped into me the moment she melted the chalice.

Our clothes didn't survive the flames, yet the jewels carved into her skin remain. Her chest and arms glint with precious stones, their alloy links glowing red-hot, creating the illusion of armor. She looks formidable—untouchable—while I stand before her, exposed and vulnerable.

"What have you done?" I manage, the shock of seeing her again nearly eclipsed by the horror of what she's become.

"I changed the world for the better."

"You're burning down our childhood home. Hundreds of innocents will die. You...you killed our mother."

"Sacrifices need to be made for the greater good." She gestures toward the center of the Eternal Hall, where her marital bed once stood. "Every single one of them—besides maybe Elio—would have died tonight if not for your meddling. The rising tides would have cleansed the Continent, a fresh start without alliances and politics poisoning everything."

"Why?" My voice cracks. "Without the Chalice, anyone with ambition and a sword will think they can claim power by force."

"Better that than forcing children and grandchildren to become pawns in a lifelong quest to maintain it." Her gaze hardens. "The system was broken, Aidan. Wicked. Now every king and queen of

Faerie will be chosen by the Gods—not Ethan Lightbringer or anyone like him."

A heavy sense of guilt weighs down my heart. "I'm sorry I couldn't protect you from him."

She scoffs, her lips pursed in a bitter pout. "The real Aidan wouldn't have stood by while that man used and abused me. But they took the fight out of you, didn't they? Washed away your memories and toyed with your essence. I tried to cure you, but nothing worked. I was so miserable that Ezra helped me fake my death just so I could escape."

The mention of my old friend sends flames down my neck. "Where is he?"

"Gone. Vanished. Probably dead." She doesn't wait for my reaction. "Beth wouldn't have survived without your magic—the shared power of the Summer King." She bites her bottom lip, her gaze narrowing as though she's slowly coming to terms with the ramifications of Beth's unlikely survival. "When did you marry her?"

She's right. Beth's ice magic barely slowed the flames, and even Elio, wielding the strength of a glacier, struggled to contain the blaze.

"Last night. On your boat."

She nods, her expression unreadable, a mix of relief and disappointment. "I guess even deceitful moths can be queens in my new world. I'll have to make my peace with that."

"You used to love her," I croak.

"That was before." Her voice is flat. "The Lord of the Tides doesn't have friends—or a brother. The sister you knew is truly dead."

"I can't let you go."

"Fire can't hold fire, Aidan. And I never meant to kill you. If I've known one thing, it's that you were always meant to rule."

"I thought the Tidecallers wanted a democracy," I say.

"Democracies are dying, too," she replies coldly. "No elected politician can do what needs to be done. There's no vision, no long-term planning—just fear of losing the next election. A true meritocracy was always the answer. You just got crowned as the new Summer King on merit alone, and so will the other crowns follow once all the usurpers are vanquished. Don't forget, there used to be eight thrones in that room, but since the Mist King fell, no one dared crown a successor. They trapped his magic in the chalice, letting it fester."

My breath catches. "A new Mist King was crowned tonight?"

She gives a sharp nod. "As soon as the Chalice melted. The Islandtide's Hawthorn is small and sickly, but now that its magic flows freely, its people will return and rebuild. The sins of our ancestors can finally be wiped clean." She takes a meaningful pause, close to tears. "This fire will burn itself out soon, and the Summerlands will look to you for guidance." She turns, hands clasped behind her back, a casual gesture in stark contrast to the devastation around us. "You should thank me, really. I gave you everything a phoenix needs to shine: a tall, enormous mound of ashes to rise from."

"What about you?" I ask, my voice trembling.

"Because of your meddling, I still have a lot of work to do. I won't rest until Ethan Lightbringer is dead."

And with that, my little sister—or what remains of her—vanishes in a flicker of light.

CHAPTER 48
CHILDREN OF THE REVOLUTION
BETH

The Lunar Cascades rush around us, washing away the ash that clings to our skin. The silver light of the moon reflects off the water, its beauty at odds with the hellish glow of Summerlands Castle burning in the distance. Flames devour the spires, sending embers spiraling into the blackened sky.

Elio holds Damian upright, his face pale and streaked with burns, while I press a hand to the Shadow King's chest, desperate to find his heartbeat.

Survivors huddle in the shallows, their eyes wide with terror, their clothes soaked through and clinging to their trembling bodies. The scent of smoke and charred wood hangs thick in the air, mixing with the sharp tang of the mineral water. I clutch the edge of a jagged rock for balance, my lungs burning from the effort of escape, but my gaze keeps drifting back to the inferno.

Aidan is still in there.

Freya is weeping beside me, her sobs breaking the stillness of the night as she clutches the lifeless body of her lover, Thorald Storm. Deep red and black burns pepper her usually beautiful face. Strips of melted skin expose the muscles of her arms, and yet she doesn't seem to notice, her eyes vacant with grief.

I think of Seth, still on the boat, unaware that his father died tonight. That his mother might not survive, her wounds grave enough for her life to be in danger. The thought hangs heavy in my chest. How quickly everything changed, how everything we thought we knew turned to ash.

"What about Ethan?" I ask Elio.

"There's no sign of him, but he still lives. I feel it in my bones."

I open my mouth to say something, but a tall, masculine silhouette emerges from the inferno. My heart bleeds as I recognize my husband among the flames.

Aidan marches out of the ruins of his castle like a god reborn, his short, soot-laden hair messy and wild, framing his sharp features. He's unashamed of his nakedness, the phoenix tattoo curling up from his thigh to his hip—its wings spread in exquisite detail, flames etched in gold and crimson that shimmer along with his long strides.

His chest and stomach are streaked with ash and sweat, every line of muscle defined by the cinders embedded in the grooves of his skin. My breath catches at the sight of him. There's purpose in his step, his chest rising and falling with a controlled intensity, each movement exuding strength and resolve. His eyes meet mine, molten and unyielding, and I can't look away. Aidan isn't just a warrior or a king in this moment—he's a force of nature, and every nerve in my body hums in response.

The surge of energy that courses through me as I step toward him eclipses everything else. My clothes are in tatters, barely hanging on. The world narrows to the two of us amidst the wreckage of everything we've lost. His warm, steady hands slide along my arm before wrapping around my shivering frame, pulling me closer. There's no hesitation, no words needed. His lips meet mine, and everything else fades—leaving only the taste of fire and blood. The world burns around us, but I've never felt more alive.

"Are you alright?" he asks.

"I'm unharmed, thanks to you."

"Willow escaped." He grabs hold of my chin and kisses me again, like he can't believe our luck. "But we survived. Who else is unaccounted for?"

We catch him up on the body count, the grim reality of our survival settling in. Hundreds of courtiers, servants, and guests didn't make it out.

A woman with white-blonde hair is sprawled over Damian, crying quietly and clutching him for dear life.

"Is he—"

"He lives, but barely. His wife healed him in time," Elio answers, his voice steady but strained.

Lori is with her, gently patting the woman's back, offering what little comfort she can. The two of them were among the servants and guards who managed to escape the castle in time.

By a cruel twist of fate, most of the High Fae foreigners escaped through the mirrors, while those without a Shadow mask—the less glamorous courtiers and commoners—were left to their own devices. We now have to reckon with the ones we couldn't save, the ones we lost to the flames. The simple fact that very few among the elite guests invited to the wedding deigned to help seems to—at least in part—justify the attack. And yet, even though some royals died, the common folk paid a higher price, as always.

"Did you find Willow?" Elio asks Aidan.

"Yes, but she escaped."

Elio's skin is burnt in patches, the ice frosting along the margins of the burns as if it's trying to keep them together, a fragile attempt at healing. "Willow was able to fool Ethan, which means the jewels of the Mist King make her more powerful than the King of Light himself. She might be able to save my wife."

"Willow wants to kill your father at any cost. So whether or not she could help you, the new King or Queen of Light might," Aidan responds, his gaze hardening. "And after what we all witnessed tonight, I'd say your father deserves to die."

"With Ezra gone, who could the next King of Light be?" I ask, my mind racing. "Helios, the God of Light, believes in hereditary monarchies above all else."

"My father has other children. Tons of them, in fact, scattered across the realms," Elio says, his words striking us all like a blow. "We might even know some of them. My father loved to spread his seed in every royal line, as a game. If Willow wants to kill him, I'll gladly help her in any way I can."

With two dead monarchs, the chalice melted, and the symbol that was the Summerlands castle destroyed, the rebels have managed to spark a revolution.

War has come to the Fae continent.

I once thought Aidan would burn the world down for me, that he'd sacrifice everything, even his own destiny, to protect me and keep me close. But it's not about destruction—it's about rebuilding. Together. The world is broken, but we'll forge something new from its ruins, something stronger. Something worthy. And this time, it's not just his fight, his home, his future. It's ours.

Aidan and I tend to the wounded as we wait for the flames of the brazier to relent, for the inferno to burn itself out before we lead everyone out of the Lunar Cascades and down the path carved through the mountains toward the streets of the capital below. It's a brand-new world out there, one forged in fire and ash.

"As King and Queen of Summer, people will look to us for answers, for a way out of this mess," Aidan whispers.

"We'll find one," I say, gripping Aidan's hand. "And we'll do better than those who came before us."

"Together," he replies.

I give him a sharp nod. "Forever."

The story continues in The Crown of a Fallen Queen.

Printed in Dunstable, United Kingdom